MEMOIRS OF A TYRANT

L. Edward Toole

Copyright © 2018 by Lonnie Edward Toole
All rights reserved.

ISBN: 978-1-77280-165-1

Published by Lonnie Edward Toole

Printed by Ingramspark Print-on-Demand
Second Edition: April 2018

MEMOIRS OF A TYRANT

This book is dedicated to Stephen King; without him I would likely never have developed any interest in reading let alone writing. Through his books I learned that imagination can have a profound effect on a person which ultimately shaped me into the person I have become. Thank you for all you have given I only hope to try to make you and others proud.

Special thanks to Tara, my wife. Without her this entire book would have sat as a lame handwritten short story in some little green notebook with barely a beginning and no end. It was words of "just finish this" that has led me to this point.

CHAPTER 1 – LET ME BEGIN...

It seems hard to find just where to start; there are so many things to say, so logically I guess the beginning is where to start, it seems so simple to say that but in many ways things never seem linear in your mind as you try to remember people, events and places. Given that; you will have to excuse me if this does not seem overly chronological or even organized, I will try but I make no guarantees. I only have a scant amount of time to get everything out and I kind of have to go where my mind takes me. Memory is sometimes fickle that way.

2012, that was the year. 2012 was prophesized as the year the world as we know it would end by the Mayans, Hopi Indians, Chinese, Nostradamus, and probably numerous others. Every single crackpot, prophet, fortune teller, psychic, and savior seems to have some day that they will warn you about. A day to fear. Get your ducks in a row before this particular day, well 2012 was just one of those kinds of times. Well everyone who said 2012 was the year to fear was wrong, with the date at least, not the end of the world. Before everything went downhill I had seen documentaries talking about how the Mayan calendar was not predicting the end of the world but was merely an end to the calendar, after which a new calendar would begin; no different than rolling from December thirty-first to January first. This is really a moot point as the date for the "end of the world" was wrong, but the world did end, so to speak. Now, the actual phrase that was said so often in those predictions was that the "world as we know it" would end. The world still exists, obviously, people still exist, just not the civilizations that we treasured so much. Basically, people just ignore the parts that they don't want to hear, so the world as we know it disappeared, leaving behind another world; a much worse world depending on your outlook. Or better, there is a certain kind of purity in having society licked clean from the plate that is Earth. Civilization has been called things like decadent and corrupt for generations by various intellectuals and malcontents. The only people who ever seemed to truly enjoy the world and its accompanying civilizations were those who were above the worst of what happened within them. In fact, it often seemed to be the people who created the negatives in civilization that did not see a real problem (or did not care) with it. The rich, the famous, the politicians, the leaders. You never read in the history books of the emperors from ancient Rome, wanting to excise the corruption from the Senate for anything other than to put themselves in power or maintain themselves in power. That is probably the quickest example I can think of, and really, I think you get the point.

The year that the disaster happened is kind of irrelevant now. Not the year itself, just the number, after all time is arbitrary. You start at some time that is picked because of the significance it has to one person but really may not be of significance to others. Take the difference in dates based on if you are Christian or Jewish. I am not even sure what basis Jewish people based their years on, but Christians of course have the Birth of Jesus as year one. So really things like dates, time, places and the like I will mention them if they are really relevant but for certain ones it just doesn't matter. Now in that year there first came the solar flare. Scientists had been thinking it was just going to be a summer where there were a large number of electrical disturbances, satellite disruptions and black-outs from electrical networks failing under the electro-magnetic waves radiating off the sun. The sun runs on an eleven-year cycle during which the frequency of solar flares and the strength of the same would ebb and grow. This is one of those weird facts that I just seem to know. Now what I didn't know, and the scientific population didn't seem to know is that every once in a while, like once every five hundred thousand years there is an even more powerful version of the solar flares, and every 50th one of those is a super flare. It's like the idea of a rogue wave, I don't recall the number of waves, but every X wave is stronger that the ones before it. I believe there is almost some kind of cumulative thing where every X times Y wave is exceptionally strong. Same idea here but on a solar level. In any event, I think I am getting off topic. In short, there was an extinction level event, it happened to be a solar flare and it utterly devastated the world. The cycle occurred just as the scientists had originally expected but then, as the piece de resistance, the solar flare kept growing, kept spewing out radiation. The flare had started on the far side of the sun, the sun having a rotational time of around 25 days (This I had to look up) but seemed very quickly to swing around to face the Earth. Like someone holding a flashlight and swinging it around to look behind them. There was really not a whole lot of time to prepare, I mean the end of the world seems like it should take a fair bit of planning, especially if you would like to survive past it. Additionally, the news networks kept bringing in their own "experts" who claimed the solar flare was going to be nothing more than some red herring (I think I'm using that expression correctly, it has been so long). People were constantly told that there was nothing to worry about, they could just go about their lives and nothing would change, so they did. This flare was the next global warming, a theory just waiting to be disproved. So, there were all those so-called experts telling people to go about their business, and they did as they were told, it was not until it was too late that a lot of people realized those so-called experts were wrong. The flare, it kept growing, kept spewing out radiation; the flare grew so large it was almost lapping at Mercury, a flare millions of miles long. In reality, it is hard for a person to fathom just how huge something has to be to stretch from the surface of the Sun to Mercury. And the Earth flew right into its path. Think of someone throwing something; we did not get hit by the person's arm but by what he threw. And the sun, well it threw a whole lot of stuff at us. Those who had had any sense tried to take some sort of shelter, hardened bunkers, mines, basements of buildings but it could not just be any building, it needed to have a lot of metal in the structure above to filter out as much radiation as possible. If you have ever seen a metal object put in the microwave, it throws off a lot sparks, having the metal in the structure does that same thing, sparks everywhere. But what you want is for the radiation to hit the metal above you and not just hit you. I guess that analogy only works if you were around before the end of the world and managed to see a microwave but if you haven't just take my word for it. Those who did those smart things in a large part survived. In reality, we are lucky anyone at all survived; the planet could have been totally incinerated. I just wish I had taken a whole lot more science courses when I was in university, because I would just like to know how we survived at all.

We could have had even more people survive; if it wasn't for the chaos that had ensued once the story of the solar flare being a real threat had reached the airwaves. One day the "experts" were espousing how people could go about their day without interruption. Then some new fact got mentioned. And another. And another. Until finally enough information got leaked out that those experts could not hold back the tide of the truth. The truth was we were all about to be in a giant pile of shit. Steaming irradiated shit. In an instant the entire world stopped. In a manner of speaking of course. It really all happened in a matter of just a couple days, panic then more panic, fear begets fear. There was no more food at the grocery stores, the truck drivers saw no real reason to deliver more food when the world's impending doom is fast approaching. And every person who is now seeing that impending doom on the horizon feels the needed to stock up on provisions. There was nothing left on store shelves in a matter of hours once people understood the gravity of the situation. Not everyone thought this was a reality; some still held out hope that the experts would be proven right, but panic is the kind of thing that spreads like any other plague. One person calls in sick, then four, then the company is on hiatus because no one showed up, it almost doesn't matter when it is only a day or two before the end of the world, it was more of just an indication of the situation as people saw it. It happened all over, in all facets of society, huge line-ups for no gas at the gas stations, no one answering the phones at pretty much any business that you called but that didn't matter because no one had anything to sell anyways. When I was growing up it was long after the rationing that had happened during the wars. And by wars I am referring to World War 1 and 2. There are more than enough paper books left on this subject so I am only going to touch on it but I am going to say that countries like Great Britain, the United States, Canada, Russia, France, Germany, etc. were all involved. The majority of the world was in on them, hence the names. Pretty much all of these countries were operating under something we referred to as "total war" meaning that the totality of a particular counties production was meant to help with war effort for that particular country. For example, things like panty hose were for a long time a mainstay of women's fashion however during the war they were rationed due to needing the material for other purposes, like for parachutes. So, as I said I was born long after that rationing had happened. I also was not affected by the oil embargos that had happened in North America during the 1970s. My having been born when I was meant that I really had no grasp of what it felt like to go without. It seemed like not many people that I knew had that experience. There had been so many years of plenty that even those who had lived through one of the wars or the embargos or some other type shortage were not used to the concept of having nothing. They had just forgotten. Now I was somewhat removed from the worst of it, as I will get to later, however I must admit that my fear was definitely piqued in the midst of the worst of the empty shelve epidemic about where my next batch of supplies would come from. Not that I was dependent on it but sometimes it is nice to have something store bought. The best analogy I can think of is the difference between cigarettes that you roll yourself and 'tailor-mades'. They both do pretty much the same thing, but one is seen as markedly better by the users.

So all that being said I do truly feel bad for those few unfortunate people who continued driving and doing their jobs, going on as if nothing was happening were driving themselves right into the middles of full-blown riots. It was like a scene out of some post-apocalyptic movie, except this was happening before the apocalypse. Drivers stopping at red lights only to be descended upon by a mob looking to take all they could from the truck, not caring if the driver was killed in the process. I remember a video from the Los Angeles riots, I think it was all the way back in the nineteen-nineties where a truck driver was pulled from his truck and hit in the head by a brick or cinder block by one the rioters, surprisingly he survived. Or the numerous riots that have happened closer to the end than the Los Angeles riots; like the ones that were started after various white police officers shot and killed black men. These end-of-the-world riots had the same flavor as pretty much all riots that had occurred before. All of those things for me just highlight how people will simply lose themselves in the moment, doing any wicked thing they can to anyone that happens along their path. Everyone was looking for some salvation, protection. People began panicking, killing those who had shelter they could be the next to occupy the shelter away from the approaching storm made by the sun, of course it was like a game of musical chairs, whoever was the last to happen upon the shelter was generally the ones who controlled it at the end. And those that didn't see an available shelter for the taking began committing every type of sin, every type of depravity, no one was safe. Mothers and their children were merely toys for animals to rape and torture, some of the men suffered the same fate. Roving gangs roamed the streets; the police, government and military were powerless to stop them. If you are reading this it is more than likely that you have never seen thousands and thousands of people, let alone thousands and thousands in the midst of a riot. It is like a tsunami of flesh; breathing, yelling, and angry water contained within thousands of people. There is no reasoning with that many people; there is nothing but a mob-mentality. One person gets to an intersection and turns left and dozens, and then hundreds of people will follow, like they believe that that one person knew where they were going. One person smashes a window and starts looting then the others join in. It is awesome to witness, and terrifying. On the news the army tried to intervene and stop one such gang from terrorizing the population of a city whose name now escapes me, it has been so long since it happened. The army unit was severely weakened from desertions of men and women wanting to spend the last bit of time they had with their families. Really you can't blame those soldiers, who would want to spend the last days of their life working, maintaining order when there is none to be had anymore. There was no longer any society. They killed a large number of the gang members, but there were too many of the scared and angry people to kill them all. Going into a riot control situation I guess they just didn't take enough ammo for a full-out battle, but that was really what it turned into. Soon they had run out of ammunition at which point the rocks and sticks of the mob had the advantage. The soldiers were killed mercilessly, stripped of their clothes and equipment; their bodies were hung from the now mostly dark light poles reminiscent of Mussolini's end, as a warning to the military or any other form of government that they were going to terrorize anyone they wished until the end of civilization. Civilization had already ended though, there were only a few enclaves where people were still civilized and those were under constant pressure, being shrunk smaller or overrun as people began turning on one another. It is kind of curious how animalistic people become in the face of danger; I guess people just want to externalize the terror they feel inside. I am still surprised at the speed at which all of this happened, but it only takes one person to do something stupid before fear overtakes dozens then hundreds. Oh well, what's done is done. It seems kind of funny as I write this as it seems like I just got to something of a logical conclusion to the horror and then well I just get to keep writing.

The next big thing was more of a problem after the flare hit but I believe it is best put when describing the overall disaster. And this was probably the most fun problem of them all. This really played havoc with the world for a fair while afterwards and really is still somewhat affecting everything as I am writing this. The world began to go dark in the path of the greatest burst of light the Earth had probably ever seen. All this happened in the span of less than a week. Why does that matter you may be asking. Well two words should clear it up: Nuclear power. There was no one manning the power plants anymore. The flare disrupted all electrical circuits on the planet. Pretty much this is the same as how there are certain times where satellite television is all messed up because of interference being put out by the sun, well crank that up to unimaginable levels. When the cooling system on a nuclear power plant gets disrupted the backup is a diesel generator. But if all the circuits in a diesel generator are fried the generator does not turn on. This means the cooling system stays off, the liquid around the radioactive cores boils off completely, usually causing an overload in pressure inside the steam vessel which may/may not lead to an explosion similar to putting a Mentos in a bottle of diet Coke. That steam explosion is of course full of radioactive material, so it is something like a dirty bomb spreading radioactivity in a giant cloud that goes wherever the wind takes it. And then finally a complete and total meltdown of the nuclear core itself. A meltdown is where all the liquid meant to cool the nuclear reactor evaporates off and the nuclear core itself starts to melt, hence the "meltdown" term. With hundreds of nuclear plants over the world all suffering meltdowns at approximately the same time means that the ultimate punch-line for all this is that in addition to the hit we took from the sun there was a long standing nuclear fall-out all over the world. Nuclear fallout is essentially just dust that spews off radiation. Alpha particles are the larger bits of radiation and while the alpha particles are not safe they are much less dangerous that gamma rays. Gamma rays are the parts of radiation that cause the real damage; they can destroy DNA of people affected. Radiation sickness is in essence a person's body melting from the inside out; it is destroyed on a molecular level. That was of course after the flare actually hit, prior to that there was the fall of society, an end to the world as we know it, in a manner of speaking. So, people who managed to survive the flare had a more long-standing problem to worry about.

Now let us just think about all that happened in and around the time of the 'end'. Can you imagine how that feels? To see the world being destroyed, before your eyes. Well in a manner of speaking since you can't really see anything wherever you managed to hide. To feel, even for the briefest of seconds that you are the LAST person on earth. You have to understand that even on those days when you want solitude, when you don't want to hear anyone else, see anyone else. Those kinds of days when you just want to have a long bubble bath with a glass of wine, not my idea of a relaxing time but you get the point. Even on those kinds of days you never quite feel like the last person on Earth. It is almost impossible to feel that way legitimately. Even people in the deepest darkest depression who feel utterly alone know they are not. They see people. They can hear people being happy outside their windows, intruding in their misery with their happiness. In short, they know they are not alone no matter how alone they feel. Now me I truly felt for a time that I was the last person on Earth. There was no communicating with the outside. Every usual means of communication at my disposal was dead. Satellite phone; dead. Cellular phones; dead. Land lines; dead. Internet; dead. God damned smoke signals might as well have been dead, there was no one nearby to see them even if I had wanted to venture out to try to make them. And when coupled with the way everything was microwaved after the flare anyone who was able to see them would have just thought some dried-up part of the forest caught on fire from two sticks rubbing together. Or maybe a lightning strike. Now that I think about it I cannot recall at this point whether there were any lightning strikes in the immediate aftermath of the flare. My mind is kind of racing, it is almost astounding I never even thought of this before, it never even occurred to me. With the loss of everything electrical did the microwaves get rid of all the charged particles in the atmosphere as well? I really do not remember. Probably not; thunder and lightning simply were not important enough to remember which is why I cannot recall now but I wonder. And I am sure I will wonder for the rest of my days. I should also mention I was underground. I would not see flashes of light through the window, I had no window. I could not hear thunder so loud that my whole house shuddered; I was just a tad too underground and someplace too solid for mere thunder to rattle it. I do recall the funny mix that I encountered upon leaving my bunker, everything was kind of toasted and crispy from being microwaved but at the same time there was a kind of musty moistness in the air. I guess having everything being bombarded by solar radiation must have boiled off the top layer of water. Made it like a green house. Even in fairly temperate areas like the place I was living the humidity was stifling. This was an area that only ever felt humid like once every two years at best, and even then, for only like a day. Not days. And certainly not for weeks on end. After that there was the whole backswing where Mother Nature tries to reach equilibrium again. It rained, but again I don't recall there being lightning accompanying it, and then it seemed dry for a while. A big dump of water to get rid of the humidity then nothing for a good while. More days? More weeks? It's hard to say. It was definitely a while before the weather felt normal. The atmosphere, well it has never felt normal for me. Not since it happened. I have talked to others about this, but no one has the same kind of thoughts. It just seems… off… to me. Like when you have a balloon that someone rubbed on their head and it has that static charge. You hold that balloon close to you and you can feel that electricity, you can feel the charge and that's how the atmosphere always feels to me. It is probably just psychosomatic but oh well. It never changed things for me, it was just a feeling. And now there is no reason to even examine it closer. It is a minor note in my life, and I was the only one that seemed to experience it.

And now you may see what I mean about the mind going where it wants to. I was talking of feelings of utter loneliness, of isolation because there was no one left, and I digressed to talking of the weather. Now we should return to my original thought. It was obviously not the case that I was the last person on Earth. There were others, and if there were not more people then who am I writing to? I guess we could explain that years of solitude as the last man on Earth left me mad but that would be too simple and really, I don't think that would make the rest of this all that interesting to read. I mean the Diaries of a Madman are always popular but there really would not be too much left to say after this if I was the last person. There was one brief second where I truly felt like no one else could have survived the disaster, I was despondent. I had nothing to even hope for, nothing to look forward to. Anything that would be new to me would just have been old news. I could look at things from the past but there would never be anything new. No new works of art to see, no stories to read, no comedies to laugh at, no people to experience, nothing. And a real nothing is hard to fathom. It's an oubliette for your mind, a deep dark hole that you cannot escape from. The only reason I did not give in to despair I think was because I only looked down the hole, I did not jump in with both feet. There were more people. They were my salvation, and I was theirs. I became their keeper and they mine.

Now after all the death, destruction, flares, radiation & diseases, there was me, not the last man standing by any means but in all reality, I could have been. Always be prepared is one of those curious little idioms that came from the Boy Scouts I think. I was prepared, as soon as I realized I was not the only one to survive I resolved to step into the vacuum and become a leader. I needed to 'fix' things. I needed to make my life mean something. Especially, since I was no longer alone. But there was a problem I quickly noticed. When you look out on a nearly-empty world there is so much that needs to be done. Laws are created by people, without people there are no laws, and lawless is not a place you really want to live in. Don't get me wrong here; acting all tyrannical is not necessarily a goal of what I planned to do; it was just a means to an end. You need rules and laws. You need order. And things need to be done. My becoming a leader was my way of ensuring that I would not be living under some wishy-washy democrat who wants to put every decision to a vote. If it needs to be done, then I want it done. And that means I want it done now. Now don't get all political here, I'm not referring to the political party that used to exist, I'm referring to someone who believes whole-heartedly in democracy. Sometimes when people are in dire straits there is no time for debate, no time for committees, and really no reason for all that if you have a leader actually leading his/her people. And I'm not going to live in some place like the oil refinery from the Road Warrior movie, the little bastion of sanity with evil swarming around it. I want to live in a fortress built on law, order, strength and power and I will make evil afraid to even get within sight of the fortress for fear of my wrath. Yes, I know you are thinking that I am being overly dramatic, but I will just have to ask your forgiveness on that. No one else is going to aggrandize me and really, I am my own biggest fan. I am awesome.

CHAPTER 2 – BEST PLACES TO HIDE

Now don't misunderstand what I am writing about, this isn't a story about survival or redemption. Any hardships that were overcome and mentioned here are just meant to fill out the story, to make you understand all the aspects. You know I could be wrong, so I take that back, I have no idea what this story is about, nor do I know how you will interpret it. It is simply my side of the story, it is me defending myself by the only means I have available going into the future.

I was one of the smart ones, I had been constructing my own place for years, deep in the wilderness, and the closest settlement was nearly 50 miles away and only consisted of a few trappers and their families. I had not been building this place out of fear or paranoia; well I guess it depends on who you talk to, if you could talk to people who would know although in all reality they are all long dead. The reason I build my place was something much simpler than fear, and far more mundane than paranoia. I wanted some place nice and quiet, somewhere I could hear my self-think. This was to be far away from the cities which were plagued with crime, corruption and drugs. I wanted someplace to raise my children in safety, without the decadent influences that came along with the cities. Given what I said before it seems like such a hard thing to want and for people now-a-days to understand, wanting peace and quiet, someplace isolated, but that is just because there have not been cities in a long time, before the cataclysm some cities were massive, with thousands or even millions of people in a few square miles. I'm exaggerating slightly, but in truth that is the kind of thing I was trying to avoid; places too full of other people, too loud, too much negative stuff. Therefore, I made my own place, off in the wilderness and that was where I was when the chaos really began. I had been building the place pieces at a time, slowly as I had the time and/or the money.

My home was a nice normal bungalow-type house or cabin I guess would be a more appropriate description. It had 3 bedrooms, 2 baths, large kitchen and living room with an attachment containing a pool and a greenhouse for growing my own vegetables. All this was built so far from the nearest power grid that it was essential that it be an 'off-grid' homestead. About 20 large solar panels and 4 large wind turbines allowed all the energy production I'd ever need, with dozens of spares packed away in my storage shed. Plan for the improbable and you can adapt. A large concrete barn was used to house the animals, nothing too spectacular, couple cows, couple horses, and chickens for eggs. The concrete here was again essential, with the entire attic section of the barn being a large water reservoir, or cistern if you want to use a fancier sounding word, where the water was caught off the roof when it rains. This is one of those things that are necessary towards ensuring that I always have fresh water available for the garden, animals and my family. Two of the wind turbines and 4 of the solar panels are dedicated to this building just to ensure that the heaters keep the animals and water contained within from freezing in the winter; winter there was bitterly cold to say the least. Putting the reservoir in the attic also had a secondary purpose, firefighting. Biggest threat to livestock is the heater in the barn catching the hay on fire and killing all the animals in the barn. It used to happen countless times every year in farms all over the world and this led to the destruction of entire herds of cattle, or flocks of chickens or whatever of pigs while still in their pens. I really don't think they were able to get out of those pens but even if they could animals, like horses for example, tend to panic and freeze in the face of fire so the reservoir that was in the attic of the barn acts as an automatic fire sprinkler system, just in case. That was never needed, but it was there. Long-term survival involves long-term thinking. As I said before, I was not necessarily building for survival I was building for isolation, peace and quiet. As you read further I am sure you will conclude that I am a liar on this subject; which is probably true from a certain point of view. I never intended to be some kind of survivalist like some sort of weird doomsday cultist. I am just an ordinary kind of person who wanted quiet.

If you are paying attention you may be thinking that a bungalow does not sound like a place to hide out in against the impending end of the world. If you are thinking that, wonderful, you are paying attention. If not, then I commend your ability to continue reading in the face of what must be your horrible boredom. I also wonder if people reading this are getting annoyed at my breaking down of the fourth wall. Well I cannot help it, I am writing this as if I were answering questions, so I am essentially writing like I am talking to an interviewer. I wish I had been interviewed, that would have been a different kind of experience. For those of you who do not understand the fourth wall reference, when a room was shown on television only 3 walls were shown, the fourth was imagined where the camera was stationed, so breaking down the fourth wall is referring to people talking to the audience on a television program through the imaginary wall. And now back to our regularly scheduled program; surviving the cataclysm. Short side note: I think for the rest of my days I am going to try to refer to the end of the world as the cataclysm, I think I like the sound of that word.

Let us now discuss the heart of my far-off homestead. The basement of the house/cabin was humungous. I had a crew come in to pour the cement; it was made essentially like an underground garage, 2 levels, all under ground. I remember the contractor I had hired to do that work looked at me like I was completely mad when I told him I wanted a huge parkade built in the middle of nowhere. At first when I did not even have an explanation, it did sound all insane. I made up on the spot a weird winding story about how this was supposed to be a high-class hunting lodge for rich people and celebrities, this 'parking' area was scheduled to be where everything was really located. From the various vehicles, they would take around the property looking for stuff to hunt to the kitchens and staff quarters. On the surface, it would look just like any other cabin, but in reality, it was a four-star hotel just with all the workings hidden away. Or should I have said five-star? Did the rating go that high, I don't recall. "Yeah I'd expect those celebrity types would have to be spoiled like that" he remarked. I was almost proud of myself for coming up with an almost plausible story on the fly.

The plans I had him follow had required an extra two feet of space in the distance between the ceilings and the floors, in order to accommodate any 'alterations' that I might have wanted to include later. A solar flare spewing radiation was one of those kinds of situations that require alterations which I honestly had not considered but it was easily combated. The whole thing was built pretty much in the same manner as any underground parking lot; it is two-levels. Oh, and it happens to have lead-plated ceilings in the unlikely case there was a 'disaster' and resulting fallout. But I wasn't paranoid, right? This is probably where you are thinking that I was paranoid, or even still am however I assure you it was more of covering angles and not an actual expectation of something bad happening. To be a little glib about it let us just say that my dream home was possibly not as bright and rainbows as other people's dream homes; but nonetheless it was still a dream home. For clarity I would also like to mention that the thinking present during the Cold War really helps you prepare for anything. For example: 0.4 inches of lead, or 2.4 inches of concrete, or 3.6 inches of packed earth or 500 ft. of air can reduce the amount of gamma rays by half. An ideal fallout shelter has about ten halving-thicknesses of packed earth, which equates to around a meter or yard of dirt. Now my shelter, on the other hand had about 12 inches worth of concrete surrounding plates around 1 and a half inches thick made of pure lead. That put it at about 10 halving-thicknesses of concrete and lead when combined. No radiation was getting through there. And that was the upper level, the lower level of the basement had around another 12 inches of concrete. If I had actually been paranoid about radiation I would have been down there all the time but I wasn't; it was just another part of the house.

So, in conclusion to this whole convoluted statement of crazy/not crazy, paranoid/not paranoid I'll just admit that I was little overzealous. The final layer of pouring the cement involved adding the aforementioned inch and half thick lead plates that were latex-coated because well, you just never know if/when nuclear war will be declared, and really why the hell not, it's not like it really truly hurt anything. But they did add a ton of weight to the floor. Well, a ton is kind of an understatement, it was tons and tons of weight, but what can you do? Now luckily, I am the kind of person who would rather have a support pole be 3 ½ feet in diameter rather than the 2 feet the contractor was suggesting. I did not need to think of an excuse for these on the spot as I had during our initial discussions, I had plenty of time to think of something plausible, but even with that I simply could not come up with anything. It in all reality was looking like a bomb shelter at that point, and really, I'm pretty sure he was just rolling with it, what else was he going to say? I paid well. I just hired someone else to bring the plates in and put them in place then had a third party pour a thin layer of cement over top, all of that in a effort to at least try to look a little less like some whacked-out crazy person. Overly circuitous but sometimes it just has to be that way. Something that looks like a giant bomb shelter only attracts attention. And believe me, not the good kind of attention, but the kind involving police and psychiatrists. Someone who knew the real plans for this place asked me why go through all this, what is wrong with just having a normal cabin with say a normal basement underneath. I could not quite answer her. It did not make sense in a normal kind of way; I only knew that I needed someplace that I could make impenetrable and self-sufficient. Nothing quite makes you feel as safe and secure as being in a place that is all but indestructible to everything short of a bunker buster bomb or a direct nuclear blast. It is funny that one of the hallmarks of someone who is 'insane' is that they don't know they are insane. By me saying that I am not mad pretty much leaves me open to being declared insane. I guess I will just have to risk it and leave it up to you to decide. Maybe the lead plates show a streak of paranoia, I will admit to that. But I just wanted the peace and quiet and self-sufficiency, I know that I could have done it the 'normal way' but that just wouldn't be me. I was right to put them in there though, it was an extra measure of safety and in the end, I survived.

The upper level of the basement was pretty much a mirror of the above-ground "house", the house being mostly for show. The fridge upstairs never had food in inside, it was never even plugged in. The beds were never slept in except by the few family members that came to spend a weekend. No clothes in the drawers of the dressers in the bedrooms. The house above-ground was a complete and total shell, a misdirection in order to give the appearance of normalcy. One of the rooms in the upper level of the basement that was not on the misdirection's floor plan was the library, the room that contained all my books as well as my armory. Essentially a large vault built into the cement wall contained my various weapons of war; swords, axes, maces, flails, and of course what armory would be complete without a large assortment of firearms. I'm not a poor mountaineer and I don't have a problem keeping my family fed, but some venison is always a nice addition to the menu. I do not even think I could name all the guns that were in the collection, I do recall there were a number of weapons which I did not need and were in essence overkill. All manner of machine guns, rifles, handguns; some made by the Russians, some made by the Germans, Israelis, Americans, etc. My favorite of all these weapons in the collection was my .50 caliber rifle. I will not say that machine guns are not fun, they are so much fun to shoot with, but there is really nothing like firing massive bullets out of a rifle. This is the kind of weapon that if need be can take out a man from a mile away, but that is the kind of stuff that will be brought up more at the appropriate time.

The lower level, the dungeon as I more than often referred to it as, contained all my contingency plans as well as a lot of extras. By descending a spiraling ramp from the outside going all the way down you come to the lower level of the basement. This level was meant to be a back-up temporary barn in the event of the aforementioned non-occurring fire in the barn. As well there was another large section of the dungeon that was set-up to be a rarely used as indoor grow-op which would probably be the envy of any man growing marijuana, assuming anyone had an idea of what was contained in that room; it came complete with UV lights, an irrigation system which could be fed from my reservoir or the nearby underground spring, this area was large enough that I could feed my entire family in the event of a [nuclear] winter where not enough light got through the clouds to use the green house. The freezer, pantry and storage room were in this lower level, enough food and provisions to last 6 months easy, a year if we were not worried about eating random meals made up of random ingredients. Reflecting now I don't think I even know how much provisions it held, it could have been more if I had tried to stock it better, but let's say 6 months for sure.

I feel I have gotten terribly off-track; let's try to bring things back a little to what I was speaking of earlier, such as my talk of 2012 and the Mayans and all that. I found that Armageddon prophecies were always interesting to read and interesting to ponder; "How will the world come to an end today?" which is why I always liked reading the works of men like Nostradamus. Watching Al Gore's movie about how we are destroying ourselves, he was of course wrong in the actual manner we would get destroyed but it was still interesting. I remember reading Stephen King's 'The Stand'. This is a massive book, something like 1200 pages. I was so enthralled with this book that I read it from cover to cover in two sittings. Then after I was done reading I watched the movie version, all the while I was thinking of how great it would be for the world to be cleansed of most of these people, so we can finally make the kind of civilization and society where you do not have to worry about how your kids will be growing up; predicated, of course, on people surviving the destructive event. In my mind, it was a 'tabula rasa' kind of thing. Now unfortunately for me, that was the absolute best I could ever hope for, for the world to end. Simply put, people of my station do not tend to get to be the people in positions of power, not without some extraordinary event. The only way I could ever be anything more than just a cog in the machine is for one of those events to actually happen and for me to seize upon the opportunity to make something of myself. Can you say the end of the world is a fortuitous occasion?

I'm sure to some reading my ranting here they may conclude that I am indeed crazy, but I have spent some time thinking on this and I feel I have a solid argument against that assumption. Since crazy people don't know they are crazy; to them the purple fish chasing after the invisible cats in their living room are completely real, and hence they are bonkers. There was a list that I printed from the internet, you know, before it went away forever, and although it is point form-ish it does give quick and dirty version(s) of my crazy. You know, I really miss the internet, not the porn upon porn upon holy fuck that is bloody sick porn but just that any fact that I pretty much ever had the desire to know, it was right there, all I had to do is look it up. I just realized that pretty much anyone reading this will have next to no idea that the internet is/was. In short, it was pretty much every single piece of information you could ever want, plus everything else. There were computer games you could play with people from all across the globe. There was… There was, well there was porn, I seem to have forgotten everything else that it could be used for. It was very handy, especially if you wanted the quick dirty and/or sometimes biased version of a particular piece of information (this is not meant to be a pun on the mind-boggling amount of porn on the internet).

So anyways, back to what I was talking about. The list I printed off. It was some Great Phobia List. Firstly, there is of course agoraphobia which is the irrational fear of open spaces or of being in crowded, public places like markets and/or the fear of leaving a safe place. This is one which I will readily admit to having. On a couple of occasions, I have had panic attacks at family events due to this, which was naturally before the cataclysm. Too many people in a small space just did not agree with me.

After most of the world's population died, everything just seemed to feel so much less crowded. I know you are thinking that it was less crowded, but what I am saying is that it didn't matter if I was in a room by myself or with dozens of people, everything felt open, I felt as though I could breathe. And you could also say I have anthropophobia which is the fear of people or society, but really, I do not fear society or people I simply don't want them near me, crowding me. And that belief would probably lead a psychologist to haphephobia or in words that everyone can understand the fear of being touched. This is another I will admit to, to a degree. Everyone has their personal 'bubble', the area around themselves that they do not want people to invade. That initially started evolutionarily as a defense mechanism against attack from rivals, or I guess more accurately it was a priming mechanism, if someone is in your bubble it pretty much used to mean that you were about to fight or have sex, I guess it could totally have been both. It just so happens that with my personal bubble, it is bigger than most people's and I really really do not like people breaking into it. And why do I not want to have people breaking into my bubble? Well that leads to mysophobia, the fear of germs. If you kiss someone the DNA from the bacteria in their mouth can live in your mouth for the rest of your life. You become a host for the germs that they carry around with them. And that is just the beginning. People are dirty, random objects. There is kind of no other way to put it, we are filthy and completely covered in germs. We are simply walking and talking Petri dishes. Take any object that has not been thoroughly sterilized and you will find it is covered in germs. When I was in university a micro-biology class took a swab from the door handle to the girl's bathroom and they managed to grow and isolate gonorrhea. The door handle of all things. Not the toilet seat, not the handle to the bathroom stall and not the tap to the sink. And this is from the girl's bathroom; they are supposed to be the clean ones in our species. You would expect the toilet seat to be more disgusting although the door handles did prove to be grosser, at least in that particular instance.

The rest of my phobias kind of run along the same thread and are pretty much intertwined, there is sociophobia, and like it looks like it should be, it is the fear of society or people in general, catagelophobia the fear of being ridiculed and one that almost sounds like sociophobia, social phobia which wonderfully is the fear of being evaluated negatively in social situations. Pretty much as far as I can see it I have pantophobia, in essence the irrational, illogical, unreasonable fear of everything. And hey for good measure how about I throw in hippopotomonstrosesquipedaliophobia which coincidentally is the fear of long words. I do have a degree in Psychology and one of the first things they tell you when you start taking those classes is that through the course of your studies you will essentially become a mental hypochondriac; you will read your textbooks about schizophrenia, bipolar disorder, depression, sleep disorders and the like and you will think, Holy Shit, I'm a depressed schizophrenic with bipolar disorder who has narcolepsy, when really you are not. The basis for a 'mental disorder is that in short you have to be debilitated by your disorder, which is really the source of my own difficulties in categorizing myself as crazy or not. I think everyone else would characterize me as being crazy, but really, what do they know. On one hand, I functioned just fine prior to the flare, I was able to go to town for food and whatever supplies I needed, I could walk right into the crowded grocery store, make my purchases and walk out, without suffering a panic attack. I could shake a person's hand without freaking out and slathering myself in hand sanitizer all the while screaming about how they are filthy. I could do everything that anyone else did, I was just uncomfortable while doing it and given the option (which I had) I chose to remove myself from most of those situations.

So now to keep beating that dead horse; am I crazy? Well according to everyone around me right now I am completely fucking sane. It is funny, on one hand you always like to know that you are sane, that the purple fish you see really is in that fishbowl. On the other hand, well you can get away with a lot of shit if you are just batshit bonkers, I mean look at Vince Li, he cut a guy's head off, ate bits of his victim (eyes, nose and ears if I remember correctly) and then walked to the front of the bus and in front of police dropped the head on the floor like it was a sack of potatoes. That all happened on a bus, with dozens of other passengers, the latter half right in front of the law enforcement and he in legal terms got away with it. He got sent to a psychiatric facility and they were debating whether or not to give him like day passes to go out for a walk like 2 or 3 years after all the business on the bus happened. You want to know what is crazy. That is bloody crazy, letting crazy out of the cage. And that is the kind of thing that regularly happened in the world before the cataclysm. People getting away with shit based on technicalities. Crazy people who were deemed as being too crazy to take responsibility for their own actions. Don't people know that if you just let those people out they will be infecting everyone they meet with crazy; there will be an epidemic of cosmic orgasmic proportions of loony walking down every street. People will hear voices, voices will hear their own voices, it's a vicious circle of nuts that can't undone, once those people have spread the insanity it will just be there permeating everything. But that is a politician for you, thinking more about looking like they actually care about a crazy person's rights then thinking of the greater good. The primary goal of what a leader should be doing is thinking of the greater whole and letting a crazy killer out for any stupid reason is just stupid. I think that may have been one of the tenets that I initially adhered to when I told everyone in Republica that I would be taking full control of the city-state. That old saying absolute power corrupts absolutely, yeah it kind of does. I would just like to point out that people who are crazy or have some sort of deficit should not have a free pass on their actions. Crazy (or whatever) only *explains their actions, it does not excuse it.* And unluckily for me this is the kind of standard I was being judged under. In hindsight, that never did bode well for me, oh well too late now. Either way, I would have ended up right here.

There is something to be said here about the bad guy in this story being a coward at heart which, like I have pointed out I think is not really true. Yes, I have irrational fears, everyone does. Some people are afraid of snakes; ophidiophobia. Some people are afraid of spiders; arachnophobia. Some of clowns, coulrophobia, and I actually think that one is completely valid; those painted-faced fuckers are truly evil. But you can see the contradiction here; I am supposed to be the great evil bad guy here, the one who was the tyrant. Maybe all that I did was my coping mechanism, I really should know that but it is one of those things, someone with an irrational fear is not going to just admit that it controls their lives. And anyways I'm all over that.

There are times like now where I wish I could just go back to my library and do nothing but read, start at one end of the room and follow it around all the way to the other side then go back again. You can get lost in all that knowledge. If knowledge is power would the solution to stopping Adolf Hitler have been to give that man a library card? Simply give him the power he craved in book form.

Having nothing but quiet is what I wanted all along and lucky for me my wishes appear to have come true.

CHAPTER 3 – NEIGHBORHOOD BARBEQUE

I remember on the day that the flare finally hit Earth there was a kind of eager anticipation among seemingly everyone who was not engaging in hooliganism and out looting to watch the arrival of the flare on TV. A hope that everything people had been told was going to happen would not come to pass and all would be sun and roses. That sun of course not being a sun that would try to kill us all. There was a wonderful CNN special report where they harkened up to the International Space Station, so they could get the eagle-eyed view of the expected splendor of the auroras across the globe. The special report did not go as planned. This led to one of the last things being broadcast over the airwaves on the television before the signal went down was the screams of the astronauts (and one cosmonaut) up there in the international space station as they were bombarded by the flare and micro-waved alive. I guess someone from NASA had said the shielding they had up there would hold or something like that. It didn't, obviously. It was a horrible event that rang in my ears for days. I couldn't believe they let it across the air, but one can only assume that the guy with his finger on the button to cut the signal was daydreaming or did not quite realize what was happening. Screams can sound like cheers I guess. I really shouldn't be trying to make excuses for some long-dead person. He or she could have saved me a few nightmares if I had not heard that scream in surround sound. After the probably 15 seconds it took to cut the feed they brought the view back to the news anchor who had the same stunned, shocked expression that I expect I had; it was probably another full 15 seconds before she composed herself enough to be able to mutter something about technical difficulties. I am not sure how long the signal stayed on after that, I was no longer in the mood to watch TV.

Back to microwaving. Have you ever put a metal bowl in a microwave oven? It is quite a show; there are tons of sparks that fly off that bowl. Microwaves, the waves not the machine, are a type of radiation but are different from radiation such as gamma radiation in that they are not energetic enough to really penetrate the body and therefore cannot cause the same kinds of harm as the more lethal kinds can. I assume this is the reason for the sparks being thrown off; it has something to do with the density of the metal, or possibly just the reflective qualities of the material, either way it interferes with what microwaves are designed to do. Microwave ovens have a coil or something inside that actually creates or emits microwaves (to be honest I am not sure just how the insides of it work); those microwaves hit the object (usually food) inside the microwave oven and actually cause the molecules that make up that thing to vibrate. I used to think that the molecules rubbed against each other, but it turns out that the simple act of moving those molecules and making them vibrate is enough to cause it to generate heat and therefore "cook" things. And since it is using what is essentially a mild form of radiation to cook that is why you can find that things will be cooked and rubbery on the outside while still cold in the middle; the microwaves were not strong enough to penetrate all the way to the middle and cause the molecules there to vibrate. More than likely that is do to water content or something like that, which is why if you let it run long enough then the whole thing will be dry and rubbery but will manage to actually cook the center, one the water on the outer edges evaporated out then the waves were able to get to the middle.

It was actually kind of surprising that the signal still managed to be transmitted from the space station to the ground; I guess that radio must have been made in Taiwan and not China. Really what were they expecting, the space station even with modern composites is probably still 95% metal. I wake up some mornings still, like today, this morning I woke up and I was back watching that same broadcast, hearing those screams. You can't scream in the vacuum of space, but you can scream from it. But I am getting off my main topic, the survival. My survival. God, do I even have a topic? This is truly all just the ramblings of a madman, a *MADMAN*. I am just going to imagine you smirked at that.

The night before the flare hit us full force I spent the entire night outside taking down the solar panels and wind turbines so they did not get fried by the radiation. With that much solar radiation, even before it hit full on, the aurora borealis, the northern lights were so bright it was like being in the middle of some city at night with all the street lights shining. And the color was dazzling, a normal northern light looks is a varying blend of blues and greens and all the other colors of the rainbow, it looks almost like a floating ethereal reflection of the ocean, which is probably what it actually is. What we saw that last night was dazzling but also terrifying, the same floating ethereal reflection but this was one color; blood red. It was not as bright as daytime but was getting damn close. The day the flare hit us full force I was downstairs, tending to the animals, picking through the garden for some nice carrots to treat them with, I had spent the better part of two days moving most of the plants from the greenhouse down to the hydroponic garden. At the height of the day the flare hit the earth full on, I was sitting in my library, reading Macbeth and drinking hot chocolate. Not that I was trying to be all coy about the death and destruction going on outside in the rest of the world. I wasn't being callous as others may say. There is simply a point where you know there is nothing you can do for the masses at large, so you might as well try to relax, keep your own calm and not run all panicked and depressed feeling into the noonday flare as kind of a suicide by sunlight. I must be very cynical in my old age, because that actually sounded fairly funny. It's like if someone just wanted to do a 'cry-for-attention' and half-ass their suicide attempt they would slather on their SPF 5,000,000 sunscreen and go outside to get a wicked sunburn.

Now really where all that this book is leading is to where I am now, which is something that we will get to I assure you, I am just trying to cover all the lead-ups before we get there. I used to hate it when stories used to essentially start mid-story and not give us the backstory, the whole reason the story began. The idea of the panic I just mentioned is one that I think I should elaborate on, since really this is kind of the 'beginning', my start down the path of evil, the march to the anti-Christ. I'm obviously overstating things but you probably understand what I mean. But in reality, what I am going to be talking about now is one of the real turning points of my story. The real gift of any successful dictator is to be able to make things happen, even if they are horrible things. To make the populace in general want you to be in charge of them and their lives. To make the problems disappear. Right now, what I am talking about is the first real problem that "disappeared", right in front of everyone. With their consent. And once something has disappeared, well, no one can really say anything then.

Do not ask me why this popped into my head at this point, something must have triggered it. There was a news story on the Discovery channel maybe? I don't remember, one of those educational channels most likely, and the program was talking about how some wildlife became scarce in the time just before the flare hit. They went on and on about the change in animal behavior and the host of the show completely dismissed all of these events. Hell, I wish I had made more of an effort to take them seriously. Now you see it has been documented that animals act differently just before an earthquake strikes. I am not sure if this is true or not, but they did point out in Phenomenon, oh that is a movie by the way, it has something to do with ultra-low-level sound waves or something just before the quake. Really, I am not even sure if that was reality or just Hollywood science, but it seems to make sense. I don't know how the flare relates to that, it could be anything really, and animals are so much more in tune with nature than we are, but they acted differently. I had noticed on my ride from my house to Republica there was nothing major, but a deer and a few birds singing, but when you think of it that is astounding. People were sheltered, at least a little and were virtually wiped off the planet, whereas the wildlife were all exposed, possibly being under a tree in some forest which is now brown and dead but for the most part just out in the open and they survived. And since then I have obviously seen many animals, the one that seems to be a tad light in terms of representation is man's best friend. Dogs. I guess it happens that being the oldest domesticated animal happened to make the dog want to be by their master's side, even if that meant being cooked alive. I remember there was this one time I had a dog come charging out of a neighbor's house, and I had been less than 15 feet from the door. This dog charging straight for me caused me to…jump. But this was not a jump that led me up a tree and away from the dog but in fact I managed to jump right into my karate stance, which I think is funny. I hate karate but the kids that happened to see all this happening remarked that they thought I was about to karate chop the dog. See that really led nowhere and had nothing to do with my ultimate ramble but that is where my mind led me. It's your fault for even reading it; I warned you that I would go off on random tangents.

One of my definitely less popular policies, right from the announcement of it, was the outlawing of eating meat. To me it seemed completely valid and the smart thing to do. Believe me, I am not a vegan, or even a vegetarian. I don't love animals so much I won't eat meat. I just hate plants that much. That was another joke. I think I am not doing very well at being a serious writer. I am not totally sure if joking at a time like this makes me more human as I try to allay my fears through humor; an unfeeling monster who just doesn't care; or a socially inept person who has no idea when the appropriate time to make a joke is. In my estimation, I would say it is around a 65/35/20 split but really what does it matter. The real reason behind the outlawing of meat was simple and practical. As I mentioned before I had a few animals that I kept alive and most people did not take the same steps that I did, meaning that there were few farm animals left, definitely not enough to go around butchering. Even with the wildlife that I mentioned, there were a few of this and that but not enough to just go around killing indiscriminately. In order to have the ability to hunt and eat meat in the future we needed to let the surviving animals rebound. And they did; it took a few years for the numbers to get back up there but it did happen, at which point hunting things like deer was again allowed. It was a temporary ban that meant survivability for our entire community for the future. We even were able to find more farm animals to breed with the ones that I had saved, meaning that for the future we were able to keep having things like eggs and milk. There was also another very practical reason to have people eating more plants and less meat. The amount of effort it takes to grow even a pound of meat is far greater than the effort it takes to grow a pound of fruit, vegetable or grain. Any plant really. I do not remember the actual statistics, but it works out to something like 100 pounds of plants need to be fed to a cow in order to get 1 pound of meat off of it. I am positive I do not have that number right but it is something astronomical like that. Thinking of it like that the amount of plants needed to raise a cow to adulthood such that you can butcher it we'll say is something like 15000 pounds of grass or hay or whatever; that number really seems too high but it does not diminish my point. The point is that to get a cow that weighs like 1500 pounds you have to feed it lots and lots of food. And that 1500 pounds of cow is not even all meat, that includes the hooves, hair, bones, organs, etc. At best, we'll say you get 750 pounds of meat off that cow at the cost of 15,000 pounds of plants that you fed to it. You can feed a much bigger population with 15,000 pounds of food than with 750 pounds. And that is the ultimate reason. That and I hate plants and love animals.

As I mentioned that was not a popular policy as everyone wanted a steak I guess. Not that I did not want that either, I would simply prefer to be able to have something in the future as opposed to only now. People are so short-sighted when they want something. But think about it, there is so much in human history relating to extinction of other species. Some people say we hunted things like the wooly mammoth into extinction, although I kind of doubt that one. The aurochs, termed the primal cow, was essentially the bridge from wild cattle to domesticated cattle, went extinct in Poland in like the year 1600. Dodo Birds, wiped off the face of the Earth within decades of their discovery. The American Buffalo/Bison was nearly wiped out. Elephants were in danger of being wiped out prior to the cataclysm. Same with both White and Black rhinos. Tasmanian tigers; gone. Carrier pigeons; gone. And countless other species. Now not all extinctions are the work or fault of humans, but too many were. It was not even necessarily over-hunting, poaching for ivory or horns but could have been other things, habitat loss, pollution of their environments, who knows what else. Main thing is I sure as hell did not want there to be more extinctions especially if they could be avoided. I am not the first kind of person to think in this way. You can look at two different massive populations from the past and how they dealt with the issue. China embraced, in my mind, the short-term gain idea. They would eat essentially anything, many things that people in North America would have turned their nose up at. Things like turtle, snake, dog, cat, pretty much anything that moved and was made of meat. The other side of the coin was India. A country that made things like cows sacred, the kind of idea that essentially necessitated a move towards vegetarianism; making an animal sacred is in my mind simply a means of stopping people from acting on their own. Both of these places, pre-cataclysm, had over a billion people. And yes, billion with a B. Again, I know it is kind of hard to fathom that many people. So anyways, how do you feed that many people? Either you eat anything that moves and supplement it with plants or you eat more plants; which as I pointed out earlier is kind of the easier path. I guess I followed the Indian example. There are all types of lessons that you can learn if you pay attention to things and think about them in a critical way. As a further example let us look at another oriental culture, Japan. There were so many people that turned up their nose at the idea of eating sushi because, it is, you know… raw fish. Just a side note, sushi refers more to the rice in a roll as opposed to whatever was in the roll and it did not have to be fish at all and can be cooked. Japan was an island; and when compared to the size of its population, a very small island. Things like wood could be completely depleted in no time if people used it as freely as it was used in other parts of the world. Meaning that unlike other places, they could not burn wood for fuel for everything, meaning that they had to learn alternative ways of preparing food. Now it just so happens that fish can be eaten raw with fewer consequences than other meats like pork or chicken when they are raw. And that is my point, a culture learned to adapt with what they had, what they could use and made it work. Same idea with eating rice. Rice was a staple food in many cultures, including the oriental ones. Originally, I thought that they grew/ate rice due to topography; since it was a lot easier to grow food that took advantage of the marshes like a rice patty, then it is to drain a marsh so that you can grow drier crops in that area. However, I was mistaken and that is not why they did it; the real reason they grew rice in wet fields has to do with weed control; rice can grow in marshes, weeds cannot so they have a field dedicated to food without the regular problems with pests. A very simple adaptation to use what you have in the best manner possible.

One last divergence before I get to the two things I actually want to touch on. Continuing with the idea of depleting resources, like for example wood. As I mentioned before they kind of found an alternative way of thinking in Japan to deal with the lack of disposable wood. There are a couple of good examples of places where they were not so brilliant and really lacked sufficient foresight: Easter Island and Greenland. Easter Island was well known in my time for being the island full of stone heads. Those heads weighed many tons each and were constructed by people without the aid of modern machinery. The stone being quarried many miles from where the heads eventually rested. They were moved there being rolled on logs, which essentially acted like wheels. Very simple and effective. I am honestly less knowledgeable about the reasons why they lost all their trees on this island, but the end result was that the loss of trees led to a change in the ecosystem of the island. That led to famine, which in turn led to something of a revolt or rebellion as the people of the island tried to appease the gods who had suddenly forsaken them. This led to many more deaths than just the famine caused; some due to sacrifices, but

I would venture a greater number being due to plain and simple murder. One person wants the food that another person has, that person doesn't want to just give it away and eventually one of them is dead. The population in modern times was significantly less than there had been when the stone heads were erected, now I will not go as far as to say it is all due to the loss of their trees but at the very least it played a part. Now my other example I do know a bit more of the details. Greenland, while not really green as the name says although it was a little greener when they first discovered it (that name was an intentional misdirection orchestrated by the discoverer of the island that was meant to make other Vikings want to move there). Greenland upon discovery had a fair number of trees which were cut down for various reasons; building materials for making their buildings, fuel for both heating those buildings and cooking. Swaths of trees were also cut down in order to make room for farm animals as Vikings were primarily farmers; raping and pillaging was more of their hobby. After they were done cutting down effectively all the trees well it turns out that Greenland is less hospitable than before. There was no more wind-break to cut down the north wind coming from the Arctic, there was no more fuel to heat their homes with and nothing to make more homes with. And on top of this they did not learn the lessons of the people who were already living there on how to survive in a very cold environment. Those people are ones formerly called Eskimos, and then I believe it went to being called Inuit, then something else I think. I'm not even sure if it matters anymore, in all this time no one I have come across has reported anything about people still alive in the Arctic. I guess it is possible, with the tilt of the Earth and all they could have effectively received less of a dose of microwaves than the rest of the world, but who knows. So those were my two examples which at the very least kind of allude to how people without proper foresight or ability to think outside the box can really screw themselves over. That is the reason meat was outlawed for a time. People needed to be self-sufficient and utilize re-useable resources. And in the short term after the cataclysm animals were in short supply and there were not enough of them to be considered renewable.

Looking back to the beginning of this bit I am writing now it seems weird how I have gone from talking of the last astronauts and the horror of their final moments being sent across the airwaves to what was my first kill as leader. There was a time when I was just kind of a respected leader type who people just gravitated to. Most people actually cannot tell the difference between legitimate competence and confidence. If you appear to know what you are doing or have answers they will look to you as being a leader. I was confident enough and able to think outside the box well enough in this brave new world to seem very competent I guess. Everyone I came across asked me questions like I had all the answers. They asked what they could or should do now. I told them and that just became the habit for me telling them what to do.

I am not sure if I am even framing this turning point in the proper kind of light. In my mind I really did see the events at the time as a move in a positive direction; it was not until later that it became negative and tyrannical; although even then I did not really see it that way. So, going way back in what I have already written I mentioned my farm animals, specifically here I am referring to my cows. Jokingly I called them Cow Number One and Cow Number Two because you should never name anything you may have to someday kill. It saves you from getting too attached to them. Their actual names were Blackie and Battie. Battie was called that cause when she was still a calf she kind of batted her eyes at me the first time I saw her. Blackie was obviously named for her colorings; pure white. Did I mention so far that I have a weird sense of humor? I don't believe that I did however I apparently do. It is really kind of pun-based or based on contradictions but hey it works for me. Blackie was the elder at 7 years, with Battie being just over 3 years when the cataclysm happened although Battie was the bigger of the two. I am sure this is likely due to difference in breeds however I really don't know the difference between most types of cows. All I know is they produced milk which is what they were there for. I may have planned further into the future to turn one of them into food however that was not in my immediate plans.

Before I had even enacted my moratorium on meat, people had been hunting the animals that had survived the cataclysm in the area surrounding our town. I initially did not have a problem with it, I didn't even think about it. I was more concerned with building the town up. That was until one morning I walked out of my house to find Battie dead in my backyard. She had her throat slit sometime during the middle of the night, which in a way was not surprising. Killing in that manner was quiet, meaning that I or no one else would have been alerted to what was occurring. As well Blackie and Battie were very domesticated. You could walk up to them and they would barely flinch; the worst thing was that once you started petting them they would not want you to stop, especially Battie, I had seen her follow more than one person who dared to walk away to do something else after they had started to pet her. They would walk, and she would follow. They would see this and begin to jog a little, she would begin to sort of trot; they would run and she should run…for about 3 seconds before she remembered she was a cow and not meant to go fast. That is a wonderful thing to remember, it kind of takes the sting out of her ignoble death. It was plain to see the person who had killed her was in a rush; a fairly sizable piece of meat had been hacked from her exposed left side. I remember my first reaction to seeing her was utter disbelief and shock. I panicked, looking to see if it was some other mysterious cow that had wandered into my yard in the night, but no of course it wasn't. It only took mere seconds for that panic and shock and sadness to turn into anger. I was always close to all of my animals and just because she was a cow did not diminish that at all. I can still clearly remember gritting my teeth together so tightly that my jaw hurt for a week, my teeth actually throbbed for a day or two. I grit my teeth together so hard it astounds me that I did not break a tooth. At this same time my mind was moving, thinking. How will this play out? And like that my face became placid; I smirked a little. It was show time. Like an actor setting himself up to read lines in an audition; I just turned off all my outward emotions and became calm. Well, appeared calm at least.

We had someone in the town that had done some hunting in the past; he was well versed enough with it to be able to properly skin an animal, cut it into useable pieces of meat. He was not a butcher per se but he did the job, the real 'butcher' was the one that had killed Battie in the first place, he had really done a piss poor job of cutting off what he did take, that was much plainer to see once she was being cut up properly. I sent word around that there would be a barbeque for everyone in town at the square, with of course meat provided by yours truly. In any other context this would have been seen as buying votes; which it may have been in a way however this was partly pragmatism, partly a way to flush out the person who had really done it. In the end I did not even need to do it so it ultimately was just my gift to the people; a way to placate them a little as I delivered bad news.

While the meat was all being prepared, a fire pit of sufficient size was dug in the middle of town, with tables and chairs brought in to accommodate everyone. Condiments, and side-dishes. Potatoes wrapped in foil were lined up. We even had table clothes brought out to give the whole thing a more 'homey' feel. Everything was being done so I decided to take a walk around. Much to my initial surprise I came across a smell that should not have been happening just yet. The smell of cooking meat, smoke and burning hair permeated the air. The burning hair part was kind of mild but it took away from the pleasantness of what I smelled. That and my anger, I mean it was my animal that had been killed so really I was none too pleased at the outcome. I simply made a note and moved along. I knew who lived in the house the smell was emanating from. I could even see the wisps of smoke coming from the backyard. They say that revenge is a dish best served cold. Well I am patient enough that I will not do anything like that when I am hot but cold is a little too long for my liking. Luke warm is close enough. The only reason you would wait until it could be described as 'cold' is so that you are not acting rashly. So, you properly plan things out. You can get away with it. That is not something that I had to worry about at that point. John Thomas lived in that house and he was going to pay.

John was a selfish man, and I am not just saying that because he killed my cow and stole off with some of her meat in the night. No, he was one of those kinds of people that found someone else's shelter and through one means or another stole it from them. In talking with others I learned that prior to everything he has been married four times before he was 40; pretty much with each marriage seeming to be in between stints in prison. He was a thief and a liar. Really not the kind of person anyone would want to be around anyways but in the interest of fairness he was permitted to live among us. Everyone deserves a second chance, right? Wrong. You deserve a second chance if you make a mistake. If you make an error. If you, in the heat of the moment, do something regrettable. He used up his chances in my mind. He did not just kill something out of hunger or by accident. He made a number of conscious choices to do what he did. He came in the middle of the night. He chose a silent weapon. He killed in a manner that would not allow for the animal to make a sound. He cut her open. Every single one of those things were a decision and he kept going. When I walked by his house he was cooking what he had stolen, hell by the fact that I could smell burning hair meant that he did not even do it right and he just threw a piece of meat on a grill without even taking the skin and hair off.

John was 5'10''. Brown hair and eyes. He had been heavier before the cataclysm but now was obviously a little thinner; his skin seemed to hang off of him a bit. That should be a little expected as there were no more fast food restaurants, grocery stores or convenience stores operating, meaning that he would not have had the abundant access he once had to fast/junk food. No diet works quite as well as removing all sources of food except canned goods and dry items. I mean you can survive on those things and many people did however it is not the best thing in terms of diet. In any event, John was a fairly normal looking person. He did not seem to have any real outstanding features other than his skin no longer fitting him as snuggly as it once had. I had seen him before around the town and he always seemed to be one of those people that just did not want to follow directions. Despite being a normal, relatively healthy person he seemingly did not have any skills or ability to perform even the easiest of tasks. As we tried to make everyone in the town a productive member of society he lagged behind always having to be essentially dragged to keep up with the rest of the people. And now it was obvious why; he would rather take from others, take the easy way instead of a more difficult way. The way that benefits more people than just himself. I mean, it's not like it is the most beneficial thing however a cow producing milk is much more renewable in the short term than killing one half of the total number of cows available. I sat down the street watching; every once in a while, I would get a slight waft of the smell of cooking meat as the wind shifted almost imperceptibly. I do not even know long I sat there exactly. It was right until the barbeque was starting when he finally came out of his front door. His lips seemed to glisten with the grease still on his face from Battie. I walked, sauntered if you like, behind him as we walked to the middle of town. It did take a lot of effort in order to be patient. I had already decided what I would do, and to do it properly required a crowd. I needed the people to see it. He was going to be an example. This was the start of a very pivotal moment in my life.

Upon arriving at the middle of town the barbeque had already started to get into full-swing. People began to congregate. I waded through a sea of people, each thanking me for my generosity, and my caring and my love for the people. It was like I was an actual politician from before the cataclysm, where I was just shaking hands and kissing babies. In my mind that always gets switched around to the funnier/more disturbing 'shaking babies and kissing hands'. I walked slowly through the crowd, not even bothering to keep an eye on John, he was not going anywhere. As I neared the small stage type thing that had been hastily constructed I made eye contact with my two "henchmen"; Jason and Will. Now these two had up until this point been not much more than helpers and something akin to runners, spreading my orders throughout the land but this was enough to secure their loyalty. They had heard me talk on countless occasions; they were well aware of my plans for the future. Not for taking power and holding it with an iron grip, but for rebuilding and making things as much like they were. Always building upon the strengths of the people here towards making a more fair, just and functional society than we had had before the cataclysm. With their understanding of my plans in all reality it was quite easy to get them to do anything that I required. I motioned to

Jason and Will with a gesture meaning for them to pay attention and wait for my signal. They had no idea what was going on, I had no chance to explain it to them, so in a way I am truly fortunate that things worked out as they did. It could very easily have gone sideways. They both nodded to me in unison just as I stepped up on the stage.

"Thank you all for coming. You'll have to forgive me, I am not necessarily the best public speaker, so I will just say what I need to say then we can get to the food. I think this is long overdue, my inviting you all to share a meal, and I would like to thank everyone who has taken the time to contribute food to this, I am sure everyone here will enjoy it and appreciates it as well. I want everyone here to get to know each other better, we need to know who we are living with. As you all know we have new people trickle in fairly regularly, generally one or two every couple of days, so we need to make them feel welcome and make them part of our community. That being said we also need to feel secure in our homes. That is something that was sorely missing before the shit hit the fan and it is something I want us all to foster here. In order for that to be fostered here I think we need to have not only law, order and accountability but also truth among us. We are a community that should be working to build ourselves collectively up from the ashes, not picking through the ashes of another person's life."

You could see the faces of the people, everyone happy and smiling going towards more serious with increased nodding as they agreed with what I was saying. Everyone wants to feel safe and secure. As much as people do not like law or rules they sorely miss it when it is not there. Not to say we were a lawless type place with no rules but it was definitely a little lax before this point. This as I said was a defining moment. I was looking over the whole crowd of people yet still managing to keep John always in my peripheral vision. His expression changed from joining in with everyone else in the joy of the moment to looking more and more concerned as I continued speaking. I mean I was only supposed to speak for a short time; I am not comfortable public speaking, right?

"Everyone here remembers the ills of the past; there were murders, corruption, thievery, violence, hatred, affecting all walks of life. No one was immune except the perpetrators. Well I had hoped we could not have to deal with that however I am being proven wrong."

Everyone was obviously getting more tense, it was almost palpable. I could see quick sideways glances as people searched to see who looked guilty. Everyone was looking around except John. His eyes were firmly affixed on me, searching for a hint from me that he should begin running. That I knew it was him. I was never that great of a poker player, but it seems that on that day my poker-face was superb. Jason and Will had slowly begun to move through the crowd on opposite sides. They had ascertained what I was probably wanting from them at this point and they were astutely obliging. No one really spoke but me yet there was a collective murmur from the crowd as people seemed to gasp as they came to the realization that life was not as pristine as it was seeming until that moment. Maybe pristine is not the right metaphor to use here. It was like taking something that was tarnished and cleaning it. It was not yet glistening, but it was definitely shinier than before and getting shinier the more time you spent on it.

"I am telling you all right now that if you want to have the kind of place that we thought we were building that you are going to have to work for it. And we are going to have to fight against those who want something else. We have to take what we want so we can keep it pure for the next generation."

I closed my fist as Jason and Will got within feet of John and they suddenly stopped. John was completely unaware; his eyes and attention were still firmly affixed on me. The terror in his eyes was something I had not really seen up until that moment. I will admit that at that moment I felt the most powerful I had in my entire life. I had someone's life in my hand, they were completely helpless and all I had to do was squeeze. I think this was the moment that John managed to finally break the spell of fear I had cast on him and he began to turn around.

"JOHN THOMAS"

He cringed at the sound of his own name, like a turtle trying to retreat into his shell. Jason and Will quickly grabbed his hands and shoulders, spun him around and kicked the back of his legs dropping him down to his knees. I was actually quite impressed with them, their adeptness at doing that would have made one think that they had done it before. John's panic was now tangible as he was sweating profusely. The crowd parted around like the Red Sea. I bet that is a metaphor that is greatly overused in literature. Lucky for me there will not be too many literary critics reading this.

"John, stole from me and consequently stole from all of you. While this meal was a surprise for most of you it was apparently not a surprise for John as he chose to steal some of the meat for himself, attempting to take more than his fair share. He stole my gift to all of you before I could even present it to you. He is the kind of person that we do not want here. He is an embodiment of the corruption and greed that permeated every facet of society prior to the end of it."

John's eyes were darting from me to Jason to Will to the crowd of people around him as he started to tear up. He could not focus, in his panic he was looking for one person to seem like they were in disbelief of his guilt. One person to give him the courage to argue. To lie to the mob about what he had done. Just as he opened his mouth to speak I put my finger against my lips, shushing him, which was followed quickly by Will punching the side of his face. I looked across the crowd as I continued.

"April. Donnie. I assume what John was about to say was a lie denying what I have just said. Could you run to his place and bring back any evidence." They both stood motionless before nodding and heading off towards his house. This moment was surreal. It felt like something out of a play or a cartoon. Almost like it was not even real; as if it was contrived in some way. The crowd stood there motionless. It was quiet; the only things I could hear were John's whimpering sobs and the slightest hint of rustling leaves on the nearby tree. I would have suspected it would have taken a lot longer than it did before the two I sent off for evidence had returned yet they managed to be back in mere minutes. I guess the whole situation was shocking enough that the adrenaline pumping through their veins allowed them to sprint the whole way. I also did intentionally pick the two people that I felt were the quickest. April, a young girl in her late 20s; she had blond hair that was just barely shoulder length and some very beautiful hazel eyes. The area right around the pupil seemed to be a bright orange color. In bright light her eyes almost seemed to burn; I'm sure the same could be said for when she was angry however I do not think I was ever up close to her when she was angry. I may have possibly been but if I was I certainly was not interested in her eyes at that moment. I had seen her jogging around the town early in the morning; she was obviously the kind of girl who had always been concerned with her health; when we met the only clothes she had were workout type clothes. Runners, yoga pants, sports bras, etc., all contained in her faithful gym bag. She still had the old keycard for her gym hanging off the zipper. Donnie was older with his silver hair giving away the secret that he was over 50. He was a man I could never have even hoped to match. He said that before the cataclysm he had run over 20 marathons. His stamina was absolutely astounding to me, and still is I guess. The other notable thing about him was his personality. He was by far the single most positive person I had ever met. Picture a motivational-speaker version of Mr. Rogers. Just happy; everything is awesome; there is always a bright side to the bright side. He was a walking pile of sugar.

They both returned carrying the items that I had wanted. Skin from the piece of meat that he had taken; most of it with the hair singed off but enough hair was left to still see what color Battie was. Half an uneaten steak, a large knife covered in blood as well a bottle of barbeque sauce. That one is kind of comical as I think it was unnecessary but in the heat of the moment, with their adrenaline pumping I guess it made sense. Now in addition to those things they also brought other items that were of interest that had all been noticed as 'missing' by other people over the past few months. Jewelry. Trinkets. Small electronics like mp3 players and cellphones. The kind of electronics that would have likely survived along with the owners as everyone would have taken those items with them into their little hidey-holes. Those were just the things small enough for them to carry back. Afterwards, we did a much more thorough search of his house and it was almost exclusively filled with pilfered items. He really did not seem to make any effort to fit in and be a contributing member of society.

"Do you all see this? This *man* is not a friend to anyone here. He steals from you. In this case, he actually stole food from your mouths. He is greed incarnate."

I was probably spreading it on a little thick here. Oh well, it is in the past, not like I get a do-over on this spur-of-the-moment speech.

"This is not acceptable here. Everyone here got a second chance at life after the end. You chose not to change and now you will have to live with the consequences. Everyone take note, IF you can not live among us, then you are NOT welcome HERE. John you are hereby….BANISHED."

One last solemn whimper escaped his lips as he heard that was being banished. Again, I felt like I was watching a movie as he was being dragged off by Jason and Will, the crowd yelling at him, shaking their fists, I think a few even threw things at him. Was there a pile of rotten tomatoes nearby? I don't recall, however I doubt it. I am not sure what was being thrown now that I am thinking about it. John was starting to yell, telling everyone that "we got the wrong guy", "I was set up", "he's lying" and so on. All lies really, he was just spouting off trying to save his own hide. If there really had been a set-up then honestly it was perfectly executed. But I truly doubt it. It would have been a lot of effort to assume that I would have noticed the smell of hair burning and meat cooking. It could have totally backfired. Or who knows what other unforeseen thing could have happened. In my opinion it was just that John was careless, stupid and an all-round asshole. He caused his own problems, much as he had for most of his life. This is not the kind of place where you could really debate with me on the merits of nature vs. nurture, especially since if you are reading this then you would simply be talking to yourself but just indulge me as you read this when I say that anyone, regardless of past or current circumstances has a choice in what they do. Even someone who has had a horrible past filled with abuse and neglect has a choice whether they rob that convenience store or smoke that crack or stab that person. Nothing excuses your actions; at best, it just explains them. People should be held accountable for things they have done; especially when they should have known better. That is probably an odd statement coming from someone who is writing their memoirs in an effort to be able to explain and justify their past actions but in all reality, it is what I believe; the problem with perspective is sometimes, depending on your outlook, things that are wrong to one person are correct and valid to another. When you are done reading you can judge for yourself, either way you decide will be irrelevant for me, I won't be there as you read it.

I finally stepped off the podium and walked towards Jason, John and Will. The crowd got quiet again, once more parting like the Red Sea as I marched through. I came close to the trio, John still being gripped firmly on both elbows by Jason and Will. I whispered into Will's ear as he nodded that he understood. "TAKE HIM AWAY". I motioned off towards mountains off in the distance. The crowd cheered. I do not believe I had ever actually had a crowd cheer for me before that moment. I was still angry, furious even. But the cheer it just filled me with such, I am not even sure I know what emotion it was. Joy maybe? All I know is I was smiling. That was my first real taste of power. And from that point on I understood why everyone craves power; why those who have power fear losing it; why people will do anything in order to make the world as they wish it. Now unfortunately, I can say that power is like any other drug. You are always 'chasing the Dragon', trying to get the same high you felt the first time you felt powerful I believe that is why all those past dictators who were known for being so horrible actually got that way, they were trying to assert their power more and more, which led to doing more and more horrible things. Asserting absolute dominance over people.

"Save those two some food, everyone else let's eat". And with that it was time to eat. It seems that everyone in town thanked me for exposing him, patted me on the back for doing what I feel they thought needed to be done. I did hear slight grumblings about people thinking we should have done more, banishment was too light a punishment since the world was starting to come back to life. They felt he would be fine without us. They wanted punishment. One person said we should have stopped him sooner. That I should have stopped him sooner. Maybe they were right. Maybe they were wrong.

You learn a lot from the past if you pay attention. There are some things that us people in modern times just do not have real experience with. Take torture for example, they pretty much knew some of the most horrible ways to interrogate people during the middle ages. Medieval times as they are sometimes referred. Hell, most interrogations were the kinds of things people did not survive. Regardless, of if they were innocent or guilty. Confessing did not undo the damage done. Most people confessed just to make the pain stop. If they did manage to survive the ordeal, they were often crippled in some way. The term 'trial by ordeal' refers specifically to a person's guilt or innocence being dependent on them enduring some unspeakable torture. Pick up a red-hot piece of iron to show that your hand is unburnt? Yeah that is physically impossible. Metal that hot is enough to effectively flash-fry your hand. Extract a rock from the bottom of a pot filled with boiling oil? Even if you can manage this, the oil is viscous enough that it clings to your hand, continuing to cook you even after you have pulled your hand out. There are so many examples of this kind of sadistic thinking that I cannot even recall a tenth of the ones I have read about or seen examples of. Drawing and quartering was one that was quite popular. This happened to the most nefarious, treasonous bastards in history. I am of course talking of them in those terms as history is written by the victors and well if someone was drawn and quartered then they were obviously not on the side that one. William Wallace from medieval Scotland is my favorite example. He rebelled against the rule of England, in an attempt to get them out of Scotland, which did happen eventually, but not in his lifetime. He was caught, hung, cut down before he died, disemboweled with his innards burnt before him before he was beheaded and his body cut into four pieces that were taken to the four corners of the realm to serve as a warning to others as to what happens to those who rebel. That was popular in the past, it creates quite a spectacle. It was all a show for the audience. Not my favorite though. Flaying. Now that was a punishment that I would not say I enjoyed per se but in John's case I felt it was apt, and I think it in my mind is still attached to the feeling of euphoria over my surge of power. It is messy though. And you should probably wear ear protection; the victim can be a little loud during. Flaying is also known as skinning, while the person is still alive.

Jason and Will followed my whispered orders to take John to an old barn about 10 miles outside of town. I made my way there after dark. Long after the meal, when everyone had had their fill, gone home and totally forgotten about the excitement from earlier in the day. My anger was still there. I am not even sure how to say it other than to say that I was very not pleased at what had transpired over the past day or day and a half. Walking into the barn I could see that John had been 'roughed up' a little at some point, whether it was before, during or after he was tied up did not even matter to me. I just stood there for a moment staring John in the eyes, my anger bubbling and subsiding; ebbing and flowing. He tried to speak at one point during this; I again just shushed him with my finger on my lips. Finally, once I felt I had control over the ebb and flow I stepped back, so we could finally have our little chat.

"Why did you kill Battie?"

"I-. I didn't. No. It wasn't me. You got the wrong gu-…" My disapproval must have been apparent as Jason hit him. Hard. I think he broke his jaw actually; as a stream of blood and at least one tooth came out almost immediately.

"You do not seem to really appreciate the situation here. I am not asking if you are guilty. I know you are. I was asking for a why. However, it does not matter. All you need to know is I am not happy. These two here. Are not happy. They missed a great meal with friends today. Sorry guys, it was pretty sweet." The disappointment on their faces was pretty comical given the situation. They did brighten up a little as I told them they had pounds of left-overs for each of them sitting at their homes. Watching their faces briefly go from disappointed to excited to angry again was interesting. That is a wide range of emotions for anyone to go through in a matter of two or three seconds.

"Well I guess we might as well get started, John's gonna have a long night. Gag him". His mouth was stuffed with some old rag that appeared to just be sitting around. Everyone finally had their first look at the tools I had brought for our 'night-out'. I unrolled a cloth full of various surgical instruments and random tools. Scalpels, a butcher knife, some sort of giant looking hunting knife (a bowie knife? I think that might be what it was called), 4 different pairs of pliers, a bonesaw, a rubber mallet along with 3 small hammers. I do not even recall everything anymore. All I do remember for certain is that duffel bag I brought was pretty heavy for all of the things I brought. Most of those I did not even use. I did crush one toe just to get things started. Then I cut it off.

With no power to the barn we had to do a little improvising. An old oven put on its back can make a decent fire pit. I realized that was necessary after cutting off his toe as well I cut an artery and vein. The blood was not stopping on its own. We had to cauterize it. We could not have John bleeding out and dying before we got past the appetizer. I am actually going to spare you some of the more gory details but just so you can somewhat picture how things played out; I started peeling him from the burnt stump of his toe, going up his left leg. I paused at his crotch though. I may have been angry and sadistic at that point but I was really not prepared to castrate him, so I peeled around it. There were two pieces coming off him at that point, one going up his torso then other coming off his right leg. He passed out more than once during the ordeal but was brought back with some smelling salts I had made up a while back. I never would have expected that I would have been using them to bring someone with half of his skin taken off back to consciousness. Jason, admittedly did not have the stomach for what we were doing, he left twice to throw up outside. After the second time he just stood in the back so he did not have to see anything. Will on the other hand was right beside me; I am not going to say that he was an active participant, mostly because I did most of the peeling, but he was definitely…interested… in my work.

Just before dawn we were done. John had stopped breathing just as we were getting up around his neck. There was a giant pile of pale skin lying on the ground beside him, all of it covered in bits of hay, or remnants of cow shit and blood. I changed out of my clothes, dropped it on the pile of skin as Jason and Will were set to torching the building. I knew that there was a good possibility that the smoke would be seen by the townspeople. Not that big of a concern; after everything got cooked and dried out we had seen more than one fire start in fields far off so the likelihood of someone coming to look were remote. Even finding a burnt husk of person would not raise a lot of alarm, I doubt anyone would be able to identify the pile of skin beside him as just that. It would impossible to tell that he had been skinned while alive as opposed to having had his skin burnt off in the fire. The sun, a giant ball of nuclear fire had cleansed the Earth; I was going to recreate that on a small scale by cleansing the world of John.

The three of us returned to town quietly, no one seemed to see us. No one talked if they knew we were gone. No one asked where John had been 'banished' to. The only mention of John really was people murmuring about him taking their stuff and the hassle of having to go through his house to reclaim it. No one seemed to remember the incident after even a week. No one, save me. I remembered, I remembered the feeling of power, determining someone's fate. The smell of blood and hay and cow shit. The sound of the barn roaring and crackling as it burned. Some parts of that day are so vivid.

Later that day I handed down my decree. No meat, for the time-being. People were not happy but I think there was the understanding of my rationale. We had more than enough to eat in terms of plants that we could let the animals recover a little. Patience is key sometimes. If you are farming, you really need to wait until it is time to harvest before you bring in the crop; anything sooner and you are just shorting yourself. Same idea here, let the animals breed and recover their numbers. There were more nods in the crowd then people frowning. But that did not matter. I was in charge, I was telling them what to do. I doubt they knew but next time someone killed something without being allowed to they would have not liked the result. And next time I had to punish someone it would have been in front of the crowd.

CHAPTER 4 – METAMORPH

I am not probably moving into this next topic properly, but I almost feel like I should now highlight the contrast between who I am and who I was. I hid from the radiation in my bunker home, my cocoon; going in as a mild-mannered person, I came out with all that was necessary to make a tyrant. I had developed a sense of myself such that I had become an uncompromising man. Everyone lived through hardships, through death; I was the one who took control. Even before I became hardnosed as a leader I was still in charge. All I had to do was stand before everyone and say my way or no way. I was the first to do so and really, I had done it on purpose. My mannerisms were calculated and thought out; simple, direct, quick and most importantly uncompromising. That is really a far cry from the man I had been. There used to be tons of jokes referring to men being in the 'friend zone'; which is a polite way of saying that they were relegated to being friends with girls/women and could never quite attain a relationship with those said girls, no matter how hard they tried to flatter her, make her special or accommodate her whims. I was the kind of man who pre-cataclysm was perpetually in that friend zone. Always a bridesmaid, never a bride. Now, in spite of being that type of person I did manage to get into a relationship, start a family, etc. People meet in a variety of ways and places although most often people meet in places where they are forced to spend a lot of time together. School. Work. Church, if that is your sort of thing. People become attracted and attached to those they spend the most time with. Since you cannot really quantify 'love' there was an old scientific standard that I think works perfectly. Proximity-seeking behavior. This is most easily seen with young couples or newlyweds. The kinds of pairings that involve two people being 'attached at the hip' with each other. They will do anything to be in the company of the other. Well it works the same way when you are trying to find a partner in the first place, you will seek out opportunities to be in their presence, your behavior will change to allow those kinds of encounters and then possibly, eventually something will happen to allow people to come together. A few dates, lots of talking on the phone gradually morphing into being inseparable. I don't think there is anything particularly interesting in my relationship. I was able to live the good life. For a time.

Now what could I tell you that would make people understand just who I was beforehand? I came from a normal home that only became broken after I had moved out. It was not really all that dysfunctional beforehand, my siblings and I did not even have a real idea there was an irreparable problem. I was second of four, the other 3 being girls. I had middling marks in school which I think would likely have been attributed more to boredom then lack of ability; I had actually been in the program for gifted students for a time although I dropped out of it once I realized that my marks were suffering severely since I was no longer in my usual classes to do the work. I was incredibly lazy at the time. I only ever did the work during class, I never actually managed to do 'homework'. Home time was not think about school time. My marks were good enough however to allow me to go to college and get a degree. That is where I met my wife. My wife, was not technically my wife, but for simplicity we'll say she was, like there is anyone to check the records anyways. We were essentially just two parts of a larger group of people that just hung out in the cafeteria between classes. There did not seem to be a real common thread through the group, we all just coalesced. A few were gay, a couple bi, the rest straight. Some science students (myself included in that), some arts, hell some that never even appeared to ever go to class. Both guys and girls. I was brought into the group by a girl, that I believe was a history major, who happened to share a class with me. Our friendship started as we both tried to cram the last little bits of information into our brains in the final minutes before a mid-term exam. After the exam we met up again to compare answers. As I recall I had many more correct than her but at the time it was irrelevant. Our conversation just ebbed and flowed from there; moving from the hallway outside the exam room to the cafeteria where some of her friends were already sitting. And that was it; I just became part of the group. Eventually, the one that would become my wife was integrated into the group. I, for the life of me, cannot recall the circumstances of how she became integrated but given how I became part of it I'm sure you can guess it was something similar. Eventually, she and I became a separate part of the group, having our own conversations, our own little inside jokes. But I was of course in that aforementioned 'friend zone'. At one point I had even helped her move in with her boyfriend, although that relationship dissolved shortly afterwards. The impetus for us to actually become a couple was simple and subtle; we just spent time together until we were a "we". And that was the beginning of us. I was essentially told to move in within a month or two since I was there all the time anyways. Within a couple of years, we had both graduated, and begun our careers. Within a couple of years of that she became pregnant; and just under 5 years after graduating we had our daughter. It had always been a point of discussion among us to have more than one but I think the burden of just one child was enough to convince her otherwise. In the middle of that, within a few years we were well enough off that I was able to acquire the land necessary to build my house, off deep in the nowhere.

She came with me, stayed while we built the house, the home of my dreams. My dreams, not her dreams and she emphasized that emphatically on a number of occasions. It would be funny if not for the arguments that were spawned over it. She had been there encouraging me from the outset, helping me design the whole building, helping go over the blue prints to make sure that things had been planned for in advance. She was the one who actually picked out the site where it was to be built. She stayed during the entire time it was being built; at the time I kind of used her as eye candy or a distraction for the contractors. It was inconceivable for a madman to have a woman here, dressed in a business suit, overseeing the construction for some large unnamed adventure wilderness tour company. She was even present after the construction was completed and stayed for a time. Then one day she just started getting antsy, getting cabin fever, until finally she said she wanted to leave. She had lived there with me for 3 years then one day she was gone; this was shortly after it was finished but before the news of the flare erupted.

Keep in mind I'm not a horrible man; well let me say I was not a horrible man, people around me now have their own opinions that I cannot control. I never hit my wife, never called her names, never was abusive in any way, she simply wanted to be around more people. A social butterfly she called herself. The part that upset me the most was that she wanted to take my daughter, well, our daughter. She didn't want her to grow up in an isolated place like this, with no real contact or communication with other people, blah, blah, blah. I honestly understood the sentiment, but she wasn't willing to compromise, let her come visit me on the weekends, or over the summer. And it's not like legally I had a whole lot of ground to stand on, there was no real proof I was the father. Except for getting a DNA test done however I in all honesty was scared of what could happen. What if she was not actually mine? What if our disagreements scarred her for life? One thing I do know about divorce is that it is not the act of separation that really upsets the children involved but the fighting between the parents and them fighting over the children. Not to say that the separation is not upsetting just that it is less traumatic for the children than the fights.

I think she had managed to convince me that they would both be better off without me. My daughter was not even old enough to know me yet; there would not have been something missing in her life because she would never know what she lost. And that was it; the whole issue had been decided for me. Then she and her mom were off to some city with 'lots of people to meet'. After the news of the flare was announced I waited everyday for that phone call asking me to get them, to save them. My wife knew what this place was, but never called, never came back. I only was left with the other end of the equation, the huge regret. The world ended, and I was alone, knowing that my wife (ex-wife) and daughter are both dead, that I am utterly alone now. It's depressing. It's heart-breaking. Even with all the things I have already mentioned about feeling alone and despondent this is the only real one. Since the cataclysm in an effort to avoid the inevitable pain I tried to be thankful and happy that I survived; really though that was a selfish thought and a horrible thought which only served to make me feel worse about everything. Knowing that our time was counting down and never getting the call to get them; that was the worst feeling I ever had by far. It's the kind of stuff that really almost made me try the whole suicide by sunlight idea.

When I came out of the cement and steel cocoon that I had made for myself (and my family, even though they did not use it) I was a new man, a stronger man than I had been when I entered. I will admit that I never really got over the loss of my family. And in all honesty, I think that would be the case for most people. It is hard to simply move on from something like that. I was angry, cynical and oddly enough, determined. I'm sure if there was someone around to dissect my actions and thoughts they could say exactly what was going on in my head however I cannot really figure it out. I know that I was crushed and broken emotionally but that seemed to lead me to aspire to having power and control and I was damned determined to succeed. Anger and hate are probably considered the worst emotions however in terms of fueling drive they must be the strongest. Putting it in writing like that pretty much highlights what would more than likely be the conclusion of anyone examining me; I was looking to exact control over others as a compensation for not having control in my own life. I would create order around myself in an attempt to fix the disorder that had disintegrated my relationship. Seems like a fair assessment although maybe a little simple and clichéd. Maybe the reason I am reluctant to see the motivation behind my motives is that it would require me having to admit that I was a wrecking ball through other people's lives even before the cataclysm and that is just a hit to the ego that I cannot bring myself to admit just yet.

After the cataclysm I waited until I was finally sure I could leave safely before I rode my motorcycle through the deserted cities looking for other survivors. On that initial run I did not actually see anyone. On my way into and out of each city I passed the obligatory eternal traffic jam left over from people trying to flee the cities in their cars to go…. where? Anywhere? There wasn't many anywheres that weren't affected by the flare and then the fall-out. So really all those people were all roasted and irradiated in their little Volvo easy-bake ovens, in their Rav4 roasters, their Hummer barbeques. I thought I heard things as I roamed the empty streets but when you are in a city that used to have 500,000 or a million people in it and is now suddenly silent I think your mind just tries to fill in the quiet with something. Or maybe I really did hear people whispering and stuff being knocked over. Given the percentage of people that did survive I'm sure it is likely that there were people alive there. Their reasons for not saying hi are a little unclear though. Perhaps I looked too biker-ish; being dressed in leather whilst riding a motorcycle. Not that I had necessarily planned it that way, I was more of dressed like one would while riding a motorcycle. In hindsight there is only one person that can be blamed for that and it is me; given the way things went in the chaos between the announcement of doom and the actual cataclysm I probably was looking more like one of the degenerates than one of the 'good guys'.

There was one thing during my travels that really did hit me and hard. There was a humidity that was everywhere, making everything feel moist and sticky however that was not the worst thing by far. No, there was an almost indescribable lingering odor that permeated the entirety of the world it seemed, to the point that a breeze could not even wash away the smell; it was a disgusting mix of rancid meat (the people rotting) and a wonderful hint of ham (the people cooked). It is unfortunate for me that this smell now reminds me of Christmas. If the end of the world had happened on one of those faithful prophesized dates then it may have been more relevant, instead it just serves to taint one of the times from before the cataclysm that I would have been able to hold onto as a good memory.

I was working in a hospital in the Emergency department late one evening and I had the joy of being the one in charge of opening the "Silver Door"; our euphemism for the morgue. I cannot honestly recall specifics anymore, we are talking about something that occurred probably 25 or 30 years ago at least but I do recall that it was either Christmas Eve or Christmas Day, possibly right around the cusp of switching from one to the other. The entrance door usually used by ambulances that led directly to the silver door was not working for some reason. Possibly it was frozen or the lock broken or maybe one of the many construction projects that are always on-going at any hospital. Again, I am fuzzy on some of the more peripheral details and the reason for the door not working definitely falls into that category. That door being unusable required that those who would normally be brought into the morgue through the back door now had to enter through the emergency department. The big difference for me is that when you use the back door, like normal, I simply open it from the inside, we sign what needs to be signed then the body is brought in and left in the morgue. I am essentially away from the whole thing, I only facilitate the transaction. When the door is not useable and it comes through the emergency department then I am opening doors for them as we take the body through. Not that being around bodies are a particularly big deal. Even at that time so many years ago I had seen hundreds of people after they had passed. Without an emotional attachment there is not anything particularly upsetting or interesting about dead people. Only rarely did a dead person come in that had already started to decompose. Then you have to deal with that smell. It is unpleasant to say the least but something that you can get used to and actually shrug off fairly easily. On this particular day the problem was not the usual kinds of unpleasant smells you associate with dead bodies; piss, shit, decomposition. It was the smell of baked goods brought in by nurses, freshly cooked ham, some hot chocolate that I had been drinking and the peppermint flavored throat lozenges I was sucking on. All the smells of Christmas. Happy Holidays and all that it brings. I don't eat ham anymore partially since we do not have a particular overabundance of ham around right now. I also did not eat it before the world ended. My reasoning for not eating ham was not due to any kind of religious sensibility and as I noted above I am not opposed to eating animals; it is because of how it smells and I'm sure you can guess where this is going. The meat from a pig is close enough to the meat of a person that most people wouldn't be able to tell the difference and I'm just not taking that chance. The supper being served that day in the cafeteria was turkey; I know that because that is what I should have smelled. Instead, I smelled ham; people who are cooked/burnt smell like ham. I will assure you that the reason I know that is not something horrible; I have never to the best of my knowledge tasted the flesh of a person. I say to the best of my knowledge because well, things happen. Robert Pickton was probably not the only psychopath with a pig farm.

Now we get to the sad story part; the portion I now associate with Christmas. Turns out a Christmas tree had been adorned with some old faulty Christmas lights which shorted out and caused a fire. I have no idea if the tree had been artificial or real, if the house was a two bedroom bungalow or a townhouse, if there were a giant pile of presents under the tree or just a few. All those kinds of details never made it to me. The only reason I know that the fire was attributed to the Christmas tree was from a newspaper article. But I did get to see the consequences of the fire firsthand. I got to open the silver door 5 times that night; the entire time walking behind the gurney, smelling that smell. Each gurney seemed to be carrying a smaller figure each time. First the father, who before being cooked likely stood over 6 feet tall, now it was kind of hard to tell; he had been cooked into a contorted shape, like a misshapen pretzel. He seemed to have tried to get out of bed but was overcome by the smoke halfway off. Next was the mother, followed by a son, probably twelve or so judging by the size, a roughly 8-year-old daughter and a little one. That was the hardest and I think the part of the whole memory that really imprinted that smell on my brain.

And that is what I was smelling after the cataclysm; a musty moistness with a distinct hint of ham. And it was everywhere I went. There are three fairly sizable cities nearest to where I was and I went through each looking for something. A sign that someone had survived and all I got was nothing. Not one person tried to talk to me. Not one person waved at me to stop. Not one person came out to see what sounded like a motorcycle. I had faint hopes as I rode through that not only would I find people but I would find my wife and child. But, well, see previous statement.

Now just to switch gears here there is another thing that I feel is somewhat related that I think I will mention now. While there were not many cases that I am aware of there were at least a few people who really did not know how to deal with the end of the world. They do not know how to get food unless it comes from a supermarket. Meaning that they needed to solve their starvation problem which they did Donner party-style. We don't like your kind here, those kinds being cannibals. Only six people in my community admitted to eating people at the beginning of my civilization; a civilized society. I'd like to say they regretted it, however I think it would be more correct to say that they regretted admitting to it. One thing that I do not recall is whether those who were eaten were already dead or is they had been killed by the cannibals. The reason I do not remember is likely because we did not ask them; which seems odd reflecting on it. It is kind of a big difference between people who eat meat that is available and just happens to have been a person and people who kill someone in order to eat them. Although in the context of when I was establishing my civilization they were little more than a convenient scapegoat. The easiest way to make yourself the trusted leader is to give people something to fear. A group to fear. And then attack them. Bring their worst nightmares to light, twist those into something that is real and tangible, place it right in front of them before changing yourself into the white knight to vanquish the foe. You could almost characterize it as I was the cannibal slayer. It was not unspeakable pain that the cannibals endured; however given the tone of the first person I had killed I think you know where it went without me having to elaborate. I am sure there is someone who would prefer me to talk about it and I may still discuss it if I have time although it does nothing to advance my past.

It does not seem clear to me if I managed to really contrast myself in the manner I had intended. The scariest part of that thought though is that I am actually hoping for there to be a drastic change in the kind of person I am. As if that would be the kind of thing that would justify things because I am not the man I used to be. Well regardless of who I am nothing can really justify it. At best I can say that I was acting in an extraordinary manner during extraordinary times. Although perhaps there is not as much of a difference as I had hoped, maybe I was always like this but just never had the 'outlet' to express it. I would like to state though that I truly believe that I am a changed person from who I was before the cataclysm. I'm not sure if that is the truth of just my own skewed way of viewing things. I guess that will be for anyone reading this to judge. When I look at things I see that my change in outlook and demeanor and way of dealing with people or things is fairly evident. I can even kind of get an idea where the change originated. The Tarkin Doctrine. Most people won't get this reference or any number of other ones that I make. I see it as being for one of two reasons: 1) no one ever paid attention to the movies and entertainment that they saw and heard or 2) they weren't alive back then. Now, Tarkin, was the anal retentive old man in charge of the Death Star in the original Star Wars movie; played by Peter Cushing I think. This was movie #4 that was first. He had said that "Fear will keep the local systems in line, fear of this battle station". Now I am not trying to control a star system, even if I was I don't have a battle station. No, I am just trying to control my own little corner, my civil civilization, my imperial town. I was prepared to be uncivilized in the name of civilization.

CHAPTER 5 – THE TOWN

At the end of my initial run through the nearby cities I arrived in a small town far out in the middle of nowhere, a hilly region, hidden if you don't know where to look. And if you know where to look, and you're there then you have a good view of those who don't know where they're going. That was why I chose to put my bunker where I did. I wanted this place to be mine, it was a nice place. I had spent time here before during a nice little vacation. The main thing that caught my interest was its big green yards, the soil is good enough that you can actually grow food in it; the nearby hills are good for grazing animals. This is where I chose to live out the rest of my life; after my ride looking for people and finding no one I had resolved to come to this town to live out my life alone, as long as it may have been.

So, I came out of my cocoon, my chrysalis, arrived at my new town, the throne of my civilization, and promptly tore down the old town name sign. There is no more Hillview. No more population 3243. There is only a population of 1. It was 4 actually but I didn't know that just yet. I did not do it at the time but I did of course rename the place; what better way to stamp something as 'yours' than to name it. It's like adopting a puppy; you can keep the name the shelter gave it but in my mind that just means you are being little more than a long-term babysitter. To really own something you have to name it. Of course, I am not some kind of pathetic monkey who will do something like calling a place Georgetown (King George) or Stalingrad (Joseph Stalin) or Jonestown (Jimmy Jones) or the probably thousands of other examples that I would not even bother to try to name. Once I realized I was not alone I decided that this was to be the bright new center of the universe and was to be named Republica. Such a nice rouse I thought, the seat of such a tyrant being named after the idea of a republic, ruled by the people kind of idea & name, the irony amused me. Although if you think about it pretty much every Republic that I can think of became an empire or dictatorship or something similar. Roman Republic became the Roman Empire under Augustus, the first French Republic became the first French Empire, and the Weimar Republic became Nazi Germany. The United States of America, was a republic and I would venture given more time it would have twisted into something more authoritarian, especially given the way things were turning in regards to terrorism, the debate of the 1% versus the 99%, the disparity in living conditions and injustice between the races, and whatever other hardships I am neglecting to think of. At some point the good ol' US of A would have had something akin to a second Civil War and out of that would have arose the American Empire. Now whether that would have been a good thing is debatable, but it would definitely have been something to see. It would have been a world changing event, and possibly even less destructive than a solar flare with complimentary nuclear fallout; possibly.

I arrived in Republica and looked at the empty desolate place, a number of its former citizens had died here, many many more had run off in search of safety that didn't exist. There was an old Catholic church in the middle of town, the good stone kind with stained-glass windows. The giant crucifix on the wall is all painted to look more life-like, so when you pray to be saved, you'll feel that you're praying to one that will care enough to save you. Half a dozen people lay on the lawn, with that rotting putrid ham smell surrounding them. It looks as if they were all kneeling to the cross on the outside to save them when the flare hit. Perhaps they were hoping for a last-minute rapture before they got the ultimate tan. Or were they feeling their skin burning thinking it was Jesus' divine providence touching them? Who knows. The pain that they would have been feeling as they were starting to be cooked would have dissipated shortly afterwards as their nerve-endings died and suddenly they would be without pain. I'm sure between the pain and their ultimate death that blissful nothing would have felt like salvation. I was not out to see it so I really cannot figure on how long the pain lasted, how long the nothing lasted before dying but time is relative. It seems to slow down with increased intensity. The pain would have been excruciating. And like I said I think that would be excruciating. And who knows how long it would have truly lasted. Likewise, the relief from that pain would be like the ultimate form of bliss and probably would have felt like the most wonderful eternity before the person was just cooked. Almost sounds poetic. That is a more fanciful way of looking at it. Conversely, perhaps the heat of the microwaving was so intense that it was an almost instantaneous death, which I think is actually more likely. When people die from a fever it is often because their brain actually overheats. The body purposely causes fevers when you are ill as a way of trying to kill the infecting bacteria or virus. Most of those little things can only live and multiply in a specific temperature range so if you raise the temperature of the body by a few degrees then they are no longer able to live and/or reproduce, meaning that they die off leaving the body without the offending organism. The problem with that strategy is kind of two-fold. One the body does not simply turn up the dial a notch or two, sometimes it just goes until the infection is gone even though some things do not die off so simply. The other problem is that our organs, be it brain, heart, liver, etc. all are made to work in the usual body temperature range that microorganisms like. Meaning that you raise the temperature to the point that it kills the little things and you are not having your own organs really working. Problem one plus problem two equals things like your brain no longer working properly. When that happens, then you start having slight problems like the brain not sending the proper signals out. You don't get those signals going out to your heart for example which means heart attack. I guess either way it is kind of irrelevant how quickly or slowly they died, or how slowly it felt. Either way there is a definite end to all of their stories. I have always wondered if these people were outside instead of in because they had been locked out. Which is not very inviting wouldn't you say? Now just a side thought, why do people always want someone else to save them? Whether it be God, or a politician or your local neighborhood tyrant. Why does no one just save themselves? That would make the most sense. No one else cares about you as much as you do.

I came upon the church not because I was looking for my own salvation nor because I was looking to see who was faithful up until the end but because I was planning on making this my new home. Without the population of the town this place was just as nice as any in terms of quiet. And I did like a couple things about it. Stained glass windows always intrigued me. I love that you can have a whole story contained in one or two windows and they give a kind of nice ambiance to the whole place when the sun shines through. As well when you take out the pews you have a nice big open room that you can do whatever you like with. Hell, throw a football from one end of your living room to the other just because you want to. I'm sure you are wondering why I left my home and chose to stay here. I am not totally sure why. Maybe because I was hoping for there to be more than just me left in the world and this is a better place than home for coming across people. I would always have it as a back-up if I desired to go home. The only thing I can think of for why I stayed here is that the library in this town is more expansive than mine. Having an entire rest-of-my-life by myself will get rather boring so I'd need something to do and I must be too lazy to go and move all the books from one place to another. One thing is certain though. With the world ended, it did not matter where I was exactly, it was quiet everywhere.

Suddenly. Surprisingly. I can hear noises coming from the back of the church, down stairs I can hear the faint whispers, the desperate "what's that?" kind of questioning like the bogey-man or Jason Voorhees is upstairs, followed by the low hissing of the person being hushed. That was my first indication that others had actually survived. I had been prepared to rule an empty town for the rest of my life but this was certainly more promising. My heavy boot steps turned around and walked out the way I had come in, walking out those big wooden fortress-looking doors. I notice there is a chain and padlock lying on the floor near the door; I pick them up as I walk out the door. I walked around the church looking along the ground, looking for windows or storm cellar entrances as I do my lap around the exterior. There is an old storm cellar pair of doors, low and slanted along the base of the barely visible amongst the overgrown brown grass. I take the chain and slowly, quietly wrap the chain around the handles of the door, putting a bolt that is in my pocket through 2 of the links, locking the door; then I continue along my walk. Returning to the front doors I can almost sense a change in the mood coming from inside the church. A fear, a panic, I can imagine the whispers from the basement. They heard a noise at their escape door, they tested it, and it is locked. I stand at the open door, just sensing their panic, I can almost hear them whispering, clawing at the door trying to push on it, trying to escape. I actually catch a bit of a whisper on the slight breeze as I step inside. I walk slower than before, stepping heavier this time, drawing it out. The more scared the whispers are now. In reality I was thinking I was just going to get the full attention of whoever was down in the basement. At this point there was no need to do anymore than that.

Back to the present for a moment. I am no longer the head of the government, no longer the emperor of the People's Republic, I sit here, in my cell, waiting. Waiting for what you wonder, well nothing. There is an impending execution date, and after that there will be nothing. Or something. I guess I'll soon know the answer to that eternal question. My people are enlightened now but they did at least learn from me how to get rid of a problem permanently. My punishment for dismembering and killing is to sit in a jail cell every hour of every day until I am no longer part of this world. To think of how I "destroyed society and decency". I am supposed to remember how I "took advantage of people in their weakest hour". I am expected to be sorry for all of this. I know there is a need amongst some of my former flock to have me apologize and beg for forgiveness but that is not going to happen. Here is the thing, I made this society, I made it safe from without and within. No one will dare let another like me in charge here again. None of my former citizens will allow someone to invade, force their way in and be the new tyrant. Once I took over that became my goal; I would be the worst person any of these people had ever experienced, make them disdain someone like me so much that they'll fight to keep their society fair, equal and most importantly safe. The reason I bring this up is again showing the contrast of my true beginning as the guy in charge and my eventual end. How the mighty have fallen. It has happened so many times throughout history, that leaders and dictators have been overthrown in some sort of revolt or coup d'état. From Muammar Ghaddafi to Benito Mussolini to Saddam Hussein to me and every other one that I will never remember. All brought down from leader to nothing.

I sit here all the time "thinking and regretting" but in all reality, I'm perfectly content. My plan could not have worked out any better if I had planned it this way. And I did, sort of. Another nerd reference. Palpatine. Another Emperor, kind of like me, if you think grandiose enough. Another man leading both sides, like me. Difference is he was playing both sides to weaken them both until he could have complete control over the Galaxy. I, on the other hand, in playing both sides, expressly with the goal of taking the strong one and essentially transferring it's strength to the other side, making the weaker side stronger. You'll understand what I mean as I go through this; but sufficed to say I helped make the weaker side the stronger which was just a side effect of what I was doing. All evilness and wickedness, well that will die with me. I am so hated here that you couldn't possibly get a more communist, Christian ideals kind of mood amongst my subjects. Everyone is polite, helps each other, everyone is equal. No discrimination. I am the strict father of a whining, screaming child, who molded that brat into a polite, considerate adult. It's a job well done. God is my gardener. They are my garden. I am their God, their fallen angel, their Lucifer, the Infernal Tempter. Only by rejecting me shall they obtain salvation. They rejected me; I hope that was enough to secure their salvation. Now why did I feel the need to mention this? It's simple; I'm giving a tidbit of how the story ends. This is a reassurance that the tyrant does not pillage and plunder forever. To let it be known that there is a reason for being terrifying. And most amusing of all, to make people scratch their heads before they can finally figure out just what I am writing about.

0.0956%. That is the percent, I did the math. The percent of Republica's population that I killed. 234 out of 2541 people. And 16 of those were the cannibals. 218 ordinary people, well 218 dissidents actually, paid the price for a truly just society. It was all spaced out over the course of a couple years. They were leaders of little whispering groups. Each died more brutally than the last. There was no one willing to oppose me, for years. This is kind of the side-story in all of this, the how and why I got overthrown; it should all become fairly apparent just how things went as we go along, we'll get to it all in time. And now back to reminiscing.

So, there I am, walking into this old stone church. The stones used to build this church apparently have some sort of metallic component to it. That's why I'm hearing whispers; these people were hidden and shielded from the radiation. Walking slowly, breathing shallowly, and trying to not taste the putrefying piles sitting just outside. That is impossible by the way; the taste, the smell, that almost oily moist film that hangs in the air, it goes everywhere, it stays everywhere. I'll taste the stench of those putrid piles for days. I'm deciding as I walk, terrifying and scary or old and grizzled with a little angry and temperamental thrown in for good measure. Given what I've already said you would probably guess terrifying but no. For the first meeting grizzled and temperamental works fine. Standing at the top of the staircase to the basement I stand and wait. No noises. Not even the hissing of someone being hushed, I always was told about but never saw the final episode of M*A*S*H and how the episode involved Hawkeye and a Korean woman hiding with a baby from a group of North Koreans. That woman suffocates the baby to stop it from crying. It drove Hawkeye mad, his mind snapped. I ponder whether there is some bad parent down there suffocating their child, some future asylum resident unable to deal with their own actions.

"I don't have time for this; there is work to be done. Get up here!"

One… two…. three…. Waiting sucks. Patience might be a virtue but that does not make impatience a sin. I am actually quite patient, but you know, I am playing temperamental.

"Don't make me come down there…If I do there'll be hell to pay". Waiting, they aren't breathing, not the slightest sound is coming from the basement. Now I am angry. There is a point, when I'm extremely angry where anything will turn it into a full-blown Incredible Hulk kind of rage. I'm getting there, I understand no people for months can make people paranoid and fearful but quite simply I couldn't stand the smell. It was making me feel greasy, dirty. Down into the dark, one stair after another.

"I'm not here to hurt you, I just want to get started fixing things and I'll need some help". A flick of a switch and we turn on the grizzly old grandpa demeanor.

"I got food" And I see a foot move from behind a pile of boxes just inside the shadows. It looks like a little pink shoe. A girl's shoe. She noticed her own movement and there was an almost inaudible gasp, my hand reaches into my pocket, grabs what's inside and I toss it by her foot. A chocolate bar.

"I'll wait outside for ya".

Sitting on the stairs looking out down the main street of my new Republica. The various trees and grasses are all still there, but sun burnt, dried, dead and brown. I can hear footsteps falling behind me. Slow ginger footsteps. More hiss hushing and 'stay back'.

"Where did you come from?" comes out of the shadows just inside the church.

Smiling, I slowly stand; take the last few steps down, turn around to face the darkness within. I'm pointing vaguely off to the southeast behind the church. My farm is about 100 miles that way.

"How did you survive? We haven't seen anyone else since it happened."

"I think ahead." I was prepared I think to myself while I smile warmly.

There is a park near the church; we sat there for hours around the fire I had made with some dry wood. Really who am I kidding; it's all dead dry wood. They wanted to go back inside, after the sun tries to kill you it is kind of understandable, but I convinced them it was fine. No more flares, we can survive just fine outside now, like it was before. I had brought some hotdogs with me, they voraciously ate the entire package. Hours went by, with them not knowing what to make of me, frightened still, before they finally spoke; a deluge of questions.

Lisa, the mother figure, was the only one speaking that night. 'Food? Do you have more food?' She was a brunette, short, like 5'3''. 'How did you survive?' She is wearing a black ratty sweater with all the edges torn. 'You still have electricity and came here?' Looks like she used to have a nice figure, but malnutrition can kind of take that out of you. 'Why did you come *here*?' She was actually quite pretty with that completely puzzled look on her face. 'Who are you?' Her nails look like they used to be perfectly manicured; now they are ragged from being chewed on constantly. 'Are you by yourself?' Her hair was all knotted and greasy from being unwashed, but then again she has not had any running water in months. 'Have you seen anyone else?' 'Are we the only ones left?' 'Where will we go?' 'Do you have any more chocolate?' 'Do you have any more water?'

We slept that night, under the stars, away from all those putrid fetid smelling houses. All those rotting greasy bodies on the church lawn. The stinking Mazda microwaves. We slept, and it was wonderful. This was the first night since my wife took my child away from my "craziness" that I slept and the last time (at least up to the point I am writing this) that I slept a goodnight's sleep. I had gone a whole night without waking however this night was peaceful. As for that so called "craziness" I was right though, I was right, I was prepared and I lived, if you call this living.

The following morning I arose just before dawn, just as the sky was beginning to change colors, beginning to drive away the darkness, replacing it with something more clean, more pure….brighter. At that point even with knowing better that it was safe the dawn was still kind of a tense time. I had memories of all the dawns I remembered from before the cataclysm that were just the dawn of a new day. Conversely, there was a dawn that few were left to see; the previous dawn having been the last for so many. As I sat there, waking up, I looked over to the pile on the other side of the smoldering ashes, the silhouette of Lisa, lying there under her blanket shivering slightly. It had been a cold night that night. Her blanket, not a blanket really, it was ragged and torn; dirty and colored with age, it seemed to be missing half of its stuffing looking like a flat deflated balloon. I think it was a quilt; a crazy quilt specifically. I think is the term used to describe those kinds of quilts. Mostly red and black. Random shapes and shades of red all stitched together, no discernable pattern, yet if you look long enough you'd swear all you have to do is step back a few steps or cross your eyes and the picture would suddenly come into focus. A couple of times during the night I had almost moved myself under her quilt. She was so sweet, beautiful, prettiest girl I had seen in months. Again, who am I kidding, I hadn't seen anyone in months, and with my previous isolation that made it even longer for me than her. Fortunate for us though, fortunate for civility, for morality that her blanket, 'crazy quilt' it smelled of the rotting parishioners on the lawn, like the commuters driving their mobile microwaves forever now.

I awoke 5 feet further away from Lisa then I had fallen asleep, no doubt my unconscious self-consciously slinking away from her smell. Sitting there I notice the girl is gone. I'm wondering whether this is a normal kind of thing. Is the girl a sleep walker? Have insomnia? Have to pee? Or just went back to the security of the church basement.

Looking across the park I can see a slight shadow coming from the swing set, beginning to streak across the whole park, a little girl's shadow is 50 times longer than the girl is tall. The polite thing would be to say good morning cover the pleasantries that I should have done yesterday, once she emerged from the dark of the church. Rudeness is unforgivable; it is not to be tolerated. But pleasantries can still wait, I have to pee.

Emerging from behind a brown roasted shrub I can see she still has not moved from where she was sitting on the middle swing. I slowly walk up behind her, stand for a moment before taking the swing to her right, apparently she never heard me. She gasped as the gravel ground under my feet as I sat in the swing.

"Nice morning, whatcha looking at?"

'Nothing, it's just warmer in the sun. I'm not supposed to go out in the sun anymore. I'll get burnt, like everyone else if I go out in the sun. We only go out at night.'

"I think the sun isn't harmful anymore, you'll be fine being outside during the day now. What's your name?"

'Aurora'.

"As in light? Interesting. I like that name. Well, my little lightning bug, how about we go have some breakfast, we got some work to do today.

Silence. She has stopped her slight swinging. Even I can tell from beside her that her eyes are welling with tears.

"My daddy used to call me lightning bug…. He's gone, like everyone else." Her eyes showed that she feared that he was sunburnt, just like the rest of the world.

That morning was longer and more disgusting than any other that I can remember in my whole life. I had Lisa help me start making this a place that I would want to live, starting with the church. We finally cleared the bodies away from the church and opened it up wide to begin airing it out. I honestly do not understand why Lisa had never done that before, I mean, that smell was deafening. And yes, I mean to use that word; the smell was so bad I swear it overpowered your other senses. Getting the smell out of the yard was more difficult. The very fat of the parishioners had in essence seeped right into the ground. I had wanted to try to burn the left over grass in that yard, hoping that it would pull the fat out of the soil like a wick on a candle but…my experiments did not go as planned. With that much dryness it was almost impossible to stop even the smallest fire from becoming a raging inferno. That is why I used a quarry that was a short drive out of town to burn the bodies. With all the death and toasted vegetation it was easy enough to get a pyre going for them, but that pyre would become a wildfire with little to no provocation, on the slightest breeze. But to get the fat out of the ground ultimately took the patience to just wait for it to happen.

The fat came out of the ground on its own. It did rain eventually and that washed it out. By getting rid of the bodies I was able to get the smell more or less gone. However, until the rain washed the fat away the smell was still there. Sometimes you would only catch a miniscule whiff but you would still catch it nonetheless. It is extremely comical in an utterly disgusting sort of way how the fat floated up to the surface during heavy downpours. The grass as it started to rebound and grow back was covered in a greasy whitish slime that would slowly meander down the ever so slight slope. The first time I recall it raining after the great burn it started in the middle of the night, slowly spitting then erupting into a full storm just before daylight. We heard a crack of thunder so loud it seemed to shake the whole building. Aurora was so excited for rain she was screaming "oh my god" over and over. Running back and forth from one end of the church to the other. Until finally the building could not contain her anymore and she burst forth out into the yard. I have no idea where she intended to go and likely she did not know either. But running full tilt on a slimy greasy lawn... well, that does not work. She slid faster than I ever saw anyone go on a slip-and-slide. Clear from the front of the church down that ever so slight grade until she hit face first into the hedge at the side of the property. The next sound was just astounding. She laughed. Loud. I did not even know a girl that young could laugh that loud and heartily. It is understandable; she had been living for months in a world filled with death, this was her first chance to feel real relief from that. She lived mere steps away from the smell that I found so repulsive, she was used to the smell that she was face-down in. And it was funny once you get past the idea of what she was sliding on. She spent the next 20 minutes running from one end of the yard then sliding to the other end, each time getting a face full of crispy dried-up leaves and laughing maniacally. It was fine, she was happy and I knew she needed that. We burned the clothes she was wearing that day.

There was more work that needed to be done after cleaning out the front yard of the church and it progressed slowly. There was only the two of us adults and even then, I ended up being the one who did the majority of the heavy lifting; an emaciated short little woman is not going to be a lot of help most of the time, but at least she tried. We went house to house, room to room. Most places were empty and that was easy enough to deal with. My main task for myself was making the pyres, burning off the former residents of the town. Trying my hardest to burn the smell out of existence. I was already thinking further along the line so Lisa's primary job was to unplug things. We took the rotting leftovers from inside the fridges and freezers that we found and tossed them outside to the wagon destined for the quarry. The flies had not yet returned in full force in those initial days in Republica, I'm sure if they had we would have needed to think of a better strategy, that wagon would have been covered in a swarming buzzing mass. We opened cupboards and medicine cabinets, taking all that was useable and/or edible and throwing them into shopping carts that we had acquired from the only grocery store in the town. Again, why Lisa did not do any of this before my arrival I will sincerely never know. Everything was being stored such that we would have edibles for years; we actually ended up throwing out tons of food that had gone stale as there were just not enough mouths to fill at that time. We had medicine that would expire long before we had a chance to use it all. Most of it I actually destroyed in my pyres as I would prefer there not be a temptation of having things around that can be abused. I did for sure keep the antibiotics. It would suck to get an infection and die of blood poisoning after going through all the effort of surviving the end of the world.

I was fine keeping Aurora away from the worst of it. That was not due to her gender if you are wondering, I think that kids should be able to try to grow up with as little trauma as possible and at that point she had experienced enough so there was no reason to unnecessarily re-traumatize her repeatedly with people who were long dead. She was tasked with things like taking the seeds that I had brought from home and putting them in cups full of dirt and watering them; starting our garden. I had brought food but not a large amount. I made a run back home in order to get more a few days after arriving in the town; mostly for meat, dry goods we had in abundance. Really though, those two were ravenous.

Everything now seemed nice, picturesque, it seemed tranquil. That, of course was about to change. After I had arrived in town it seemed to begin to burst with all kinds of little pathetic life. Was I simply the first pathetic life form to come here or are pathetic things attracted to me? Either prospect seems kind of insulting but I am the one saying it so I guess I will have to just not take it personally. Lots of ants, bugs, mice, squirrels etc. Each day a new creature rediscovered the light, each slightly less pathetic than the last. Finally worked up to seeing a cat, slowly quietly stalking an unwary mouse, a little bum jiggle then... dead mouse. Next day a mangy skinny whimpering version of a German Shepard skulked up to the front of the church, my newest home. Head down, tail between it's legs, its eyes, puppy-dog eyes, crying for any food. I'm sure it must have been in this area before; why didn't it just eat the parishioners? Or any other person that it happened upon, there were literally people everywhere that there were people before the cataclysm. I guess it doesn't want to be around putrid rotting people either. I throw a pile of meat on the ground at my feet, it gingerly takes it, and I now have a life-long friend, a protector. I call over Aurora, make her feed him the rest; I need the friend now, not the protector.

I am not sure if I have mentioned this before or not but I am going to mention it now; Aurora, one of my first two charges, became one of the dissidents that overthrew me. From my understanding she had in fact been a ringleader in this most recent group that disagreed with me. Now you're probably wondering what I did to this little girl that would make her want to depose me when she finally grew up. I am slightly disappointed with her as she was not in favor of the fate that I have been meted down. They have imprisoned me and I am now scheduled for execution (28 days, 4 hours 2 minutes before that by the way). She was on the side of life imprisonment which in all fairness is not a good plan. Leaving someone like me alive is…dangerous. What if I still have a supporter? What if they break me out of prison? What if I start all over again? Take my revenge on the community that betrayed me? I am not interested in any of those things, but they don't know that. I am content to live out the rest of my days here in my cell, writing; even if someone was to break me out I think I would honestly break their neck, leave the body lying in the hallway to my cell, me sitting calmly at my desk and the door open just to prove the point of I am not going anywhere. Not that I am looking to kill anyone else but things happen in the moment sometimes. Going back to Aurora and before your mind runs into the gutter I did nothing bad to her not directly at least. Everything I did to her was suffering directed towards others that she empathetically took on to herself. This is fine, she did as she was taught, empathy for others, love, co-operation, etc. etc. When it came to everyone else she had a bit of a reputation of being a girl who is not to be fucked with. It's kind of a wink-wink thing. We'll get to that later.

CHAPTER 6 – LOSING PATIENCE BEFORE THE END

Obviously, I have now kind of given away my ultimate end in all of this although that is more or less what this whole memoir is about; I am hoping to stitch together things coherent enough that when you finally have all the pieces in front of you it all makes sense. Not just the simple things that are probably straight forward but also all the little countless reasons. Everything happens for a reason. I am not saying that in a religious sort of way I'm saying it in a mechanical kind of sense. What I mean by that is there are hard-wired paths in our brains that determine in essence the way we will react to things. It is the old fight-or-flight idea used when discussing the instincts used by people when they have a rush of adrenaline. If someone is able to actually think-out the situation then they can change the way they react but for most people, they will simply run on instinct. And that is what I mean by everything happens for a reason; there is a pre-planned evolutionary way of preserving people, so they can continue on. Propagate the species, etc. etc.

Thinking of this idea brings to mind again the time period just prior to the cataclysm. When panic was king. I think when people are faced with a truly dire situation, like the end of the world they can operate on both sides of the fight-or-flight spectrum. As I mentioned before, people panicked in trying to find hiding places and then attacked those who had them. So panic is one that I think I should elaborate on, since really nothing is totally as it appeared. This is kind of the 'beginning', my start down the path of evil, the march to the anti-Christ. I'm obviously overstating things but you probably understand what I mean. Who put that princess in the tower? Why did they lock her up? What drove the white knight to becoming a hero instead of just a jousting champion? Where did the dragon come from? Even when you read the beginning of a story there is always the stuff that would have had to happen to set up the story that you never get; unless someone decides to go back and write a prequel... or just write a chapter or two in a memoir about things that happened before what is really relevant. Prequels just give a broader scope to things that happen later. Whatever. Just continue reading, you may see what I am getting at. Or it is just another story.

Prior to the flare arriving I was preparing to take down the solar panels so they did not get fried by the flare although thinking now I am not totally sure why I was doing that; I mean I had more than enough panels that I could have left it all to chance. And that would have saved me a fair bit of work, I could have gone on the idea that the flare would not be that bad and they would be fine. It would have saved me a fair amount of work. Now you have to keep in mind I live in a very isolated place; a place with a lot of bears, cougars, wolves and the like around. As well, there is always the problem of people who like to break into summer cabins when the people are back at their usual residence. To keep myself safe from those sorts of things I had a security perimeter, if you will. Without actually seeing me around there or the animals roaming around it is quite likely that someone could mistake my place for a weekend cabin that people go to in order to get away from their usual hum-drum lives. In all reality it is irrelevant if someone wanted to try to break in to this place; this place was a fortress and not just from flares and nukes. As I said before the house on top is all just a rouse anyways, there is nothing up there of value other than furniture that is collecting dust; someone can break in there all they want and they will walk away being disappointed. For someone to get into the heart of the place there were only a few ways in and really none of them were easy. Firstly, there was a secret elevator in the pantry of the [fake] kitchen. If you do not know what you are looking for you would never ever find it. The pantry is just like any you would ever expect to see; and thinking of it that was like the only room in the whole fake house that actually had anything in it that were not just for show; mostly just a pile of canned goods, some dry goods like pastas and also, I think there was a tin of oats for making oatmeal. Those things were there for show in that they were just there to look at and were somewhat of a distraction from the rest of the room, but they never moved. I used to have to go fairly regularly to dust everything in there so that there were not any tell-tale signs of just where the trigger for the elevator was. Dust is not helpful for that. I don't think I could really describe accurately where the button was exactly; it was on the bottom of a shelf on the left, it was kind of disguised as an upright for the shelf. You simply pressed it and the wall in front of you opens and you step into the elevator. I made sure when it was put in that it was big enough (and hence the pantry had to be big enough) to accommodate something large, like a couch, cause well why not. That is most likely the largest thing that will need to ever be moved in this way. If something larger was needed then there is the ramp coming from the outside but even that was never used. The really large things that I required were put in place as the whole place was being built. The walk-in fridge and vault for my weapon room were both put in during construction. The elevator was all kind of part of my security planning; it was designed to sit on the main floor for quick easy access in case someone did manage to get in and I needed a quick escape. Going up from the basement I can wait the few seconds for the elevator to come down to me but going down it just made more sense for it to be immediate. So that was one entrance, another was the ramp that led outside; the door on that was solid steel and essentially barred closed unless you had the 8-digit security code to get it to open; which would only leave someone wanting to break in the option of cutting through the steel with a plasma torch, which is totally possible, however unlikely as who would think to or want to carry around a plasma torch like that. And that leads to the last 3 exits. They are only openable from the inside and are really escape tunnels; the exits are completely camouflaged and under a layer of dirt and grass. You cannot even open them manually; they have a hydraulic ram that will push the entrances open, thereby negating the weight of the dirt, grass and other debris hiding them. There was one each going north, south, west from the lower level. To the east the lake was too close so there is not a tunnel exiting that way. Each of the entrances to those tunnels were readily accessible from the weapon room just in case there was someone that was trying to plasma torch their way in through the big door. My plan would have been to be able to shoot whoever was getting all gung-ho to get into my place from afar; this is something I obviously never utilized. I know I am sounding very paranoid again; it is kind of late to change how things had been planned out. I just like contingencies I guess. In fact, I kind of disdained the idea of shooting people like that it was more of a last-resort kind of plan; I prefer to just deal with things more head-on if possible.

The security perimeter itself was mostly just a simple set of motion sensors meant to help stop me from walking face first into a grizzly, which I did once when the property was about half developed and I was out scouting around for berries or other noteworthy things. Don't scoff at what I am saying, coming face-to-face with something big and angry looking was a possibility. I startled it and it ran off which is good; if that had been a female bear, with cubs, it is likely I would not be here to relay this story. All these sensors are routed to a little beeper thing I have in my pocket, again just a simple heads-up. As well there are a total of 7 cameras around the property that would allow me to see who or what was nearby without having to ever step outside. This entire perimeter was dead after the flare. I had made the effort to get the solar panels in but not the cameras and motion sensors; to take down everything would have been too much, power was a priority, security as much as I enjoy it was not.

As I was saying I was preparing to take down the solar panels just before dawn on the second last day before the flare and it was right as I was stepping out of the barn to go start my work that an alarm was set off. However, this particular warning was not a grizzly or deer grazing in my yard. No, this was a group of 3 men and 2 women. Now I was clearly not expecting them, although really, I should have. Only one of the men I recognized, the one leading the pack, waving the group over to me and towards my house. He had been one of the workers who had helped make the house that sits on top of the 'basement'. I knew this was going to be a problem when he was still working here. He did too much snooping around, looking at where the ramp leads to and not doing enough actual building on his part. Mark, I think his name was. So he brought this group here, which as it turns out consisted of his girlfriend, 2 drinking buddies and some chick they happened to meet at a fucking truck stop. So we are all standing on my lawn as the sun is getting closer and closer to cresting over the horizon all the while this 'Mark' guy is telling me that I have to let him and his posse in. I got all the sob stories one would expect during a time like this. The only one I recall was his assertion that his girlfriend was pregnant. He was telling me about how it is my responsibility to make sure that they all [as well as the unborn baby] survive. In fairness, I was never going to be persuaded to allow them into my home, but I would have at least tried to think of a way to help until 'Mark' had assured me that if I didn't let them in then I would not be surviving either. And, after all he knows I have a 'bomb shelter' and 'it would be a shame if the nearby town found this out'. Even at that point I had gotten past the majority of my fears and insecurities and well I don't react too well to threats. I stood there while he talked, all the while looking him dead in the eyes. Everyone's attention was focused on me.

I do not remember exactly what was said that brought the whole argument to a head, but I am guessing Mark finally realized that I was not going to acquiesce to his demands. With all the attention focused on me I think I was the only one seeing Mark's right hand moving around curiously to his lower back. To me that was an obvious sign that things were escalating and quickly. From the angle of his arm I was guessing he did not have a gun; more than likely a knife. He pulled it from his back, twisting in the air about a foot from my face. A bowie knife with what looks to be a bone handle. I know enough of situations like this that this is the time to not get tunnel vision. Keep an eye on everything, use your peripheral vision to watch the entire group. My hands go up, "surrendering" as I step back slowly. I stop looking at his eyes; they will not tell me anything. At this time eyes might as well be dead. His shoulders are what are important now. Any kind of strike, whether that strike a punch, slap or stab, will all appear first in the shoulder as it tenses before the person lunges their arm forward (or around in an arc) depending on the type of strike. My steps are small and slight but just enough to increase the distance between me and Mark even with him advancing; all the while still twisting the blade in the air, spewing profanity about how I'm a fucking asshole. 'Just take it easy buddy'. A step back. He's going to fucking kill me. 'Just take it easy buddy'. Another step back. I'm a piece of shit. 'Just take it easy buddy'. A step back and slightly to my right. Moving to his left moves me further from his right hand and hence further from the knife. I'm a selfish prick. 'Just take it easy buddy'. A step back and to my right again. He'll gut me and let me fucking bleed here in the dirt. 'Just take it easy buddy'. A further step to the side. As I see his shoulder begin to tense I know I am already out of range for him to effectively strike. He was focused on my eyes and I don't even think he realized how much I had moved because his eyes had been on mine the whole time. He lunges while shouting "GO" as what was evidently meant to be the start of their taking over of my hiding spot. They did not know that they would have died here without me regardless, they would not have been able to get inside. Chaos ensued. His entourage tried to rush towards me at that point but…. But everything stopped when I fired my gun into the air just above their heads. Everyone stood wide-eyed looking at me; Mark's knife was barely halfway to me just hovering in the air. Still. It seems that I now had his attention as he was no longer twisting it in anticipation of stabbing me. Not one of them had been watching my hands; they had all been looking at my eyes. From the 'surrender' posture my hands had been slowly lowering to the level of my waist. Each time he had hurdled a profanity at me I had countered with 'just take it easy' my hands had made a slight 'stopping gesture'. After each gesture my hands had returned a little lower, a little closer to my body. A little closer to the holster at the small of my back. I am not a quick-draw champion by any stretch of the word; I needed as much of a head start as I could get. The light was still creeping closer to the horizon; it had felt like hours since my alarm had sounded, and I first saw the silhouettes coming towards me but I think it had likely been less than five minutes up to this point. Time is relative, so it is hard to get a real handle on it. Just as time flies when you're having fun, it slows to a crawl in a crisis; assuming you have the wherewithal and presence of mind to deal with it. It is the only way you could ever really handle something like this, otherwise you would only be able to run on instinct like people who panic. Like these people.

I am glad that when I chose to take a weapon with me around my property; which I always did after that first face-to face, heart-to-heart meeting with a bear; that I chose a semi-automatic. A revolver would have done the job, sort of. To me, having 17 shots is very much preferable to the 6 shots that I would have with a revolver. It allowed me to be able to point my pistol at Mark and fire twice. Leg shots, kind of like in the movies. With a revolver I would have only had 4 rounds left for 4 people. I mean, it is workable but sometimes you miss... That would require for one or all of them to be willing to attack someone who is still holding a gun. If they had been thinking they would have to be able to think that two shots were fired and there were only four left. They would have to be willing to take that chance. Worst is that in a time like that they may have taken those steps. Again, semi-automatic eliminates part of the possibility of someone trying to continue the situation. With shooting Mark, I eliminated the other end of that possibility. If you are ever confronted by a group of people, they are only as brave as the loudest member of the group. Remove the mouth and the rest will fall. And you don't even have to actually touch or hurt any for that, the act of telling a mob who believes that they are invincible you only have to address the one. If he believes that you are willing to stand before that entire group, get beat, get killed, whatever and your only intent before the whole thing is resolved is to take out the mouthpiece then suddenly the mouthpiece will feel very small. Very alone.

Their only strength is being part of the group. Being the lead in the group. Single them out and make it seem as though you are willing to sacrifice yourself to eliminate them as your dying wish and their devotion to the cause will diminish greatly. I could have done this. It may have even worked. My way was a much quicker solution. Take the leader out by no longer allowing him to lead. After getting shot he could say nothing other than 'oh god' over and over again as he went back and forth from holding one leg to the other. Mark was 'fine'; I just winged him. I mean he still would not be walking too quick, or at all really. Crawling; that he could do. The smell of gunpowder lingered and a little strand of smoke was snaking out of the barrel as I eyed the group.

"You have two minutes to get off my property." Really 2 minutes was not enough time, but as long as they are going that is fine. The two drinking buddies start over to Mark to drag him off. They are again frozen when I point the gun in their direction.

"He can make his own way. Better start running; only a minute and a half left." They all run, even the girlfriend. She didn't even look back.

I knelt down beside Mark looking at the fear in his eyes. Even with all this time we have spent together; the emotional gambit we ran together; the feelings we shared I never actually looked into his eyes as I was now. There was a wisp of brown hair laying over his eyes as he lay on the ground. I brush it aside, so I can look directly into his brown eyes. Looking at him man-to-man. "You are Mark, right?" He nods his assent; a little whimper escapes him as he has clearly come to the conclusion that he has pissed off the wrong person. "I'm glad we have these few minutes to talk before you have to go. I'd like to give you the hope that they will come back and help you but..." looking off towards the edge of the field as his posse is just getting to the edge of the woods. "that is not going to happen. They don't care about you. Even the pregnant' one" I use my air quotes to him as I speak. "I would put money on the fact that if she is pregnant it is not yours; she never even looked back". That statement seemed to hurt him, a little tear seemed to well in his already teary eyes. "Take all the time you need just get off my property. Oh, and for the record if you had not pulled out that knife you could be running away with them right now, keep that in mind for your last little while." I grunt slightly as I stand, "I am not as young as I used to be." I stand looking over to the east; the sun just peaking over the horizon, its one great beam of light looking like a laser streaking across the lake towards us. Mark has started crawling off in the same direction that the others ran; his strains to move being punctuated by grunts of pain. "You and I both know this world is going to die, that is why you came here, but you came to the wrong place. This is for my family not you. And now you… you are going to die along with the rest of this world. You will get a front row ticket to the show. If you live that long." He did not; I checked on him later that night he had crawled probably half the way to the road, which all things considered was pretty impressive. It was apparent that even before the flare the sun was ramped up, his skin was burnt from spending all day out in daylight. It had already started to peel, I would say that it must have been excruciating although with his being in shock from having been shot likely meant that he did not feel the majority of it. They never did come back for him, not even an attempt. The police were never sent to my place either. This meant either society was that broken that a phone call about someone getting shot was lost in the pandemonium or I was right and his girlfriend was banging one of the drinking buddies and couldn't be bothered to call the cops. Oh well, either/or, it is kind of funny.

If you are paying attention you will likely note that I referred to Mr. John Thomas as my first kill when this was chronologically first. And that would be a fair assessment; in truth I had kind of forgotten about this episode until I reminded myself of it and then wrote it down. I guess the reason I never really include it is that this one was self-defense, and against a real threat, not against some dissidents who were only talking about being a threat at some point. Also, I just don't want to include this one, of all of them, this is the only one that I could've been justified in but at the same time I regret it. As well it seems kind of lackluster. I mean, shooting some guy in the legs and letting him bleed out. Very unimpressive. Not like there is a competition for that sort of thing and even if there was I would not win anyways. I see your skinning someone alive and raise you some cannibalism. My answer is C: Genocide. Final Answer. I'll take impaling thousands of my own people for 1000 Alex. See, I am not the worst, just the most recent.

And now to return full circle to the beginning of this story; panic. Fight or flight. Mark and his posse were in a panic, that led them to me and trying to hide (flight); desperation and my stubbornness led them, well Mark, to try to take my place by force (fight). It all had the same route. Panic.

You may also have the thought right now about how I had said something previously about how I was proud of my former people as they were now more along the path to egalitarianism, they were all helpful to each other. I had made something close to a true communist society where everything was for the betterment of the community. These ideals, which I am proud of others having, were not being displayed by myself prior to the cataclysm and you would be correct to recognize that. I think my best value as a role-model is what not to do. I do really think that communism is a good idea but people destroy it. Greed makes people not want to give up stuff for the good of the community. I have never said I was perfect so obviously I have a problem with greed. Or just my introversion was stopping me from allowing others into my home. Either way nothing can be changed now.

CHAPTER 7 – TEACH A MAN TO FISH…

Now where should I go from here? Should I bore you with stories about how the crops I was growing on the lower level of my home looked so good, probably better than I could ever get them above ground? No, that would not be overly interesting although it is amazing how a confined space does make it easier to concentrate. Should I tell you about how one of the horses managed to get into the garden area and sat there and ate most of my lettuce? Still haven't figured out how that Houdini horse with no thumbs got out of its pen. Should I regale you with stories of how I managed to read dozens of books in a couple days? No, of course not, that is not why you are reading this. You're not even reading this so you can find out how I helped save what was left of the human race from itself and make my people the strongest around. Their character was impeccable, honest and hard-working people for the most part; and those of course were the ones that I was ultimately making this place for. You want to read about the death and destruction. You want to read about the horror and the aftermath. Depending on your outlook everything from just prior to the flare could be construed as fulfilling those roles with kind of a meandering up and down to it, a retreat and advance. The actual full force of the solar flare only lasted for 3 days, but it had a longer build-up and just as long of a cool down. At the point I am writing this things have, to a great extent, normalized. People have normalized. Society goes on, life continues. It has truthfully been so long that I don't even know how long it has been, my guess is at least 15 years, maybe even getting close to 20. This is one of those kinds of things that were relevant before the cataclysm when there were places to go and people to see; that is not a huge concern here. Most of the people are sedentary farmers growing food, or some form of craftsman making things necessary for everyone.

So, we might as well discuss a few years after I settled Republica. I honestly don't know how people initially found out about my little town or if they just randomly wandered until they found a place that had no abandoned cars cluttering up the streets, no fetid rotting corpses strewn about, no mummies left baked and dry in what used to be people's homes. I, and eventually we, took care of all that. All the cars left abandoned were towed to a nearby farm with the pair of tow trucks that used to operate in the town. All neatly parked, unlocked, keys when we had them were left in the ignition. We had a giant box full of old keys that we found here and there around town. Each one was eventually categorized into house or business keys; and vehicle keys broken into rough categories, Chevy, GMC, Ford, Dodge, Toyota, etc. and then systematically tried in each of the vehicles until the proper one was found. This was another job assigned to Aurora. Simple enough for a child and a good way to keep her distracted from some of the other things that were going on. Even as time wore on she never mentioned or complained about the smells that she would encounter on a daily basis in those cars. I admire her for that. People who do not complain are few and far between. I have even caught myself doing it from time to time although in my role as leader I have to be very careful about it. If something bothers me then that breeds doubt. Not just in myself but others in me. There was no danger in having a little girl do this as I had all the batteries taken out; they can be useful for other things, like when electricity is not readily available. A car without a battery will not start, so she just went about her business trying keys, picking flowers, gazing at clouds and butterflies. All the gasoline from the vehicles was siphoned from the tanks; it can be used elsewhere. If you leave the fuel in the gas tanks all it does is varnish the inside of the gas tank and become a totally useless inert liquid. Given enough time gasoline will essentially break itself down into something wholly useless. I do not know of a way to explain it for people who do not understand what it is like to be reliant upon fossil fuels. Many alive now have never been able to just go to a gas station and fill up their car. There was honestly a lot of freedom in that; the ability to simply get a tank of gas and go as far as it will take you. Not to say we did not make due; you can learn to make biofuels. You can get oil from vegetables that would then be used for some purpose like cooking before being filtered and used as a type of diesel fuel. The vehicles we have now run on that. I cannot take credit for making this happen; at best I set the stage and prompted the people with know-how to actually do things instead of just surviving. Every house was systematically checked, every room, every closet, every basement and crawl space; for things of use as well as for the remains of the former residents; we needed to clean out the houses and get rid of the remains of people in addition to making sure that we had things for those still alive. This was all done for two simple reasons. One: there are no more operating factories that I am aware of at least. Everything that is made is usually made by hand but someone handy with some sort of thing like people who can knit making clothes or someone that used to do all kinds of crafty stuff making soaps. We had a blacksmith, a mechanic for working on the few vehicles and a man who used to make birdhouses as a hobby is now making most of the furniture. This was a prime reason for finding and storing useful things; it would all get used eventually, in some manner by someone. The reason for removing the remains of the former residents was not just for decency's sake but it was also a health issue. Having rotting flesh everywhere and not removing it is just asking for there to be an outbreak of disease. Could be the kind spread by rats (i.e. bubonic plague) or something mold based or just some out of control bacteria colony. Who knows, it is irrelevant either way. My town did not have enough people in those first few months in order to be able to rebound from having even half the population die. Well we would have probably rebounded the same as after the cataclysm but why pile one disaster on top of another. Whilst we were getting all the former residents out of their homes and looking for useful things to stockpile we were also packing up a majority of the belongings that would have reminded people of the former residents. Again, I will remind you that this is of a practical nature as opposed to being something more spiritual; like how so many former cultures used to bury an individual's personal objects along with them so those things could accompany them into the afterlife. It was thought that everything they needed in life they would continue to need in death. The Vikings, Egyptians, Celts are the ones that most readily come to mind that acted in this way although more than likely they were fewer cultures that did not practice things like this than did. People did not have the same kind of idea as we more modern people have. 'You can't take it with you' was a fairly common phrase referring simply to the idea that real objects do not transfer into the spirit world. That is a little more philosophical than I want to get. Who knows? Maybe they were right, maybe the more modern ideas are right; maybe there is nothing at all. I'm not going to judge that. Not at this point anyhow. The items that we brought with the people to be cremated along with them tended to be of a more personal nature; pictures, bills, pets, toothbrushes, hairbrushes, all that went with them. There is no reason for someone if they chose to inhabit a new home to go and then have to see the pictures of the previous owners when they were happy; at weddings, on vacations, sitting with their children on their laps. You know, before they were cooked sitting in their favorite armchair waiting for it to be safe to go outside. Everything was loaded up, moved out to the quarry and burnt. Here is where the gasoline was used. Now don't mistake my current matter-of-factness with there being some sort of insensitivity at the time; I gave it a measure of ceremony and respect although it is more than likely there are a few who would not have wanted something akin to a Viking funeral pyre for their cremation, but no one was available for me to ask. It's not that I was a monster, at least not at that point; it was more of a personal feeling of mine that this is what we needed to do with the former residents. It was also just a matter of practicality. Graves are time consuming and space consuming and made so people can visit them. That is why they have markers, with names and birthdays and all those things that people loved to have on them, those little sayings and inspirational things. We didn't always have that in the first place; names as much as we feel they are very concrete things, we personalize and internalize them are in fact just an abstract that we use. Someone saying I am John, I am Dave, I am Helmut, I am Nancy; are all just ways that we envision and label ourselves. We hold on to those ideas, but they are in fact intangible. If you are never told someone's name, never read it, never hear it spoken in conversation would never have any idea what that person's name is; they'd just be 'Guy' or 'You'. There was for example a couple that I would have characterized as elderly. They looked like they were probably in their sixties or maybe seventies, but honestly it was hard to tell; exposed to a super-flare and then exposed to the elements for so long they looked more mummies than anything. They had been sitting on a bench in a park and were still holding hands when we happened across them. No identification. All we could say with any kind of certainty was that they were probably married; she was dressed in a plain white dress, very old looking, but quite obviously a wedding dress. He was in what was probably his best suit, a dark grey with thin pin stripes; a burgundy and navy striped tie around his neck. Their [wedding] rings matched, he wore what looked to be a Medic Alert bracelet on his left arm; I did not bother to check to see what he needed people to know. Not important to us. I am certain that with some sleuthing and checking pictures in random houses, public records, etc. we could have determined who they were but what for? Who would that have been for? The people in Republica had no idea who they were; they would not be remembered for anything other than a touching story of love and devotion. It was better to cremate them, let their ashes float up towards the heavens and they can be united eternally in that manner; much as they were united in life. So that couple along with every other person we found was moved to the quarry. All of those who left Republica in this manner were given as proper a service as could be expected and every night for almost 3 weeks there was a great funeral pyre in that quarry. They and their belongings made the night seem bright. The heat was reminiscent of things that most of us there would have preferred to have forgotten. If there is a god and a soul then maybe that could mean there is some form of a tangible item from their lives that could go up in smoke with them, wisps of pictures floating to heaven.

I know there are still some people who are reading this that probably think that they should have been buried instead of burned like a pile of garbage and they may be right although the time for debate has long since passed and I would have been the one digging a trench a mile long; it would not have been worth the effort. On top of that I do feel that if we were going to do it right we would have to give everyone a headstone. Even though we generally had no idea what their names were, or birthdays or even favorite colors. And another important question, who would make the headstones? No one had the time or the skill to carve those. And where do you put all those people? Space is at a premium when you have a little town and no outside sources of food and no place you can import fruit and vegetables from. With no grocery store you cannot just walk in and buy your food. Without those kinds of things you need all available space to grow and graze your own food. The yard of every home was a garden, with the simple basics everyone can do, carrots, tomatoes, onions, and the like. Every place we could get that had decent sun indoors was used to grow things that needed a more tropical climate. Hell, we even turned a room attached to the local pool into a tropical hot house where we grew bananas and those kinds of fruits. The humidity was the key to getting them to grow properly. Every person was, of course, responsible for the garden directly attached to their house and helped out the community with the more public ones. The public ones did have kind of a communist feel, things were rationed and were given evenly throughout the populous. This worked out most of the time, but when people have next to nothing it becomes very easy to be tempted but also very easy to incur the wrath of a community. Once, and only once, did someone decide that he would take more than his fair share. This actually amounted to almost a quarter of the bananas that were available at the time. He just packed them up and took them all home. Once the community at large heard about this there was of course an uproar. He was brought before me for punishment; he was bruised and according to those that brought him to me "fell down, multiple times". I'm not necessarily a fan of bananas, nor do I feel particularly slighted by him taking them, it was more of a way to keep the people happy. Bananas were one of those simple little pleasures from a better time. And there is also the idea that all people under me should be equal. So, he was brought before me, or more correctly dragged before me, and my citizens asked for his punishment for stealing from the community, punishment for making their lives worse again. Demanding his punishment for just being stupid. I think his accusers were a little surprised that I made him confess before I even made the attempt at giving them justice. And they were even more surprised by my decree. You see normally I have most things set out as kind of a barbaric corporal punishment kind of justice system, it has much more of a deterrent value than the old ways. If you have not figured my logic on the dealing with miscreants it is very simple. No one will dare go into someone's home and steal something if they will have to spend a week in the stocks then have their hand cut off. No one would think to beat his neighbor to death because that neighbor's dog shit on his lawn. The penalty for murder is death, and not the pre-fire kind of death sentence. There is no such thing as prohibitions on cruel and unusual punishment. I am the only one that makes prohibitions like that. Well this man's sentence just happened to be the most apt I could think of. Expulsion. Permanently. With a twist of course.

I know some of you completely understand after all it makes sense when you think about it the right way. His crime and sin was greed and gluttony and what better way to punish him then to cast him out, he will never again have the luxuries that he experienced here. Now here is the fun part. The part I thought was above all funny was where he was sent. We had a working plane, nothing fancy or spectacular but functional. It had a range on the order of 800 miles, but with a few modifications that was doubled. He was flown about 1500 miles north, above the tree line. It would seem that this was a massive waste of resources but at the same time it was done for effect. Anything worth doing can be worth overdoing. He was taken to the desolate lands, cold tundra, with no shelter or food and he was dropped from the plane by parachute; it was a death sentence but with more flare than just killing someone outright. I learned later from the men who dropped him off that the banana thief was afraid of heights, all the better though. His hands were cuffed with a key sewn into his pants and he was pushed out of the plane. It became our own little urban legend, the man who stole bananas, a morality tale for the kids to be fair to all those around them. It worked, I'd like to say you can't argue with results, but people will always try to. In my town there was essentially no such thing as crime. People can and will be fine upstanding citizens, it's just sometimes you have to put a gun to their heads to make them want to be that way. Those were of course the early days, when I was just leader by default, the 'first' one here and the first one to step up with a plan. Becoming the tyrant is something that would happen a short while later.

My first tyrannical act was not even mine. It was just perceived to be. I would say it was around 4 years after the cataclysm when we were having a town meeting where I was telling the citizens of my plan to start having a tax of sorts taken from everyone in the form of a portion of their vegetable crop in their gardens. This was done for the greater good, not for my benefit. There had been a few families in the previous winter that had almost starved to death. This was due in large part to their own failings however a person failing is not something to punish. I am willing to help someone as long as they make the attempt to help themselves. Their biggest failing was not being able to get things to grow, which was more than likely due to a lack of knowledge which was as compounded by a lack of knowledge of the fine art of canning. I proposed this tax to the masses one of my subjects decided he wanted the floor to speak and didn't care how rude he had to be to get that privilege. After being interrupted twice I relented and let him speak. He railed about how he is not going to help the others in the community, how he is not going to keep people alive to save them from their own incompetence. I understood his point, but really there was no reason for his acting as he did. Also, I am not amused by rudeness. The amount of vegetables I was talking of was nearly negligible, only worked out to probably 5% of their total crops. But he had to be heard; I let him speak for almost 5 minutes on the fairness of every-man-for-himself and the survival of the fittest. Finally, I had enough and ordered him taken out of the room, so he was escorted out. He was absolutely livid. After I was done talking whilst on my way out he decided that was a good time to continue the debate. I had none of it, I had already made my decision and all the other citizens said nothing against my plan; most actually liked the idea of having a safety net not just for others but for themselves. Later than night the trouble maker's house burned down. Again, this was not my fault. Turns out he had faulty wiring in his house and that started the fire, which burned him alive. But everyone thought it was me, and I just went with it. That whole episode was forgotten though. And my taxation plan ended up having a much more beneficial effect than I had planned. It seemed that it was a way of fostering a sense of community within my people. Those that had a hard time the previous winter had that safety net of being able to eat but in the end they did not even need it. Their neighbors, their peers around them took the initiative to help them do it right the first time. They got taught how to plant things, fertilize, tend them, look for parasites, harvest, can, prepare, really the whole process from start to finish. Those people no longer had to not rely on the kindness of others. Instead, the kindness of others ended up being kindness for themselves as we ended up having sufficient food for the whole town to have a feast around what we guessed was Christmas time. A community is not just a bunch of people living in the same area, breathing the same air, it is a bunch of people who care about one another; who try to make their lives better by helping someone else come up to their level as opposed to stepping on their head to take one more step up the ladder. Caring.

All emotions turned the right way can be useful at times; some are just easier and quicker to use. Fear can be a great asset. If you harness emotions and funnel them properly they can be very useful. I used fear as one of my greatest motivators for the populous. After this first incident it really hit home for me and reminded me of those thoughts I had before the world turned to shit. Power does not have to be real. It can just be a perception. If you make someone fear for their life they will do anything, but additionally you can make someone do almost anything for 'love' and love's evil cousin hate. If a man loves a woman you can get him to be your dutiful enforcer or serene gardener if you make sure that he has the means to provide for his newly beloved. I guess that could be greed, but the underlying emotion that is driving the need for some form of wealth is, at its essence, love. There have been many more publicized examples for the opposite emotion. From the crazy person on the street hating how you look and attacking you. To the Nazis having millions of people killed by their soldiers, many of whom were not overly hateful, because they hated their 'impurity'.

In the beginning I did not have power; there was no 'power' to be had. People were terrified of me anyways. It doesn't take much really, look angry, and do not laugh at stupid jokes even if you find them funny. Just look at people, look through them, it makes them scared. People fear what they do not understand and if you do not explain anything then there is so much more for them to fear. This is not to say I did not find a lot of the jokes and whatnot I heard funny, I just simply had other things on my mind. A family gone, a world scorched and burnt; a hundred people who bloody well need direction and purpose and have to be told that they need it. I often would walk through the town, not doing or looking at anything in particular, and I would pass people and they would look down as they walked by or would suddenly become really engrossed in their gardening. I was like the boss everyone hates, the bad guy who will fire your ass for taking too long on a coffee break. Every once in a while, I would even stop by one of those people gardening and just stand there. At first, I was waiting for a hello, but then that really did not seem like the best course of action. My main goal is to make these people, and by extension this town survive. It cannot survive if people are starving. And people work twice as hard if they think they are about to be fired. Perhaps while still alive. In their house. While they slept. See, I even made a joke there. Anyways, it came that I would stand there and essentially give them a tongue lashing. Work harder. Pick out those weeds. Go to the compost heap and get some more fertilizer. Place a half empty beer bottle on the ground to catch the snails. Yeah, I might have been a bit of a jerk, but no one needs wishy-washy leader in the aftermath of worldwide devastation. Ned Flanders is not a help, he is a hindrance. Indecision and being hesitant are the kind of things that can bog down a rebuilding effort. Sloth is not just a deadly sin worthy of getting you killed in a Brad Pitt movie, it is worthy of getting you killed in my town. I don't think I ever actually had someone killed for it but there were a few 'lessons' that had to be taught. Medieval kind of stuff, a day in the stocks that kind of thing.

We had someone who tried to take advantage of the tax that meant to help feed the less fortunate. I believe this was a man named Ron. I think, again long time ago and not a significant portion of my life was devoted to him. Of course, we are talking about him because he ran with it in the total wrong direction. On more than one occasion I walked by his home and saw nothing but weeds in his garden, soil totally untouched. I honestly thought the house was one of the empty places; it still had the red star painted on the front door saying so. I thought this until he happened to be coming out as I was walking by one day. I stopped him, asked him what he was doing in the empty house, where he was off to, etcetera. He almost kind of scoffed at me, saying it was his house and he was off to the neighbors for a drink. I looked at him, nodded and walked off. I made sure to check that house every day for the next week; I even checked the back yard just to make sure he didn't do all his gardening back there. Nothing changed. All the other houses at this point had yards full of vegetables, the people who had been lacking the knowledge the previous winter had been taught by the more knowledgeable ones on the ways of farming. So on the seventh day I did not rest, but he did. He was dragged from his house and taken to a set of stocks I had one of the people in town with carpentry know-how make the day before. I had them nice and prominently set up in the middle of town. People all came to see what was happening. I yelled at them all to go see what sloth brought his garden, to see the fruits of his labors. Everyone went to see. Everyone came back with the same look, a look of disappointment and revulsion. For him, of course. None of them looked me in the eye. So I made my decree, 'No man that shuns his own garden in that manner shall be fed by the community. Any person found providing him with food or inviting him over for dinner or helping him in any manner when he refused to help himself for so long shall forfeit their own work to the town'. I left him in the stocks for 3 days. At dawn on the third day I walked out, knelt before him and asked him what he had learned. He said he had learned the error of his ways and he was going to be the hardest worker in the town. That might have been true. But unfortunately, it started to get cold every night shortly after. I think it might be like the fable about the Ant and the Grasshopper. He just did not take it seriously until it was too late. And to their credit I do not think any of the townspeople agreed to help him. He just disappeared one day and left the town. It could not have worked out any better for him, with no one willing to give him food his only option would have been to steal from another, and he knew that would have been a death sentence. I will not fuck around with people like that. To be honest I always wondered if he survived, found some source of food to last the winter, and found another town, I wondered if he truly learned his lesson.

But ultimately, I am not a Ned Flanders kind of guy, I made decisions. In Ron's case it quite possibly meant his death and was in a way contradictory of my earlier thought of providing for the less fortunate. But then again, he was not less fortunate. He didn't have poor soil quality and a lack of farming knowledge. He simply did not want to work; he would rather enjoy the fruits of other people's labor. People really do not follow ideas, but they do follow action and directness. People will often mistake confidence for knowledge or skill; this was not generally a problem for me in that I was able to exhibit confidence as well I seem to know a thing or two. I was able to be confident enough that no one questioned me; say it once and with authority and the masses will just scurry off to do whatever and not say another word. There at least. If you tell someone to do something they will more than likely do it and they will for sure do it if they fear the consequences of not doing it. I think that despite their fear of me people are happiest when someone else does their thinking for them, at least on the big issues. If I say to my people we need food, go grow it, they do. That is the kind of direction people need.

Our little town managed to attract all types of people. As I said in the beginning people just flocked here on their own, like moths to a light. Afterwards people started venturing out; meeting people out in the 'world' and bringing them back. We had a doctor, electrician, plumber, a few people in various construction fields, an electrical engineer plus a large number of people with 'hobbies'. Those are the kind of people that we truly needed. Not because of their skills, although those were helpful, but because of their drive and dedication. They inspired people to try hard and work hard and make everything work out. And everyone was pretty much given the best apprentice we could provide them. There was no real schooling in our town. It was made sure that everyone, boy, girl and adult could read and write and do basic math, had a general grasp of the world around them and how to make things works but education past that was kind of a luxury and had to be handled in a more on-the-job kind of manner. No one is unable to learn and there is no reason they should not be able to so we ensured that it was the same for everybody in that they did get the basics. It is just sometimes there needs to be different methods taken to ensure they learn; some people learn better from books, some from experience, some tactile, whatever; we adapted to their needs so they had what they needed. And everything we did was pretty much focused on the future, from making sure we had a doctor 20 years from now to making sure there was power and clean running water going to the retirement home that we converted into a full-on hospital. That did take a bit of work and planning; you can't just turn any room into an operating room. In order to do it properly you need a way to get it sterile and maintain that. Filtration for the air. Filtered water. I'm sure dozens of other things. I was not really part of that, I just decreed and let it happen. I decided it was time to stop living so primitively. There was a river nearby, which by the point I made my pronouncement, had begun to flow again. We had everyone in the town pitch in with whatever skills they had and firstly built the water wheel then built a dam with a kind of trough to drop the water on the wheel. I'm sure that has some particular kind of name but I honestly did not need to and still do not need to know what that name was. All I knew was that method was supposed to be the most efficient for transmitting the kinetic energy of the water to the wheel and hence the most effective method of generating electricity. Now I am obviously over-simplifying the amount of effort and skill it took to make this happen as well as the effort it took to make it worth the while, because in the end having a generator that could not put out enough electricity is going to do nothing. All the 'modern' conveniences in that town were things I had to actively spurn to get the people to do. Now if you remember when I said that Lisa was turning things off this is why. I had thought about this before doing it and it made sense that everything should be turned off or unplugged if you are unsure if it is on or off so if/when we finally had power running to the town there would not be an instantaneous overload of the whole system as every appliance in town suddenly turned on at once. Most of the wires were completely screwed from the firestorm but it was not something that I was comfortable leaving to chance. That much radiation and spare electrons running around just overloaded every wire, not totally sure what it did but needless to say it was a mess to fix but we managed it. And that is what I had experts for.

Hardest part of attracting all these people is actually a left over from the old world. People want to be paid for their work. It makes sense when you think of it but when the economy you have is at best described as a bartering system, it is just not totally possible. I mean certain things were easy to accommodate; the doctor got paid in food as he was not able to work on his garden as much as others so to supplement his deficiency he was fed. Totally fair. She did need a bit of an education in fairness though as she was still thinking the old way and in essence wanting to overcharge. What good is doing an emergency appendectomy and saving someone's life if you will take literally all their food and starve them out a little while later. I think once it was explained in those terms she got the fact that we want everyone fed and alive which means sharing to meet everyone's needs not taking.

So that is our place, our home, my town. Looking at it I'm sure you are reading this and thinking that with the exception of a few moments where I was a dick, I was not being the tyrant that I have so far made myself out to be but don't worry, you will understand everything soon enough. The problem that I am having is that in all honesty I never really saw what I was doing as being that bad, I was looking out for the population as a whole, that was the appearance at least, but I was looking

out for just one person. And oddly enough it was not me that I was looking
out for, I was looking out for my little girl; Aurora.

CHAPTER 8 – A VESSEL OF …

Of course, at this point as you are reading this, you probably think I went all M. Night Shyamalan on you. He was a movie director who was known for putting some shocking twist into his movies, no matter how absurd the twists were. They were entertaining. But that is the truth, I am her father, and yes, I knew from the first moment I saw her again in that church all those years ago. Why did I not tell her? Why did I not wipe away her tears that first dawn after we reunited? I was still seized by the thought that she was better without me. In all honesty, I froze. I just could not bring myself to say it even though I wanted to and then as time wore on I just could not say anything. The further time wore on the more it seemed like I would have just been playing a horrible joke on her and she never deserved that. It is like when you miss someone's name or forget it then at a certain point it becomes too embarrassing or insulting or uncomfortable to tell someone that you have no idea who they are. In all actuality I excelled at dealing with people like that; I was able to go weeks without ever knowing someone's name, I would just be patient and eventually someone else would say it or I would see it somewhere. On a piece of mail. A pay stub. A list. Somewhere. It did not matter where exactly. Now don't think I am so callous that I referred to everyone as buddy or pal. I am more intelligent than that. You simply have to phrase things in a way that you do not have to use names. I kind of got past the point in the conversation where you need to use names and then just run from there. Act as if they are already a friend, even if they are not. You could just meet them but if you talk to them as if you know them then firstly they will feel more at ease talking to you but there is also no need to use names. Best friends never use names in a sentence when talking to each other; they only use names when trying to get the other one's attention. That was essentially the principle that I operated under and it worked exceedingly well. This was a necessity for me as I can't, for the life of me, remember names. Not until I have practiced it in conversation. Or seen it written down somewhere. I really think that reading is the way I remember names best so I am obviously one of those kinds of people that learns best that way. That is the only thing I can figure as I am able to retain hundreds of random facts years after I read it or watched it on TV or was taught it. My memory is by all accounts pretty extraordinary with pretty much any piece of information I get, except names. Just a small side-note here, the only reason I remember the names of most of the people that I have mentioned so far is that I wrote them down. I listed every person that died as a result of my words or actions. I would like to say that it was meant as a way of trying to cleanse my soul or pray for the atonement of my sins but as I have already established that would just not have been me. Not my motivation. History is written by the victor. If I won then I had to be the one to write history going forward. That was the initial motivation. In the end it just became a huge Nixon-esque list. No real history in there, just a list of names.

I wonder if as you are reading this if you had been pondering things out of the scope of this writing. Stuff more personal to me. Like what kind of person was he beforehand? Was he really as fucked up as he made himself out to be? What did he do? Where did he learn all those random things? Was he as smart as he tries to portray himself or was he just a really good actor? How could he afford to build that compound that he was so proud of? Those are the kinds of things that I would have been asking myself along the way as I was reading this.

I think most of those are open to interpretation and will become apparent as we go, but here are a couple tidbits that will maybe tie in a few loose ends right now. The place that I loved so much that I lost my family for. It was the product of someone with a good healthy dose of anxiety and social awkwardness suddenly having too much money on his hands. It was my inheritance from my grandfather passing away. I guess I should also mention here that my frivolous spending of my inheritance was something else that prompted my ex to take away my Aurora. I was not spending the money as she had wanted. On her. Making her life perfect and luxurious. I am not a jewels and caviar kind of guy so that kind of thing never really entered my mind. So anyways, I was "selfish" and did things as I pleased and it cost me a lot more than money. The rest of that whole period I think I will leave in the dark; it is either completely immaterial to what I am saying or has already been mentioned so why keep beating a dead horse. The other tidbit I will offer up right now is where I learned all these wonderful and random facts. I had always referred to myself as a "Vessel of Useless Knowledge" which sounds almost exciting but really is not; there really should be emphasis on the useless part of that title. What I know is mostly only good for trivia games or impressing people.

I went to university like so many others, thinking that more education would land me a dream job. Things do not always work out as planned. At the start of my higher education I was enrolled in the science program. I was going to be a biochemist. Make drugs and shit. That plan quickly changed half way through my first year when I got extremely bored with chemistry, which is just a tad integral to biochemistry. I do not know how I can really articulate it for someone just how I felt at that time but obviously I am going to try. In short, I would have to say it was the actual work involved. Taking a normal chemistry class you are required to take a 'lab' which is where you practice doing experiments. Now these are nothing exciting, simple mix this solution into this solution until you get something with a certain pH, or the color changes or it heats up. Whatever. Once you got the desired result then the "fun" starts. The calculations. That is where I got lost. An experiment may take an hour or two or three; the calculations may take a week. It was just too much. Too many numbers. Too repetitive and boring. Now don't get me wrong I can do a lot of math in my head, I think my brain is geared for that kind of work but yeah…months of chemistry calculations and I knew I was in the wrong place. I finished off my year then I changed my major and my focus. Sociology. It's perfect I had thought. I will be able to study people and finally understand them; there are billions of people, hundreds or thousands of different cultures to study, I would never be bored. I could investigate social dynamics and behavior patterns and it didn't work. I mean I learned and was able to understand things better than I had before, but parts of the whole sociology field just did not "do it" for me. The kind of big concept stuff either seemed too simplified for me to take seriously or just did not seem to work and fit. Well... third times the charm, right? History. It is nice and simple. Dates, names, events, places. All very ordered and simple, yet expansive. No matter how much you think you know about something you can always seem to find something more detailed. New perspectives. New interpretations. I had finally found my 'passion' and I ran with it. I graduated with a degree in History. Not an honors degree though, again not for lack of ability just lack of effort. Having to pay my own way through school meant I did not have the time necessary to do the extra work necessary to complete such a task. A history degree though is not the most useful degree out in the real world. I ended up having to work a variety of jobs from cleaner to dog walker to convenience store clerk to security guard until I was finally able to get a job that at least somewhat was related to what I went to school for. I got a job working in a museum; setting up displays, doing cataloguing, arranging for archaeologists to bring in exhibits. All kinds of random things. And there I got to finally feel like I was happy. Sort of. The whole place got stale after a while. On a few occasions I had to cover for when our tour guides were ill and I ran the tours. I was able to recite each exhibits plaque verbatim. As well those tourists were given my little additions to the tour; they got the benefit of my knowledge obtained from other perspectives and interpretations. I think that is why once I had the freedom to do as I pleased I ended up making the library such an important place in my house; for me the learning was the most important part, so I just wanted to learn on my own.

Now you see why I was initially trying to be the new writer of history was because I was the keeper of history before the cataclysm. A list of names is not history though. History is stories. It has meaning. It is something you learn from or are doomed to repeat it. Relate that to what you are reading and some good can come of all my ramblings.

As time plodded along there was a return to 'normalcy' which I have to use loosely as the world was never going to return to normal in the sense that I would have been thinking. Maybe I should use the word stabilized. Or returned to homeostasis. I'll just stick with normalcy for simplicity. Things were not going to go back to how they were though. That would be almost physically impossible. To have a stable genetic population of people you need something on the order of forty thousand people which would allow enough genetic diversity for a population to survive indefinitely. In all of North America there might have been something around two hundred and fifty thousand people. I am of course guesstimating but I think it probably works out to be about right. Collecting enough people in a single area would be difficult given that much of what used to be used for transportation is not going to operate properly for one reason or another. Gasoline degraded. Car batteries dead. Highways in eternal traffic jams. Miles upon miles of dead trains sitting lifeless on the tracks. Flying could possibly work I guess but then you have to find somewhere to land. Planes aren't really effective for transplanting a whole population anyways. So people were stuck where they were more or less. Or they could go on foot or bike. Wander around until they came across a place like Republica. Make a home for themselves. Raise a family. Grow stuff. Have a 'normal' after-the-cataclysm-kind-of-life. Nothing in the normalcy of our existence gave a reason to ever tell Aurora who I was, why I never said anything before, why I was gone. The longer from that first dawn the less it mattered. I still watched over her as her father would have. I protected her. I taught her. I raised her, at least in part.

I was with her when the situation arose that would lead to my becoming the official leader of Republica; as opposed to the de facto leader that I had been beforehand. Not solely her but in a way it was just us. Everyone had their purpose in rebuilding the world and I was no different. My part was a little more forward thinking, planning for the future. Teaching the children; not that I was necessarily qualified for this but it was something that I had started almost as soon as I met back up with Aurora, so it ended up just continuing as more and more people arrived in the town. Being my daughter and my first student, I am sure I always favored Aurora over the other children. It was not necessarily intentional. It was something like when you bring a baby home to meet the family dog. Depending on the breed of dog; that child will have a protector for life. I started this relationship we had while sitting on those swings. I was going to protect her and nurture her as only a [surrogate] father could do. That particular day class was reviewing the math lesson taught the day before, when there was a knock at the door. I remember having a dumbfounded look on my face as I was being relayed the bad news. People were sick. Since last night there had been 14 people brought to the nursing home to see our "doctor", more were expected, they were doing wellness checks on everyone to see who else was sick and just not able to get themselves to the home. I say doctor in quotes as at that point the best we had was a nurse. She was still good and helped a lot; I will not diminish anything she did in those early days. I was told that she had been an operating room nurse for years so apparently, she picked up a few things.

It would seem odd to think of a time in Republica when I was not in control but there was a time; a time when I did actually give a measure of freedom in what was allowed. In the beginning my biggest concern was making sure that the basic necessities were available for people. We had enough food for everyone, we had reasonable access to healthcare, water, shelter, heat in the winter, clothes. All those things were handled. Not by me personally of course. I just set things in motion, mostly through suggestions or sometimes if the person I was talking to was a little more on the daft side some convincing was necessary but overall I just pushed the dominos and let them go. And this worked for some time. I was never a micromanager, nor did I ever aspire to be. If you make the goals simple and clear enough then there is no need. My assumption that people would work well without any measure of supervision and only a directive to get things done was one of my largest mistakes. We had a number of people die, however they are not on my list. I take no responsibility in their deaths as they did not die as a result of my words or actions. At best it is only through my inaction but after being funneled through the incompetence of 3 or 4 other people my inaction becomes much less important. There were a number of failures up and down the chain of command and the only part of the responsibility that I will truly accept is that after knocking over the first domino I did not watch to see if they all fell. People got lazy and it lead to problems, that I don't think anyone could have really foreseen; even I did not figure on these kinds of things occurring in my wildest fantasies.

The problem that cropped up was a multi-layered problem which I think only coincidentally started to converge making a large problem all at once. One of those issues was something that I mentioned much earlier but never said anything about since. The nuclear fallout. I will not even claim to have a good idea as to how it really affected things, but I do think that at our latitude we actually hit fairly light from it. I'm sure there are other things like wind patterns, jet stream and tons of other factors that would be an entire volume in themselves if I was to really try to document them and delve into them as they should be addressed but that is unnecessary. Radiation is dangerous due to a few things. Alpha (α) particles are the largest thing thrown off by radioactive dust. It is generally fairly easily combated, you don't even need that much of a barrier to stop them. Beta (β) particles, slightly smaller and therefore slightly more difficult to stop but kind of the same idea. Not the biggest concern. Gamma (γ) rays are the really bad ones. These are as the name suggests actual 'radiation' akin to x-rays. This is the big one that needs to be stopped. Refer back to the radiation halving thicknesses if you need a reminder. When things are radioactive there are a number of things that happen to people the most important being radiation burns which are similar to sunburns but on steroids; physical effects like nausea and vomiting which are the parts of the 'radiation sickness' with weakness, hair loss and those kinds of things coming later on. All of those in themselves are the kinds of things that can be overcome and moved past but that is not really an option. Picture a bunch of pool balls all nicely racked up before a game of pool begins. That triangle of balls would be the representation of your deoxyribonucleic acid; DNA, the stuff that makes you and everyone else what they are. DNA is the real thing that separates us from the animals, albeit only by a few percent points. Do not take these numbers as exact but they are close enough to show what I mean; a chimpanzee has something like 97% of the same DNA sequences as humans, horses are 92%, mouse 90%, even a sea cucumber is like 75% the same as humans. Everything on earth started at essentially the same starting point and branched out from there. Evolved from there. That again is another expansive discussion that I am not going to go into right now but just trust me that is what happened.

And I am off track again, I apologize. In any event the rack of pool balls is the DNA and the cue ball the radiation, in whatever form it may be; α or β particles or γ rays, it does not matter all that much. The cue ball hits your DNA and knocks it around. Your body will naturally try to repair the damage, rack the balls back in the way they were but sometimes a ball has gone into a hole and is no longer there or the order is not the same as it was in the beginning. Holes in DNA will get filled by one of the amino acids that make up DNA; sometimes the body gets it right and puts the "A" back where it came from; sometimes a "G" goes there, or a "C" or "T". The real problem is that just filling in gaps does not make things better. Putting things back together in itself does not make things better. It is like listening to music. Put any piece of music in your mind, regardless of what kind as long as it has actual notes in it. As I am writing this I am actually thinking of Ein Klein Nacht Musik by Mozart but the actual piece just does not matter; main thing is that you know what you are thinking of. Now take a note in the middle and change it. I guess this would make more sense to someone who actually plays music, but it is probably the best analogy I can think of at the moment. Changing one note drastically right in the middle of a song can actually change the mood of a song; change the flow. Do that more. Hit more A's when they should be D flat. C sharp in place of E minor. Go up a whole octave for one note then down two for the next mistake. Eventually you would no longer have a song, you would have noise; like a toddler banging on a xylophone; incoherent noise, when compared to original. And now the other problem, putting the piece of music back together but not in order. Really it would come out feeling the same; instead of something wonder and beautiful and uplifting you would get something disjointed and unintelligible. People's minds are actually made to identify and enjoy music, something like I am describing would almost be painful to listen to. And that is essentially what is happening to your DNA when you have been exposed to radiation. The musician (that is your body) tries to play the music that it thinks it has and all that comes out is garbage. Your body dies because it can no longer function as it is supposed to. You melt and fall apart on a cellular level. The old comic books lied to use, radiation does not give superpowers, what it does give is a painful death. Good news though. My people were not sick from radiation poisoning. I was simply using people as a stand-in while I illustrated what was happening elsewhere. As I said our latitude and whatever other number of factors led to us not being terribly affected by the radiation and what radiation did appear we dealt with as best we could. Layers of top soil were stripped off areas that were used frequently by people as well as out of most yards since that is where our food was grown and used to fill in a mine about ten or fifteen miles away from town. The mine was chosen mostly because it had the least chance of contaminating us or the surrounding environment more than it already was. So my people were safe from radiation, the rest of the world was not. And this included our water supply and there is the culprit in all of the illness.

During the flare things died, most of everything really. Almost the world. Most fish live within something like the top twenty feet of water, half of which boiled off, meaning that water levels were lower than normal during the event. There was a greater likelihood that the majority of fish would be affected. And now not just the fish were affected. Every crustacean, insect, plant, plankton, whale, cephalopod and so on within every body of water was affected with most of them dying off. That is a lot of dead material. Prime breeding ground for bacteria. All those things being dead in water were not overly helpful as that means that once those bacteria are done eating they can float and move around until they coalesce into colonies. There were giant masses of bacteria in the lake that served as our reservoir. I would assume it was the same in every other body of water throughout the world. Slowly this dissipated, the dead fish and other water-borne creatures all having long since died; food was scarce for those bacteria as well the fish and other things began to make a comeback. Everything rebounded just some slower than others; I think fish were one of the quicker things. Around the same time that those bacteria were floating in the lakes, rivers and streams the nuclear power plants started to blow their tops. Radioactive dust was blown around the world, some settled on its own here and there. Some settled right onto those bacteria colonies. Some of it stayed up in the atmosphere until coming down as precipitation. Have you ever wondered why your car is dirtier after it rains than before? Despite what we may think rainwater is not 'clean' as we would like to think. Moisture in and of itself will not do anything in the atmosphere. Think of when you exhale on a cold day, if all you needed was moisture and a drop in temperature for water to glob together and make rain then you would have a mini rain storm in front of you every breath but that does not happen. Each tiny raindrop started as a miniscule grain of dust high in the atmosphere, if there is enough moisture in a particular place, like for example an assemblage of water vapor like you would find in a cloud then that little speck of dust will begin to attract water to it, eventually building enough of it to the point that gravity takes over and it falls to the ground as rain. Sometimes the wind is stronger than gravity and the fledgling raindrop gets held aloft longer than normal making larger raindrops. Sometimes the convection of the wind is stronger than even this and the rain gets pushed higher and higher through the cloud, over and over again. Each time it rises it attracts more water. Each time it rises it gets colder. It freezes. Gravity takes over and it falls only to be pushed up again, gaining more water vapor to itself, like rolling a giant ball of snow across a field to make a snowman, more and more snow is added to that ball as it goes. This happens until even the wind is not strong enough to keep it in the air and you find small dents on your car from the falling hail. Regardless of what form it came down in those bits of radioactive dust became radioactive rain or hail or sleet or whatever. Well where does that precipitation go? To the ground; swelling the ground water, eventually flowing into streams, then bigger streams then rivers, lakes, bays, harbors and the oceans. The dust itself can stop at any point along that journey, if it makes it to a body of water it may flow along or settle somewhere along the way as silt. But the damage was already done. Everything that bit of dust touched has already been contaminated. It is already poisoned. It could already kill you. Or fish. Or bacteria. Thing with bacteria is they do not have the same kind of mechanisms as larger organisms do. They cannot just rebuild themselves. No instead they reproduce. Why fix a broken paramecium when it is just as quick and easier to make a whole new one. And they did. Entire colonies of bacteria were dying as they made the next generation. I have tried to understand just how they survived at all using that mangled song they had for DNA, but I honestly do not know. But what I do know is the effect they mutated bacteria had on the ecosystem. Everything goes from bottom up in life. Bacteria are eaten by larger bacteria, which are then eaten by small insects, then larger insects, then frogs, fish, birds, etc. So, the whole ecosystem was irradiated and passed it along. Each time getting more messed up. Sometimes things were still functional like a fish with a spare fin on its side, sometimes not, like a frog with no legs. With bacteria it just did not seem to matter. They reproduce faster than the radiation kills them; non-functional ones were evidently outweighed in number by the functional. And now this is just my opinion, but it seems that that kind of forced adaptation and expedited evolution just led to stronger and more virulent things. I have no idea just what it was that actually made people sick whether it was amoebic dysentery or E. Coli or typhoid or what but when it hit my people it hit with a vengeance. We had not really planned for or even considered an outbreak of disease as being a problem that we would be dealing with. Short-sighted on our part. On my part I guess.

You are probably wondering if that short-sightedness is the reason this outbreak was at least partially my fault. Well that was obviously an oversight on my part but you cannot live going after every what-if scenario that comes your way. You'd go mad if all you did was think of things that will go wrong. No, the reason this was other things that were neglected. Stuff that could have ameliorated the whole outbreak before it got that far. My town was clean and organized starting from the time I cleared out the first house of dead bodies and began emptying the streets of abandoned cars. Even when people started coming that is where it kind of stopped, at the town limits. More than that it felt like trying to change the world and that was too much for me. And for all of us in that town, we got settled and complacent and it backfired on us. The furthest that we went outside of our town to try to fix things was when I had sent a crew of men out a year or two before the outbreak in order to find whatever was restricting the water flow in the river than ran near the town. This river was also the source of our water and in the end the reason for the outbreak. I am fairly confident that unblocking the river of all the logs and debris that was hindering water from flowing was not what unleashed the bacteria upon but in the end who knows, it is within the realm of possibility I suppose. The blockage was somewhere around 5 miles upstream and that was the furthest extent that we tried to change the world at that point.

In the beginning what we had done in order to get people power to their houses was cannibalize my own place. All those solar panels and wind turbines that I had worked perfectly when transplanted to my new hometown. In time those ran out, and even with breaking out all the spares I had in storage we just could not keep up with the demand. We needed to start thinking more outside the box, being more creative and inventive. We made a small waterwheel power station that dipped into that river that just happened to be close at hand and that was able to serve a few houses. As well we had some sort of mechanical genius in our midst, damned if I can remember his name, began taking every single alternator out of every used vehicle we had parked in our wasteland, rebuilding them and then bolting them together, attaching some sort of transformer and voila we had more wind turbines than you could shake a stick at. Clearly not helpful when it is not windy out but as you may recall we did have a giant stack of batteries which were likewise rebuilt and utilized as battery power. So eventually every house had a wind turbine or two plus a pile of batteries in the basement or crawlspace or wherever was convenient and that is how we kept the lights on. We were again kind of "normal" in that way; no longer living like it was 1716 again. That is just a random number, don't bother looking it up, there is no code in it. That was wonderful of course but it does not leave a lot of extra for other things. Like, for example, water purification. I had an idea way back around the start of Republica of all the things that I thought we would need. I do not recall most of that list, I'm sure it has all been covered by now but one thing that I am certain was on that list was a means to purify water. In reality, I could care less how it is done: filter it, boil it, voodoo it, who cares what you do; the main point being that when someone goes to drink it should be clean. That is one of those 'first-world' kinds of things that we all got used to and I am not sure about you but that is one that I would prefer to keep around. I stopped short when it came to pushing that through. I allowed people to just go about their lives and not be concerned with a basic necessity that we had. In the end we had 73 people get sick with 19 of those people dying, including our builder of wind turbines. Lucky for us he had been given an apprentice some months before he got sick and died. Unlucky for us that apprentice did not learn a great deal during his time with our mechanical genius; he was often times used more as a janitor then a tinkerer; and that set us back a little.

Now you can criticize me for what I did or did not do prior to the outbreak but what I did during, I think, is something that really defined me, especially in the eyes of my people. My response after being called out of that classroom all those years ago was multifaceted but there were a few main ones that I will mention now. It took a little bit of actual investigating for us to figure out just where the problem originated; if it was water-borne or food-borne or air-borne. But after elimination of all the problems that did not seem to be the cause of the illnesses then all that was left was water-borne. At that point we took action to address that. As I just finished pointing out there was an obvious need for water purification which we handled in an efficient and thorough manner. I had builders make an addition to the wheelhouse structure that allowed for an improved water pump (our water pressure up until that point had been atrocious) as well as all the water that went through was filtered, cleaned and sterilized. That was the most glaring deficiency that we had. Another was our power problem which needed to be addressed. The wheelhouse did not produce enough power for what was needed nor could it really be expanded in a way that would allow for further growth. Turns out the area where there had been that blockage in the river was well suited to putting a permanent kind of power plant in. That expansion allowed us to properly clean the water, so it was suitable for drinking as well we even had enough excess power to have streetlights. A further return to normalcy. The last big feather in my cap involved the actual illness itself. Our "doctor" was able to do the usual medical kind of things, put in IVs, check blood pressures; she could even perform some surgeries, although since she was mostly doing them single-handedly they were clearly only ever done in absolute emergencies. Making IV fluids is fairly simple, it is just a saline (salt) solution but other medications were much harder to come by. Even the ones I did not destroy, such as antibiotics, do have an expiry date, after which they are no longer useful. An expired antibiotic is actually kind of worse to use than none at all as a weakened antibiotic has the potential of allowing the bacteria or infection to develop a resistance to the antibiotic thereby making it harder to get rid of. 'Dr.' Karen used what she had to treat her patients but it was not doing the best of jobs. I, as the resident vessel of useless knowledge, oddly enough had the solution.

Cantaloupe. Penicillin; the first great leap forward in dealing with microbes is made from a fungus. The best strain of that fungus was found growing on the skin of a moldy cantaloupe. Again, something random that I know that would normally never be useful in any context other than for answering some trivia question. In the end of the world it is very useful. It also helps if you specifically plan for this and cultivate it. Personally, I hate cantaloupes along with every other of the melon fruits. They have a strange texture that I just cannot get over, so I never eat them, but the animals liked them so that was a good enough reason to grow them in my home. As well you never know when you may need to start growing and producing your own antibiotics. When I moved myself permanently to Republica it was one of the things that got transplanted from there to here. It took a little while but the 'doctor', a chemistry student and myself all worked to develop and grow our own source of penicillin which was therefore administered to our ailing population.

So that was the key to my being made the leader of my fair town but it did not clinch it for me. For the year or two prior to the outbreak I was just a cog in the running of the town government. I was seen as something of a respected elder amongst the population, even though I was at that point about the median range of all our survivors. The respect I garnered was due to my handling of things before most people got here, it was due to my tendency to help other people and providing that kind of take charge leadership that was needed in emergencies. That was why they got me when everyone got sick, but I was not the leader at that point. I was actually only an advisor to our council. We were ruled essentially by an oligarchy. A collection of 'wise' men and women. They were the ones that had the actual power. They made the decisions. They failed the people here by not ensuring their safety. I did not really make any kind of waves afterwards but when asked my opinion I did point out that with appropriate direction the town banded together and made everything necessary to ensure that we had fresh and safe drinking water within two months; the further perfection and refinement of what we were doing was completed within another four months. In six months we had eliminated the illness, the cause of the illness and almost the memory of the whole event. People did not really seem all that inclined to dwell on the bad memories associated with people dying due to a sickness. There had been enough death for most people I would imagine.

Shortly after the last person left the nursing home with a clean bill of health everyone decided that they would hold a barbeque. Somewhat akin to after the Battie/John Thomas incident, except this time no one stole anything, and it was a more pleasant affair. Unbeknownst to me our town council had been talking of just handing over the reins to someone with a measure of vision and respect. In the middle of the meal suddenly I begin to hear a glass being clanked. Then another. A chorus of them.

Someone behind me stands and starts talking "A toast to 'our great friend' who helped us all find a new place to live. He found this town, made it something for all of us. A place to begin anew. He went further and has helped us survive again." At first, I had barely been paying attention but by the end of the toast I had stood to nod and bow before the people. I was still not comfortable with being the center of attention, but I knew the role that they wanted me to play. Sometimes you just want someone to thank. Someone to cheer for. A hero. He continues "I hope you will all join your town council in asking 'our benefactor and savior' to officially become our leader. He has been here from before the end (he apparently did not know history all that well) and he will undoubtedly be here for us for the rest of his life". A swell of cheers and clapping erupts around me. I bow. I begin to shake hands as I walk up to the man who has been talking.

"Thank you everyone. Under me I will ensure that we will continue to grow and continue to thrive. We will return to what we once were." That was it. I was not really big on speeches. Especially when I was unprepared for them. And with that I was the leader. A tyrant voted-in by popular demand. That is not uncommon. You can never really get to a top level without having support. At that time, I had all the support I needed.

CHAPTER 9 – CREEP

I don't know if you can recall something that I had mentioned a fair while ago but did not delve into. I had said when I entered Republica there had been a population of one (just me, which is what I had originally thought) and there were actually four. I mentioned two people; Lisa and Aurora but did not mention number four. I'm sure there are some people who would have assumed that the fourth I meant was the dog but that is not the case. There was a fourth person in the town at that time. He had arrived just a day or two prior to my getting there. I am not totally sure just where he came from or what his goals were, but I would overall venture that he did not have the best of intentions. I guess he had been seen skulking around when Lisa was doing one of her late-night attempts to forage for food in the nearby houses; she was still afraid to get too far from the church lest the sun pop out in the dead of night I guess. He by all accounts had been trying to find and corner her, even going as far as to come in the front door of a house as she ducked out the back. She did manage to keep her home base a secret which I guess was a good thing. That was apparently what the chain and padlock were for by the front door of the church; they had been locking the doors. The faint far off sound of a motorcycle had scared them enough that they hid rather than secure the doors. I asked Lisa months after our first meeting why she had come out for me but not with the miscreant who arrived before me. She said it was because they knew I was a different person. I was not trying to just grab her; I offered food. Fair enough I guess. A simple difference in our approaches when meeting new people.

I had a feeling that I was being watched the first three days in the town but I had just assumed it was an overall discomfort about being around people again. It was not until just as dusk was happening on the third night that I saw something. Just a shadow moving through a house as I passed by it. It was "nothing" or so I told myself. When I got back to where the girls were preparing supper I acted the same as I had the day prior. Stretching, lamenting at how my back was sore and needed to lie down for a few minutes before eating. As I lay there I was kind of doing a 'this is what I did today' play-by-play, omitting the more unsavory parts for Aurora's benefit of course when I mentioned my odd sensations of being watched and how I thought I had seen a shadow move behind a curtain as I was walking back. I must have prattled on for a minute or two before realizing that both of them were just staring at me, not saying a word. Barely breathing. Once you have seen fear in someone's eyes, and I mean real fear, you recognize it again instantly. If it had not been for that look on both of their faces I would have been half chuckling as my confusion took over and I repeatedly asked "what?". It was at that moment I realized that I had made something of a tactical error. I was overjoyed at finding Aurora alive and I had reveled in that knowledge. I had assumed that other than Aurora, Lisa and I the world was dead. And in that assumption, lie my error. I had completely forgotten the possibility of there being other people. Others who would take instead of give. The kind that will harm someone for a hiding spot. The kind who were probably more likely to survive. I told the girls to calm down and we'd think about it. And we just sat there. No one said anything while we ate; it was definitely a different tone from the last night when they had been happy to have the company of another person. The only sounds any of us made was the occasional hiss to get the attention of one of us who started looking around too obviously.

After eating I looked at them after I had scanned the sky. "Looks like it could rain tonight, I think we should go inside.". Lisa nodded, in a kind of exaggerated manner that at the time I thought was rather odd. Kind of robotic and awkward but after a little reflection I had realized that she was already thinking in the same manner as I was. In her mind she was thinking that we were laying a trap for our mysterious neighbor. I was thinking about luring him but it was not an actual goal of trapping or ambushing him. As far as I was concerned I was quite willing to let him live as long as he was not being a threat. We returned to the church that night and slept behind barred doors. It was a restless, interrupted sleep. The girls had retreated to the basement while I slept where the reverend or priest who formerly presided over this congregation had slept. I am going to assume it was a him as the clothes and shoes left behind looked as though they had belonged to a man. His bed was uncomfortable; the edges seemed firm with an overly apparent groove in the middle, this mattress had likely been used for decades and no one decided to replace it despite the fact that it seemed to have a dead coil. Or three. Also the room had a musty smell reminiscent of tobacco and something else. Maybe old newspaper. I could not put my finger on it but I was aware of it every time I woke up that night. I like having a plan for things and I will admit I had been distracted so I had not even fathomed what to do when someone seemed to be stalking the people I was with. And I surmise I was being stalked as well. Around 4 or so in the morning it occurred to me that I was making things too difficult. I was making the coat draped over the chair into a monster in my unlit bedroom. I got up just before dawn and rummaged around the room looking for paper. There seemed to be no blank paper in the room; I ended up using the backside of an old poster for a church yard sale. It was over three years old; at first it seemed as though the reverend did not seem to be serious when it came to cleanliness although as I looked closer at the pieces of paper in that pile it became more apparent that he was a collector. He had more posters from old yard and rummage sales along with other posters and pamphlets in the pile. Christian day camps, making money to help with little Timmy's medical bills, advertisements for a Christian couples counselling, helping to convert the people who have not yet found God in the rainforest, whatever. It looked like 20 years of memories were in that pile. Small little things to me but obviously they meant something to him, you could see the tattered edges on the lower older posters, there was an obvious smudge along the side where he had been thumbing through the pile of memories.

On the back of this sheet I wrote in large letters with the side of a pencil. I did this, so the lines would be thick and easy to read. I guessed that our mystery person would either not come too close to the church where we were and try to keep catching us alone or he would come in the dead of night when we are all asleep. I hoped that by writing to him and communicating we could get something going. End the stalemate. No more hide-and-seek.

'YOU DONT NEED TO HIDE WE WONT HURT YOU. It was simple and succinct. I was hoping to at least be able to talk to him. See his face. Get his story.

Three days that message was nailed to the door of the church. I felt something like Martin Luther when I was nailing it up there. Not that I see myself as a religious icon or something. For those three days Lisa and I did our work in more or a spiral pattern near the church as opposed to going down the street as we had been doing. We had Aurora always nearby; within sight at all times. It is hard to do that while working so the clean-up in those places took longer than usual but we did what we had to do. They walked by the sign nailed to the door multiple times each day and every time it seemed to be reminder that there was something ominous and possibly dangerous lurking in town. It was quite possibly not dangerous, but safety requires a measure of caution, especially when dealing with people who would not make themselves known. After the first night I had sprinkled a bit of flour from the reverend's kitchen onto the porch area of the church. I wanted to see if our little guy was coming to see what was written. Each morning I examined the flour and it was evident that he had been on the porch, he appeared to be wearing size 10 skate shoes, they were slightly smaller than mine so that is my best guess. He had seen the note. On the second night he had slipped slightly on the flour. Not surprising, the wood was painted and when coupled with the flour it did make it kind of a slippery surface to walk on. After 3 nights I started to believe that nothing was going to change; he would keep checking the church, he would keep watching us. Stalking. Until he found an opening to pounce on. Like a cat. The fourth night there was a new note for him to read.

'STOP HIDING OR LEAVE THIS TOWN'. Nothing changed. Still footprints in the morning. We were still working as a group. I still watched Aurora at all times. We barely spoke during these days as we were always looking around, scanning the windows, seeing which curtains moved as we strode by. We listened for creaks in floors of the houses across the street. We ate in the same park every meal of every day as it seemed to have a kind of safety in it. You could see all around us. It was exposed but it was the one habit that none of us seemed to want to lose. We had food and were sitting in the sunlight and not dying. I was growing impatient and the girls could tell, even without having to use words. A more purposeful walk and a kind of scowl on my face; I would not even try to presume that it was not visible to anyone who was seeing me. That impatience was uncharacteristic for me, even from before the cataclysm, impatience leads to mistakes and like I said I prefer a plan. Well my plan was not working as I had hoped. Another night passed and this time instead of broken sleep I simply had none. The hope of resolving this whole situation quickly and simply was not there anymore. I no longer had the expectation of waking in the morning and having a new person to talk to. And really it was getting downright creepy. You'd think someone would try to do something instead we were just left with an omnipresence of something in the shadows somewhere in the town. I heard the door rattle that night as he tried the door; it was 3:17am according to my watch. He tried the slanted cellar door; it was 3:19am. With the moonlight behind him he cast a shadow as he appeared to try the window that was beside me; it was now 3:24am. There was complete silence in that church and surrounding it. The crickets had not rebounded yet. I was hearing his footsteps outside the window; soft and slow but deliberate. He tried the window on my right. The floor beneath me squeaked ever so slightly as I shifted my weight, so I could turn towards that window. His footsteps halted. In that moment I was not thinking about where things would go from here but perhaps I should have. I cocked my pistol. Until you are in dead silence you will never know how loud that sounds. The steps stop. I can see his shadow slightly hunch over. He must be thinking. Evaluating what to do next. Seeing if I'll pursue him or start shooting wildly through the window. I hear a mocking huff and the steps begin again; away from the building. We were in the clear. He left. There were no more footprints. No more testing of doors and windows.

By my reckoning it was two days later that the dog appeared. I fed it as I already said and allowed Aurora to feed it the remainder of its meal. Normally, I would be wary of a dog that is as bad off as this was. I have seen dogs that have never had a care in the world be aggressive around food. Growl at its master as they put their hand near the bowl. Snap as you try to take the toy out of their mouth to play fetch. In my experience that tended to be the smaller dogs that acted that way; like they know how small they are and have a Napoleon complex about it. That is actually a misnomer; Napoleon was not as diminutive as people believe. Napoleon was likely around five foot seven or eight, which would put him around average height for a Frenchman in the early 19th century. This dog right from the outset did not seem to have that kind of behavior. He approached with his head bowed, tail between his legs; he was submissive. He took the food from my hand and while hungry still made the effort to be gentle. I have always had a way of dealing with dogs when I meet them that usually involves me making the same kinds of soft shushing sounds that you would make to an infant before they start crying. I have no idea why I did it or if it even worked as I assumed it did but it seemed to work and that is good enough at times. I gently stroked its head as I gave the meat to Aurora. The dog was burnt slightly along its back and to a greater extent over his right hind leg; he walked with a slight limp from it. I wish we could have done something about it although the damage was already done. I figured that this dog had found someplace to hide that was just a tad too small for him leaving his hip just near enough the doorway to get burnt. This left him with some scarring over that hip area that never seemed to loosen and that in turn is what caused him to limp. The fur over the rest of his body, especially his back grew back once he was no longer starving; the burns in those other areas healed like you would expect from a normal kind of sunburn. Only his scarred bald thigh belied what he had gone through; once he started to have a full belly again he was happy. He played with Aurora; slept with her, watched her and never left her side. It felt nice that she had a pet. I do not know if her mother ever got her a cat or a dog or even a goldfish but I would guess it was unlikely. If she had been given a pet, it likely ran away or starved; her mother was not the most attentive of people. In any event Aurora never spoke of any pets before this one and I never asked.

She named him Princess. I told her multiple times that he was a boy. I even showed her. I think she did it to play with my mind. I like that she seemed to have the ability to still have fun and make a joke even after everything she had been through. Also, I was known to be a bit of a prankster myself when I was younger, so I could relate with her if that is indeed what she was doing. I tried to change it tacitly by referring to him as Prince. He would raise his head at hearing Princess and not Prince. She was steadfast about Princess and in the end, all I could do was shake my head and accept it. And he accepted it. I was not going to ruin her first pet for her with technicalities. Anyways, a name can be anything you want it to be. I always contended that you can even take something like DRAUYPHE and say that it is pronounced DAVE. Now that is not adhering to any kind of language standard, it is just what you can say. The R is silent, the PH sounds like a V, the Y is, I dunno, silent too. It does not matter. It is like the difference between a Brit and an American saying the word 'ladder'. Brits would pronounce the double D as a harder sound than the Americans would have. I don't know. Probably not one of my more profound thoughts and I don't think I really defended it all that well; not like it matters anyways. Moving on.

I wondered where this dog came from. Did it arrive with our creepy friend? Did it come here on its own? Was it here all along? Just things to ponder that will never have an answer for me and will never matter in the end. Our routine returned to how it had been before we were being watched. Lisa and I kept ourselves busy cleaning out houses; categorizing things; stockpiling; burning. Aurora did the stuff we set aside for her, always with her Princess along for the walk. It was easier to be comfortable when you know she has a guard dog with her. Even without the police dog type training she was still protected. At the very least he was an alarm system that followed her around.

Republica was perched kind of in the middle of what you could call foothills, on the top of one of the bigger ones. There were mountains visible off to the west; the hills seemed to get larger and larger until they just became mountains off along the horizon. The highway going through the town was kind of diagonal when you think of it on a map. It comes from the south-east and exits in the north-west, or vice versa I guess. Over the years the majority of our people came from the south-east. That made sense as the majority of them came by foot or bike; there were not a lot of vehicles that were operational as they were after the flare. It took a bit of work to get them back in working order so most people travelled by people (or animal) power. I was an obvious exception as my motorcycle had been in my underground garage and was therefore unaffected by the radiation. If you are walking or biking I doubt you would want to go up a mountain unless you absolutely had to. Up a hill is more plausible. Jason was the first permanent fourth resident of Republica and he came from the south-east. While having supper in the park one day I saw something glint off in the distance; to the south-east. It appeared to be just at the crest of the next hill over. It was a momentary flash, but it got my attention. Was it our creeper friend coming back? Was it some other scoundrel? I walked towards my motorcycle without taking my eyes off of the crest of that hill. Taking the binoculars from the saddlebag I looked to where I thought I had seen the flash. There did not appear to be anything there but in reality, that hill was so far away it was not surprising that I could not see anything. I stood there motionless for what was likely twenty or thirty minutes, looking for the light. There was nothing. The rest of the night I continued to glance over there, scan with my binoculars. Lisa had asked me what I was looking at and I recall saying I thought I saw something flutter by, maybe it was a bird or a leaf, although I was not sure. She smiled and mentioned that she would like to hear a bird sing again. I only replied 'yeah' as I looked out to the highway.

That night was again restless for me, most nights are restless but that night was closer in feeling to when the creeper was around. Dusk could not have come late enough and dawn could not have arrived any sooner. Darkness makes things uncertain. It's like the fog of war; you just don't know what is out there, out of your grasp. There was a movie many years ago called the Matrix that kind of perfectly highlighted this whole idea. In short, the whole premise of the movie is that people were living in a "computer-generated dream world" which was essentially real for them in every way since the things that people see as being "real" are just nerve impulses that your brain interprets in different ways depending on which nerve it is and what part of the brain it goes to. I'm sure there are impulses going along your optical nerve even when you are sitting in pitch black, but you'd never know. Your brain interprets the black as essentially nothing. And that is how it feels when you cannot see something. To me it felt like that far off light was a person but that person was not real until I could see them. Until there was something tangible about them. I was already awake as dawn finally broke the darkness; I made my way to the same place I had sat when I saw the flash of light. We were finally getting to the point where we had drank all the coffee I brought with me, and were going to have start getting out the stuff we had been finding and stockpiling. One of the few luxuries I brought with me when I left my house was some 'good' flavored coffee; nothing that we had found, to the best of my knowledge' compared although even this coffee was somewhat ruined by having to add whitener to it. I miss having cream or milk. It was at this moment where I was thinking it was about time to take a run home in order to get my animals and bring them here. This was a place that would be as safe and sustainable for them as home was. As I was leaving home I left the gates open, the automatic waterer on, the barn propped open; they all had free reign to go wherever on my property they pleased, it was more than big enough to allow them all to graze their hearts out and still have food left over. I look again at the highway, slightly snapping myself out of my thought/daydream. It is still hard to see that far away which is made even more difficult by the slight haze that seems to be off on the horizon. But there it is. What I had been waiting for since the day prior. A figure on the road, I would assume walking closer but at that exact moment and from that distance it was hard to see any movement at all. I watched mesmerized as I confirmed that yes that far off figure was moving towards us, I began trying to do some mental math, thinking how long it would take someone walking to get here from there. How far was there? Not extremely far, maybe a couple miles. He would likely be here in less than an hour but possibly longer. Who knows just how tired he/she is.

Aurora was the first to join me outside. She was not pleased with again having the same choices for breakfast; oatmeal or cereal with powdered milk. That was another reason it was time to go home. There may now be a number of baby chicks in that coop. With no one taking the eggs each day the hens would have just sat on them until they hatched. Fresh eggs would definitely be a treat. She chose as she normally did, eating some sugary kids' cereal with the powdered milk, it was quicker than making oatmeal. Aurora had also grabbed a can of dog food from the stockpile in order to feed Princess but quickly looked confused as she say down beside me at the picnic table looking around for something to open the can with; she had not thought to bring the can opener with her. I put the binoculars down as I take the can out of her hand and start opening it with the can opener built into my pocket knife. I was still looking off to the distance, not speaking.

"Whaf are you loofinf af?" she said with a full mouth as she tried to put another spoonful in. I could see her trying to squint to see what I was looking at.

"Don't talk with your mouth full. It looks like there is a person on the highway coming this way." I sighed heavy as I finished saying that. I hoped that I was right and there was someone there. Otherwise it was just me going all crazy and seeing mirages. Aurora continued to chew her food but it was obvious that she had gone pale. "It'll be fine." I assured her. "This is not like the last one; this guy is at least taking the road. He's not skulking around. Swallow your food." The dog was sitting patiently staring at me as I continued fiddling with the can opener. When I was finally able to get the can open I turned it upside down and listened for the *schloock-ploop* of the food coming out of the can and hitting the ground. We'd have to get that dog a bowl soon enough but at that time I don't think Princess cared; he was more than fine eating it off the brown grass. Aurora took another few spoonfuls before putting the bowl on the ground. Princess tried to eat her food while also eating the remains of the cereal and powdered milk. "you shouldn't give that to him, he'll get diabeetus."

"What?" she responded as Lisa came up behind us. She had been quiet, I was not even aware she was there or if she had been there long. I waved my hand at Aurora while muttering 'never mind'. The dog was done everything and was now licking the grass.

"That's not a bird is it?" I shook my head as she put her hand on my shoulder in order to reach over me and pick up the binoculars off the table. She followed my line of sight and zoomed in. "Do you think it's that guy? How long do you think it'll be before he gets here?"

I look at my wrist and sigh before responding. I still do that occasionally even though I never wear a watch; I haven't worn one in likely 30 or 40 years. "My guess is probably about 45 minutes away at this point, he seems to be going pretty slow."

"And he keeps looking behind him." We sit there another 20 minutes not speaking just watching; each taking turns looking through the binoculars. Each of us seemed to be trying to get the first real look at who we were dealing with. Our mysterious stranger disappeared behind a tract of trees at the bottom of the little valley between the hill he was on and Republica's hill. It was really real at that point, we all knew that it was going to be not too long before we had a visitor. Before he disappeared from sight I could tell that he was wearing a long trench coat, or maybe a raincoat as well as a large backpack like you would use if you were going on a long hike. I had already decided that if this person was not creepy, not strange, not a stalker, not dangerous then if he so wished he could stay. There would of course be a number of questions I would need answered before I was secure around him.

By the time the man had returned to view he had already started up the hill which seemed to have slowed his pace even slower than it had been before. As he neared the town you could see he was dragging his feet; the weary walk of someone who has walked too much. There was also a noticeable limp, likely from a blister that had formed due to his extended stroll from wherever. He continued to turn and look over his shoulder; not often but often enough that it was noticeable, especially after Lisa had noted it earlier. What was he looking at or for? Was he still thinking like before as if he was on just another hitchhiking excursion and any minute now someone would pick him up? Was he being followed? Was he looking to see what had made that flash of light? Maybe that was not him. I sent the girls to a house to the north of the church. I said that I had already looked through it for people and there was none so they just needed to grab anything useful from there. As they walked off I knew they would not be doing a substantial amount of work and would likely be sitting in a window watching as the stranger walked in. I hoped they would work though it would at the very least keep them distracted. Princess had of course followed the girls while they worked; he'd likely curl up on the couch while they sorted through the cupboards and cabinets. He seemed more than willing to sleep through that kind of banging but I had seen his head pop up as soon as he heard a squeak in the floor or a door open. Calm but alert. Exactly what you would want from a dog that you have entrusted to guard your daughter.

As I was lighting a fire to make something to eat while I talked to the stranger I could see him coming across up to the town sign. He stood for probably over a minute, like he was trying to process what he was reading. It was apparent at that moment that he was now sure he was not alone. His head turned slightly as he first caught sight of smoke coming from the fire I was lighting. The unfortunate thing about the end of the world is that all the conveniences of food that you are used to no longer exist. Frozen foods by that point had all thawed and started to rot as the power went out and freezers stopped working. Many things like bread were no longer edible; it just does not keep that long. Dried goods were generally ok as there tended to not be a lot of moisture in those foods meaning that they just got drier, although that did seem to make some things go stale quicker; if you were making something like pasta or 'macaroni and cheese' (which by the way is gross when made with powdered milk and using something like vegetable oil as a butter substitute) you never really noticed if it had gone stale or not. Canned goods, while the best preserved in terms of maintaining their past flavours and consistency did occasionally have one slight problem; those same microwaves that killed off damned near everything also sometimes managed to get some cans hot enough that the contents of the can started to boil. That boiling led to steam, that steam led to an increase of pressure and that pressure, if it got high enough led to an explosion. So many times did we find cupboards smeared with the remains of a can of chicken noodle soup or baby corn or some other thing. Not always though, sometimes the pressure just popped the seam on the can and the insides came out more as a dribble; just enough to relieve the pressure. For our incoming stranger I was preparing a can of vegetable soup; nothing extravagant but fairly good in terms of nutrition and still light enough to not shock his system if he has not eaten in a while.

He followed the smoke towards the park. His pace was quicker than it had been although still kind of slow, hampered by the blister on his foot. I sat on the far side of the picnic table watching him. He waved as he stepped off the road onto the dry grass, I could hear it crumbling under his feet as he strode towards me. I raised my left hand enough to acknowledge him without showing any enthusiasm. Although I was excited. This was the first new person I had seen in a while. First one that was actually willing to meet. My first new conversation. It was like being a discoverer or something. "Hello friend." He said as he was about ten feet from the table.

"Hi." I replied as he stood just on the other side of the table. "If you don't mind I would feel more comfortable if you'd drop your bag and have a seat so we can talk." He frowned slightly; I am guessing he had expected a hug from the get go. He did as he was asked though, as well he took a large hunting knife that he had in a sheath on his hip and placed it on top of the rucksack which was a few feet from the table. He nodded as he showed it to me, I responded in kind. "Soup should be ready in a few minutes." I said as I looked him over. Jason was white, probably early thirties, fairly scruffy-looking, His pants were like heavy duty work pants, almost like canvas; shirt was a plain white t-shirt that had been covered in grime until it just no longer got clean, the sleeves looked like they had been torn off, but it was hard to tell until after he took off his long coat. His hands looked quite rough and his steel-toes boots were very well worn. I recall my first guess being construction worker or something like that. He seemed to likely be a smoker beforehand as his teeth and moustache both had kind of a yellow-ish tinge although I did not smell any smoke other than that from the fire, so he likely was out of cigarettes and had not gone and "acquired" more from a gas station or wherever.

His eyes brightened, "What kind of soup?" I turned the empty can around so he could read the label. He smiled, "Well at least you know my favorite kind. I'm Jason by the way." He was quite willing to answer all questions I had and only seemed hesitant a few times, which was understandable given the questions. I had been enquiring as to where he was going exactly; it seemed odd for him to be going along the road as he had been. He said was going to his hometown which was the next town along the highway, around another 20 miles. He was going to his parents' house. He had been in a small town around 300 miles from here working in a mine, looking for nickel I think. When the flare had hit he was underground working the night shift; the metal in the surrounding rock meant that he escaped completely unscathed by the radiation. Morning came that night and he was stuck down there. He did not have any food with him though so that was a hardship. He had been with two other people both of whom left the mine after the first night and never came back. One of them he was sure had perished; when he finally left he found that co-worker's body in one of the trailers used by the mining crew; the other guy he saw no sign of but assumed likely suffered the same fate. After being in the mine for a week he thought it was finally safe to go out. He said that he initially only travelled at night until he got caught somewhere that he could not find shelter and was surprised that the sun was warm, inviting and totally not deadly. He hoped to find his parents at the end of all this. He was hoping they were still alive although he was unsure if that would be the case. He said that I was the only person that he had seen, although… he trailed off and began to look uncomfortable. "Do you believe in ghosts?" The question seemed so out of context it honestly took me a few seconds to even process it. He sat motionless, anxious for my answer. All I could do was shrug. He continued "Two nights ago I was sleeping on the side of the road under my tarp and I thought I heard something but I could not see anything when I sat up and I did not hear another sound. I- I- I'm not sure what it was. All I know is when I finally got up in the morning my rifle was gone. I was totally convinced it was ghosts that took it until I saw you. You and I are the only people left alive."

"Not quite true. There are two others here; a girl and her mom." I sat watching his expression at that knowledge. He seemed to brighten. Everything was making him feel like it was more and more possible that his parents were still alive. Sitting in their house on their rocking chairs, drinking tea and talking about the "good ol' days" when there were still other people alive.

Save a few prompts or questions from me to get him going I simply let Jason ramble on about this and that. People will tend to just keep talking if you say nothing; it is like they feel they did not say enough when they were first talking so they keep going. Eventually they just think that is how their conversation with you is supposed to go and they keep talking. You can learn a lot by not saying anything. In the span of around an hour I learned that he was single, his last girlfriend cheated on him around 2 years ago, since then he had just been working and not thinking about dating; he had no children; he had a dog from when he was 15 or so that died when he was 28 and he would have loved to have gotten another one but he tended to not be home enough to care for it so he felt it as unfair to get one. My main goal had been to see if he was dangerous, if he was one of those kinds of degenerates who lost his mind around the end and I just did not get that impression from him; overall my impression of Jason was fairly positive. He was open to discussing things and it did not seem that he was lying. Not that I was an expert on lying but I did watch way too many crime shows and profiling shows and what-not so I think at the very least I had the basics down. Who knows. The fact that all this time he had talked and not asked very many questions seemed a little puzzling but I think he was just happy to be able to have someone to talk to instead of just muttering to himself while he walked down the highway.

He said for right now his plan is to keep going home. He needs to see if his parents are still alive. He planned on burying them if not. He needed to know either way. After that he said he had no plans. "What are you and the mom and daughter doing?"

"I think we are just going to stay here and make something of this place. Rebuild. Grow food. Make us civilized again. Turn on the electricity. Put on a nightly Swan Lake ballet performance." He was nodding as I talked until the last one. I think he was unsure if I was joking or not. Then a giant smirk across flashed across his face and he began laughing as he pointed at me. He kept repeating 'You got me'.

The girls finally came out of the house once I started walking with Jason to give him the basic rundown of the town and what we had done so far. That pretty much confirmed for me that they had been watching all along. Really, I am surprised that they waited that long, if it had been me I might have popped out after no one got killed ten minutes into the conversation. He seemed to be excited to see more people, again reaffirming for him that he is not alone, which is always nice. As Lisa and Aurora got closer Aurora began to slow slightly, hanging back and starting to 'play strange' around a stranger, who would have thought. The last ten feet or so Jason began walking very quickly towards them; a giant smile across his face and hand already outstretched to shake hands. Lisa glanced at me quickly before shaking his hand, surely to see if I would give her some clue if she was in danger by doing so. "I'm Jason." "Lisa", she replied with a nod. He went to step beside her to meet Aurora who was at that point around five feet further back. Princess was already her protector and Jason just moved to quickly and erratically. Without even being able to really see it happen from where I was Princess darted from behind Aurora to standing between her and Jason. The hair on his back was up, lips quivering without actually baring his teeth. Such a low growl it was almost inaudible. Jason, understandably, came to a screeching halt there before taking several slow steps backwards. "You have a dog? Oh my god, she is so cute." A pause. "Could you make her stop growling at me?"

"It's a him and his name is Princess." I spoke as I continued to walk to beside him, past Lisa. He looked at me sideways, lifted a finger and opened his mouth to speak before stopping himself and saying nothing. Whoever owned Princess before the cataclysm did a good job of training him. A snap of the fingers and he immediately sat down. Still watching Jason intently but without the threats associated with an angry dog. Jason just slightly waved at Aurora. "Hi. I'm Jason." She stood there looking at him, not speaking although not even seeming afraid; just standoffish.

"Her name is Aurora." Lisa said. "Did you guys eat everything or is there something left for us?"

I motioned towards the table. "There is a little left in the pot now and I already opened up the next can, so you guys can make more. We'll be back in a bit I'm just showing him around. We walked up one street and down another, the entire time I am essentially selling him on all that we had already accomplished, what the plans were, how we were going to achieve them. To be honest I took a liking to Jason from the outset. I figured he could be useful in helping rebuild; he's enough of a hard-worker and handyman type that he can help us do things that need to be done. He was however going to find out about his parents. He did suggest the possibility of bringing them here if they were still alive. He shrugged and said he was not sure if his dad would leave their house; I tried to sweeten the pot by telling him they could have their pick of the houses after all we have a whole town to choose from. It was a good point to note.

We returned to the park for the remainder of the day, no one was going to be able to get anything done so we did not even try to fight it. We were all sitting around the picnic table talking of this and that, nothing exciting really, I can not even remember most of that stuff, it was all chit-chat that is now indistinct in my memory. Princess warmed to Jason fairly quickly once we were all relaxed. I trust a dog's intuition about people and Princess' reaction to him that only reinforced my liking of Jason. If Princess was willing to accept him, when he is not being too upfront and moving hastily towards Aurora then there is no reason I can not accept him. He allowed Jason to pet him but always returned to Aurora's feet to lay down. Such a loyal dog.

Jason chose to stay out in the park under his tarp that night while we returned to the safety of the church. I think he was accepting of the idea that people can be cautious of strangers and that is not rude but rather prudent. He just bid us good night and said he would see us in the morning. Not the best sleep that night for me though, I was still wondering about what he had said about his rifle disappearing. I chose to not mention it on purpose to Lisa as I felt that would just ramp up any anxieties she had already. I am feeling pretty certain that it was not a ghost that took it just someone who acts like one. Our (friendly?) neighborhood creeper. While Jason had been going through his rucksack I noted a number of things that got pulled out of there. Nothing extreme; mostly clothes, books, a play station, a pile of DVDs. No glasses that I saw, no binoculars, I don't even think he wore any jewelry. The only thing that to me looked like it could have be used to make a flash of light as I had seen was a DVD but that would not have made sense. He did not know we were here so there would have been no reason to signal us from afar, and if that had been what he had done it was more likely that he would have done it more times than just the once. I was more and more convinced as I reflected that more than likely the flash was from the person who had left Republica suddenly not so long ago. That was not a good prospect. The rifle was taken form Jason two days ago; I saw the flash the day before; he had been moving consistently closer to us each day; meaning that the creeper was backtracking. And now he was armed. I was wishing that I had my own rifle here I could have been on the lookout for him. I will still be guarded in my actions just right now it is more likely that I will be two steps behind.

That next morning came time for Jason to continue on to his parents. We had oatmeal that day although Jason was really the only one wanting it, the rest of us were kind of sick of oatmeal; Aurora was right on that count. I initially had considered giving him my motorcycle in order to complete the journey quicker but I had plans for myself that would require the motorcycle. He was given a bicycle to at least try to make it a little quicker for him although I do not envy him trying to ride a bike uphill and where he is going is pretty much mostly going upwards after you leave Republica. It was still better than walking on a foot with a huge blister on it. He was told not to worry we'd be here when he returned if he chose to. A few hand shakes, a few cans of soup for the road and he was off.

Lisa was the first to stop watching him ride away. "Do you think he'll be back?" I shrugged at her as I turned away as well. "So we should get back to… what are we at? Number 35 now?" I looked down the street, trying to remember which house was which.

"I think that was the one you guys were in yesterday. I thought you were done." They both looked down and shuffled their feet. "Uh-huh. I get it 35 it is." I began walking with them towards the house we had work to do. I would like to say that my 'spidey senses' were tingling walking up to that house but they must have been in the shop that day. I opened the door and walked into the living room. The house was modest and quaint. A floral-patterned sofa sat off to my left with a TV directly across from it. I recall thinking that was one of the ugliest couches I had ever seen, then I recall being on my hands and knees. I have never been hit like that before, but I will tell you getting slammed with the butt end of a rifle is not a pleasant experience. My head hurt from just behind my right ear going straight across my head to the left temple. Everything in between seemed to be screaming in pain and almost vibrating. If I was knocked out it was only for a second or so, it was more like a skip on a record than a fade to black. I looked up and to my right to see our not-so-friendly neighborhood creeper.

When you look at your life everything seems to be dragging slowly. Nothing ever goes quickly. Even when 'time is flying when you are having fun' you can stop for a second and really appreciate things. When something like this happens it really does go too fast to process. You react. I was in the process of looking up and about to grab my pistol out of its holster as the barrel end of the rifle was put in my face as my reaction stopped. I just knelt there looking at that man. The only way I can describe him is to say, meth addict. He was pale, skinny; half of his teeth looked to have rotted out of his face as he sneered at me. His clothes were probably two sizes too big for; they were dirty and torn, especially around the edges. The smell coming off him was indescribable, how we never found this guy by his smell alone I can not even understand. It was something like rotten fish and meat which kind of blended with the overall pervasive smell, along with some super bad breath and maybe a hint of shit thrown in for good measure. He could not hold the rifle very steady, whether that was his nerves or the adrenaline pumping through his veins does not really matter. He made the mistake of lunging forward from behind the door to put the rifle barrel directly into my face, within grabbing distance. When someone has a gun on you the only possible way of really fighting back and trying to ensure that you don't get shot is by controlling the muzzle. Another instant reaction and I was grabbing at the barrel, pushing it off to my left as I turned to face him, away from the door and the girls who were still behind me. So close, to simultaneous, that I would say both things happened at once the rifle went off beside my head and Aurora screeched. It was close enough that I could feel the bullet exhaust blowing past. The pop was directly in my left ear which instantly added to the pain I was already feeling. The good thing is I know that a bolt-action rifle only has one shot before you have to pull back the bolt, eject the spent round and put in the next one. I jerk the rifle out of his hands as Princess literally jumped on Aurora and sprung off her grabbing him around the left elbow. I am barely able to do more as the shock begins to take hold and the whole world begins to swoon around me. Everything is getting fuzzy. Further away. An echo of reality. I crawled on the floor, moving myself closer to the sofa as Princess continues to shake and bite as the creeper screams out. He somehow manages to stand with the dog continuing to hold onto his arm. Lisa runs straight at me trying to get to me before he can get another weapon. She makes a sort of baseball slide that ends with her at my side. At first, she tried to wrest the rifle from my hands although admittedly in the state I was in I had a death grip on it; there was no way it was leaving my grasp. She grabbed the pistol on my hip and fired. The whole room stopped moving at that instant. Princess released his grip on the creepers arm. Aurora fell backwards landing on her ass. The creeper, stood with a trickle of red coming through his shirt where he had been shot. It was one of those "flesh wounds" you see in the movies, which by the way are generally more serious in real life, getting shot is not something you skip down the road after. It was up near his right shoulder, directly beside his clavicle. He stumbled slightly as he fell out the door and began trying to run although his legs were no longer working as he was accustomed to. Princess was seemingly confused at that point, he wanted to chase the creeper and continue the attack meanwhile he was trying to keep the three of us safe.

I awoke around 15 minutes later, according to Lisa's reckoning. She was still holding the pistol at the ready, moving like a squirrel, twitching from window to window to door to hallway and then repeating. My head was pounding. "Where is Aurora?" I mumbled; I am surprised

Lisa was able to understand me, it felt like my tongue was not even working.

"She's on the couch behind you." I looked above me to see her sitting on the couch, happy and content, brushing Princess' fur and kind of gazing out the window. My mind was cloudy, but I was still thinking that she must be in shock to be that calm. I tried to get up only to fall down again. I used the rifle that was still in my hand as a cane and brought myself to my feet. Shuffling my feet as I go towards the door I chamber the next round in the rifle. It's only a .22, a gun better suited for killing things like rabbits or chipmunks than people, but I doubted Lisa would be giving me back my pistol anytime soon.

"Stay here." I leave and begin following the bloody droplets. From one yard to the next, over multiple roads. Every once in a while, you can see where the creeper fell. There was usually an accompanying bloody handprint. The trail led me to an old looking house. This looked as if it had not been maintained at all in the past twenty years. And that was before the house was baked in the cataclysm. Behind the house was an old single detached garage, it was in an even worse state of disrepair; the roof was half caved in, there were a few boards missing from the walls, the windows were so dirty with grim that the glass was no longer transparent, more of a translucent. I was still a little wobbly as I kicked the door and stepped back. I could not hear anything coming from inside as the door slowly began to close. The wind generated by the door being opened forcefully had kicked up dust which was now swirling inside the slightly open door, which I began to steady with my foot. I stepped inside slowly, this time much more cautiously, looking for any sign of someone hiding behind the door. In the corner. Behind a box. I swung the rifle around the room as I searched the dark and dusty space. It was apparent that this garage had been more of a storage space than a place for a car before the flare. The musty/moldy smell was overpowering. At the far corner of the garage, behind a pile of boxes, was what appeared to be a work bench. Walking wide as I looked behind the pile I could see a pair of feet sticking out from underneath the bench. I simply stood there, watching. No breathing that I could see. The was not real blood pool either. The dirt that composed the floor likely soaked it all up. Rushing forward a few steps I stomped on his ankle. Hard. I could hear the ankle bone snap. I did this with such a force that I almost lost my balance; my balance at that point still being quite precarious. No movement. He was dead. I dragged his body out of the garage and left it outside the building before returning to examine where he seemed to be running to. There was a false panel under the workbench leading to a small room underground. 'Room' is being rather generous when I describe this little cell. The room was around 4 ½ feet wide and 5 feet long; not really even large enough to stretch out in and the ceiling was just over 5 feet high, I could not even try to stand and was essentially forced to move around the room on my knees. I have no idea if the creeper had been the original owner of the house/garage or just happened upon it but it seemed as though he had been staying here for at least a while, likely from before the flare. I am guessing this had been the shelter he had survived in but I am not sure how, dumb luck maybe. The walls were plastered with all types of images involving bondage and torture. Even more disturbing were the books stacked in the corner. They seemed to have been read thoroughly and repeatedly; the pages being tattered and dog-eared. Real crime books discussing Jack the Ripper, BTK, Ted Bundy, Gary Ridgeway and others I no longer recall. I knew who all of those people were, what they had done and given the tone of the rest of this room, those books were instructional manuals to the creeper; definitely not 'light-reading'. If the creeper had not been a dangerous person before the flare, he would have been given more time in the old world. And he certainly was after the flare. I tossed the creeper's body back into the garage as I set it ablaze. It was better to just get rid of him and everything in there. I realized how big of a mistake that was after it had caught, I quickly tried to determine which way the wind was blowing. An errant spark could easily take out half the town. There was barely a breeze though.

I returned to number 35 through the backyard. My legs were becoming more solid underneath me as time wore on. I had become more aware now that shock and adrenaline was starting to wear off that my head was still hurting more than I had ever experienced before. There was a small amount of dried blood on the back-right side of my head and a very large lump. Opening the back door, I yelled in to Lisa that he was dead. Princess hops off the couch and trots toward me; a low rumbling growl coming from her throat. I kneel and extend my hand allowing Princess to smell and lick my palm. First security check passed. "Lisa?" Silence. "Lisa, I am coming in. Don't shoot me." Walking through the house I can see that Lisa is now sitting in the corner of the front room away from the door. The pistol was still in her hands, pointed to the floor between her legs. Her face was not expressionless but instead belied a deep exhaustion. It had been a long day so far. Kneeling in front of her I tried to get her attention. I was honestly scared of scaring her while she was in her own mind only to have her come rushing back into reality and start shooting. I knocked on the floor hoping she would feel the vibrations through her feet and make eye contact. Princess let out a little half bark. Lisa's eyes slowly rose, blinking as if she was waking. Taking the pistol gently from her I stand up pulling her with me. "Come on guys, we're done for today."

Walking out in the light both Aurora and Lisa shield their eyes from the sun. Number 35 was much too dark. A short distance away the fire continues to burn; they can see the smoke gently rising over the interceding houses. "He's dead?" Lisa asks.

"Yes. And I burnt down his place with his body in it just in case I was wrong. He's not coming back." We walk to the church not saying anything until I open the front door for them. "You guys go lay down. It's been way too exciting of a day. Rest. I'm gonna take a quick ride back home to pick up a few things." I had never really told them about my place at that point, but I knew there were some useful things that could be had I would prefer to get them prior to Jason returning. I liked him but did not trust him. Trust is earned, and you do not get it from a few hours of conversation.

"Why? For what?" Aurora put her left hand down to her side with the palm facing the ground; Princess nuzzled up under her hand. The dog was already a comfort and support for her when she was scared.

"Don't worry I will be back soon. I'll be bringing more food. Fresh stuff." I winked at her. "Plus, I think we could really use some lights." They both exchanged puzzled looks as I pat Aurora on the head. "Trust me, I'll be back soon."

Aurora muttered "Liar" under her breath as she walked away. That was one of those instances that I really wanted to mention who I was to her but I did have a sense of urgency. I did want to be there and back within the day, I had already thought out what were the most important things to bring back other than the animals; some turbines/solar panels. Seeds, I had a pile of them frozen in my freezer. Every kind of plant we could want; hell, there may even be some plants still alive in my indoor garden. I doubt it though; they had not been tended for a while. We needed to get that started; growing things so there would be something fresh to eat soon. Obviously, some more weapons would be useful.

CHAPTER 10 – A TURN OF A VISE

So that was how we began to stock things up here in Republica. As more people arrived and I became more secure in Aurora's safety I took more and more trips to my home until I had stripped it of everything that could be useful in my new home. I'm sure some have wondered why I left there in the first place considering how well equipped my fortress was. The reasoning is that as great as my home was it was, in essence, over-engineered. A big thing in terms of ensuring that I have enough water for the crops and animals was that cistern built into the top level of the barn. It was a great idea. The rain that hits the roof of the barn is collected, stored for later use and like I said earlier it was also handy for any possible fires that happened within the barn. Now here is the problem; the cistern itself was a single large container sitting on top of the barn. It had a few inlets that allowed water to flow in as well as a number of sprinkler heads within the barn to allow the aforementioned possible conflagration. When the flare hit, as I keep pointing out, it microwaved everything. Well when you have a large container holding water like that and begin microwaving it you soon have a large container holding a lot of steam. Even with the pressure somewhat being released through the inlets there was no way to really stop the pressure from building within that cistern. Due to all the radiation the cameras were dead outside so I did not see what actually happened, but I felt it, even underground in my hardened home. It was sudden and unexpected; an enormous thud that shook everything. The pressure in the reservoir built so high that it literally cracked then blew off a corner of the barn. An entire 4-foot by 5-foot section near the junction of the roof and the corner of the wall was sent flying in dozens of pieces. The largest piece of this disintegration of my barn was approximately 400 pounds. It was thrown from the barn into the side of my 'distraction' house. It acted as a cannonball; hitting the wall to one of the smaller bedrooms squarely, ripping a hole into that room. It ricocheted off the bed making a further hole into the kitchen area before finally stopping next to the unplugged and never used stove. I could not hear any of that down where I was; it only came through as one large thud and shudder. The impact actually moved the whole distraction house almost a foot further from the barn. This had a number of unforeseen consequences. Well, that is kind of an understatement. The barn exploding was unforeseen, and all this happening was tied in with that same occurrence. The elevator ceased to work as the shaft in which it ran was now bent. There was a crack in the ceiling of the main area of the barn which meant that most of the water that remained within the cistern would just drip down into the animal pens. The barn was ruined, I could try to continue to use it but soon enough it would have just been a cement building with that musty/moldy smell of a wet basement. As well there was a crack that actually managed to appear in the ceiling of the upper layer of the basement. Not a large crack but enough. I mean if you have any understanding of the kind of force that it would take to make a real dent in that building, well let's just say that cement cannonball sure packed a wallop. There were other things that I noticed but they are not really important. In any event it became apparent after that steam explosion that my fortress might not have the unlimited sustainability that I had planned for.

Every return to home in order to pick up supplies was something of a reminder for me of my own failure. I had tried to plan ahead and my planning was essentially my own undoing. As I said, it was over-engineered. I needed to simplify. That became one of the hallmarks I think in what I was going to try to do within Republica. And I mean that in everything. If there was a way to do something simply I would generally prefer that method just for the simplicity of it. Food was something that was covered in a few ways but again was basic. We had our vegetables that made up the bulk of the diet of every person in town. We had fruits like bananas and cantaloupe growing in that greenhouse but also things like apples, watermelons and pears growing outside. Gardens full of things like blueberries, raspberries and strawberries. The main idea with what was being grown was that it could be eaten with as little preparation as possible. Grains for example are more intensive than fruits and vegetables which can often be eaten right off the tree or from the ground. Protein, while supplemented by hunting wild animals, chickens and eggs, was primarily covered for our residents through eating fish. We had a whole system in place for the growth, reproduction and harvesting of fish. Tanks specifically for fish eggs, others for little fish, larger ones for juvenile fish and the community center swimming pool was utilized for adults. Breeding was done in separate tanks so the eggs could be easily collected for the egg tanks. We ensured that each stage of their lives they were given the best chances of survival so that we always had a ready stock of food. This meant removing the larger fish from the smaller ones. Fish tend to not be overly picky about being cannibalistic and will devour anything that they can fit into their mouths. The citizens of Republica were provided for. They had all they could want in terms of food that is except for those whose taste in food was different from the rest of us.

As people had been filtering into Republica there were a few things that were initially more of a concern than how people had survived. We were focused on our continued survival as opposed to dredging up the past. As people happened along the town they were welcomed, given a general tour and then interviewed. This was something not unlike a job interview although no one was ever really rejected during this stage. It was more of an assessment to try to see where people fit into our society. To see what they can contribute to the community. Standard things like what kind of education do you have, past job experience, hobbies were all relevant. There were also questions regarding criminal past. Which often was something that people are much more reluctant to answer. Just because the flare wiped the world clean does not mean the slate has been wiped clean. Again this was not an area that we rejected people for the most part, unless there was some very blatant lying, and the only thing that was a real hindrance to entry was something like having been a serial killer or sexual predator however no one ever admitted to that on their own. We therefore had to rely on what people said. There are no records to check. No references to call. No people to vouch for someone, other than if they have traveling companions. We had a system in place for new entrants to be screened on a more ongoing basis after they first arrived. They were given a house in the middle of a number of trusted citizens who were tasked primarily with following, befriending and documenting people in their first weeks in town, as they settled into life here. This was quite effective in discovering people who were brazen enough to try stealing from neighbors or had happened upon a large stash of crack cocaine prior to entering the town or leaving their house in the middle of the night in an attempt to stalk and presumably attack women within the community. That particular person had a 'rape kit' with him when he was apprehended. While technically only circumstantial it was enough for us to get rid of him, permanently. Exile was the usual method of punishment for these people but the stalker was not the kind of thing we wanted to unleash upon the remaining world, so we didn't. This system for checking on our new people was not foolproof however as people obviously got through, like John Thomas. Also, the cannibals got through.

As I said there was not initially a need to investigate everything that had happened previously; rebuilding requires forgetting or ignoring things that happened before or shortly after the end of the world. 'Are you a Cannibal?' was not a question on our interview back before it became relevant. Hindsight is 20/20. I was told after the whole debacle that when the first of the cannibals had arrived they had appeared to be following someone returning from scavenging in a nearby town. This is not uncommon, you see someone you follow so you can try to meet up with them, join their town. It happened many times before and after. But this one was different. The scavenger was not so much as being followed as being stalked. As well in a funny 'coincidence' the stalker along with two of his friends all appeared at the same time. All coming from different directions. Again examining it through hindsight they were stalking in the same manner a lion may do. One is visible from behind while the other two approach from the flanks slightly ahead of the prey, catching it unawares in a pincer movement. Almost immediately upon discovering the town one left to go get their friends who all arrived around six hours later. They were given the usual treatment in terms of assessment and supervision and passed everything quite well. The group as a whole was somewhat promising as they included an electrician, plumber, and carpenter all of whom would be quite useful in maintaining the buildings within the town as well as constructing new things like our wheelhouse. As well they had a homemaker who knew how to make soap, a knitter, a man who was an ornithologist, another who ran a fishing lodge until he retired, a botany student, a paramedic and a butcher. Probably others who deserve to be mentioned but I think you get the idea; they were a fairly diverse group of people who were all useful in one way or another more so than ever as they arrived a short time after our illness crisis, so we had lost a few skilled people.

The newcomers were separated into a few houses and observed as we did with everyone. Nothing out of the ordinary for those first few weeks meaning that we had no reservations with moving them out into the greater community; they were then promoted up to getting their own places around town. Everything went swimmingly. Until it stopped going so well. Who knows if it took a week or a month or months after they stop being observed on a constant basis. I will admit now that not all of these people were bad, for some of them it was guilt by association, but something needed to be done. The first indication that something was amiss occurred around 4 months after they arrived. Despite the medical care that we could provide we were hampered by a general lack of personnel or supplies. Our doctor/nurse was capable of doing some of the things necessary but especially at that point she did not have a lot of help meaning that if an accident happened that required surgery to fix it would have to be done by one person as opposed to the usual team of doctors and nurses. In our haste to get the wheelhouse and water purification building up and running certain safety procedures were bypassed. Roger was an older gentleman who had been something of a handyman throughout his years. I believe his actual occupation had been working as an engineer on a train, but it was his carpentry skills that were of more interest to us. He was atop the frame of the wheelhouse affixing the roof structure so the building could be enclosed. Things were running simultaneously on the construction, which is I'm sure how things always work in construction. According to others on the site a gust of wind was all that was needed to overcome Roger's equilibrium and send him tumbling down. A simple safety harness and rope would have prevented the accident although no one bothered to try to have Roger wear it or even try to get one. He survived the fall and if it had been on a plain floor would have just led to a broken bone(s). The cement floor had been poured with bolts sticking out of the floor to which the generator would eventually be secured. Those bolts were thick, likely ¾ of an inch across with around 12 inches sticking out of the cement. It was surprising with Roger being impaled as he was that there was so little blood surrounding him however it was the pressure he exerted back onto the bolt that kept the blood flowing inside him. Like destroying the entrance to an ant hill the whole area suddenly became a swarm of frantic activity. Some people were trying to perform first aid as best they could, some running from place to place like chickens with their heads cut off and some just staying out of the way and helping as they were needed. Just another example of how some people cannot handle stress and panic well. Roger was unconscious from the fall which was very fortunate for him as I am sure the bolt sticking through his torso would have likely been excruciating; he would have passed out from the pain if he was not already unaware of what was happening. At least he never had to endure that pain. After some panicked minutes our new paramedic friend arrived on-site to help prepare Roger for transport to the nursing home. The bolt was somehow cut underneath him allowing the bolt to be taken with him, in hopes that it could be removed allowing him to retain as much blood as possible within himself. A number of blood donors were arranged among those who knew their blood type as being O negative. No one was certain of Roger's blood type, so we had to use the 'universal donors' to avoid any donation complications. Right now, if you ever receive blood from an incompatible blood type you might as well kiss your ass goodbye as the two bloods interact leading to an enormous clot that stays in you until it gets to your brain and causes a stroke or goes to your heart causing a heart attack. Either way you are fucked. Nothing short of anti-coagulants will help although even that is not a certainty. Using O negative avoids that issue as anyone can get blood from them. The paramedic was with Roger the entire way to the makeshift emergency room. He "assisted" the "doctor" in removing the bolt from Roger however they were unable to stem the flow of blood from the wound. Whether it was incompetence on his part or her just covering for her own failings we will never truly know however according to our doctor he behaved as someone who was wholly unfamiliar with surgery and medical practices, which is completely contrary to the reports from everyone at the job site who said that he was thoroughly knowledgeable and took charge in a way that ensured that he was able to get to the nursing home alive. Maybe they were both right. Maybe he was a very good paramedic but was unable to transfer those skills to the operating room. Or maybe as we began to suspect later he purposely had not tried his hardest. Either way Roger's fate was sealed and he died having never regained consciousness. The most disturbing thing that I was told after the smoke had cleared from the cannibal crisis was that after Roger had expired; our new paramedic was seen casually walking back to his house licking the blood off of his fingers. Contrary to the usual way of doing things when people died there seemed to be a growing sentiment that those who die should be given a proper burial instead of cremation. As leader I was more focused on the town than minute details. I was not really part of the decision to bury Roger. How much of the change in attitude towards cremation was fomented by the cannibals I can never be sure, but I would venture it was likely due to one or a number of them as it was never an issue before or since. I would say the service was pleasant, not overly religious but not discounting Roger's faith which was apparently quite strong. There was something for everyone to take away from his death. A few were 'born-again' after hearing of his devotion to the scriptures. Some gained a renewed sense of community seeing for one brief moment the entire population coming together to try to help one man in need. There were a fair number who grabbed a hold of his work ethic, wanting to bring the best of themselves out when they worked to help out everyone around them. Some just got a much-needed day off. Whatever it was, they got something that they needed. Unfortunately, this even included those whose needs ran against the rest of us.

'We are gathered here to remember our dear friend Roger Spencer'. The ornithologist, the paramedic and the fishing lodge operator were their own little group during the service.

'Roger was a man devoted to his family before they were taken from him'. I was not the only one to notice them as others seemed to be upset at the disrespect shown by talking during a funerary service.

'He showed a rich love of life that came out not only in his laugh but also in his kindness with others; he was always willing to help, always there to lend a helping hand or give you the shirt off of his back'. Whatever was said amongst them was obviously amusing as they all had a smirk across on their faces for the duration of the service.

'Roger spent his years working with trains before retiring to travel and spend time with his grandchildren, God rest their souls'. There was an occasional chuckle from the group or hand rising to cover their ear-to-ear grins, at this point everything was out of place and disrespectful but not extremely alarming.

'He will now be reunited with his family that he cherished so much, together to spend an eternity together with God in Heaven'. Laughing at a funeral is very poor taste but at the same time perhaps they did not really

know Roger all that well. He was an older man; it was highly likely that they were in totally different social circles.

'*Ashes to ashes, dust to dust*'. They might have never met him prior to his nosedive from the frame of that building; without his accident they could have likely gone months without ever really meeting.

Amen'. Never knowing each other's name.

Back in World War II the Germans had laid siege to Leningrad which was the second most populous city in the Soviet Union. Prior to the Bolsheviks taking power in 1917 this city had been the capital city of the Russian empire and was called St. Petersburg. The city was renamed after Vladimir Lenin, the leader of the Bolsheviks, making it Leningrad. Given its 'importance' Hitler made it a goal of his Russian invasion to utterly obliterate this city from the map. No citizens were to survive; he did not want to have to worry about feeding and evacuating people from the city. As the defenses around the city stiffened; it was decided to just surround the city by cutting it off from all supplies then bombarding and starving the inhabitants until there were none left. I do not recall the numbers of dead but it was hundreds of thousands. Those that were left did the best they could to fight against the Germans while simultaneously not starving to death. One of the things that were noted for having been eaten by those residents of Leningrad were loaves of bread made with sawdust. Now this is not a loaf made entirely of sawdust, but it was a significant enough amount. The rationale behind this was to take limited resources and stretch them. Makes sense and in times of utter hardships it is reasonable. Getting something into people is better than nothing. However, there is an obvious problem with this solution. People cannot survive eating wood. It is indigestible. It is literally something that just passes from one end to the other without giving anything to the body. When you think of it sawdust bread is possibly even more harm than good to someone. With the body taking nothing from it but still making the effort to try to digest it you are expending calories, at least where the wood particles are concerned. The other ingredients of the bread may make up for that, but it still does seem to be a problem in my mind as it takes something on the order of 2500 calories each day to help maintain not just your body weight but also other vital things. I am primarily thinking of body temperature. Russian winters are noted as being particularly cold so when you couple someone not having enough food energy coming in to maintain their body temperature along with a lack of fuel and/or shelter what you have is people dying in droves. Again, I do not remember the numbers although I would venture that there were likely ten times as many people that died from starvation and disease in that city than died directly from violence from the Germans.

So, during this siege one of the solutions to try to stop people from starving was to take food and stretch it but there were a number of documented instances of cannibalism. Again, this is in a way an understandable solution that some people reach in order to avoid starvation but at the same time most people not in that situation see it as reprehensible. After the siege was lifted by the advancing Soviet army instances of this were investigated and dealt with. There was a distinction that the Russians made which I did not bother with, although I was aware of the different nature of things. One group of cannibals were found to have been corpse-eaters, meaning that they only ate from those who were already dead. Most of the people found in this category tended to be women, along with their children. They would eat someone who had died either from starvation or maybe a bomb being dropped. Who knows. I read that the children often did not even know what they were eating; their mother would leave to get food and return with meat that would be made into a soup or stew. People in this group tended to be punished by being sent to the outer reaches of Russia, like for example the dreaded Siberia. In a way it was likely something of a blessing as those people, I would assume, would probably not want to be staying in someplace that was that close to the invaders. Even if they were not pleased with that result they still got off better than the people-eaters who were routinely shot in the back of the head. The difference of course between corpse and people eaters is that the people eaters killed for their food. Even in a war as savage as WWII that was not something that was 'cool'. The main reason for the differing reactions was related to peacetime. Both groups of people had eaten other people for survival. But that manner of death on the part of the meal was very important. A corpse-eater, even if they 'developed a taste' for people are not likely to find bodies just laying on the road once the area is no longer a warzone; the people eaters actively went out and killed people. They do not have that problem of eating humans being inconvenient, they can always go out and find someone that looks tasty. If they develop a taste for it then in theory the only thing keeping people safe would be that person's self-control. How long would it take before they justify killing and eating someone because it was 3 days to payday and they were hungry?

Roger's grave was found to have been disturbed two or three days after his burial although no one is sure if the cannibals waited that long, he was likely up and out of the ground the night he was buried. The only reason we knew about this was simple carelessness. There was no reason initially to assume that there had been anything truly disturbing happening. He had been dug up and the dirt replaced back into the hole afterwards, but it was done in a rushed manner. When his grave had first been excavated the soil had been put onto a tarp so it could be easily returned to the hole above Roger. The grave robbers had just dropped the dirt beside the hole then made a half-assed attempt to fill it back in. My guess now is they were likely startled by something and chose to not return as that would have increased their chances of getting caught. Roger's body was to be exhumed in order for us to try to understand why his grave had been disturbed. Not surprisingly it was not there. I would like to say that we had an idea after that discovery about what had happened but then again, we did not. It seemed odd. Roger was not buried with any valuables and even if he had "valuable" is a relative term. You cannot even sell a gold ring in our town, the economy is just not made for it, meaning the only thing you could do with it is wear it and that would be suspicious. Also, there is actually a pile of jewelry we found in the houses in our stockpile that people have access to. It is mostly seen as a pile of 10k and 14k junk; it has no purpose or use and kind of gets in the way when you are tending a garden. A watch may be useful but again same thing we have them available if you really want one. It did not make sense. Eventually, the whole issue became something that conspiracy theories were made of and was only discussed in hushed tones. One of those rumors involved me, which while amusing in its own way was not funny at all. The rumor was that I had taken his body to be used as a prop for the cult that I was trying to start within the town. I have no idea where this idea could have come from as I never once made any hint at trying to start a cult nor would I. Cults are too 'shower-cappy" for me. In any event this was something that faded from people's thoughts but not their fears. It seemed odd and appeared to forebode something sinister.

A further few months from then, there began to be reports of shadows moving around at night, following people out late. Stalking. This was reminiscent of our neighborhood creeper. But at the same time, it was different. This was more organized and dangerous. The thing that made it so in my mind was that it was not one shadow seeming to follow you but rather two or three shadows working in concert. It did take a little bit of silent thought on my part to remember the situation that had brought the paramedic and his party into our midst. I remembered the apparent pincer movement that brought three of them here at once. I remembered one leaving abruptly only to return later with more companions. I remembered the talking and smiling during the funeral. All of it circumstantial and a very tenuous connection at best but I could not shake the feeling that I was looking at the solution, however I was still not putting it all together. I mean in my mind cannibalism was not even a possibility. After three straight nights of shadows following someone I was told that there had been an actual attempt to grab this last person. And well that was it, there needed to be something done. Each of the suspects, the ornithologist, the paramedic and fishing guide, were all grabbed during the middle of the day and handcuffed immediately before having a bag put over their head. They all ended up in the basements of different houses. We waited. No one talked to them; they were kept locked in their respective basements, until the next night passed. No shadows following people. No boogiemen trying to corner people. I was much more confident that we had the right people.

Each was interrogated in turn. Again this was not a pleasant experience. Not even for the men present with me. I took a primary role in the questioning not because I particularly had a need to but I thought at that point I should. It was my theory. We're talking all those 'enhanced interrogation techniques' along with some golden oldies. The longer the interrogation took the angrier I got. That led to more and more pain on their part. First was the ornithologist. I specifically went after him because he seemed to me more of the weak link in the trio. A slight man, probably only in his mid to late thirties but he looked much older. His hairline had probably started receding when he was 20. His glasses were thick, meaning he was likely almost blind without his glasses.

"Were you following someone the other night?" A panicked look from him when he made eye contact with me. The vise is twisted a quarter turn. He screams as the tip of his pinky finger is starting to be crushed. "Were you following someone the other night?" No matter how angry you may be as an interrogator it seems to actually help if you remain outwardly calm. They need to see that nothing matters to you in this conversation. You are fine with any outcome, including ripping someone to shreds if you do not get your questions answered. It is ominous for them to see someone completely not caring about their pain. I did care of course and like I said I was angry; I was always able to maintain a plain tone of voice. No excitement or regret. He nodded furiously as my hand went towards the vise handle. In all fairness this was a little disappointing, I had not even really begun, and he was already beginning to crack. "Why were you following people?" He opened his mouth repeatedly like a fish out of water, trying to get a breath, trying to speak but no sounds were forthcoming. Another twist on the vise. Screams. Well I was now sure he would be able to make sounds. The tip of his finger was crushed. I had William reposition his finger putting the teeth of the vise on the first knuckle of his pinky. Blood ran onto the vise from the tip of his finger as it was released, the pressure had been keeping the blood in, now that there was no more pressure the area under his nail where his skin had split was now allowing the blood to flow. His lips loosened as the blood dripped from his finger.

"W- w- we were just playing around." I was looking at him eye-to-eye. My expression was not changing. I knew something strange was happening. I said nothing, just watching him. The longer the silence; the more panic he started to display. It was probably only thirty seconds of silence total before he realized I was not going to be that easily deflected. "It was Cliff's idea, he said he was hungry." Clifford, was the name of the paramedic. I was having trouble remembering it until now but thinking of this had jogged my memory. The paramedic was Clifford; the fishing guide was Glenn and I was talking to Robbie the ornithologist. "We were just looking. It was Cliff. He made me taste his fingers"

"What do you mean... hungry?" This idea was off-the-beaten-path for me. It was all right there but still not making sense. He shifted nervously. I think I actually bared my teeth at him, belying that my subconscious had put the pieces together before my conscious mind had. "Taste what?" My hand moved to the lever of the vice. "You better start explaining things, because this is only going to start going faster."

"We were out of meat. We needed to get more." He paused which was quickly followed by a twist of the vise. Screaming. This scream was longer than the last; going until he was completely out of breath. Robbie sat there panting in front of me, sobbing, begging; 'No more. I'll talk. No more' he kept repeating. "After Roger died Cliff found me and took me over to his house and said 'remember this' and he stuck his finger in my mouth. It had Roger's blood on it. I remembered the taste from before. We started to get hungry. It was all we could think about. We just talked about how much better we ate back then. Glenn came over and Cliff told him everything. He just kept licking his lips. He said he was sick of vegetables and eggs and wanted real meat. We were just hungry." I let a sigh out as I was absorbing this. I turned to look at the other people in the room. Everyone was standing with their mouths open, shocked at what they were hearing. Stephanie, the woman who lived in the house next door to Robbie, had slipped into the room at some point. I was not sure when. She was one of the people who had been seeing shadows. She was pale and green at the same time. A mix of fear and disgust. I nodded towards the door and Jason grabbed her by the arm and led her out of the basement; having someone vomit during an interrogation is not something that I want to happen. Smelling puke would annoy me. "We dug up Roger." I turned back to him as he began speaking again. "We brought him back to Cliff's." He began sobbing again. "We cooked him. He was in the freezer and we kept cutting off parts and cooking him. Until he was gone. But when he was gone we just could not stop thinking about it. We wanted more. But no one was dying. So…" A pause. And a turn of the vise.

"You ate him? Roger? You dug up Roger to cook and eat him? What the fuck? Seriously. What the FUCK?" I was done with acting calm. I swung hard and punched him in the side of his face. The force was enough to move his chair across the floor. His finger which was already mangled by the vise tore completely off where it was being held. Blood began flowing liberally; getting blood all over the chair and floor. He was now just screaming. High pitched and shrill. Looking at William I tell him to get me something to stop the bleeding as we were not done talking yet. Robbie was trying to shy away and not look at me. He was still screaming and sobbing. I had begun to reclaim my calm after the outburst. "You were looking to find someone alive to kill cook and eat; is that what you are saying you guys were doing out the past few nights?" Robbie meekly nodded as William wrapped a towel around his hand. "So just You, Glenn and Clifford. No one else was doing this with you?"

He shook his head as he whispered, "It was all of us."

"All of us who? Who was doing this with you? For fucks sakes talk or we will start again with the vise on the next finger." A new round of bawling and begging to 'please don't' began. And that is why we started with Robbie. He was the weak link and broke. Not to say that I would not have broken if I was in the same position, but it did seem to be very quick; he barely resisted at all. We got a list of names; Cliff and Glenn numbers two and three behind Robbie himself. I won't make it seem like I can remember all the names on the list but I will assure you that the list consisted of that one group that came in at the same time. Sixteen names total. I still have that list, framed. It was a source of power for me but also a license to do all that I did. Any doubt that I may have ever had was erased by looking at that list. I had cleansed the town.

I had thought I was going to see our fishing guide Glenn after finishing with Robbie, but I changed my mind as I stepped out of the front door of the house Robbie was held in; turning right instead of left. I wanted to just go right to Cliff. He had always seemed to be the leader of that group. Instead of poking around the side of the snake I was just going to look it in the eye. Descending into the basement he was put into I quickly came to realize that this location was not going to work for me. It was too small; the ceiling was only like 4 feet off the floor; the floor was just packed dirt. This was not even a real basement, more of a crawlspace. Despite the lack of room and inability to maneuver someone had already begun 'softening up' Clifford. His left eye was black and puffy, only a slight slit was still there for him to see out of; it also appeared that he was missing a few teeth which were now between his feet mixed in with mud and blood. My discontent with that development was palpable. I simply looked at the two men who had been in the basement with Cliff while grinding my teeth. Maybe I was getting too Alpha there; they touched something that was mine. Maybe it was just that they were not even interrogating, just beating to a bloody pulp. It was not helpful for me. "Bring him!" I yelled as I walked up the few steps leaving the crawlspace. One of the men dragging Cliff along was having trouble holding him; he had broken his hand while beating a cuffed man. I could care less about his pain as I marched back to the house where Robbie was being held. I had a noose fashioned out of an electrical cord strung between the beams of the basement, overtop of a pair of cross beams near the corner of the basement. Robbie was stood up and put in the noose. He was not going to die there; it was more of a way to keep him contained while we asked Cliff questions. Quite simply it was just that we needed the chair.

I covered all the same questions that Robbie had already answered. It only cost Cliff four of his fingers to get that far. Robbie could be heard at times sobbing; at other times trying to scream through his gag to tell

Cliff that he did not need to keep the secret. He had already told us everything. We ended up going further with Cliff. He had killed 6 people since the end of the world. 3 men, a woman and 2 children. It took 2 more fingers and a thumb to get that information. At that point though he was past resisting; there were instances where he had passed out from the pain and we were just crushing a finger without even a twitch from him. Once he was just too busy screaming and crying and blubbering to answer anything, so we repositioned his hand and started on the next finger. This was truly the messiest thing I have ever seen. Even more so than flaying someone, I am guessing it is like the difference of having a steak that is bloody and ground beef that is bloody; the bloody drips off the steak onto the floor making a little puddle, in the other scenario the blood drops to the floor with some of the meat just a pile of person mush staining the cement.

During one of the times that Cliff passed out I asked one of the men who had been with Cliff in the crawlspace, Adam was his name, if he wanted a chance to redeem himself. He nodded emphatically. Two others were working with Cliff trying to bring him back to consciousness while I looked Adam in the eye. He was told he would be going with Jason to start tackling the list of names we had been given. He was given the strictest instructions that if anyone he brought here looked like Cliff had then we would be asking him questions next. He just stood there as I spoke. Adam's Adam's apple repeatedly made hard and long undulations as he swallowed. I wonder if Adam's mother foresaw that he would have a large Adam's apple in his neck and I wonder if she had named him that intentionally. As Cliff was made to smell the homemade smelling salts I waved Adam away as if I was royalty while I am holding eye contact with Jason; nodding at him to go out, my hand outstretched with the list for him to start collecting. "Nine and seven first" I told him just prior to the basement door closing. I inhaled deeply before returning to Cliff who was now awake and sobbing again.

Cliff at this point needed no more incentives to talk, he was pushed past the limit that he could resist and the information was simply spilling out. He said that his entire group had participated in the consumption of those people although not all had killed. As well they had scavenged a number of bodies whether it had been friends or family that died or just people they found dead on the side of the road. It was only him, Robbie, Glenn and two others that had hunted and killed people. Jack and Joe. Those two were numbers 9 and 7 respectively on the list; that group of five were the real people-eaters; the rest were more of corpse eaters. They only ate once someone was already dead. All but 3 of that group had eaten Roger, the three that didn't were the ones who had not developed a taste for people yet. They had secretly met in his house at least once a week to roast pieces of him in the fireplace. He said they did it in the dead of night so no one would see the smoke. They only did it when the wind was blowing towards the east since they were near the east side of town and it was less likely that someone would smell it. Really, they had put a bunch of thought into this, they planned to consume and were doing all they could to get away with it. They knew it was wrong.

Joe was the first to be brought to the basement next to where I was and was shortly thereafter, followed by Jack, Helen, Randy, Brian, Angela, Chastity, Monica, Tim, Tom, Rory, Michelle and Ashley. The list was there in its entirety and in order; with the exception of number nine being before number eight. Each was being lined up and essentially hung from the ceiling in the same manner as Robbie had been. Of course, each was confused and scared. All were gagged and hooded to avoid any possible way of them looking at or communicating with each other. All had varying degrees of bruising or blood running from their heads due to resisting arrest; that is if you can call what we were doing arresting people. A couple were completely naked which is I am going to assume how they went to bed although I am not totally sure. Working as I was you do not tend to attract the most honorable people, so it is possible that it was not as innocent as I had thought at the time. The naked ones were all given clothes; it often did not fit but at least there were somewhat covered.

Glenn was now on the 'hot seat', as it were, having been brought from the house next door to the one we were currently in. He could see both Robbie and Cliff hanging along the wall, a puddle of dark blood on the floor, covering their feet. It had gotten to the point where it was getting gel-like and tacky. No longer the bright red life-giving fluid now it was a maroon reminder for them of where they were. I was honestly at that point feeling exhausted. I was having more trouble containing myself although I did manage to not have a real severe outburst with Cliff as I had had with Robbie. Glenn was much luckier in that he could see what had happened to the other two. In fact due to his relatively close proximity he had heard the anguished screaming coming from them so he knew what was afoot. There was a constant chorus of sobs and sniffles coming from the two behind me as I warned Glenn that I was not going to tolerate his lying to me or not answering my questions. Glenn tried to say that he had never killed anyone as soon as I implied that he had been part of the sub-group that had, to which I replied with a turn of the lever on the vice. With little hesitation he recanted that lie and began from the beginning of his introduction with the cannibals. According to his story they had all been living in the city that I had last rode through prior to getting to Republica. The group had started as Cliff, Jack, Helen, and Monica along with a mother and her three children. They had been raiding a local grocery store although it was mostly empty from the pre-cataclysm looting; once that ran out they began foraging in nearby houses and buildings although they were not able to find enough to eat. This was compounded when Glenn was incorporated into the group along with his two new friends. Soon enough they had no food, and according to him no real way to get anything substantial as they had too many mouths to feed. The youngest of the children, probably only 6 years old, quickly became weak from malnutrition and was unable to combat whatever sickness soon befell him/her. That child died in the middle of a room full of starving people who apparently could just not live with that feeling anymore. He described a situation where everyone looked at the little body and justified the greater good of the group was more important than their disdain of what they were suggesting. They ate the child. Even the mother who was initially weeping and crying out for her lost child sat next to the fire, plate in hand, watching as her offspring was roasted on a spit as she waited to be served.

From there he said everything just became scarier and more horrible. No one even made attempts anymore to go out and find food. All they needed was right here in front of them. There was nothing to eat and they began eyeing the children, looking for signs of their next meal although both of them seemed to be healthy. A day of watching the children laugh and play turned into two which turned into five then a week. They were all getting weaker without one being the 'weakest', the children seeming to be the strongest of them all. At some point someone suggested not waiting for nature to take its course and suggested some manner of sacrificing someone for the good of the group. Drawing straws. Playing Russian Roulette. Eeney-meeney-miney-mo. All of those were "unacceptable" as everyone at that point was only worried with self-preservation and no one was willing to "take-one-for-the-team". It was constant; the children were always the solution that was offered when other ideas were shot down. At first the mother was against the ideas, simply putting it aside as a No, before she began to see the sideways glances always looking at her kids. She became more vocal, angrier as people kept looking at her children, suggesting they eat another. According to Glenn's version of the story Cliff was the first who made an attempt to go directly after one of the children, the eldest, a boy. The mother quickly stepped in front of him, stopping his momentum. He was dumbfounded at what to do; his mind had been so focused on his next meal being the boy that he could not comprehend the mother being in front of him. Jack then stood from behind her, looking Cliff in the eye, saying that the boy does not need to die for them to eat. He seemed to grab the mother in a embrace of solidarity before stabbing her in the back. Cliff apparently had smiled as she fell to the floor, a trickle of blood escaping from the corner of her mouth. The boy was ten and had tried to stop everyone from cutting her up to be cooked but was quickly subdued. Everyone ate that night and no one said a word against it. Glenn had his head lowered as he recounted all of this. The boy and girl were tied up in the room next to the main one. He said they were kept in a room without windows so there was less chance of them being able to run. A sinister chuckle escaped him as he said they were always fed parts of their mother before everyone else, often by force, so they could be strong for their turn to be on the spit. Often times when people engage in cannibalism for survival they avoid eating the parts that seem "too human"; the face, hands and feet. It partially makes sense as those are not meat-heavy parts of the body, but it is more of a psychological thing where people avoid feeling like they are eating a person. The children were fed those parts first; he remembers how he had tried to convince them that their mother's thumbs were chicken wings. It was a way to break their spirit I guess, to let them know they no longer had a protector. When they "were not hungry" Glenn said he would beat one child while telling the other to eat before reversing the target; when even that would not work they would take pieces of chewed meat and spit it into the mouths of the children, as a mother bird would feed its chicks. They soon enough stopped resisting. They did as they were told. It is a phenomenon called "Learned Helplessness" which is significantly different from "Stockholm Syndrome" which is a much more popular psychological problem. While Stockholm Syndrome has those that are captured by others adopt and join their oppressors Learned Helplessness is characterized by a complete loss of the will to fight. They learn they are helpless. Many years before the cataclysm, back when there was significantly less ethical oversight on experiments, a study had been done with rats. Essentially what was done was rats were held or wrapped up such that they could not get away. They were held that way until they became exhausted. This was repeated until the rat learned that there was no reason to keep struggling, it was helpless. The time it took for the rat to stop struggling became less and less until it learned to give up immediately and not even attempt to try to move or get away. This extended right to the end of the experiment where the rats were placed in a bucket of water and drowned. They had become so used to not struggling and trying to get away and survive that they just let the water envelope them and they died. The children ate. They complied and when it came time the boy simply walked in front of Cliff and waited for the slash across the throat that killed him. A week later the girl was up for sacrifice for the good of the group. Glenn recalled a savage scene as there were now bones, black from the fire, often broken to release the marrow, strewn around the main room that the group congregated in. The room with the fire. The had set themselves up in some sort of store, as if they were waiting for the next truck to arrive with a delivery of food; this was to never come. Another group had happened along as they were cooking the last of the girl; he figures they were attracted by the smell of meat being cooked. That same kind of ham smell that pervaded everything. How they were able to discern one from the other I will never understand. These were the final people needed to make the group of sixteen. They had feasted along with the others before they were told what they were eating. Glenn said a few seemed horrified the rest were just happy to have food in their bellies again. None complained. At this point Glenn said they began looking out the windows again; their place had come to seem more like a cave that a Neanderthal would inhabit as opposed to civilized people. He felt they were no longer looking for easy meals but instead looking for anyone that was alone. They began trying to lure people into traps. Or stalking those that were still alive and foraging for their own food. They only managed to catch one meal in that way before the troop decided it would survive best if they began hunting, following their prey. They followed behind one man walking outside the city, finally catching up to him some twenty miles outside the city. He was murdered by the 'hunting party' before being brought back to basecamp for the group. The next was some 10 miles past that again brought back to the group who lagged a few miles behind, all the while keeping a fire burning so they could begin cooking at any moment. They kept moving along the highway, until the scouts found a lone man walking along the highway. He seemed strange to them as he did not seem to be carrying all that he owned with him. He had a water bottle, a sweater tied around his waist, and nothing else really remarkable. They quickly came to the conclusion that he had a home. A camp. With more people. Glenn said they called us a "Smorgasbord". They many times had the chance to kill him and bring him back but instead they felt it was better to stalk him. Use him a way to definitively find the town. This was actually quite fortunate as he notes they would have missed the turn to find this town if they had just been going their own way. Once they had scoped the town and seen people moving within it they split to try to catch their prey before he entered the town but were too slow. Back-up plan was apparently to enter the town and try to eat from within. It was not until they were inside that most of them realized they could survive without killing people. Without murder. We had all they could want.

I had sat through this entire story, with my chin resting on my hands, trying to not let my personal feelings invade my thoughts. I was absolutely enthralled while simultaneously revolted. I said how many of your sixteen people did not partake in eating Roger's body. I turned to look at Robbie and Cliff hanging off behind me as he spoke; "Michelle and Ashley didn't eat." My teeth gritted as I glared at them. Both were frantically shaking their heads, bowing their knees as they tried to beg for their lives through the gags. "…and I think Brian was not there." That was it. The same three names I already had on my list as having not participated in the desecration of Roger. I stood and walked over to the two men hanging from the ceiling. Looking into each of their eyes, they shied away as if that would save them. I knew what it was; they hoped I was not going to return them to the hot seat for another turn.

Returning my attention to Glenn I began walking towards him. It was only a dozen or so steps from Robbie and Cliff to him but those were purposeful steps. I undid the vice from his finger; he seemed to have forgotten it was partially crushed until that point, he slowly shook his hand, wincing at the pain from his finger. "Gag him." I instructed the man behind him as I put his whole hand back into the vice. I twisted the lever as he bit into the gag between muffled screams. His fingers quickly turned purple as the blood vessels were all ruptured by the pressure. The bones in his hands were quickly reduced to a pile of jagged bone chips, all digging into the nerves in his hand. I stopped turning as I saw the skin on the back of his hand begin to split. He was unconscious at that point. "Take him over there" I pointed to the corner that was designated as where those I was done with would go. "And get Joe in here." I walked over to Jason who was standing near the stairs to the basement; yawning. I could see that he was getting to the limit of his alertness. I had not noticed that he had at some point returned to the basement to watch the interrogation, obviously it had been during Glenn's story which we were all absorbed in. I had been probably the most captivated. "Do you want to go to bed?" He shook his head 'no' while simultaneously shaking his head harder trying to wake himself up. "Well too bad. Tomorrow is going to be a long day I think. I got one more thing for you then you can go lay down for a few." Jason opened his mouth to argue before nodding and asking what I needed. I just mouthed a name while making a cut-throat gesture. He nodded and walked off. Jason at that point knew what I wanted. And man was he loyal. Not even a lick of real hesitation.

I could see light begin to start poking from around the towels that had been used as curtains in this basement. Those streaks of light told me that I had been interrogating for hours. I looked around at who else was in the basement with me as Joe was being dragged into the basement. He was still struggling until they tossed him down the stairs, likely dislocating a shoulder; his arm was sitting funny after the fall. William had been sitting off near the back corner of the room; I was unsure if he had been trying to just stay out of the way or if he was avoiding the interrogation. Either way I needed a rest so I waved him over. "Billy. Have you been listening to them?" He replied that he had. "Do you have any questions?" He shrugged. As I stood there waiting he could see that I was not going to just let it go at that, I wanted an answer. He shook his head. "Really? No questions? There are no gaps in the story?" He again shrugged. "For fucks sake spit it out!"

He leaned forward to whisper "I just wanted to know why they killed the kids." I clapped him on the back. That is a good question I told him. Joe was just sitting in the chair at this point. His hood was off so he was finally sitting in the light again. He was having trouble keeping his eyes open due to the brightness of the fluorescent bulb above him, for the first time that whole night I noticed the slight hum as the light flickered. I wheeled around while keeping my hand on William's back. I motioned towards Joe with my other hand. William looked like a deer caught in the headlights. Joe was still squinting and trying to open his eyes.

"Go ask him." William sighed then nodded. Joe was not able to tell him what he wanted to know, he had not been there until after the kids had been murdered but that was kind of irrelevant. The main point was I wanted him to be asking hard questions. I did have to keep goading William on as he kept turning to me saying that he did not think that Joe knew anything. It works the same as the psychological experiment concerning obedience. In short the point of the experiment was to show that if you have an authority figure who tells you to shock someone else every time they get a question wrong most people will "follow orders" right up to the point where they shock someone to death. This is despite the fact that they can hear someone screaming and each shock as they incrementally get higher and more deadly. In reality all the people that were getting shocked were just actors and the ones doing the shocking needed therapy when they saw how far they were willing to go in the name of obedience but that is what happens. That is how you can explain why the majority of Germany, a country of 80 million people, was willing to either participate in or tolerate systematic genocide. The Nazis and especially Hitler knew the value of playing on peoples need to obey. I was doing the same thing. Not that I am particularly proud of that but considering the fact I am making it overly apparent I guess could be construed as pride. Whenever I needed people I could trust and well making them feel like they have no choice but to obey pretty much is exactly what I needed to do.

Joe was the last interrogation of the night. I continued along with my regular schedule until approximately 10 in the morning when one of my good citizens came running up to the building I was teaching in. He huffed as he leaned against the door. Each breath he took he tried to start talking, each time there was nothing coming from him. "Calm down. Take a deep breath." He inhaled deeply. "Good. Now what is going on?" He began pointing towards the east.

"Someone was killed." He was distraught at this. I could see his hands begin to shake which he tried to cover up by wringing them together.

"Who was killed?" I remained calm, even-toned. This is the difficult thing about lying. In order to lie effectively you either need to believe what you are saying ("crazy" people are particularly adept at this one); you need to not care about the situation or you need to control yourself very well. Despite my earlier assertions that I was crazy I don't think I am crazy enough to qualify in this area, nor do I have lack of emotional investment in the situation which meant all I could do for the time-being is to just control myself. Play it cool.

"I don't know. Someone said it was Ashley. The brunette one. You know she was like short and her hair... was like at her shoulder. I- I don't know. I di- didn't see anything. God. What's going on?" He was starting to hyperventilate with wherever his mind was wandering to.

"Shhh." I hissed at him. "Remember to breathe. Kids we're done for today. We'll pick this up tomorrow." I waited as the kids walked out before I guided my panicked citizen over to one of the children's chairs. It probably wouldn't have helped his breathing to be sitting with his knees up near his chin but he was not going to be sitting that long regardless. "Ok. Tell me what do you know? What are people saying?"

"I don't know. I don't know why they sent me to get you. They saw her over at that guys place. The one... the guy... ummm..." I was losing him. He was getting himself all worked up and was not focusing. I snapped my fingers in front of his face; it seemed to snap him into reality. "Yeah. It was that guy. The guy that was an EMT. She is dead at his place." I nodded and helped him stand up.

Patting him on the back as we left the room I told him "You did good. Go get some rest. Or have something to eat." I walked over to the place where Ashley's body now was. I thought to myself today was going to be a very long day. My body tried to yawn repeatedly along the way. Each time I grit my teeth together, holding my mouth closed. I did not want anyone to think I had been awake all night. The town itself had a very different feel that morning though, and not just for me. And not just because of the fear of a mad killer on the loose. No, it was the lack of activity. There were definitely fewer people around. Whether everyone was crowded around Cliff's house or just sleeping in or hiding in their houses away from the boogieman I was not sure at that point. All I knew for certain was I was feeling alone again; I generally did not walk down a street without seeing someone in their garden, or walking to some job they had to do, or talking to a neighbor. It was odd.

Arriving at my destination I could see Jason standing at the front gate of the house. While I was initially upset at his not having gone to bed like I told him to I was feeling pretty good that things were going to fall into place. There were a few people standing on the street all asking him questions which he was calmly and politely telling them that "We'll get to the bottom of it." I strode past the group of people, getting close enough for him to whisper in my ear. "It's all set up, sir." I nodded and addressed the small crowd by asking them to return to their homes while we figured out what was going on. They all looked confused as they shrugged at each other and began walking back to their respective homes. Jason quickly ushered me in so he could go over the story he had concocted. In truth, it was kind of what I was thinking but I guess he had put a little more thought into it as my mind had been pre-occupied with other things. "I kind of took what they were saying and I made it look like they had taken someone to eat. She's over in the kitchen. I said to the people that I was walking by this morning and saw something strange; when I knocked on the door a bunch of people bolted out the front."

"Perfect. Get everyone you can to start telling people to lock their doors and stay inside. We'll start 'searching' the houses. Everyone can stay inside until tonight. That is when we will find our quarry and interrogate them. Sound plausible?"

Jason nodded and turned to walk out but paused at the door. "What are we going to do with them afterwards?" He spoke over his shoulder.

"Leave that to me, I have an idea." He nodded again as he left the house. I walked into the kitchen to see just what I was dealing with. What I would have to explain to my fair citizens. I was actually not prepared for what I saw. Jason had prepared an entire scene for anyone who came into see this. I could not tell how Ashley had died although I will venture a guess that he likely slit her throat. It looked as if someone had started butchering her and was interrupted in the act. Pretty much exactly the story he had relayed to me. She was in pieces. It was rather gruesome. I thought to myself that no one actually needed to see that; the fear was already going to spread through the town and I was going to be the savior who would deliver the people from the evil that had insidiously infiltrated them. At least that is what they were going to be told. None of the normal people would know any different. I walked to the hallway leading to the bedroom, looking for a linen closet. I was disappointed to open it as there did not seem to be anything of use in there. Cliff's bedroom was the next stop; I ripped the sheet of the mattress and brought it to the kitchen to cover up Ashley.

I had teams of men scour the town, entering every house, "looking" for the killers. The rumor mill was already putting out that Cliff's whole group was now missing. No one knew where they were. Every time a pair of men searched an occupied house 'for their safety' they retold the same stories to the occupants. Sensationalizing as much as they wanted. It is like that telephone game we used to play as kids where someone says something and after it gets passed from person to person down the line the story begins to change as people mishear it or simplify it or elaborate it or just outright lie. By the time the story made its way back to me Ashley was not the only one that was dead. There were 3 dead women; and they had already begun consuming them. A pot of woman stew was on the stove. A lampshade was made of skin. All lies but it helped the cause; hysteria was promoted. That night everyone in town went to bed afraid, sleeping behind locked doors. In the morning their fear was gone. We had 'caught' the killers. They were being interrogated as everyone was assured they could resume their normal activities.

At noon they were all paraded out to the center of town. It was apparent to all seeing them that they had been beaten and put through incredible amounts of pain. No one cared. They were booed. A couple of them tried to speak to the crowd through their gags. Things were thrown at them. I read to the people the 'charges' against them. Murder. Cannibalism. Rape. Theft. They had all 'confessed' I told the citizens. The shouts and jeers were wicked; the crowd demanded their heads. I waved at the crowd; trying to 'calm' them whilst at the same time trying to keep them riled up. When you are utilizing your 'monsters' to advance yourself you can't let them seem human; they need to remain as monsters. As vile things. As something evil. Bringing Glenn to the front of the accused I whispered into his ear; telling him that if he did not answer properly I would be making the past day seem like a summer camp compared to what I would do later. Addressing Glenn and the crowd I yelled "Glenn. Are all of these charges against you and your friends true?" He hesitated for the briefest of seconds. My heart skipped a beat. Then began emphatically moving his head in agreement that it was true. He began sobbing again and tried to beg forgiveness by dropping to his knees. William quickly swung something that looked like a broom handle at the back of Glenn head before grabbing him and dragging him to back with his friends.

The corpse eaters were all lined up under a tree at the side of the town center. Jason had prepared some nooses for them. Each was stood on a platform, had the noose put around their neck and were pushed. All broke their necks and died instantly except Michelle I think. She was a little too light. There is an actual formula for hanging people. It pretty much goes by weight; if you weigh X number of pounds then you need Y amount of rope. Too much rope for the weight and you can have the head literally pop off the body. That never happened with us, but it is a horrific concept. Too little rope for the weight of the person and you get this scenario; a girl kicking her feet, trying to breathe through a crushed windpipe. It took almost a full minute for her feet to stop twitching, not good but not a worst-case possibility, I have read of people who lasted many minutes hanging and more or less they just had to keep kicking until they were dead. These were likely the lucky ones. The people eaters had a much more dreadful fate awaiting them. And funny no one even seemed to notice that they were not among those being hung.

The end of the people eaters came outside of public view. Even the majority of my loyal people were not permitted to be around for this. Certain things can haunt people even if the person they are dealing with is reprehensible. So, they were kept out. I and Jason were the only ones present for the entirety. I think Jason was trying to prove to himself to me that he had as strong of a stomach as I did. Not that it was a competition. Each of the people eaters was, in turn, put into the back of a garbage truck that still had the hydraulics functioning. The others were chained up to watch as we slowly would move the ram door a few inches at a time. Some would try to move around inside the back of the garbage truck as if they could get away from being crushed. I know that is not it but people panic and in their terror they resort to acting on instinct. Like I mentioned before. There was no thought in their actions just futile attempts at self-preservation. Jack was first. He had not even gone through what the others had in terms of answering questions. The door closed on his left foot first; from inside the back of the truck you could hear ever so slight pops and cracks as he was crushed. His screams echoing in the hollow metal chamber. Joe followed. More of the same. Robbie tried to kick against us as he was grabbed to be thrown in the back. It did not help him. Even trying to crawl underneath the truck to freedom was not going to do anything. Jason had a firm grip on his belt and pulled him back out before hoisting him into the back. He was laying on top of the crushed remains of his two friends along with the garbage that had been sitting there prior to the cataclysm. I don't know if he just gave up or figured that going headfirst would be quicker but that was what happened. Glenn and Cliff were both put in, there was little fight left in either of them. It was a kind of rat in a bucket scenario. They just sat there, eyes closed as the door closed. There were still the echoing screams. I still hear those screams some nights while I try to sleep. Sleep rarely came those nights. I never spoke of this instance until now; it was my own burden to bear. I caused my own problems and I have accepted them.

CHAPTER 11 – A NEW GAME BOARD

I'm sure that you may be thinking that I am truly a sadist. I can neither confirm nor deny that sentiment. It is really based on your personal opinion of me. I will however say that I was greatly disturbed by the incident with the cannibals: not just what they did prior to entering Republica, after they entered by eating Roger and then stalking the residents or my actions towards them. It bothered me then and still does now. I will not make excuses for my actions, which would likely be deemed inexcusable as I went above and beyond seeking justice and was searching for a measure of revenge. Why I needed vengeance is hard to explain since I did not actually know Roger all that well, I did not have a personal stake in what happened to him after his death. The only thing that somewhat makes sense is wanting this place to be safe for those who remained, which obviously includes Aurora. There were a number of times I felt the safety and stability of my town was in jeopardy; we have already covered the creeper and cannibals. Those I feel are things that came from outside the community as the creeper was never part of the community and the cannibals had just tried to ingratiate themselves into the community before turning on us; in much the same manner as a cat that allows you to pet it for a few seconds before turning to hiss and scratch you. The other times it was members of the community, people who had embraced our values who turned on us. They were much more insidious. Much harder to deal with. It is difficult to punish someone that everyone in town has known for years. Someone that they ate with, talked to, joked with, recovered from hardships with. Not to say that it can not be done but it is considerably more difficult than making a demon out of a group of cannibals or a potential sexual predator.

I have dealt with a couple of potential revolts in my time. The first one, I think requires more explanation so, I will actually deal with it next but before that I will talk about the second revolt which was more of an 'almost'. If you could really call it that. This one barely ever got off the ground as it were. Now, the term salon has a different meaning now than it used to. Back prior to the French Revolution it was a meeting place for intellectuals; the first seeds of revolution against the monarchy were likely fomented in a salon, it was fostered and grown in other salons until it spilled out and took over the whole country. It led to not only the revolution which depending on your outlook was a good thing or a really bad thing. The revolution led to The Terror. Tens of thousands of French people were executed by the leaders of the revolution, I can not totally recall but I think it was called the Directorate. In any event that is not important, what is important is that those French people were guillotined for holding views contrary to those of the revolutionaries or just not being revolutionary enough. This happens really in any major shift in government. The Soviet Union had their purges throughout their history starting right from the Russian Civil war, Reds versus White. The Chinese communists had the Cultural Revolution which was kind of a backlash against the counter-revolutionaries. Even the United States of America had a bit of a backlash against the Loyalist faction that had supported the British during the War of Independence; I don't think it was to the extreme of the French, Russians or Chinese but it was still there. In any event, I brought up the original meaning of a salon because that is analogous to how the second revolt against me began. Discontent was whispered in the background. In back rooms. Among two or three people, expanding to five or six, then eventually it got up to a dozen people. In the grand scheme of things this was nothing to deal with, just some idealistic people that had no idea how to run a town, how to control people or how to maintain order. I had been a hero to all the citizens for what I did with the cannibals, as far as they knew I had just dealt with it, most did not know the extent to which we had 'dealt' with them. I proved to the people living here during that time that I had their best interests at heart and that sentiment carried over to the people that would arrive later on. Every new resident was given a tour of the town when they arrived; I was inevitably included on that tour as 'the saviour of the town'. Then as 'the benevolent leader'. Then just 'leader'. Then 'the guy in charge'. As time wears on people forget the good you have done and start to only remember the bad things. It is a "what-have-you-done-for-us-lately?" kind of thinking. And who can blame them. Making a home, cleaning it out, starting the gardens, getting rid of the cannibals, providing power, water, sanitation, a hospital and providing education to the children. All of those things I did. And once they became part of the expectations for the town they were taken for granted and in part forgotten. There were other things that I did for the good of the people like taking away the freedom to hunt whatever and whenever you like; the restriction on moving as you please; the controlling of every aspect of people's lives; those things persist long past the incidents that precipitated them.

This almost revolt began due to a woman named Nichola; although she generally went by Nixi. This was a girl who was what I would consider to be, a born-again hippie. She was Caucasian, had long brown hair that was done up in dreadlocks. She wore glasses which the frames had long since broken so she had fashioned her own frames out of some sort of stiff wiring. She was quite industrious; her clothes were all-natural fibers that she had managed to weave and sew-together herself before she ever came here. Her shoes were made of hemp, one of apparently a half dozen pairs that she had bought years beforehand, the soles upon wearing out had been replaced by recycled radial tire tread. Very industrious. Very useful in many aspects. But also entitled, privileged and idealistic. I recall a time shortly after she arrived in my town that I talked to her while on my walk around town as she tended to her garden. She spoke of how she had been protesting against climate change, globalization, government being too conservative and invasive in people's lives. She had also lamented that she had been too young to be at the Occupy Wall Street protests but had wanted to join them. Now I say that she was entitled, privileged and idealistic not necessarily meaning to denigrate her but more of showing that she was in fact very wrong about things. As much as I was completely willing to give to the community my time, blood, sweat and tears I did not do it simply because I wanted to. I lead by example. I expect people to contribute to the community as a whole and I feel that while things like electricity, water, sanitation, etc. should all be things that we expect as "modern people" those are not things that are "free". I know I am repeating myself, but we don't have an economy based on currency; things only have as much value as they intrinsically have. A piece of paper or a small metal disc; no value anymore. Food, clothes, tools, fuel, services; and a slew of other things I can not even think of right now are all much more valuable because people can use them. Education, has obvious value as well. And I am not just saying that because I am the one who primarily did the teaching but because it is the truth. Thinking towards the future: if we did not bother with keeping up simple standards of education then what happens when the doctor gets ill or dies? What about the plumber? Electrician? Those are all easy examples of people that are very important and while not irreplaceable do require knowledge and an ability to learn in order to be replaced. Even with the program for apprenticeship that I had put in place there were still problems. For example, when Roger died he was in the midst of teaching an apprentice, but he was not done, that apprentice had not learned all he needed to know. While there were other people who could help instruct the apprentice on some of those things he had not been taught; the remainder of lessons he needed to learn they did not know how to do properly. So our choice was for a collection of people to try to muddle through something and proceed by trial and error or finding another means to learn how to do something. In this particular instance it is a fairly easy solution; obtain a "do-it-yourself" book that deals with things like construction and maintenance and learn by reading it. Well to the best of my knowledge there is not a real Entire-Electrical-Grid-for Dummies book. Or a viable Home Dentistry Manual. Or a Do-It-Yourself-Heart-Surgery book. Learning from a book is useful but experience and hands-on learning is just as important. That is what the apprenticeship was meant to do. And without the basics of education even if those manuals did exist they could be useless if the guy can not read the book.

Now here is where the problem came up with Nixi. When talking of employment sometimes people got to do the things they wanted or were trained to do; other times they were essentially "volun-told" what they would be doing. Believe me; I know this is not always the best solution however necessary in some ways. Take Jason for example, he was working as a miner before the cataclysm. This was not a profession that we needed after the flare so he was made to adapt. When he is not doing things for me as leader of the community he works as a mechanic. Something he had a little bit of experience with but really had next to no interest in doing, however it was necessary, so he did it for the good of the town. Thanks to him we have a number of serviceable vehicles that can be used when we need to do heavier things like moving equipment or lumber for building, those kinds of things. Nixi due to her overall ingenuity was utilized making clothes. Fashioning shoes. Knitting. Sewing. All those kinds of activities. Maybe her growing dissatisfaction is really our fault as we essentially thrust her into a sewing circle. Although I always believe that people need to take responsibility for their own actions meaning that regardless of what was done to her in this regard there was another way she could have been dealt with the whole situation. Although in this case I think it would be easier to just blame her parents. She rebelled against her parents although they never stopped giving her money and allowing her to live as she pleased and Nixi never stopped taking money from them. They were apparently very well off which permitted her to never have to work a day in her life. Up until the cataclysm, then everything changed. The game, the pieces, the board, the table everything is played on and the players themselves.

She began foraging near the place she had been living, eventually having to branch out to the nearby wilderness to try to survive. Nixi had been living in a forest for years, alone. She sustained herself by eating berries, whatever other edible plants she could find and some insects. It was not what you could call a luxurious diet. Nixi had an admirable drive to survive; by the time she became introduced to us she was emaciated and filthy. She was managing to survive, in a sense, as she had lived for years in that manner however she was near starvation by the time she happened upon one of our people while he out on a permitted hunt for meat. The clothes she had been wearing when the cataclysm happened had long since wasted away and fallen apart; being replaced by clothes that she had stockpiled before the end. She had made large purchases of natural cloth, bolts upon bolts of hemp, wool and cotton cloth that she had planned to fashion into her own line of natural hippy clothes. The clothes she was wearing when she was found allowed her to be perfectly camouflaged; it was all dirty earth-tones; what had previously been a dark green hemp cloth now looked more like a military styled camouflage shirt. She was able to blend into the surroundings almost perfectly such that she was nearly shot by accident. She was spotted while eating the few berries off a bush. According to any hunter safety course you ever take there is a huge problem with looking for prey through the scope of a rifle. It narrows your view. You get tunnel vision, pretty much literally. That is how she was almost shot, the one who found her saw movement and fired. Luckily for her, he was a piss-poor shot and missed; unluckily for the community as a whole he was a piss-poor shot and rarely brought anything edible back. As the round whizzed past her head she turned to look at her shooter; he saw the whites of her eyes at that moment. Her eyes were massive and filled with fear. And that was totally justified, pretty much any sane person would be afraid at that. When the hunter ran up to her he began apologizing profusely. As he neared he noticed that Nixi was frozen in place, standing in a puddle of piss, berries half chewed in her mouth, juice still on her fingers. She apparently was near catatonic and did not talk the entire time he was bringing her back to town. I guess it was fortunate for her that he was not the kind of guy who would take advantage of someone in that state.

Nixi arrived here and began to integrate into the community for around 2 years or so before she started gossiping and complaining behind closed doors with the other malcontents. That is likely not accurate, as I am sure she was gossiping before that but it only came to a head and to my attention at around the 2 year mark of her living here. From the reports I got, Nixi began complaining to a woman named Rita as they worked making clothes for the inhabitants of the town. The original complaint was that there was too much power in my hands. I made people do what I wanted with no concern for what they wanted. Nixi did not want to make clothes, she felt that she should be in charge of the town; it was I that had forced her into a life of making clothes and shoes. I can say that in all fairness when she arrived in town she was just as qualified to run the town as I was. Before my arrival here I had never run a city government. She was just as qualified in that sense; however, by the time she arrived I had been doing this a considerable amount of time and I had dealt with all the things I have already mentioned. I did the things that she was actually espousing like making things equal for people, ensuring that everyone was healthy, had food, had as much of the modern experience that was possible after the end of the world. Her real issue was with being a mere cog in the machine as opposed to the operator of it. I can get that, it makes sense. No one craves to have a life of mediocrity but there is a difference in what I did to become the leader and what she was trying to do. I was moved into this position by strength of will, by perseverance, by popular demand and by being here first. There was a problem with her aspirations and it was not just that there was already someone doing the job that she coveted. While I was not necessarily "qualified" for the job I was willing to learn new things. I was willing to work as hard as I expected everyone else to work. I allowed people to play to their strengths; we moved people into positions and apprenticeships based on what they already knew, had an interest for or had an aptitude for. Her plan was really to become the entitled little daddy's girl who gets all she wants handed to her without having to work for it. Like the trust fund her parents had set up for her all those years ago. Before money and banks became useless.

Margarita better known as Rita was an older Filipino woman who had been stranded in the basement of an office building she had been in working the night shift as a cleaner. As the flare appeared over the horizon that last morning of civilization she took cover in the only place that she felt was dark and dank enough to avoid the sun. Luckily for her it worked. The cement and steel of the underground parkade coupled with the glass and steel of the high rise above her provided all she needed to live. It was her and 3 other overnight employees that survived the flare. Like everyone who found themselves in the city after the dust settled she soon came to realize that the city was not a place to try to rebuild. Cities are a mark of civilization; burned-out cities are the mark of the apocalypse. She knew where she was. To her, being in a 'dead city' felt as though she was living in a modern Sodom or Gomorrah. The skyscrapers were just pillars of salt. In her mind everything that had happened was God's retribution for our sins. It was what was foretold in Revelations. The world had been wiped clean in preparation for the second coming of Christ. I was never honestly all that clear on the writings from the Bible but to me it seemed as though Rita had been kind of interpreting the writings in a manner that suited her beliefs and conclusions. It's fine. She had the right to her beliefs. And a healthy dose of religion is always nice for a person like me; if I play things right I can come off looking like the second coming of Christ. I did not do that so well; I ended up looking more like King Herod to her but some things just can not be helped. Not that I had a desire to be the next Christ. While I was trying to remake a world in the best way I could, I ultimately was not trying to become the poster child of a religion. I am just a person. In my opinion the best person in decades but that is just my opinion. Also, Christ is a very curious title anyways. Not only Christians but other people as well had gotten into the habit of calling him Jesus Christ when that was not his name. If anything, he would have been Jesus of Nazareth or Jesus of Bethlehem. Christ means "the Anointed One" so really when people were calling him Jesus Christ they were actually saying Jesus the Anointed One. It just annoyed me that people acted as if it was a name when it was not. And that does not even bring into play the other possible discussion regarding Jesus' name; which was that Jesus was not an actual name used in Judea around the time of his supposed birth, meaning that his name was likely something closer to like Joshua which over time was distorted into Jesus. Regardless this is me getting off track again. Rita along with two of the other survivors who came with her were actually some of the first people who found their way into the town. When she arrived, tired, hungry and despondent, she initially praised me as a great man. She prayed in the church, thanking God for bringing her here. She prayed even though it was no longer a church per se. The pews were firewood and replaced with more comfortable furniture. There is no reason you can't pray from a leather couch apparently.

Nixi and Rita were some of the people who would make and repair clothes for the people in the town. Most of the people who were our seamstresses tended to do their work alone and bring the finished products to the warehouse where they would be distributed to the masses at-large. Nixi and Rita were neighbours, doing the same job, so naturally they came together to tackle bigger projects, to work as more of an assembly line as well there was a need to socialize while working. There was nothing wrong with this for almost two years. Then it began to be noticed that Rita's companion, Manuel, began shirking his other responsibilities to the town as the electrical engineer in charge of the water wheel. Not that it really needs constant attention. He should still have been making sure that things were running smoothly. He did this in order to spend more time with Rita and Nixi. This trio was soon joined by another person. And another. Soon we had an entire sewing circle. A group of half a dozen people meeting was not something to be concerned about but it was the contents of their discussions that began to concern me. It was just little things about not liking how things ran. Conspiracies about what I had done. What I made others do. There was a rumour among these people that I was in fact a cannibal and had eliminated the other cannibals due to not wanting competition. To not wanting to share. And not wanting my secret to come out. That was not true of course.

Even complaints and conspiracy theories are not a huge concern. It was when the tone of the Nixi's rants turned towards 'gaining support', finding a way to get rid of the tyrant and installing someone better in charge that my interest was piqued. I always used to make jokes before the cataclysm when there was drama in whatever workplace that I was in that "my spy network was better than your spy network", with the 'your' being whoever I was talking to at the time. And that was usually true, I always tended to know a lot even though I was not part of the drama. It was a hard tightrope to walk in order to be informed of everything, usually from both sides of the drama, without being sucked into it but I somehow managed. Don't ask me how, I don't think I could describe in a manner that anyone would be able to replicate it. At the time of Nixi's mounting insurrection I, in truth, had a better spy network because I actually had one. Nowhere near the extent you would expect from MI5, the KGB, the CIA or the Gestapo but it was there. Although when you consider the fact of how few people we had in the town you could actually say that I had a more massive spy network. In a place small enough for everybody to know everybody having even a few spies is very handy. Having a person come right up to me and say "Nixi is saying this and that" really allows you to deal with things head on.

By the time her little backroom sewing circle had reached fourteen people I was actually in control of three of those members. They were told to be quiet, observe and not help or hurt the movement being grown by the people who were there of their volition. Just observe I kept saying. Do nothing and report to me. Each had their own method of getting what they knew to me. One would leave a letter in a 'dead drop' every couple of nights. A dead drop being a hiding spot where someone will just leave something to be picked up later by someone else who is also aware of the hiding spot. Ours was a hollowed-out board on a park bench that I would occasionally stop by while on my rounds of the town. Another method of communicating was one of my spies would bring snacks to the children in class each day, during which we would have a brief 'what's-going-on' chat which tended to look more like flirting than anything as the kids ate their cookies or apples or whatever. My third spy was the best while simultaneously the worst. She would simply stop me in the street whenever she saw me. Her information seemed to be the most complete and useful. She seemed to know nothing of subtlety. It was always my belief that she was one of those gossip-monsters that every workplace seemed to have. She needed to be in the drama and would even create it if it was not there. If I had only been getting information from one of these sources, I might have had an interest but not particularly cared. It would have seemed insignificant but having 3 spies all reporting the same thing meant that I had to at least take it a little seriously.

This went on for weeks. Each report said the same thing. 'Nixi wanted to take him down'. 'Nixi should be in charge, things would be different'. 'We need to get more people in here.' 'We should make our move.' I was not certain if what I was hearing was something real or not. I mean could some little girl barely out of her twenties be so conceited to think that she had the solutions? Apparently so. But for a while I was skeptical, I thought there was a possibility that Nixi was just not liked to the point that other women had begun to try to make her into an enemy. This is a common thing with females; while males tend to show actual aggression to each other when there are disputes females tend to use covert bullying or social aggression as a way of hurting and ostracizing other females; socially taking them out of a group or using an entire group to harass and bully a disliked peer. The more I watched and waited the less this seemed to be the case, Nixi really was trying to garner support for herself in some sort of play for power. It was cute. A group of seamstresses with a couple of other people are not the kind of people that you would expect to be leading a revolt. Not a successful one at least.

After three weeks of reports Nixi did not seem to be slowing down on her rhetoric and had even seemingly been gathering some more support as she had been hoping so hard to do. It became apparent that I would need to take action to nip this in the bud. Over time I would say that I mellowed in not just my outlook but also my response. For good or for bad. Nixi was a focus of the attention now directed to this group although I do not believe that most of them had any kind of a clue that they were the focus of anything. The least of all was Nixi. She seemed to have blinders on; she believed that she was a genius and was pulling the wool over everyone's eyes while lining herself up to be the next leader of Republica. In my mind normally, I would respond by assuming that this whole uprising was some sort of hydra that had to be dealt with by killing the body as well as the heads. But alas three weeks of notes and flirty discussions told me this was just a snake; a small weak snake at that. You can cut the head off this and the whole thing will die with barely a twitch of the tail. Simple and direct.

It was a brisk autumn morning that I took my usual walk around the town. Looking at gardens ready to be harvested. Talking to the random resident here and there, mostly about the weather and our guesses on the severity of the coming winter. I would likely classify this day as being a sauntering type of day; I had a purpose and a place to be however I was not in a particular rush. I passed Artie as he was leaving his house to go to the warehouse that we stored things in. He was a clerk; a really nice guy although he did seem kind of dim at times but was steadfast in his dedication to his work. He worked even on a day like today when no one else was working. It was a Sunday. And he was happy to do it. There was nothing to complain about from my end, if he wants to spend his spare time cleaning a warehouse or reorganizing things that it totally his prerogative. I nodded an acknowledgment of him as he returned the favor. In the years that I 'knew' him this was our usual interaction; I think we had only exchanged five words in all that time. Next, I saw Mrs. Rose and waved to her as I strode by; she was an older woman who had a simple grandmotherly feel to her. She has since passed on, which is unfortunate as she was a sweetheart, just as she had often referred to everyone who came to her house. The cataclysm seemed to have almost not affected her; she always had some form of baking waiting for her visitors, a pot of tea ready to be put on, and a smile. Mrs. Rose sat on her porch, gently rocking in her chair as she sipped her tea out of a wonderful little tea set. I remember remarking to her once while I visited with her that she made the best tea I had tasted in years. That was true; it had been years since I had tea before that but more so it could likely have been the best tea I had ever had. I probably should have asked what she used to make her tea with before she died but no one had expected her to die; she had been the second oldest person in town but always seemed so full of life and vitality that no one saw the heartache that killed her coming. Last before reaching my destination was Suzanne, a young girl at that point of roughly 10. She had come to the town with her mother and aunt. All three had suffered from severe sunburns although they all managed to recover from them with only slight scarring. Suzanne was very conscious of her scars meaning that the cooler weather that presented itself in the fall was welcome as she was now able to keep her shoulders and legs covered without being overwhelmed by the summer heat. I smiled at Suzie, reminding her we had school tomorrow and she should have her homework done. She giggled and laughed saying 'she knew' before smiling back at me with that giant gap where her two front teeth had been. Her homework was not done by the way. I only frowned at her when she said it was not done. Kids sometimes get to just be kids.

Along the way I had passed by Nixi's house. I had barely paid attention; it had not been my destination. I was walking to what had been the only mechanical shop we still had in town. To see Jason. It is becoming very plain to see that Jason was my go-to guy for any matter that needed to be dealt with. This was much the same as other times that I had needed his help; his discretion and loyalty are indispensable. I walked into the front of the shop as he was under a truck draining the oil. Grabbing a wrench from the nearby bench I tapped a barrel containing some sort of fluid, this was our signal that we needed to talk. It was a quick interaction. "Do you know who Nixi is?"

"Dreadlocks. Brunette. Smells like BO. Nice big tits." He made the gesture for breasts as a smirk slipped across his face. Jason knows I am not particularly a fan of crude talk but does also know that I do have a sense of humor, even if I don't show it all that often.

I sigh at his attempt to be funny. "I never noticed her tits but yes that is her." His eyebrow cocked up as he gauged if I was just being funny or if I was playing coy. He quickly came to the conclusion I was joking and the smirk got wider. I had noticed her chest; it was nothing special.

"I need you to bag her tonight. Quietly." A pause as I tried to think of her block. "Which basement nearby would be empty?"

Jason's little hamster-wheel began turning as he also thought of her house. "Um. The gray house. Shit... wait... no- that guy from down south just got put there. Maybe the house with the missing front stairs, but I don't know if it has a basement. There is always the dark house." Dark house being the euphemism we began to use after the cannibal incident to refer to the house that we had used for the interrogations. "It is not that far away."

"Not really what I have planned for tonight.... On second thought. Do that, I'll be there at midnight." Jason nodded as I turned to walk out. We had a plan and I was going to resolve this little hiccup. "Oh, and disarray please."

That day was an unsettling day for me. I had an entire day to role-play things in my head although I knew there was no urgency. It was still difficult to get the thoughts out of my head. My mind always returned back to things like Robbie, when my emotions had gotten the better of me. I do not particularly like that feeling. Not being in control is out of the ordinary for me. My wanderings around town had me come to the edge of town three times that day; my mind was so engrossed in thought. It would seem that I was anticipating this as something that I was beginning to look forward to. Had I become a person that was no longer able to be compassionate? Was everything truly this black and white? Where had I gone wrong? The answers are no, no and nowhere. I was fine I kept telling myself. I had a plan and it would work. A snake without a head is nothing but a tube of meat. That sounds rather dirty but it is fairly accurate. Also, it is funny; I'm just going to leave that here.

As night fell I stood on the steps of my house listening to the crickets and other creatures of the night. They had long since rebounded to what were probably their pre-cataclysm levels although I am by no means an expert on bug and bat populations. Nixi was brought to the dark house as expected, arriving a few minutes before midnight. She had the customary black cloth bag over her head and a man on each arm, dragging her limp body down the stairs. She was conscious; I could hear her gasping against the gag in her mouth. Jason and Jack swung her around before dropping her in the chair and tying her wrists to the armrests. This is obviously a different Jack than the cannibal one; he had already died by this point. "Disarrayed?" I said looking at Jason. He nodded and mouthed 'of course'. A half smile across my face as I pointed him and Jack off to the dark corner of the room, out of sight. Pulling off the hood I stood in front of Nixi as her eyes began to adjust to the light. I looked at the t-shirt she was wearing, a pair of underwear barely visible underneath. "I see we must have gotten you at a bad time. Were you already in bed?" I pull the gag out of her mouth. There was blood on the cloth meaning that either she does not floss as much as she should, or they were a little rough on her. She works her jaw back into place before she answers.

"I was sleeping. What is going on? Who are you?" It occurred to me that her eyesight was probably poor enough that she truly needed her glasses to be able to even see someone two feet in front of her. She was squinting trying to get something to come into focus for her.

Leaning in closer to her. "Well it would seem that you have a real problem with me. You think you should be in charge. I hear that you and your friends are going to kill me and replace me with someone else. Someone like you." Even if she could not see me Nixi definitely knew who was talking now.

"I- I- I-." and she trailed off. I really hoped this was not going to be a blubbering discussion, those are so not helpful.

"Well here is your chance." I began. "Tell me what are you going to do better?" She said nothing. "You are going to make things better for people here? Give them food? I have already done that. I gave them electricity, we have a hospital, and we have antibiotics because of me. What else? What else are you going to do for people here?" She still said nothing. "What did you mean by you are going to 'take me down'? Do you think that people will support you? I am the one who saved them from the cannibal clan, I made this place out of a shell of a town and now look at it thrive. You haven't done shit except make people some new shoes."

"But you can't keep running people's lives." She finally spoke. And what a poor way of starting to try to defend her view point. Telling the leader that he cannot be running the lives of the people in the town. Asinine.

"What the fuck are you talking about?"

"You tell people where they can live, what they do, how they do it, what they can eat. It is their life. You have no righ…." I was now nose to nose with her and she trailed off.

"I am going to make this exceedingly clear for you, I saved this place and I have given everyone living here a chance to return to civilization. That being said, I will not have you saying another word against me. So, let me make this easy for you. When this morning is over you will return to your house. You will go back to work, you will say nothing of tonight nor will you repeat any of the things you have said in the past regarding the leadership in this town. This is my town, I built it and I will decide who gets to stay in it. If I hear one word. One fucking word, and I mean *one, fucking, word,* about what is wrong with this place or about getting a new leader from you or any of the people who come to see you daily I am going to have your tongue cut out of your head, I will use red-hot pincers to take off your nose and I will personally crush your feet with a sledgehammer. Nod if you understand!" She nods furiously, as anyone would. "Here is what is going to happen. You will be telling everyone; Rita, Manuel, the Sams (a girl and a guy) and all the others that come to your place that you do not want them there and you think you were wrong. Am I understood?"

"Yes. Yes. Yes." She begins to cry. I put the gag back into her mouth and bag her again.

Talking to Jack and Jason who are at this point playing cards on the table in to corner. "Leave her there for now. She can think about what she has been told. She can go home at dusk."

"K. We'll do that." I left them there and returned home. Another night of inadequate sleep. There was a commotion although only talked about in hushed tones that morning as Rita and others all arrived at Nixi's house only to find that it had been trashed. Nothing broken but the house had been tossed. Put into disarray. Every one of them was in their house, looking out the window, checking to see who is walking by or what those sounds are. Nixi came back that evening and never spoke a word of what had happened. From all accounts she said nothing of where she really was all day, I think she had lied to tell people she was out for a walk and got lost for a day, so they would stop asking. The whole issue was not mentioned again until very recently.

CHAPTER 12 – NUMBER FIVE

Jason returned to Republica two days after he had left. I took longer than I had anticipated, meaning that he had returned before me. I likely made quite an impression on him as I returned to town driving a military styled truck; full of all types of useful items from solar panels to guns and ammunition to various plants and seeds, tools, jugs of fuel and a "water generator" which is really just a glorified dehumidifier. As well there was the trailer with the various animals I was bringing with me. With the exception of the chickens who needed to be a little more contained, the remainder were allowed to roam around in the field by the school. More than enough grass for them to graze on and no need to start putting up fences, they were already there, I just had to close up the gates. That was only for the time, later they were moved to the approximately six acre 'yard' that laid behind one of the big houses on the west side of town, the one that I finally decided I would appropriate as my new home.

Jason's return home had been disappointing for him. He entered his parents' house only to find the kind of thing that he wished he did not see. He thinks his father was likely sick when everything turned to shit as he was laying in his bed, in the pajamas that he had called his 'sick PJs'; they were supposed to have been some sort of ugly puke-green looking things. Jason's father's mouth seemed to have been left wide open as if he was screaming, although that was actually fairly common, muscles relax upon death moving to a relaxed position meaning that the mouth would gape. On top of that you add in the cooking aspect to the 'meat' of his father and you have a permanent scream on his face. He said months later while we were discussing something random that that was all he could remember about his father. Not his voice, laugh, posture, old sayings or sense of humor. Only the screaming face. Jason's mother had been walking from the kitchen to the bedroom; he assumed either moving in response to his father's pained moans as he was being cooked or her own realization of what was going on and her attempt to be by his side as they met their end. Jason preferred that option as it sounded more romantic. When he told me the story I affirmed that was the more likely answer, it seemed to comfort him to hear that. Jason spent his first full day after returning to his hometown digging graves for his parents in their backyard, he thought since they had lived there since they got married they should remain there, in that place together. He laid them in the same grave, arranged them as if they were holding hands. He had intended to dress them in their wedding attire however the state of their bodies did not allow for that so he simply used his father's suit and mother's wedding dress like shrouds. Their Papillion, Maxie, they had had for the last 10 years was laid at their feet; he had been lying beside his father, protecting him until the last. He told everyone in Republica at that time about how he had tried to give them a proper burial, like they would have wanted. He recited all the prayers that he could remember went into a funeral. He cried as he worried he had not remembered the right things; he felt he probably disappointed his mother. Having Lisa there in that instance was very helpful as, in all honesty, I was still too macho to be of much help consoling him. At that point I was likely fairly numb anyways. There had been nothing but death around since the cataclysm. It really did not even occur to me at the time that he would need consoling, not until Lisa walked around the campfire to hug him. In all fairness though I was not the only one; not the only man I mean. Jason's visit to bury his parents had not been a total loss; he brought our next citizen, Flynn Hardel.

I will admit, I did not take an instant liking to Flynn; Jason had known him for years, so he was not operating on first impressions. There was nothing that I was able to pinpoint as being the problem, it was more of he was just one of those people that rubs you the wrong way. I have had more than enough time over the years to really delve into my memories and see the things that I either missed or dismissed when it happened. For example, when I first rolled up into town with my truck, cargo and animals, Flynn had been laying out sun tanning. Not a crime however when Jason, Lisa and Aurora are all working, well, you should likely know my opinion on this matter by now. I was displeased with him from the outset. He did help unload the vehicle and herd the animals to where they needed to be but it took some prodding. Prodding to him, not the animals, they were pretty well behaved considering I had left them alone for a while, well maybe a little cranky.

My first conversation with Flynn, which I understand was likely a repeat from the conversation he had had with Jason, Lisa and Aurora the night before, seemed to be full of holes. He held things back. In hindsight, that likely meant that where he survived was where someone else would have survived; if he had not taken it for himself. He likely hurt someone else to survive. There is no need to point out that I am no saint in this regard, I could have done better myself. It is still a little distressing from my standpoint. I did not go out and attack someone for anything, I just defended my home. Semantics though. But it was not just that but everything, he avoided every question; deflection after deflection; evasion, defensiveness. What did he do before? I did not learn until months later that he had been a warehouse clerk at a grocery store. Did he have any brothers or sisters? Again, months before finding out he had three younger half-sisters; his mother had remarried and had more kids. He apparently did not have many interactions with them as he was already in high school when his mother remarried. Flynn was a 'stoner' who preferred to live in his mother's basement, playing video games like Call of Duty or whatever. He only had one real girlfriend when he was in high school and not much since. Flynn was in all seriousness not the kind of person I would have associated with pre-cataclysm; we were opposite ends of the spectrum I think, different values that we both clung to.

Most of what I knew of Flynn came from Jason; they had been friends since they were both in Grade four. They had lived down the street from each other and had known of one another for their entire lives but it had apparently been not the friendliest of relationships. There were various play dates that their parents had arranged that had led to fights and stealing of toys and whatever other little insignificant things that kids under the age of 10 find truly important. I was told during one random conversation about how Jason had taken the sand from the sandbox in the kindergarten classroom and put it all over everything that Flynn had. His shoes, his lunch, a painting he was making for his mother, the blanket he used during naptime. Jason chuckled hard as he told this story. It was not what he had done which tickled him so, but rather Flynn's response. First: there was a block thrown in his direction from across the room however Flynn's aim was less than stellar and he missed. Next: Flynn tried to retaliate by getting a girl in the class with them to kiss Jason; a truly horrible punishment if I ever heard one. Jason and the girl were apparently boyfriend & girlfriend for the rest of that year. Another failed attempt. There were two or three more that I cannot remember, the last one, the final successful one was Flynn took Jason's shoes and slathered them in glue, sticking them rather securely to the shelf that they sat on during the school day. Flynn was also not too careful with what he was doing so there were further things that were covered in glue; most notably was Jason's left jacket sleeve which was apparently almost permanently formed to remain straight. Jason said it took his mother many washes to finally get the sleeve to not be 'crunchy'. The funniest part to all this is Jason was blamed for sticking his own shoes to the shelf. The teacher thought he was the one who covered his jacket in glue. He was labeled a problem child by the school, given some sort of counselor, almost held back in kindergarten to give him more of an opportunity to adjust to being in school. Jason is telling me this story, almost in tears as he described his not understanding at the time what was going on, he remembers that when he had found his shoes stuck to the shelf he had actually been scared, he thought he was getting weaker. And all through that Flynn had been sitting quietly in the background, drinking from a juice box, smiling quietly to himself. He had won in his mind. Jason discovered all about this when they were in junior high together. They had been talking with other friends about the best pranks they had ever pulled. That was Flynn's example; he recited everything he had done, plus a few things that Jason did not even know had occurred. All the while Jason listened to the story. He said he had been plotting his revenge but he never did tell me how he got his revenge, if he did at all. At the end of Flynn's riveting tale their entire social circle was spellbound which was only broken by Jason's loud "That was me you did that to, you asshole!" Flynn had forgotten. The event was more important to him than the revenge I'd say. That was kind of a good example of the tone of their relationship until they actually became friends.

When they were both in grade four they were for the first time in separate classrooms. Jason was with Mrs. Engret; by his account a pleasant older woman who had a very grandmotherly feel about her. Flynn was with Mrs. Durst, a woman who was younger but in his opinion someone who was already bitter and jaded and probably should never have been a teacher. Her manner with her students was less than pleasant as she would often berate children who spoke out of turn or gave wrong answers. Jason's seat at the back of Mrs. Engret's room had allowed him to hear the yells coming through the wall from the other room. It was in that environment that Flynn's spirit had broken a little, something that had extended out into the playground. A day in late fall, just before winter, proved to be the faithful day for Jason and Flynn. At the time Flynn was a smaller child, 'weasel-like' in Jason's rendering, who began to be picked on by some of the larger children in the school. Especially "the" bully at the school. From the portrayal of him and the whole situation given to me by Jason this bully was a composite of every bully you have ever seen in TV shows or movies. Like he was a composite taking a little bit of Nelson from the Simpsons, a little Bif from Back to the Future, Stelio Kontos from American Dad, the bullies from Christmas Story and whoever else you can think of. He was overall a dick, preying on the weaker kids; as bullies are wont to do. On this particular day something set Jason over the edge at the sight of this, he was not able to tell me what it was exactly, but the final straw before he was seeing red was the sight of Flynn being pushed facedown into a puddle of dirty brackish water. Jason descended down a slide from the top of the play structure before rounding the corner to where Flynn and the bully were. Flynn was sobbing; tears mixing with the mud on his face, leaving slight streaks of clean among the dirt smeared across his face. Jason stood behind the grade sixer before shoving him into the puddle himself. The bully, who was now suddenly furious, spun around to see who had done such a thing to him. Like any schoolyard fight this one action immediately attracted the attention of everyone within the playground. Shouts of 'Fight Fight Fight' rang out as the two began to square off. Jason said that he barely remembered all of this happening, he could only really recall bits and pieces, and it was Flynn who later regaled him with the full scope of his exploits. The bully who being two years older towered (by schoolyard standards) over Jason however he stood his ground. A punch thrown by the bully was dodged. He stood there, letting whatever rage was within him build. The second punch thrown by the bully met its mark but at that point Jason had steeled himself for the onslaught. What he thinks was probably a full power shot from the bully barely turned his head. The bully's eyes opened wide as he was tackled by Jason; there was a splash of water with every punch he threw at the bully's face as the back of his head was thrown into the puddle. After three punches there was blood all over his hand as the bully's nose began to pour blood. By the eighth punch the bully was not even trying to fight anymore, he was out cold, his left arm held tensely out to his side. By the twelfth punch other kids were trying to pull Jason off. He kept throwing punches until enough had grabbed him to pull him away. He struggled against them trying to hold him back as he saw the bully begin to rise. He was on his hands and knees before putting a foot flat to begin to stand. Jason broke through the grip of the other children only to latch himself onto the back of the bully. He tried to squeeze as hard as he could with his arm wrapped around the much larger neck of the bully. More struggling from beneath him; frantic clawing at his hands, little gasps escaping from beside his ear as the bully was taking his last breaths. He became aware of kicks on his back as the other students were now trying desperately to get him to stop. Trying to end the fight they had cheered for only moments prior. They were trying to stop a schoolyard murder. Jason could feel the pulse under his forearm begin to slow. Growing weaker. He did not even care, he just kept trying to squeeze. There was suddenly a voice in his ear. 'Jason! Jason! Stop it! Let go!' A gentle hand inserted itself in between his face and the back of the bully's head. It seemed to smell of his Nana. Mrs. Engret. She had the same perfume as his grandmother. He let go. The bully instantly fell back to the ground; coughing and gasping for every breath. Sobs punctuated every few breaths. He knew he was lucky to be breathing at that moment. Jason began to cry as well; all the anger and rage that had just been powering him was gone; he was left feeling emotionally drained. Physically exhausted. He walked to the principal's office under the watchful eye of Mrs. Engret, each step rigid, almost disjointed from the last, as if he had forgotten how to walk. Jason was suspended for two weeks. The bully's father came to the school to demand that Jason be expelled completely although that quickly changed when it was brought up that the bully had in fact been the perpetrator and what happened to him was a reprisal for his behavior. The bully was beaten as soon as they were in the car alone. Jason was not sure where the bully went but he never returned to the school after that.

Following that Jason always had someone to walk with on the way home. A constant companion for whatever escapades he may have gotten himself into. Flynn had his savior. In Jason's words they were inseparable from that point on. No one ever bothered Flynn again; word of Jason's beating on the bully persisted much longer than the bruising on his hands. Jason's father had initially tried to be angry and punish him for getting into a fight; it was not what the men in his family did. Flynn's mother brought over a pan of brownies during Jason's two-week suspension, Flynn had told her all of what Jason had done so she felt it appropriate to thank him. That allowed the reprieve from two weeks of chores that Jason had garnered for himself; he still had chores just less backbreaking ones. Chores that he was happy to do. Alas, Jason and Flynn being inseparable only lasted through junior high as high school seemed to have presented different kinds of problems and circumstances. Jason began playing football, dating the cheerleaders, thinking about college after graduation. Flynn hit his growth spurt however it wasn't enough for him to begin to play sports. He was still an introvert. He became alone again. He turned inward, began doing drugs, dwelling in a basement. They hit a fork in the road and each took a path.

As Jason had been placing the dirt above his parents he heard someone from behind, a familiar voice although different from any he could remember. He recalled that he knew instantly that it was Flynn, he just felt that there was something odd in the tone he was hearing. He assumed it was depression; Flynn had until that point been all alone in a town full of dead people. Flynn spoke quickly yet cautiously, as if he had caught himself talking to people before only to realize he was having a discussion with a mannequin. It was a flood of questions for Jason, most of which he was in no position to answer; he had just buried his parents, they were all that was on his mind at that point. After all the dirt was settled Jason found some flower seeds to plant overtop of the grave. I cannot recall right now what kind but whatever they were; it was his mother's favorite. He was not sure if they would grow or bloom in the future, but he planted the garden regardless. That night they sat and reminisced under the stars in Jason's childhood backyard, just like when they were kids camping out. Jason used the fire pit in order to make 'smores, which seemed to be the only thing he could find to make, everything else had gone bad and rancid, although he was more than a little annoyed at the chocolate and marshmallows as they had both melted during the flare. He was happy with it though, he needed some comfort food after the day he had. The entire time Flynn still seemed off to Jason. He always was looking behind himself. As the sun set Flynn tried to avoid the shadows as they began to stretch across the yard towards him. It wasn't until the dark enveloped him that he seemed to calm; the only light that was really striking him was the glow from the fire in front of them. The fear of shadows as opposed to being afraid of the light was strange considering that in all reality the dark had been your friend in the cataclysm, the light was what killed people. Jason told Flynn of the people he had met, about us. Flynn was reportedly still thinking Jason was a figment of his imagination as he argued about how no one was left. Not necessarily an unfair assessment given his limited knowledge of what was going on, but it took a slap across the face from Jason before he actually began to the see the figure in front of him as a real person.

In the morning Jason awoke to see Flynn sitting on the picnic table smoking a cigarette while staring off towards the rising sun. He did not even acknowledge him at first; deep in thought. As the heat from the burning cigarette began to hit his finger he finally snapped out of it. Jason said that he was reborn, like the Flynn he had known from before. He was wide-eyed and happy to see Jason. The first thing he said that morning was "Should we ride our bikes to go see em?" I smiled at being told that, it was more promising, it meant we were less likely to have some crazy nut on our hands. They both packed up all that they felt they needed to bring from where their hometown was and began their journey. Still, it seemed to take a long time after Flynn had entered Republica before he seemed to get his anxieties under control.

As I said my first discussion with Flynn was not fruitful in the least however once I had talked to Jason and had grasped a little of the kind of person that Flynn was I made much more headway. I chose to go a different route with him. I simply had him begin working with us, whether it was clearing a house, planting vegetables, watering the gardens or tending to the animals. He took well to this; although he is still what I would have considered lazy he made an effort. At some point he almost became part of the background as he was something that was there but never really paid any attention until he began talking. The more he was involved with while he was working, the more he was hearing us talk to each other, the more he had to say. It is funny how much he was like a little child once they get past the 'playing-strange' point. Getting him to talk was like turning on a faucet then having the knob break off. There was no stopping him whether it was a discussion about a meal he had once had three years before that had a profound effect on him or just some casual insight about the shade of the paint on the trim of the church. He was interesting. I would not put him in the same category as myself when we are talking about knowledge and random facts although I would definitely say that he was intelligent.

As more and more people began to appear Flynn seemed to be coming out of his shell more often. I more or less facilitated this, as I put him in charge of meeting people as they entered. He did their initial 'interview' and was in charge of arranging for their receptions to be done. I was using each new person he met as practice for his opening himself up and talking to people. I was not expecting to be able to change an introverted person into an extrovert; nor would I want to but people should be able to find some kind of balance in their lives and interactions with others. I allowed him to be the coordinator for everything involving new people. He seemed to relish the ability to organize people, categorize them, assign them to this or that job, find their housing, etc. He was in charge of all of that for the first year or so after he arrived. It seemed to be a good fit although, again, hindsight tells me that was actually a bad thing. I put a lot of power into his hands and did not adequately supervise him. In my mind at that time I did not think I should not have needed to micromanage him, or anyone else for that matter. Everyone should have been working towards the betterment of the community as a whole as opposed to working on their own agendas. Flynn had the distinction of being seen as 'the gatekeeper'. In his mind but as well in the minds of many others it was his opinion that determined whether someone entered the town. No one was ever turned away that I am aware of. We needed every person that came along the highway more than they needed us. As a community we were stronger retaining all the people that happened along and all it cost us was some things that were not difficult to make or replace; food, power, water, etc. When talking about myself I did kind of highlight the problem that somewhat occurred with Flynn. It is still the same idea that power corrupts everyone that has it.

Flynn was removed from the job after I began to hear disturbing things about bribes being elicited from both new citizens as well as people who were already here. There was an instilled fear in all of them that if they did not give him whatever he requested they would be turned away or thrown out. Both of which are things I would not have done or condoned. The bribes were not anything extravagant, many people did not arrive with much more than the clothes they were wearing and possibly some stuff like a sleeping bags and random items. From what I understood from the people I talked to about this the biggest thing was cigarettes. I guess Flynn never bothered to realize that the reason no one else really smoked in town was that it was easier to quit than keep pining for something that was not going to be made anymore. Again, the community is more important than stupid little things like that. It is bigger than any one person, possibly except for myself. I always find it strange how it takes one person to break the silence before everyone else who has been offended finally admits that they were. I got one report of impropriety; then two more the next day. I personally interviewed all these people. Three more people came forward after I dealt with the whole thing. There were likely more but I never heard anything from those people. I get the embarrassment, guilt and whatnot that some people may feel after being taken advantage of but if I had known sooner I would have acted sooner.

"Jason, I need to talk to you." I said as I ambushed Jason on his way to the garage. Jason was always an early riser it seemed. The best time for me to catch up to him and talk to him privately was actually on his way to work as most people were not out walking around just after dawn. If they were out at all they were likely tending their gardens otherwise anyone awake at this hour was likely still having their morning tea or something; they were certainly not walking the streets.

"Sir?" He looked at me confused. I think I had actually startled him. He had likely not been expecting to see anyone anyways but on top of that he appeared to have been daydreaming as he walked. Jason suddenly became rigid, as if he were trying to stand at attention without quite understanding how to do it. I smiled at him and gestured for him to calm.

"Jay, its fine. Don't worry. We just need to have a bit of a talk." I stood in front of him. This was one of those times I really began to see the disparity in our positions in town as I could have sworn that Jason was shorter than me at that moment, even though I know we are the same height. I think he actually would change his posture in my presence as means of showing who was superior. If you see two dogs who know each other interacting you will actually see something like the more subordinate one doing stuff like licking the face of the *Alpha*, who will look away. They will actually demonstrate who is superior. Not that I was thinking of it at that exact moment as I took the Alpha role and began leading the way; I put my hand on Jason's shoulder as I turned him back to the direction of the garage and began sauntering while we continued our conversation. "Have you been hearing anything weird as of late?"

"Not that I can think of. Although... one of the new people did say that he had seen something that looked like glowing nuclear zombies along the side of the highway. He said he had passed them a like a week ago when he was coming here." My stride came to a sudden halt as I looked at him. He shrugged as he continued. "The guy did not seem too certain of what he saw. When I talked to him a little more his story changed to he heard some weird sounds. He never actually saw anything."

I breathed a sigh of relief as I pat him on the shoulder and we resumed walking. "Jeez. The kind of people that survived the end of the world. Never ceases to amaze me. In any event, that is not the rumor I had heard. Specifically, Flynn. Anything?"

"Umm. No. I haven't talked to him lately, he's been busy." I inadvertently scoffed at that. "Did he find some old stash of drugs? Is he all fucked up now?"

"Fucked up, yes. Drugs. Not as far as I know. To be honest I am not sure how to tell you this but- Well- Your friend is going. I am expelling him today."

"Wait. What? What happened? You can't! He's my friend!" I smirked at Jason when he said I couldn't. I think he shrunk a little shorter. "Can we do something? I told him this place would be safe. I said he'd never have to be out there."

"Well, perhaps you shouldn't have promised that. This is something I cannot just ignore. Listen though. It is not your fault. This is the result of his actions and this is the resultant consequence. In reality, if I had reacted as I think I should have I would have just shot him in the back of the head and been done with this; however I am acknowledging that he is your friend which is why he is being banished as opposed to shot." Jason looked puzzled and still scared. A very 'deer-in-the-headlights' kind of expression on his face. That is a bit of a misunderstood phenomena; deer do freeze when caught in headlights but not for reasons that people think. They are not afraid, well they may be, but it is not because of the light. Their brains simply tell them to stand still while their eyes adjust, which means they stand still in the middle of the highway and get run over. "Listen. Jason. Don't worry. You vouched for him, if I was blaming you or thinking you were complicit in this I would not be talking to you now. In fact, you would be joining him. I just wanted to give you a heads up because I think that is the decent thing to do because he is your friend."

"I still don't get it. What did he do?" Jason's hand brushed by mine as he went to grab my wrist to stop me from walking; the fact he only brushed my hand instead of actually grabbing me tells me that he managed to get control of himself at the last second. He still did not seem to be his normal height but was standing a tad taller than he had a few seconds ago. I took the queue nonetheless and stopped walking, turning to face him. I watched his face, looking to see something hint the truth in his eyes.

"You really don't know?" He shakes his head. I can't see anything that tells me he is lying. This was the real reason for me wanting to talk to him. I needed to see if he knew. If he was part of what I had heard, then he would actually have died right there in the street that day. It would have been more upsetting for me to have Jason being a part of extorting people as I liked him and it would have required him lying to me, which I could not just abide. Flynn on the other hand was really nothing to me. He was just a name on a ledger. "Hmmm. I figured if anyone would have known it would have been you. Well apparently, Flynn has been taking advantage of his position and making people pay for their entry into town." A blank stare. I have always liked Jason and found him to be quite clever at times but did not seem to be processing what I was saying. "He made them pay to get in. This is not a theme park; we don't charge people to come inside." We did charge people in a manner of speaking by making them work to stay, but that is really something that is only fair. In any event I didn't add that thought to what I said to Jason.

I could see Jason's face instantly get red, his jaw hardened and there were a few nearly imperceptible cracks as he ground his teeth together. "That son of a fucking bitch." I nodded with a look of amusement on my face, as if to gesture 'No shit.'

"And that is why he is going. I am going to get a couple of people to take him like a hundred miles down the highway. He'll be told if he ever returns there will not be a second chance at exile." We had resumed walking and were now turning the corner of the street. The garage was down the street to the left.

"Is there something I could do? He is my friend…. I promised his mother after I saved him from that bully I would always try to keep him safe…. I just- I want to- I need to keep that promise. Everyone I know is dead just like everyone he knows is dead; we only have each other left…. I need to keep that promise to her."

I had been so focused on whether or not Jason was a part of the whole thing I had not foreseen this turn of events. I had mentally prepared to tell Jason that he was not going to be allowed to kill Flynn; I guess I had expected him to feel more betrayed than he was. He did know Flynn better than me, in that light it is not so unexpected that he would not have been surprised by Flynn acting like an asshole. I had not mentally prepared to discuss anything other than he was not allowed to murder Flynn. We stood in front of the garage, staring into each other's eyes. Jason looked as if he was expecting us to kiss; his eyes were darting around, looking for some sign from my face as to what I was about to say. I sighed. "Well, as I see it there are three possible options here. First: I could do my original plan and just shoot him. I think that would be a good message to send to everyone else here. I have their best interests at heart. But I have a feeling you'd be a little pissed about that since it would go against your promise. And if you were to try to keep your promise then I'd have to shoot you too." My eyes narrowed on his. There was again a slight reduction in size on his part.

"I woul-"

I waved him off and continued. "Second: We do the plan I already told you, which would mean banishment. If you want to keep him safe, then you can keep the seat beside him on the ride out of town…. Of course, that means on top of losing one problem, I lose a very useful person. And a friend…." Jason perked up a little. "For the record, I think you are an asshole. I should not even be considering anything other than death or banishment. That fucker was taking advantage of people. That was never the fucking plan for this place."

"Sir, I know. I get that. This place is supposed to be an oasis. I will take full responsibility." Silence. I just stood there. Looking at him, he should have known even by that point I was not a fan of being interrupted; especially when I was rambling, it's one of the few pleasures I really have in life.

"Third option: He stays here. You take full responsibility for him. He will be put somewhere; doing something menial. I never want to hear of him like this again. If I hear anything it better be that someone nominated him for Employee of the fucking Month… Those are the three possibilities as I see them. Now I know you have already made a choice, but I am telling you to think about this. I do not want to have a repeat of this conversation.”

No hesitation. “I understand. I will take option three. I’ll take him to work with me, here in the shop, that way I can keep an eye on him. You’ll never hear another peep from him. I will make sure of it.”

“I told you to think. You already have me making a choice based on not wanting to lose a decent person from the town and now you’re making an emotional decision.”

“I know. I know. He is my friend; I have known him all my life. I have to do this.” Puppy dog eyes; who can resist those?

“Fine. I am not going to debate this all day. His life is in your hands. If there are more problems, it will either be up to you to fix it or up to me. And I will wipe the slate clean.” He understood the meaning behind clean. I nodded as I left him standing in the open door of the garage. Jason looked off to the distance as the sun was now poking over the trees. The day was getting brighter.

CHAPTER 13 – WOODPILE

I think the situation dealing with Nixi was the best possible application of fear that I had during my entire time as leader. My intentions were made, my displeasure was displayed and my word had true power behind it. As I pointed out earlier, fear is a great motivator. It is the basis of the Fight-or-Flight response. With the proper spurring of that emotion you can get anything done. That would be more of the flight end of the response spectrum; people will actively avoid having to confront a situation, so they will comply. Complicit agreement with whatever tyranny you may wish to impose upon them. The revolt before Nixi's did not respond as well with the application of fear. It was a different set of circumstances, different players, and different personalities. It just did not work out all that well; I shouldn't say that; it still worked out, for me at least, as I was able to weather the storm and come out still on top. In short, they could not be bullied into acquiescing; it took a real degree of work. Tangible consequences instead of pile of intangibles; it is the difference between actually seeing or feeling harm as opposed to just imagining it. I could not just let their minds run wild; they were kind of past the point where prodding of that sort would have a real affect on the outcome. I don't even know if I could classify it as a revolt per se, Nixi's revolt was not even a revolt. The first one I would actually say it was maybe more of a civil disturbance, it does not matter either way though because it was suppressed and I just kept moving forward. This was my true lesson in dealing with a hydra as opposed to a snake and I think my inexperience hampered my response and made it much more volatile than it had to be. And not to say that things did not change for the better following the upheaval, I am a reasonable man, I simply do not deal with threats all that well. This was a lesson that I took very seriously; I learned that basing your decisions on your emotional state are not necessarily the most rational decisions.

There were a few lists of names that I kept during my time as leader. The first and most important was the population list. It was kept in a simple black ledger that sat upon the right-hand side of my desk. On top of it sat a geode, just a paperweight really, the geode itself was about the size of a softball and quite beautiful. It was made of light purple amethysts that seemed to have a kind of cloudiness that made the whole thing mesmerizing. There were times when I drifted off into my own thoughts and just stared at the geode; many answers that I was looking for were found in that geode. That black ledger contained the names of every single person that walked into my town from the day that I first met up with Aurora and Lisa outside the church; with the exception of the creeper, I never knew his name nor was he ever a 'resident' here. I was, of course, # 1 on the list, Aurora #2, Lisa #3, Jason #4, etc. This was in many ways the record of my crowning achievement. There are thousands of names in that book; each one was a life that we gave the opportunity to flourish; whether people took advantage of that opportunity is another matter. It was the most up-to-date record of who is in the town. I had a system for those that were no longer part of the population. Exiles were crossed off in blue; natural deaths, including those that died from the E. coli outbreak were red, the cannibals were crossed off in green and all the other people that died, the ones that opposed me were crossed off in black. They were effectively erased from the list; you could no longer read their names at all.

The next list as I mentioned before was the list of the cannibals that I hung on my wall. The frame was some type of wood; it looked like oak to me although I am not good at actually identifying that kind of thing. The original picture that had been in the frame was still in the frame, just behind the list. It was a beautiful wintery scene with what appeared to be a child playing with a dog out in a field; some of the snow had been kicked up by a gust of wind, making a haze over the trees in the distance. I did not have the heart to toss the picture for the frame, so I kept it there just hidden from view. This list served as a reminder for me of how I had truly worked to save my people from a danger, as well functioned as a bit of propaganda reminding everyone else of that same thing, lest they forget. They forgot regardless of my efforts to remind them. Probably didn't help that it was not kept in a public area.

The blue names were kept on the back pages of the black ledger; they were our lost boys, they strayed from the path they were given and had to deal with the natural consequences of their hubris. I don't know if I have much more to say on these ones, there were only ever a few, mostly thieves and they got dropped off out in the wilderness somewhere. In a way they probably got off better than the blackened names but who knows for certain, none of these people ever returned.

This brings me to the last group; the blacked-out names. I took to referring to these people as 'the redacted ones' but that was only ever in my head. Those names were of every single person that I had to "deal with". It is mostly composed of the participants of the first uprising against me. I kept this list in my house, hidden inside a false panel on my book shelf. I would look at that list most nights; alone, more so in the last few years but on a fairly regular basis right from the end of the revolt. Contrary to what people thought or still think of me I was not trying to be a monster or the like by having hundreds of my own people killed but you have to understand that once someone is in power they truly do not wish to relinquish it. The thought of that is almost painful. It is frightening. The prospect of suddenly not having control is a difficult idea to grasp especially while you still maintain your control over others. Not only that, there is the inevitable likelihood of my being strung up because of things I had already done. All that meant that the only way to preserve my life was to retain my place as leader. Hindsight is 20/20 and I have found that now that I am no longer in power the transition was not as scary as I had feared. I also believe that I am weary, which is why my inevitable end does not concern me now as much as it would have years ago. You can only read those blacked out names on the list in my study; they were redacted from history as much as possible. I believe I am the only one who must remember their names as I am the one that must pay for their treatment.

The biggest problem facing my people was a problem that I fostered and nurtured and allowed to become prevalent and common-place. And contrary to Nixi's complaints this is much less something that I was actively doing; the problem was with what I was not doing. I was not being a responsible leader. I let things coast. It was as if I sent a bowling ball down the lane then never bothered to check to see how many pins got knocked down. Nor did I listen to the subsequent crashes, each giving notice of another pin or pins that were falling over. I had no idea if the ball was even in my lane anymore. It was careless. I will acknowledge that, there is no one to blame other than myself. If I so desired there are people that I could blame, and did, although ultimately 'the buck stops here' meaning that the leader is the one who needs to be blamed. I understand it and in what I am saying here I will not try to blame others. Blame however does not stop a reaction; it does not provide any measure of cessation when things have been put in motion, not for me anyways. It is the idea that once an arrow leaves the bow you can not just pull it back.

Summer was always a pleasant time in Republica; full of flowers, birds and bees and a seemingly endless amount of food: mostly fruits and vegetables although once we had shored up the population; chicken and eggs were readily available. Fish rebounded enough to be caught to supplement everyone's diet and we of course had the occasionally hunter go out to get something more substantial although this was kept to a minimum for years. I am still unsure how things like birds managed to survive the cataclysm however I am guessing that those that did manage to survive the flare were in very poor condition, much like Princess was when we found her. Each year as the leaves turned varying shades of yellow, orange and red, the tranquility and plenty of the summer seemed to begin to fade away. People began making preparations for the winter. Piling leaves against the side of the house for extra insulation. Stockpiles of firewood were piled up to help heat their houses during the cold months. Everything seemed to be coming to a head while at the same time, almost slowing down as if the colder temperatures were causing the blood in people to begin to thicken, like molasses that has been put in the fridge. I can not rightly remember what year it was that the insurrection started but I think it would be around 5 years after the cannibal episode. During the summer the usual feel of contentment that I had just did not seem to be present. I could not put my finger on it the whole time. It seemed as though the mood of the people was off; as the morale of a defeated opponent would be. Although at that time I was not being particularly harsh or vindictive. I was probably at my least invasive in people's lives, and there stemmed the problem. Not that my subjects wished to have me monitoring and micro-managing their lives, but they did want some interest. Enough to show I cared. I was oblivious to it. As I was oblivious to many things at that time it would seem. It was not until I was thanking everyone at the harvest celebration for their hard work and perseverance in the past year that I became truly aware of their discontent. What I had been sensing though was not a drop-in morale over being defeated; it was anger, seething and bubbling below the surface.

As had become custom I made a heartfelt acknowledgement of people's efforts. I was greeted with silence, very much an out of the norm occurrence. I congratulated people on making Republica a place that they could do more than just survive but live a 'real life' and I was greeted with scoffs. I extended a measure of praise for people making this a place in which they could be proud to raise their children and carry on human civilization and I was met with jeers and boos. I was perplexed. Nothing in my time before that as leader had prepared me for dealing with a crowd that was not interested in hearing me out. There was no reasoning at that moment. There began a cascade of complaints and shouting; too much to understand, it was just like being pummeled with sound. All I could see was a wall of red angry faces, advancing and yelling. My loyalists were stationed near the front of the community hall, nearest to my table as usual. It is kind of no different that going to a wedding reception where people do not have a seating plan. People will sit where they feel the most comfortable; those that were within my graces tended to aspire to sitting nearest to me. As the crowd began clamoring more and more insults began to be hurled in my direction, followed by more substantial objects that included some fruits and vegetables and other food items but also a chair. The chair was misthrown however and actually hit a small child in the side of the head; it did not cause any permanent damage, but I recall hearing she required a couple of stitches to close the wound on the side of her head. There were instantly a few people standing in front of me against this surge of people, guns trained upon this person or that. A tense stand-off ensued as both sides stared at each other waiting for one to make some sort of move. I was still bewildered. I implored both sides to be calm and disperse. Jason stood directly in front of me against the one that seemed to be the ringleader of the malcontents; Rusty. Jason heeded my order and told all the others who stood with him to lower their weapons, which they did. Rusty seemed to take that as the opportune time to take his leave of the situation, the others behind him soon followed suit.

Standing at the head of a half empty hall I demanded to know from every person that remained what the fuck was going on. My spy network was not operating if that many people were upset about something and I hadn't the slightest clue what it was. No one was answering me. Those that remained out on the floor seemed to just be trying to finish their meal before bolting out the door. My men seemed visibly shaken as they had not been anticipating anything of that sort to occur; most of them no longer seemed to have an appetite. I was angry at that point at what I had just confronted but also, I was actually feeling quite anxious. Being directly confronted by a mob, even without suffering any violence myself was quite nerve-wracking. "Jason, could you please get the ringleader of that circus and bring him to me, I need to know just what is going on here." My voice faltered a couple of times as I spoke. I began to cough as soon as I finished speaking; my throat seemed tight and rigid. I could barely swallow. Jason agreed in his usual 'Yes Sir' kind of manner before setting off towards the door at the far end of the hall. "Ask nicely." I chimed behind him as he left the building. I was not sure if he heard me, he may have nodded or waved but stepping out of the building he was consumed by the darkness of the evening.

Returning to my house I sat on the porch. Looking at the stars, something I rarely did at any point in my life. Likely that has to do with what I had mentioned earlier, how thinking about the universe reminds me how infinitely small our planet is, let alone how small we are. How fragile. I was not really looking at the stars though, I was consumed in thought. My mind was going over the past events trying to see if I had said something particularly offensive without realizing it. As it happens to everyone at some point or another. Putting your Foot in your mouth or as I used to enjoy calling it, Athlete's Tongue. Either way it means the same thing; talking without thinking it out and saying the wrong thing. I looked at my speech notes. These were the same notes I had used for years, they were slightly crumpled and starting to yellow with age. I was never a fan of public speaking, so those notes served as a security blanket for me. I rarely used them anymore; I had the framework memorized. Greetings. Congratulations to all. Special thanks to whoever. Moment of silence for those lost. Reminder to be thankful for what we have now. Please begin eating. Nothing was out of the ordinary. I had barely gotten through the congratulations part. I was about to thank Dorothy (our doctor, by that point I think she had progressed and learned enough to drop the quotation marks) for continuing to do a great job and LeAnn for learning so much from her and becoming our second doctor. Randy and Jamaal for 'graduating' from school and beginning their apprenticeships in carpentry and mechanics respectively. We had 6 couples that were expecting children within the next couple of months. I was going to wish that everyone had a happy and healthy baby. I never got to that part of my speech. My mind was unclear. I was filled with doubt. What had I done wrong? As I sat there thinking and identifying various constellations, Cassiopeia, Big Dipper, Little Dipper, Orion; Jason announced his arrival. He was alone. "Where is Rusty?"

"I don't know. He is not at his home. Everyone near him says they do not know where he went. No one is saying anything. They all just say he disappeared after the meeting." My face likely showed displeasure although that is not an accurate word for what I was feeling. I was concerned and still confused at what had transpired earlier in the evening. "Do you want me to bring in some people for questioning?"

"I do but I am not certain what is going on just yet. I think we can be a little patient. Get Flynn and a couple others to do a few patrols around tonight, see if anything is out of the ordinary." He nods and starts to walk off. "Wait."

"Sir?' He looked as perplexed as I felt. The first time since that evening's commotion that he seemed to be anything other than angry. I was having doubts. My mind was telling me to think and ascertain what was going on before acting, my heart was telling me to act as a hammer and figure things out from the shattered remains.

"Who else seemed to be alongside Rusty instigating that?" Jason was thinking and kind of shuffling his feet. More odd behavior. I was beginning to become suspicious of him. What was he holding back? What did he know?

"Damian seemed to be up front. I think I saw Tommy F. as well." I nodded.

"Ok, bring them here. Still ask nicely. I want to get to the bottom of this. Take someone with you if you think it makes sense." A new nod and he takes his leave; he just disappears into the darkness again. It was at that moment I noticed that Jason walks while barely making a sound. I was again alone in the silence, save for a few crickets chirping. Soon I would not be hearing them making noise, it was getting cold and almost time for them to begin hibernating. I was still unsure of the circumstances I was looking at. Rusty disappearing makes sense as I am sure he expected some sort of reprisal but I was not looking at things that way. I wanted more to just understand the situation. This was not a situation where I was dealing with something I could see and at least figure out. I was trying to solve a puzzle without knowing anything of what it would look like when it was complete; How many pieces are there? What does the final picture look like? Which are the edge pieces?

It seemed like hours that I was in my own mind before Jason returned. He was not alone this time, but his companion was unexpected, it was a fairly new resident named Gary. "Sir, I checked both their houses, both dark with no one around. I happened to bump into Gary here and remembered that he was near front and center too." A quick shove to the back and Gary was on his knees at the bottom of my porch stairs. I could only glare my disapproval at Jason at that moment, one of those keeping up appearances kind of things. Gary's eyes were down so there was no worry of him seeing my expression. Jason understood that we would likely be having a discussion later on about what exactly I mean when I say 'ask nicely'. It wasn't a euphemism, I actually meant it.

"Thank you, Jason. I think Jerry and I will talk for a bit. Have you told Flynn what I need him to do yet?" His eyes opened a little as Jason realized he had forgotten I had asked for some people to be doing some citizen on patrol kind of work tonight. I gave him a disapproving smirk as a father may make to a child when they are 'very disappointed in him'. "Okay, well you know what I need done. I will talk to you later after I talk to Jerry here abou-...."

"My name is Gary." More out of the ordinary behavior, I don't normally get cut off mid-sentence. It happens but not in this kind of context; if you are brought forcibly somewhere it stands to reason that you likely should not be interrupting.

"Ah, yes, my apologies, Gary and I will talk about the unpleasantness tonight." Jason shrugged a little as he turned, I must have been incredibly aware of what was going on that night as I don't normally notice every little gesture and motion people make but I was. I ushered Gary over to the bench on my porch, so we could talk, I sat on the rocking chair sitting next to it. Gary seemed uncomfortable but at the same time was keeping himself rigid, as if waiting for me to pounce or an opportunity to run away. "Gary, again I am sorry for forgetting your name, there are so many people here I sometimes get people mixed up. Also, I think it would only be courteous to apologize for Jason's treatment of you, I assure you I will deal with him." A scoff. And I pause. "I'm sorry, is there something you disagree with in what I just said?" Gary's eyes are fixed straight ahead. "Listen, Gary I am a reasonable person. I can't fix anything if I don't understand what is going on. If you could help me then we can start to work together to settle whatever is going on and I'm going to venture that you know what is going on around here." His mouth starts to open before clamping shut. He is pressing his lips together, that at least confirmed that he does know something, now we just need to get it out. "Gary, I deeply care for everyone and everything in this town, which is why I made it a place for people to come and rebuild their lives. Rebuild civilization. But I need to know what the problems are before I can correct them. You can help me. Just tell me what I need to know." He had made eye contact briefly before resuming looking off into the distance. Despite all my attempts to be patient I could feel that ever so slight nudge in the back of my head wanting to move things along. With the cannibals the feeling had been of a linebacker or sumo wrestler slamming me forward into being frustrated, this was a subtle nudge, but I could still feel it.

"A kid got molested." I was not expecting Gary to say anything; his lips were still so tightly pursed together. I on the other hand was unable to contain my shock, my mouth probably gapped for ten seconds before I noticed and closed my mouth. It did begin to make some sort of sense now. Rusty had a little girl; she was going to be three that December.

"What? Who? When? By whom? Where?" I had a lump in my throat. Aurora was older than a lot of the other kids at this point but who knows. Maybe it was her, or maybe it had been her. Pedophiles are predators and will often have a string of victims before someone finally says something. Regardless I was fighting the urge to go to her and see how she was. Urgency and panic. I was unaccustomed to feeling those things at this point; I had gotten so comfortable in my station and place. I used to feel secure. That feeling was broken and I was not even the one who would be truly affected. I wanted answers but at the same time I could feel my heart in my stomach, I was upset and disappointed. All I could do was sit; waiting for answers. I moved to the little stool sitting in front of Gary. I sat probably a foot from him, looking intently into his eyes as I let the silence draw the words from Gary. His speech began slowly like an old locomotive chugging slowly at first becoming more regular and rhythmic as he progressed.

"I don't know who. Or when. All I know is it happened here. One of your guys. And it's been happening for a while. Everyone says you don't do anything. You let them do whatever they want." More silence. I was again aware of the crickets, it was as if I had someone playing sound effects at opportune times to exemplify the mood of the situation. I was stunned and waiting for more information. I fought the urge to start bombarding him with questions, or to throttle more answers out of him. Going this far he will likely tell me everything he knows, I don't think he has a real reason to keep it from me. He is not trying to hide his own actions. He just did not understand how desperately I wanted a real answer from him, I wanted details that he was not providing. I did not see him trying to deflect from the facts; he had not eaten people nor did he seem like he was trying to place blame for molesting someone from himself to someone else. He was acting as a concerned person and I was getting a message of genuine concern from him. It is what I kind of expect from people. "They all have the big houses, like this one. They tax our food. They get everything. No one can say no, especially not the kids. They're bullies."

"Kids? Are we talking about like two kids, three?" He shrugged and muttered he didn't know. "Ok, so who are we talking about? Which of my guys are doing this? Who is taking your food? I need to know."

"I don't know. Everyone told me to keep to myself and don't stick my neck out." He chuckled a little. "Guess I shouldn't have been out digging for worms late at night." I looked at his hands, they were dirty. I had noticed it earlier but just assumed that he had gotten dirty from Jason pushing him.

"Everyone who? Who will know what I need to know? Rusty? Does he know?"

"I think so. I heard bits and pieces from a couple people, so I dunno." I rubbed my head as I closed my eyes. I was tired and at this point all the adrenaline had long left my system and I was getting a massive headache.

"Gary. Please do me a favour. You need to get someone who knows what is going on and get them to come and talk to me. Like I said I can't fix anything if I don't know what to fix." I was doing my best puppy dog eyes but it wasn't an act, they were pretty genuine; I wanted to know what was going on and fix it. "Please." I implored, hell, I was seconds from begging him on my knees.

Gary nodded slowly. "That's it?" I nodded back to him. "Um, okay, I'll go talk to some people and see."

"Thank you, Gary, just do your best, that's all I ask." He smiled as he rose from the bench. I was surprised as he stuck out his hand to shake hands. Good sign, he feels comfortable enough with our conversation to extend that courtesy. This discussion was after all a different kind of interrogation than the ones with the cannibals; none of them would have shaken my hand even if they still had fingers.

I watched as he walked off into the dark and the anxious waiting began again in earnest. What I would not have given for some painkillers to work on that headache. It was a thumping/pounding sensation directly behind my eyeballs. I was all too aware of it as I sat on my porch waiting. Twice over the proceeding hours I saw a pair of men walk down the middle of the street as they patrolled the town. They were embroiled in some sort of discussion as I waved to them both times. Each time I stared at them wondering if they were the ones who were molesting children, stealing food and bullying people. My people. My daughter? God, not that I wanted any of the kids to have to go through that I was hopeful that it was one of them and not my own blood. As the sky began to brighten I began to wonder if something had gone wrong. Where was Gary? Where were Rusty, Tom and Damian? Who was I to trust and who was to not be trusted?

The sun was fully up when the men did their next walk down the street, I lifted myself from the bench to talk to them. My muscles were stiff and sore from having sat all night, barely moving. I assumed that also had to do with the residual after effects of having adrenaline coursing through me. I shielded my eyes as I looked up to the sun. "Guys, it's about 7:30, I think you did good for the night. You can go rest. We'll try to sort things out, so you don't have another long night tonight."

"Thank you, sir." They spoke in unison. They walked off, continuing their conversation. I remember being amused as they were talking about football; a game that had not been played in years. Professionally at least, some of the citizens had at time organized little intramural games; baseball, football, floor hockey; they were all good at keep people entertained and exercised but there was not the kind of quality people would pay for. Oh well, that is a long-gone luxury. I yelled at them to tell everyone else to go to bed. The younger looking one turned and said, "Yes sir." Then they again carried on, presumably continuing the same conversation. I looked down my wrist to check if I was right about the time, forgetting I had not worn a watch in years, the tan line had long since faded away.

The streets were still quiet, more quiet than usual for this time of day although I was getting used to the silence. Given what people had seen the previous night it was understandable that they would be keeping a low profile. Hiding as if there were going to be another gunfight at the OK corral. I was still standing on the side of the street; the two who were patrolling had just turned left down a side street and were now out of view behind a house. I looked over my shoulder at my house. I sighed as I noticed that my paint was starting to peel, I guess I'd have to see if we had any paint around that was not dried into a rock still in the bucket. I grabbed my jacket off the arm of the rocking chair and began to walk to the church. The church was still essentially the administrative center of the town, I needed to look at the residence list to see where some of the malcontent residents lived; if Gary could not convince them to come see me I was going to see them. Work this out. Problem solved. I thought of how what had been the town hall before the cataclysm was some little office building in the 'downtown' part of the town, but I always found it rather small and cramped. Also, it did not allow for me to 'hold court' as it were. Usually once a week while reviewing whatever administrative duties I needed I would have people come into ask for this or that, generally some sort of assistance or permission to get a tool or something. It was really never anything exciting or noteworthy but somewhat necessary as we did still have a somewhat limited resource base, so we could not let people just grab as they saw fit. Certain things like for example a rototiller was utilized by a number of people each spring. We only had a few in the town so people had to share. It would be brought to the warehouse after use, checked out by the next person and then they would return it the next day. Everything worked like a library, checking books in and out. No fines for late items though; usually a stern lecture or being at the bottom of the list for the next item to be borrowed if you were a chronically late person. That was a natural consequence; if someone holds up the line then you put them at the back so the only person they hold up is themselves. It was a system that worked for us and everyone got what they needed as soon as was possible.

Walking towards the church my mind was drifting from this to that; from yesterday evenings commotion to my talk with Gary, to my confusion with what was happening at the harvest festival to my concern for Aurora. I was still worried for her, I still wanted to see her but I still needed answers and I needed to get things sorted out, which meant talking to the malcontents. I could talk to her after. My mind drifted back to the paint peeling from the siding of my house. I really needed to remember to ask about paint. And I guess I would need to see about getting someone to paint the house. My mind paused at that, as did my body. Should I get someone to do it or should I do it myself? I am capable and there is really no reason I shouldn't do it myself. I am just like one of the guys and what better way to make myself seem as a man of the people than by doing something mundane like painting myself. I recalled at that point there were times in my childhood when I had painted the siding on my house. I remembered how after the first time my parents were less than pleased with my efforts; I was sloppy and had painted everything one color, including the trim, which was supposed to be a darker shade. I had not known any better at that instance, I was only around 9. Also, the paint only extended to around 4 ½ feet up so it gave the whole outside of the house a half-done look. I still think I did pretty well considering. Maybe I should have asked first before I began painting. Long dead should-haves that I could have said to long dead people. I had resumed walking and was just now turning the corner to the street with the church. We had an older woman living on the corner; I say older in that she was older than me although likely not by much. She had begun a relationship with a man a number of years ago and at some point they had essentially decided they were married. Again, it was one of those things that worked for us. No need for licenses, or religious services or even a judge to marry people. They had been Mr. and Mrs. Perlmen for years. I waved to her as she was picking some corn off of the stalks in her yard. At first, I don't think she saw me, so I added in the same "Morning, Mrs. Perlmen." I always said. I startled her. It often happened. I think her eyesight was quite poor, but she never looked through the pile of glasses we had despite knowing that she could at any point. We have never had an optometrist in all the time I have lived here so the best we can do is recycle old glasses or any glasses we found, giving them to people who happen to have the same prescriptions as the former owners. Maybe if she could see the world around her better she would get frightened less.

A return wave and reply of "Morning." That was the same as normal, at least something didn't change overnight. Behind the Perlmen's house was a place that we had left vacant for years before tearing it down and using the lumber for fuel. No one had wanted to live there nor would I have forced someone to. The house smelled even after having been cleaned out and given years worth of time to dissipate. The former owner had been a bit of a hoarder; everything you could think of that was useless was in there as well as things that could possibly have been useful if you have every found them. On top of that the person had likely had over a dozen cats, likely dozens. Everything in the house smelled of mold, musty ammonia and cat shit. That was why we tore it down, if it had been the pre-cataclysm world the house would have been condemned and then torn down; we did the same without the red tape. In place of the house we had set up a little bit of a park, just a couple of benches and some gravel for a path. Just a nice place to sit. I wanted something that was just for relaxing and not necessarily for food. It is the only place in the town where you can see flowers that are just for looking at. Roses, daisies and lilies are the only ones I could identify. There are dozens of other flowers, but I have no idea what any of those are. It was at that moment that my eyes were drawn to a figure on one of the benches, it looked like a man with a hood pulled up over his face. This was another out the ordinary thing; we don't have homeless people here, everyone is given a place to live and I knew for certain at that point there were likely over 100 houses that were ready for someone to just walk into and begin living there. I diverged from my plan to go to the church post-haste in order to talk to whoever this was. It was not unheard of for new people to the town to come in unannounced like this although they never got this far into the town before without being noticed and the process of introducing them to the community begun. I was also supremely disappointed with my roving patrols, they should not have missed someone laying out in the open on a park bench; I was thinking that I would have to get Jason to break up the pairings so those two could be with someone whom they would have a less distracting conversation with.

I came up to the figure on the bench and cleared my throat. "Excuse me?" Nothing. "Sir?" Still nothing. I kicked the bench slightly, hoping the thud against the metal would be enough to rouse whoever this was. I could see the shoes were sitting in an awkward way as if this person's leg or legs had been broken at some point. I extended my arm to shake his shoulder but as I clamped my fingers down I realized it was not a person. It was just a pile of clothes stuffed to look like the figure of a person. I had just walked into a trap.

I had never been stabbed before; the pain is hard to describe. It was like a burning sensation going deep into my side, just below my ribs on the right. I felt the blade go in, starting at a singular point and expanding to the width of the knife. Moreover, I could feel the knife in my back being pulled out; the edge was pointing downwards, the same direction that the pressure on the handle was being applied. I could literally feel my skin and muscle being cut further as the knife was being withdrawn. I began to slump forward not out of pain, but partially because of it. I was already trying to get away from the pain coming from behind me. Another stabbing motion from the figure behind me and more pain, this was only glancing though, I felt my skin tear under my shirt as the blade missed my shoulder blade. I completely hit the ground, I began scrambling under the bench, at the same time I turned to see the one who was attacking me. My hand fumbled towards my holster as I was trying to push myself away in some sort of panicked crab-walk. It was little more than me flailing my legs as my ass was dragging on the ground without me using my arms to help move me. This man was wearing a dark turtleneck sweater pulled up as far as it could go with some sort of scarf wrapped around his head, obscuring his face. His eyes were fiery, and intent on getting to me as he bounded to his left to get around the bench. A flash of light came off of the blade of the knife, it was quite shiny and sharp with what looked to be a bone handle. There was a thin layer of my blood on the knife, already starting to bead a little on the metal. The reflected light had a slight tint of red on it as it had passed through my blood, which was now beginning to drop onto the grass behind the bench as well as being on the knife. My assailant let out a strange hissing sound as he rounded the bench and began to lunge forward, trying to bring the knife down in a stereotypical stabbing motion. I had barely pulled the trigger as the blade again struck home, in my left shoulder this time, piercing through the head of my shoulder muscle.

His eyes got softer and softer over the next few seconds. Laying under someone with a knife in your body and those seconds can seem like hours. Center-mass. That is supposed to be where you aim for. It contains most of the body's vital organs as well it presents the largest target to shoot at. When you are engaged in what turns out to be a quick draw contest that is all you have time to go for. The assassin was struggling to breathe as I had shot him through his diaphragm. This is a very important muscle in terms of breathing as your rib cage muscles can only expand the volume of your chest cavity so much; the diaphragm is a large muscle that drops down, creating a large negative space in your chest, thereby making a vacuum inside you, that space is then filled by your lungs which pull air in through your nose or mouth. It seems more complex than it is; it is kind of no different than sucking on a straw, your tongue drops down creating negative pressure, in essence a vacuum, in your mouth which allows you to suck in something. With your diaphragm that stuff is air. And he was running out of it. I couldn't push like I wanted to, the knife was still in my left shoulder meaning that it couldn't use that muscle as well as I wanted to nor could I push hard with my right arm; I would have pushed my attacker over the knife, as well it made my back hurt. I kind of slid out from underneath him, then I knelt beside him, breathing hard. I was going to try to pull the blade out however I know better. It may hurt but right now the knife is acting like a plug and keeping blood from coming out of that wound. I pulled the scarf down enough to see it was Damian, his skin was still dark and tanned from being out all summer; his moustache was all frazzled-looking from the static made by the scarf. He lay on his back. Struggling to breath. I knelt there, feeling shock begin to wash over me again. I still remembered that feeling from the creeper incident and I still did not like this feeling. And not just because it meant I was injured. It makes you feel odd. Detached. Almost like step one of an out of body experience. I looked at Damian as his eyes were pleading to me to help him. He was dying and he could feel that he losing himself to death. He was mouthing words to me, but nothing was coming out; not a sound. Or at least I couldn't hear anything. With the fog I was in he may have been making some sort of sound. I wasn't hearing anything. Still huffing from the exertion of getting out from under Damian, I rasped at him. "Where is Rusty? Where are the others?" His facial expression changed, it was no longer him begging for breath, he was now begging for his life. I could see him mouthing the words 'Please' over and over again. He tried to cough but that only seemed to be more painful than it was worth. I realized at that moment that I did not have the time to get answers, I was starting to feel light-headed, more so, as I was still bleeding, probably quite profusely from my back. I would get answers from someone else. I wrapped my right hand around his neck and began to squeeze. I could feel his pulse through his carotid artery. He tried to push me off with his left while grabbing my hand with his right. I leaned forward, making him try to push against my weight while I twisted his right wrist with my free hand. His pulse was getting slower, weaker. His mouth began to gape, trying to take in a breath as I was crushing his throat. I could feel the cartilage ribs in his esophagus starting to bend and buckle as I continued to squeeze. The beats stopped. I applied more pressure; I wanted his neck to be crushed. As I felt his windpipe collapse in my hand I exhaled deeply. More of a sigh. This was a trying episode.

I picked myself up and began walking back towards the church. As it came into view, I remembered that I had been stabbed and I began crossing the street walking towards the retirement home. I had tried to stick my finger into the hole in my back although that probably made things worse; the hole was bigger than I could plug with one finger but too small to put two in so I ended up just trying to ball my shirt in my hand and using it like a bandage. My right shoe was feeling wet and slippery as it filled with blood; there was that distinctive squishing sound with each step as the blood in my shoe was squished out through the lace holes. It still felt like the old west, there was no one around, everyone was still out of the way, shuttered inside their homes. This had been planned, they all knew what had been coming. Getting to the front of the retirement home I fell into the front door, it was locked. I was worried now, not only was I dying but I was not going to be able to receive help. As I turned my back to the door I leaned against it and turned the knob; the second of the double doors was open. I giggled a little as I stumbled inside, without that error I might have bled to death sitting by the front entrance of the retirement home, mere yards from the doctor.

It occurred to me as I was shambling down the main corridor that I did not have the slightest idea how this building was laid out. Or if either of the doctors are even here. Who knows, I wouldn't expect they would be; it was still just barely past dawn. I briefly took a moment to lean against a wall. A bloody handprint remained showing where I had been. I turned to the right from the main hallway; it was dark to the left and looked unused meaning that if there was anyone there they would be this way; there were lights on at the nursing station midway down the hall on the right. I heard a meek little "Hello?" come from the station, at least that meant someone was here. A chair squeaked, followed by a squeak of a shoe on the floor. LeAnn poked her head around the corner. "Sir?" A pause as she came fully out into the hallway and she could see I was covered in blood; the knife handle still protruding from my left shoulder. "Oh my god, Sir!" She screamed as she ran towards me. I liked LeAnn. When she had come across Republica she was only 14 years old, meaning that I was her teacher for around 4 years plus another 2 years where I had her doing studying on her own as preparation for her medical apprenticeship. I was at the finish line now and suddenly my entire body had become heavier than it had ever felt. I struggled to maintain myself upright; I had such a grip on the railing running down the length of the ward that my knuckles were white. The blood loss probably helped with that as well. LeAnn ducked under my arm to try to help me along, it was a nice gesture but kind of futile, she was at best 150lbs. I, on the other hand, was nearly double her weight. She quickly got the message as I started to lose the ability to hold my self up and my weight started to fall on her. She ran to grab a wheelchair from across the hall and rammed it into the back of my legs, if it wasn't for all the endorphins in my system that likely would have hurt a lot as there was a quite a bruise on the back of my legs later. I dropped into the chair and she immediately started rushing me towards the operating room. I had lost all the strength I had and my head flopped back. I could see up her nose.

I awoke sometime later. I could not say initially how long it was, but it had been hours. I was still in the operating room, lying on the gurney. Everything hurt. My shoulder hurt the worst of all. I looked over and saw the stitches that were holding the wound closed, the scar would be all jagged, and I remember thinking LeAnn needed more practice with doing stitches. I tried to sit up but I could feel the stitches in my back wound starting to pull so I ended up just curling onto my side in the fetal position. I could hear a commotion from outside the door. Someone pleading. Someone female, probably LeAnn still, her voice sounded something like what I was hearing. "Come on, in here." The door burst open as she pointed to me saying "Here he is." The door was behind me now that I was lying on my side. I was unsure if she was directing the next assassin or someone else.

"Sir!" Jason's voice. Well at least that meant I was less likely to be stabbed in the back although I was not very trusting of anyone right at that point. I flopped back onto my back. The wound in my back immediately screamed in pain then almost as quickly began throbbing. I suspected I had opened it up again. "Sir. Are you okay?" I nodded slowly as I forced my self into a sitting position, painful or not, I could not be lying down right now. I looked Jason in the eyes as I told him of the attack and where to find Damian's body. I was looking for something from him, if he knew; there would be something on his face. Instead, I got the opposite, he was surprised at all of this. He stared at me intently, concerned and fascinated. "We have to get them." He said. I nodded.

"In time, I- I mean we, we need to figure out what is going on. At this point we only have a few people to look towards; Rusty, Tom and well there was Damian. I don't think Gary actually knows anything more than what he told me." My throat felt hoarse, I realized I had probably had a breathing tube stuck down my throat while I was unconscious. "Can I get some water please LeAnn." She nodded as she scuttled out of the room. "Jason, we are going to destroy them all. But I need to know who we are going after." I sighed heavily before I shifted my weight and wincing as I tossed my feet over the side of the gurney, Jason moved beside me in order to help me to my feet. "I want you to grab two or three trustworthy guys; Flynn for sure and whoever else you can think of who'd be good. I want you to start with people nearest to Rusty, Damian and Tom. Find out where Rusty and Tom are. Also, have someone else go collect Damian's body and put it in the back of a truck, I have a plan."

Jason looked uncertain, or maybe uneasy is a better description, at the notion of having a plan for Damian's body but the good thing about loyalty means he'd do whatever regardless. He left the room without another word; he passed LeAnn just outside the doorway. She was walking slowly, I would assume because she has begun to spill water all over her hands. "Why did this happen? What's going on?" She asked as I was handed the cup. I drank it all before replying to her; it was lukewarm but at that point I couldn't have cared less. My throat was so sore and burning. While drinking I weighed my options about what to say. At this point I had only one real thought and that was getting to the bottom of who tried to kill me. Selfish, yes, but I'm irreplaceable, especially to me. I was still very concerned about what Gary had told me however who knows if it is true or just a smokescreen. After all he never came back, I still did not know why, maybe he was part of the conspiracy that almost assassinated me.

"I don't know LeAnn. There are some people who are apparently pretty pissed at me." I chuckle a little only to regret it seconds later; I was going to be sore for a fair while. "I was trying to figure out why everyone was so upset last night but at this point either we can't find anyone or no one knows anything. I don't suppose you know anything about this? Have you heard anything? Seen anything?"

She shook her head emphatically "No. What happened? I was here so I didn't see it, but a few people mentioned it late last night. Said everything was a huge riot." I shrugged a little as I started to walk for the door.

"I have no idea what is going on, but I need you to stay here. Forget that you saw me for now. Just stay safe. At this point I don't have the foggiest who is involved in this and it is probably safer to not stick your neck out right now. Be good." I patted her shoulder as I hobbled out the door into the hallway. I was still a little light-headed and woozy but I was managing. I could hear LeAnn saying something about staying in the hospital but I was honestly no longer paying attention. "I'll be fine and I'll see you later." I yelled over my shoulder to her. Stepping outside the retirement home I was nearly overcome with the intensity of the sunlight. It hurt to open my eyes, I actually had to stand there for probably two minutes just to let them adjust. I will most certainly say that due to my near-death experience I had a heightened awareness of what was going on around me. There seemed to be so many more sounds at that moment; birds, insects, a slight breeze, gentle rustling coming from the tree on my left, a wind chime ringing from far off. Everything I could see once my eyes adjusted seemed clearer and more vibrant; the bright emerald greens were contrasting against dozens of cascading shades of yellow, orange and red as the leaves were turning colors for autumn. I could smell the ever-so-slight hint of moisture in the air, left over from the shower that had happened a day ago as well as whatever residual morning dew there was. My walk home was uneventful yet nerve-wracking. I could not think of another time when I walked with my hand inside my jacket on my gun all the while looking in every direction to see if there was anyone around, purposely giving everything a wide berth, so no one can jump out at me. This was an actual time for me to be afraid. In my mind I laughed at myself for how I used to get afraid of so many different nothings. I may have laughed out loud, but I had enough presence of mind to not do that again, it would have just hurt. As I passed the park I noted that the pile of clothes was still there however Damian was gone; I was hoping that it was

Jason's doing and not one of the conspirators. I passed Mrs. Perlmen's house and saw her sitting on the porch having tea. She still didn't see me; her eyesight really was that bad. I shuffled past without saying a word, why bring attention to myself if it was not needed.

Jason along with Flynn and the two who had been walking down my street this morning all pulled up in one of our 'work' trucks as I arrived at my house. Not that we really had any vehicles that were used for things other than work; fuel was just too scarce to waste frivolously. Gasoline had long since disappeared from the town; all the vehicles still running were diesel or used to be before they had been modified; now they ran on things like cooking oil. It is the best we could do to have sustainable fuels going into the future. I also always thought there was a kind of popcorn smell that I enjoyed. I was never sure if that was from the fuel itself or the exhaust, but I enjoyed it nonetheless. To my relief they did have Damian's body, laying in the back of the truck, wrapped in some old shower curtain they had managed to find somewhere along the way. Beside him was a rather large man named Darryl. He was actually one of the men who worked on the vehicles for the town; instantly it became apparent where the truck had come from. Darryl looked at me, his eyes full of alarm; blood slightly coming out from under the gag in his mouth. Pointing at Jason and the younger guy, Ronnie, I say "Bring him." As I begin walking into the house. "Flynn. You and Dale stay out here and just keep watch, we won't be that long."

You can take the paranoid nut out of the bunker, but you can't take the paranoid nut out of the man. My basement had a secret room that was my new armoury. As Jason and Ronnie were dragging Darryl down there I was already in my room getting an arsenal out for my men. I intended to go slow figuring out who of my men could still be trusted but in the short term I at least had to give weapons to the men I had here. We were about to go hunting. Darryl was tossed down hard on the cement floor. I could hear the thud followed by his attempts to gasp for air; the wind had been knocked out of him. "Take off his gag." I said to Ronnie. He sat there panting, struggling for breath. He had almost begun to breathe normally when I walked up to him and put the barrel of my pistol into his open mouth. More alarm in his eyes. Terror, really. And who can blame him. I would likely react exactly the same if I were in his position. "Darryl, right? I am going to give you one chance to not die in my basement, so I want you to think very carefully before you answer. I want to know where your neighbour is, Rusty." I winced a little as I had moved probably a little too fast in my haste to get the gun in his mouth. I could feel Darryl's tongue moving on the pistol as he swallowed. Taking the gun out his mouth I told him. "Someone tried to kill me earlier today, so I am a little irritated; you would probably not want to piss me off more." Darryl nodded that he understood.

"He made a little cabin for himself just outside of town, to the east by the river." I nodded and thanked him.

"Take him outside and shoot him. Put him in the truck with Damian." Darryl started to kick and was screaming for me to not kill him. I sighed before shooting him in the head myself. I did not want to have a mess to clean but I was not going to have him fighting us. They struggled a little as they dragged him up the stairs; he was a lot of dead weight. I could not help as much as I normally would have. Hindsight, I should not have brought him downstairs at all; he was too big to easily be dragged back up by two guys so I had Flynn go down and help to make it easier.

After Darryl was put in the back of the truck I told everyone with me the plan. It was simple and direct. We were going to Rusty's cabin; we were going to kill him and whoever was there and rip the head off this snake. I neglected to mention what I had been told by Gary, I was still holding onto that and I would deal with it once I was assured that I would be alive tomorrow.

I actually knew what cabin Darryl had been referring to; I had come across it while out for a walk some time before. No one talked as we drove out of town along the dirt road with two bodies in the back of the truck; each bump we drove over made them thud and roll around the back.

I felt each bump as well as I could feel some of my stitches starting to pull and strain. I did not think anything of it as it looked to be just some old shack, I did not actually think it was something that was being used. I would point anytime I needed Dale to turn down some other path until we were about half a mile from where we were going. I raised my hand and the truck came to a halt. "Let's go." I said as my door creaked open. That sound along with every sound we made from that point on made me think that we were not going to be able to catch them unawares. Surprise is needed just to make sure that I am not running through a forest looking for the next would-be assassin while I am still full of stitches. We walked single file through the forest along some old deer path heading towards the cabin, as the river was bubbling off to my left. That did allay some of my concerns about being detected prematurely, the sound from the river was likely to dampen any sounds we made; not that we were not trying to be especially quiet though. It was as we finally began to reach the little clearing along the riverbank where the cabin was, that I realized I could smell smoke as well as see slight wisps of it rising above the trees. I could hear the crack of the wood as it burned; I wondered if I was still just being hyper-perceptive or if this was my senses back to normal. I was used to it either way; it no longer felt as though everything was electric. I huddled close to the guys I brought with me behind a woodpile as I told them my plan was essentially for us to blitz in and kill them all. Ronnie looked a little nervous at that, I had not looked at him in the past while to know if he had been feeling this way all along or if the notion of what we were doing had finally hit him. Maybe it was the slight splatter of Darryl's blood on his cheek that was unnerving him. It was irrelevant at that point. If he failed to act as I was telling him to he would join Rusty. The door was on the far side of the cabin from us, facing the river. The campfire seemed to be over on that side as well. I had to hand it to Rusty; this did seem like a nice place to go and fish.

We walked out from behind the woodpile still single file, Flynn and Jason went to the right of the cabin; Dale and Ronnie were ahead of me on the left. Poking around the corner it was easy to see why Gary had never returned, he was frying up a fish over the campfire, sitting with his back to us in an old lawn chair that was all tattered with a bent leg. The right armrest was cracked, leaving sharp plastic spikes sticking off to the side. I whispered into Ronnie's ear to tackle him, pointing at Gary. I pushed him out from behind the cabin towards the campfire and Gary as I rushed towards the door, followed closely by Dale; Jason and Flynn were slower but not by much. It was stupid for me to be rushing like that given that I had lost a fair amount of blood earlier in the day and was still full of jagged stitches. I turned the knob and fell into the cabin. I landed on my left side, instantly opening a few stitches in my shoulder. As I collected myself from the floor I could hear the gunshots. There were screams. Coming from outside I could faintly hear Gary yelling 'don't kill me, don't kill me'. By the time I was fully aware of what was going on it was all over inside the cabin. Rusty was dead, still sitting in the chair with two bullet holes in his chest. Double-tap, center-mass. Pretty much a textbook kind of kill. Tom was lying beside the same table, his chair had toppled as he was killed with a shot to the face as well as another in the chest. There were three other adults in the house; two women, Heather who had been Rusty's wife, and Jane who was Tom's sister. The adult was Stephen, they had all been sitting over on the bunk beds when we entered, each one had been shot multiple times. Heather was not killed outright and was executed with the last shot fired before I stood up. Rusty and Heather's daughter, Rita, was still alive; she had been on the bed, I would assume playing with the women and Stephen when it all began. She was covered in blood and screaming now. My first impulse was to shoot her as well, make the screaming stop but I did not give the order. I was never in the habit of killing children nor did I even like the prospect of it. I may be an evil person, depending on your point of view, but I am not that evil. Inhaling deeply all I could smell was gunpowder. It was a caustic smell in such a small confined space. I exclaimed "Well then." as I exited the cabin. Flynn followed shortly afterwards with Rita. I asked Jason to go get the truck as I descended upon Gary.

Gary was thrown into the fire when Ronnie had tackled him. The frying pan and fish were now overturned next to the smouldering pile of logs, half strewn about. I could see his right hand was burnt and black.

That was likely a third-degree burn and if he had a medical team from before the cataclysm he may have been keeping that hand. Assuming he lived, which was looking less and less likely as I closed on him. His hand was shaking furiously, which is more likely due to the intense nature of the burns than fear. His fear was shown by the wet spot in his pants. "Gary. Gary. Gary. What did I tell you to do?"

"I told them to go see you, so they sent Damian to go. He was supposed to tell you everything. He was supposed to help you make everything ok." Looking him sternly in the eyes I slapped his right hand, a shrill scream escaped his mouth which was quickly filled with my pistol. I looked at the blood seeping through my jacket where I had torn the stitches holding my left shoulder together.

"Damian. Tried. To. Kill. Me." I spoke through my teeth. Not like it matters but there was not even an attempt to hide my seething anger. I expect that dying could ultimately be the shittiest possible thing to happen to me on any given day and it was almost that day.

"Oh god." He said, muffled by the weapon sticking out of his mouth. I took the barrel out of his mouth, grabbed the overturned lawn chair and sat down in front of him. Flynn had taken Rita over to the river and appeared to be washing the blood off her. I just sat there looking at Gary for a few moments, composing myself.

"You disappoint me Gary. I hate being disappointed. I think you tried to kill me and I think that you know more than you told me before."

"No. N- n- n- no. I- I- I- didn't." You know that you really have someone's attention when they begin stuttering like this. Not that I want him stuttering; it makes it somewhat hard to follow what he is saying and like doubles the length of the conversation.

"Gary. I want you to think. You have already lied to me. You said you didn't know where Rusty and the rest were yet here you are with them. That upsets me; that you lied to me. I trusted you to do your best. Do you remember me saying do your best? And you couldn't even do that right. I'm still alive."

"I- I- I- didn-"

"Shut up Gary. At this point the only thing you can do to save yourself is tell me who it was that was molesting the kids. If that even happened, which I am inclined to think didn't." He looked over his shoulder and raised his burnt quivering hand towards Flynn on the bank of the river as he tried to play with Rita, despite the fact she was still sobbing.

"It's him." He let out a heavy sigh. As if a huge weight had been lifted off his chest, which I guess in a manner of speaking had happened.

"Did you know that when you were talking to me before?" I sat waiting for some sort of answer. I guess there was still a weight sitting on his chest, although I think this one was more if he wanted to come clean as having lied to me more than once.

Gary cleared his throat as if he was about to speak, then simply nodded. "Mmhmm." It was now my turn to let out a heavy sigh. My actions had been dictated by the actions of Gary and the others but I could have changed the course of everything with this knowledge being given to me sooner. Jason, Ronnie and Dale were now taking everyone out of the cabin and loading them into the back of the truck.

I called Jason over by shouting his name, within short order he was obediently kneeling beside me. "Gary, tell Jason what you just told me, tell him everything you should have told me last night." Jason looked at me puzzled; he was used to me asking him to do things, giving orders, he was not used to being included in other things. I patted him on the shoulder. "Just pay attention." Gary then began telling Jason how he had come to know about Flynn's deviance, how he had been told by Rusty that Flynn had been caught by him touching Rita. The threats Flynn had made to Rusty to get him to keep it from me. He managed to be succinct yet riveting enough that Jason ended up sitting down beside me. I simply looked over to Jason and made eye contact once Gary got to the portion of the story about how Rusty had everyone convinced that I was covering for my men. My gaze drifted towards the river, Flynn was still sitting beside the river with Rita. She was no longer crying, just kind of mashing the mud from the river bank in her hands. Jason acknowledged my thinking and rose. I watched him walk over to the river bank; help Rita stand up then point her towards me. She started walking, at first looking back over her shoulder at Jason and Flynn then afterwards she started running. It was not a scared run; she looked like she was happy. Not sure if that was she was happy to be away from Flynn or if it was just my imagination. Just before she got to the area around the fire pit where there was no grass growing she tripped; seemingly on nothing, but that is kind of typical for kids. She began to cry as she looked at the scrapes on her palms; little pebbles and rough sand were now on her hands. The crying suddenly stopped as a gunshot rang out and Flynn's lifeless body fell into the river. I picked Rita off the ground, helped brush the dirt off then led her towards the fire pit. "Say night to Uncle Gary." She hugged him before being led towards the truck by Dale. The bodies were all in the back of the truck now, mostly covered by a tarp, although there seemed to be a hand and a couple feet sticking out from underneath. Jason had started to drag the lifeless body back onto the shore, Ronnie was over helping him. I could see him whispering to Jason, likely trying to ascertain what was going on. It had never been part of the plan to kill one of us, as far as he knew. I watched as Jason told him what he had done. To anyone that did not know Jason as well as I did you'd think his face seemed blank, as if this had not affected him at all. I, on the other hand, knew better. His eyes were a little more distant, lips a little more pursed together, a slight furrow on his forehead and he seemed flush. Although the flushed look could have just been due to exertion from dragging the body back onto the shore, who knows. Point is I could see the difference, what was likely a huge conflict within him that I would have to have a conversation about later. When it was just us. Jason knew better than to question me in public, when we were alone it was a different matter. There were opportunities to talk plainly, as equals. Occasionally. As Jason's explanation winds to an end I see him kick Flynn's body before they both hoist him up and start to carry him towards the truck. My attention returned to Gary. He was still shaking, his hand was looking more disgusting than it had been. The thing about the third degree burns, is that the heat trapped inside by your tissues actually remains for a time afterwards and it gets radiated out. That is why when you get a burn it feels very warm. In this case the heat that was radiating was strong enough that it was continuing to cook the flesh. As I said before about a pre-apocalypse medical team being able to save the hand, it was looking a lot less likely at that point. Gary was experiencing shock, something which I was growing more familiar with. He was pale and clammy, his skin a pale shade of whitish-blue. I almost started calculating in my head how well he would survive if I left him alone. If he would survive. I was kind of in a bit of a bind, on one hand I did actually like him a little and he did, eventually, tell me what I needed to know; on the other hand, he lied to me twice and I was not too certain that he did not have some knowledge of what Damian was returning to town to do. I hit his hand again, a little bit of flesh sloughed off. I almost vomited right there to be completely honest. It was extremely disgusting. I think that also released a little bit of ham smell which only made my stomach turn more.

"Ow." He said it so quietly and softly that you would think all I had done was flick his ear. He looked up from his hand to me. His eyes were glossy, I was not even sure if he was looking at me, per se, he looked in my direction but I could not tell if it was me he was seeing. "I think my hand is fucked up." I chuckled a little; the obviousness of his statement was a little comical at that point.

"Dale, you know what needs to happen now, don't you?"

"I know. I didn't get to eat my fish though." Another little chuckle as I patted him on the shoulder. Breaking a neck is not as easy as it seems in the movies, overcoming the tendons, bones and muscles of the neck is not that easy. I'm sure if my life were a movie that is how Gary would have died. Instead, I shot him at the base of the skull. I hadn't necessarily thought out placement when I did that and the bullet exited out of the top of his head along with brain matter and blood like the most morbid jack-in-the-box ever. I closed my eyes as I finally had a moment to do nothing. I heard Gary's body getting dragged a few feet before someone grabbed his feet and he was picked up to be put in the back of the truck. There was a faint metallic thud as his head hit the bed of the truck. My head was starting to hurt. I realized I had not had anything to drink since drinking at the hospital, I was probably getting dehydrated, hence why my head was starting to hurt.

I walk towards the truck as Ronnie is moving Gary's foot so that he is able to lift the tailgate closed. "Jason." I breath deeply as Jason comes around to the back of the truck, he had been talking to Dale and Rita who were playing with the air freshener like it was a mobile. "I need you to take a drive, over to that clearing on the hill to the west of the town. You know what I mean?"

"Umm, I'm not sure. The one where they had been doing that clear cutting from way back when?

"Ugh. I don't know if that is it, in any event, can you see the one you are thinking of from town?"

"Should be able to. Why?"

"Dump them up there, get everything you can. Make a huge bonfire at nightfall. I am not going to have people here thinking they can try to kill me without some serious ramifications. I am going to make sure the people are aware of how I feel about this. Understand?"

"Yes." He steps towards the truck and pauses. "Sir." Time would tell but at that moment it seemed as though his loyalty was wavering. Or his mind was elsewhere. As I said time would tell. Jason opened the door to the truck before looking at me. "What about you? And the kid?" I had forgotten about the girl. My mind definitely was elsewhere. I was already essentially planning my speech for tonight.

"Right. Well I was going to just walk back but I forgot about her. Take me as far as Johnston Road, then you guys can head around the town and west and I will take Rita back to town. I'll leave her with LeAnn until tomorrow." He nodded and held the passenger door open for me, then sat behind me after I got in. Again, there was not much talking on the way back. I was dropped with the girl as planned along the highway as Ronnie drove Jason and Dale off to the clearing. "Remember, nightfall. As in after it gets dark. People need to be able to see it." The last thing I said to them before they left.

I held Rita's hand as we walked into town. She was a cute little girl who stopped at every flower we passed by in order to smell it before I plucked one and gave it to her. She walked the rest of the way to the retirement home with her left hand in mine, her right holding a daisy under her nose. She seemed happy, maybe not that happy, maybe I should say content as we entered the building. I was somewhat relieved that she was likely to not remember the events of today when she got older. She was just at the age where she is starting to develop concrete memories, meaning that even if she does have some memory it is likely to be incomplete. Easier to work through when she gets older. I was however hoping that she just did not remember her parents at all; less therapy that way.

LeAnn was excited to see me return. I noted that she or someone else had cleaned my blood smears off the walls. I'm sure that is necessary for maintaining hygiene in the hospital, but it was also nice to not keep scaring Rita further, I was sure she had seen enough blood for today. "Sir. Are you okay? Did someone attack you again?" She was pulling off my jacket. As I looked over at her frantically pulling my sleeve I realized that she was seeing the blood that was now a dry stain on my shoulder.

"No. It's nothing. I'm fine. I just ripped a stitch or two." I winced as she pulled the jacket off pulling another stitch out; it had been glued to the inside of my jacket with my blood. Fresh streams of blood began to drip from my shoulder as she ran off to get her suture kit. I sat in the waiting room area as Rita began playing with some of the toys. I picked up an old People magazine from 2006; it was crazy that something like that had survived so long. Steve Irwin's tragic death was the cover story. I remembered that whole episode. It seemed so far off, so removed from where I was at that moment. It did somewhat remind me that there was a world outside my little sphere of influence, although other than the occasional straggler we did not have much contact with the outside world. LeAnn was trying to sew my shoulder back together as I read stories about long dead celebrities. "Where is Dot? She wasn't here earlier that I saw."

"Dr. Campbell? We have it worked out where we work 3 days at a time. I just stay here the whole time and sleep in the back room. It makes it easier."

"Ahh, so you don't know where she is?"

"Nope. I wouldn't see her until tomorrow. Ugh. I'm sorry sir. I didn't do a good job with the stitches. You're gonna have a really ugly scar." She was frowning as she tied off the last stitch.

"It's fine LeAnn. It'll give me a story to tell later on. Main thing is I am alive and I have you to thank for that. So thank you."

"You already thanked me sir." She was blushing. It was flattering that she had a crush as she did but not really something of real interest for me.

"LeAnn, I need you to do me a big favour. I need you to take a few minutes and go spread the word that everyone needs to attend a town-meeting tonight at around dusk in the middle of town."

"What? Yes. Why? I will, sir." Her enthusiasm is really wonderful, although she seemed a little scattered as she took off her lab coat and power-walked out of the building. Rita had stopped playing with her blocks and was now holding the remains of an old tattered children's book up for me to read. It was only part of a fairy-tale book, the story began midway through Hansel and Gretel, covered all of Rumpelstiltskin and ends midway through the Ugly Duckling. I just started reading from the start of what I had; Rita did not seem to know the difference as she crawled up onto the couch next to me and put her thumb in her mouth as she fell asleep under a green knit blanket.

LeAnn returned a short time later after having gone around telling everyone nearby, she looked as if she had been running the whole time. Her face was red and she panted for five minutes without saying a word. "Have you eaten?" It was another thing that had totally slipped my mind; I had not eaten since the little nibbles I had stolen last night at the harvest celebration. She took the silence of me trying to remember if I had or not as an indication that I hadn't so she again went off to begin grabbing some food from the room near the old nurses' station. "What is all this about sir?" She said from around the corner. I looked over to Rita; she slightly squirmed with the increased noise but did not wake. I said nothing; I did not want to wake her if possible. In all fairness she had had a long day; and yes I understand that was in large part my doing but still, there is a point where you have to begin working forward. LeAnn came from the kitchen with a plate of cornbread, a cold piece of fried fish and an assortment of vegetables. It seemed kind of an odd combination of foods, but I had realized how hungry I was after it had been mentioned to me; so hungry in fact I really did not care if it was cold. My mind was still thinking forward despite the fact I was trying to live more in the moment; it's rude to neglect your host just as it would be rude to neglect a guest when you are the host. She handed me the plate and sat in the chair next to me. "Sorry, I did not mean to ask too many questions. I'll let you eat in peace." I chuckled at that.

"That is not necessary. I just didn't want to yell and wake up the girl; she needs to sleep." I took a bite of my cornbread then gestured for something to drink before I continued. "There are- well were- two separate but intertwined problems. First, was apparently this girl was being abused by someone she should have been able to trust. Unbeknownst to me one of my guys was doing that. Understandably, her parents got angry when they found out. Now, why they decided to not say anything I do not understand but end result was they blamed me for everything and well..." I nodded towards my shoulder.

"God. Who would do that? She's so sweet. And why are they blaming you sir?"

"It was Flynn; he is no longer an issue. And well. They aren't blaming anyone anymore." I frowned as I came to a bit of a realization. "On that note, now that you made me think of it, how would you feel about adopting Rita? She'll need someone who can care for her, someone who will love her, and I think you are that kind of person." LeAnn's face was a little pale and flat for what seemed like minutes. I think it really just took her some time to process what was happening.

"Sir. I don't- I'm not- I'd love to but- Yes." She shrugged as she acknowledged the request, not the overwhelming enthusiasm you would prefer when getting someone to adopt a child but grand scheme of things I am correct I believe LeAnn would likely do well with raising her. As well she has proven over the years to be a very good listener which is exactly what Rita will likely need as she gets older, especially if she ends up being able to recall any of the events from earlier today. I smiled at LeAnn as I continued eating the food she had provided. LeAnn looked at Rita sleeping before she disappeared to the room she stayed in while she was here in order to prepare a space for Rita to sleep. She was a cute little girl; it would be easy for her to get attached to her and that would at least give her a chance for a good life moving forward.

I sat in the waiting room of the hospital for the remainder of the day until the sun started to drop closer to the horizon; the sky was filled with a mix of light blue, lavender, salmon and orange. There were a few clouds, occasionally blocking the last rays of sunlight for a few seconds before the cloud moved out of the way allowing the sun to continue to shine as it finally touched the ground and began to dip out of sight. That was my queue. I now needed to go out and reassure the people that they were now safe, from everything, including me. I had resolved the issues that were troubling us all. I arrived ready to tell everyone exactly what had happened. There was understandably some apprehension on my part as the last time I had stood in front of a crowd of my own people it became a mob before my eyes. I ascended the little stage that was in place, so I could address everyone, I stood off looking towards the clearing that I was expecting to see a light from. There was nothing as of yet.

"Citizens of Republica. Earlier today I was the victim of an attempted assassination." Some people looking around. Some concerned, some looking scornful. Overall, not a very good beginning to this speech. "This was perpetrated by a group who were angry at one of my men for something he had done. While I understand their anger, we live in a society. We have the rule of law here. Laws exist so that we can maintain social order, without that order we would only have chaos; we can not simply go about taking the law into our own hands. I am here to assure every one of you that the man in question, the one who upset them, has been dealt with harshly, such that the preservation of our society is assured from his deviance. As well, the assassins themselves have been dealt with harshly as well. I gave you people everything; my blood, sweat and tears. Murder is not condoned, especially not the murder of the father of this community. For their attempt on my life they have paid with their own." The light finally begins to shine, off in the distance, I point everyone's attention to it. "Everyone look. That light in the distance. I want the light of that fire to burn itself in your minds. Remember the light; that is the light given off from a pyre made of a pedophile as well as by people who chose to try to murder me. I am the fire burning in this town. Just like any fire I am able to provide heat and comfort to make a house into a home. I am able to keep you warm and fed. I am the enlightenment from which you can all benefit. Conversely, if we ever have anything such as the likes of today happen again, if someone tries to murder me I will ensure that nothing is left standing as I burn you all to the ground." Shock and awe. Every face is pointed to me. Every mouth is agape. No scornful looks anymore. I have instilled fear on a grand scale. I had done it before, as I mentioned previously, but that was only ever in small groups. This had an effect on the community as a whole. It was intense. Any instances where I had felt powerful in the past paled in comparison. Having people move out of the way as I walked through the crowd was not something new but having people literally jump back so as to not be close to me was much more impressive. I really revelled in it. It was at this point that I truly realized how far I had risen (or fallen) depending on your perspective and there was no going back as I would never willingly give any of this up.

Five of my other men had been milling through the crowd as I spoke. They were looking for those who did not attend. There were more than I would have liked. Whether these were people who simply were not told that there was a meeting in the town square, they felt they could just miss it or if they were part of the group of angry people from the harvest festival (there were definitely more people who rushed towards me than were in the shack) it did not matter. Anyone who was not at that meeting. Anyone who was not there to receive the message that I needed to convey was a potential threat. And they were dealt with as such. Each night for a week there was a curfew starting at dusk. Each of those nights, as dusk fell, there was a new fire and there were a few fewer people living here. In the end I won't say it was the right thing to do, nor will I condemn my own actions. What mattered most of all is that in the end I ensured stability for this community. I ensured not just my own safety but the safety of others living here. The ones who simply wanted to live their lives, to recreate civilization as much as possible. No matter how uncivilized you had to be in order to achieve it.

CHAPTER 14 – PURPLE

I would venture a guess that someone from the outside world would now be wondering just how I managed to get LeAnn to be so concerned about me. As I said there was an obvious crush there, but it goes deeper than that. Pretty much every 'successful' dictator was the head of their own "cult of personality". Pick any one; Mussolini, Stalin, Hitler, Mao Zedong had all had their images plastered in every place they could. Their people were taught to revere them and idolize them. I had the special distinction among them all as being the only one who was literally the head of their own personality cult; the only one that I know who did the indoctrination personally. It probably does nothing to exonerate me by referring often to those that were fairly heavy on the oppression side of the spectrum, but I was essentially the head of my own Hitler Youth group. Not that I was teaching any of the garbage that they taught to their young, but I was still their teacher, I was the primary person molding the young minds. Every lesson had an element of hero worship imbedded in it. As I said much earlier, only one person is really going to aggrandize me, so I had to do it by necessity. I guess these younger ones were the ones who truly knew the value of having me in charge. They likely heard the story of finding the cannibals and removing them enough times that they were getting bored of hearing it; they were of course getting the PG-13 version of events. Same with finding this place, bringing it up to snuff. Making it a home for all of us. I did. I was the one who saved you all. I would relay the stories during every history lesson. Everything had duty attached to it. Why do you need to learn to read? Because we need you to be a contributing member of society. I made Republica and I need everyone to help make it strong. Collective effort all working towards a stronger community. There is nothing wrong with that and a little self-glorification should be forgiven to the guy who put it all together. Why should you learn mathematics? Same reason; every job will at some point at least use basic math; also there is no reasonable reason to not learn the fundamentals. History? Well how else are you to know how lucky you are; without a comparison at how bad things used to be in the past. Also, there is the usual argument about being doomed to repeat history if you do not know it and learn from it. I will admit that I did omit some of the things that would have put me in a negative light like perhaps some comparisons to the aforementioned dictators.

My role as the primary teacher began somewhat innocently while Republica was still in its infancy. For the first 6 months to maybe about a year the town grew slowly; people were only arriving at a rate of two to three a week; on a good week. It could at times be as low as one over the course of two weeks. Regardless, it was just a trickle for the first while before the faucet was opened. As each person entered the town we took note of their skills and aptitudes; those that had deficiencies especially in the area of growing food were given lessons. It was kind of an on-going thing where people would just come with me while I tended to my farm. Or helped feed the animals, or whatever. As more people appeared there were more options for having them taught. I began to take a more formal role that involved less dirt. I began teaching people the essentials that they would need in order to do whatever job we assigned them. Sometimes it was just simple things like being able to read a manual for this or that. Other times it was a little more intensive; after I covered the prerequisites then the person who would be supervising the apprentice would take over. If we had such a person. My biggest challenge during this time was teaching those who did not have a mentor on how to learn such that they could teach themselves for their new future profession. Of course, if they already had a profession then that was the best scenario as we just put them into whatever role they were going to perform.

Aurora was my first real student; which I doubt would surprise anyone. She had been too young to really teach her anything before she and her mother left but I was there for her first steps (at 7 months old) and first word (boba- which we assumed meant bottle). My real contribution to her education began even as people were trickling in. There were a small group of us who would spend each evening together, talking, reminiscing, snacking and in my case often explaining or expanding on ideas. Our initial lessons were still on things relevant to us and our new situation after the cataclysm. Things like the water cycle: evaporation, condensation, precipitation and accumulation. She had asked many times why there was so little rain so we ended up having an impromptu class, sitting in the middle of the park by the fire; me drawing a diagram in the dirt. Each person that was there that night watched as I dissected each step and what it meant. How it worked. I explained things in likely more detail than was necessary but as I talked more, every person seemed to have a question that may or may not have been totally relevant, but it still got answered in turn. I already mentioned how dust is the catalyst for rain drops falling. Another example I could point out is the reason that people sweat is that when water evaporates it uses some of the heat from the object it is attached to in order to change from one state, liquid into another state, gas. Whether the heat is taken from a person or muddy water sitting in a puddle on the street the process of evaporation cools both. As your body heats up it begins to sweat, as that water evaporates off your skin it steals those little bits of energy in the form of heat and therefore cools the body. The reason for explaining was to show that an abundance of external heat tends to lead to a higher rate of evaporation, I think that idea might have gotten missed a little in my explanation here. I'll assure you that I did explain it a little better at the time. Some things are not necessary to know, but it doesn't hurt to know. Going further I could also explain why fanning yourself when you are sweating makes you cooler faster. Of course, there is further information behind that; the air being pushed by the fan actually reduces the air pressure over the droplets of water. The drop in air pressure pressing down in the water means that it is easier for the heat to allow the change in state by that droplet; meaning it cools you off faster as more water droplets are evaporating at any given time. See, that is likely over explained and not really necessary, but it does give a real depth into why things happen. But I think you get the point overall. Each step when broken down and explained helps you understand the inner works of the things around you. Go any direction out of your own scope, whether you look at things more and more closely until you see things microscopically or even atomically. Or look broader and broader until you see the whole solar system, whole galaxy or the known universe. People always used to make fun of the 'nerds' in society but I think they were the luckiest people ever; they got to experience things in a much more exciting and fascinating way than the rest of us. I, at best, got just a taste of those experiences. Teaching others started as a passion, I was just in the right place at the right time I guess. It did also help that I was able to just anoint myself the teacher. Morphing my role as teacher into full-fledged personal propagandist did not really happen until after I was officially made the permanent leader but even before that there were little elements strewn throughout my teachings.

Now here is the thing about indoctrinating young people. On one hand, it is easy in a way; you simply limit their information to what you want them to know. You keep feeding it to them, until it is all they know. Kids are impressionable, the more they are told something the more it becomes part of their knowledge base for when they get older. I do not recall the way I had seen 'independent thought' defined so I am just going to go with my best approximation here. In short, I would say independent thought is the ability to think creatively, 'outside the box'. I am actually not liking that definition, maybe it is the ability to analyze, dissect and question all the information you are given. Whatever. I was going for the opposite of that. All of the children were expected to be 'thankful' each day to their savior. Every day began with what amounted to the Republica version of a Pledge of Allegiance, although it was not anywhere as formal as you would have seen pre-cataclysm. "We thank you, our savior; for delivering us from the chaos; for making Republica a home for all; we will continue your work to make a strong and prosperous town". This was followed by each child talking about what they were grateful for from the day before. I would of course prod them into being thankful for things that could be attributed to me: safety, a home, food, friends, etc. As well each child thanked me at the end of every school day as they walked out for saving them. The funniest part of all of this was it began firstly as just a child who entered the town and the very next day was attending classes with the other children. She was just so thankful for all that I had done that I had to interrupt her just so I could teach that day's lesson. The end of the day led to more thanking, likely having been pent up all day of not thanking me. This continued on until all the other children started thanking me as well. Whether they saw that I had really done so much for them that they felt they should thank me or if they were just following along with someone who was grateful I am not totally sure. In the end it did not matter because I took the concept and turned it into something I could use.

Obedience, duty, honesty. These were all stressed every day. No talking out of turn. Raise your hand when you want to speak and wait to be acknowledged. Stand in line when told to. No asking "why". Always do as you are told; follow the rules. Follow what you are told to do by your superiors. No lying. No 'stretching the truth'. Take responsibility for your own actions. And I could go on and on. In truth I don't know what, if anything, really separates me from the old communist regimes from the Soviet Union but you do kind of have to admit that the tranquility of the citizenry all doing the same thing, following all the rules, even if it is behind an "Iron Curtain" is nice. Compared to the world as it was during the Cold War, the world in the time just prior to the cataclysm was somewhat of a let down. Individuality run amok into tons of little hoodlums feeling entitled, all taking videos on their smart phones of kids beating up smaller helpless kids. Taking pictures of drunk girls getting raped. Showing off their new luxury car that daddy's wealth had bought them. The respect that children of the 50s and 60s had compared to the millennials…. night and day. The millennials had none that that I could see. And when they did "respect" someone, it is only because they were shown respect first. Not to say that every and all of either group; the children of the 50s-60s or the millennials were all good or bad, but I am speaking more in generalizations. In the strictest use of the term I am talking in a prejudiced manner. I feel that I am correct so just let me have this. Really, if you want a demonstration though you can look at the 'revolts' we had. I would say nearly none of the younger generations were involved in the first or Nixi's uprisings; and that just illustrates the sway that I had over the younger ones. They were not willing to break ranks. They were obedient, honest and loyal. Just like I taught them. Most of them anyways.

I had mentioned before how there was a little resentment between some of the other students and Aurora. She was seen as being favoured because she received extra attention, which given everything you know now is understandable but is still not excusable in the grander context. This was not exactly favoritism in a positive manner though. It is something like a class clown getting more attention than some of the other more well-behaved students because there is no difficulty keeping order with the others. I think the biggest part of the problem is not that Aurora was my blood, but it was because I was the one who found her and back then I was just a normal man. She saw the creeper knock me senseless. She had Princess; her walking security blanket. By the very nature of our relationship from the first time we met at the church she saw me in a different light than all the others. Aurora stood for the morning pledge the same as all the others as they repeated the same words every morning; I watched her each morning, mouthing the words but never actually making the words out of her own breath. Aurora had a different perspective on the whole hero worship thing. She was with me as we cleaned the houses, room by room. She was sometimes not there as she was off doing other tasks that she was given. She knew I was just a man, I was vulnerable like everyone. I could be indecisive. I could be funny, silly even. I was nothing special in her eyes. That was the disconnect between Aurora and the other children. The fact that she never seemed to believe any of it was the reason that she received extra attention. I am kind of unclear as I sit here writing and reflecting on what my intentions with her were. On one hand I would like to say that I was in fact trying to groom her to take over for me as leader however that was never the path I really put her down. Nor was I trying to make her into a mindless child either. There is a distinct lack of clarity for me right now as to what I was trying to do, in regards to her. My only guess is that with her I was only trying to teach her without giving her much in the way of 'brainwashing'.

Aurora would walk in each morning, say "morning" before proceeding to her seat. Princess still at her side every where she walked would curl up on a little piece of blanket between Aurora's desk and the radiator. I really loved that dog for how it made it, so I never had to worry about her. Princess was never more than mere feet away from her; never growling or showing teeth yet attentive to all that went on around Aurora. The few people that had dogs in the town all kept them at home, no one else had it walk around with them. That in itself was something special about her. I do not think any other children in town even had a dog let alone brought it to school with them. She was the envy of every child who ever liked dogs. Almost every morning when it came time for her turn to say what she was thankful for she would name Princess; who would then raise his head, receive his morning pat then lay back down again. Like clockwork. Once Aurora threw me for a loop by saying she was thankful for Lisa. But it was always in a monotone. She never had any real inflection in her voice when she was thankful for something. It was like an ongoing depression however it was not something that persisted outside the classroom. She played with the other children; ran with Princess through the park; laughed at celebrations; sang at birthday parties. All normal. In class she was disinterested. That would most likely mark how she is more like her mother than like me. If she were more like me she would have been fascinated with learning. This is not just parental boasting but she was smart; anything I could teach she was able to assimilate and spit back at me. She just didn't seem to care while doing it. She was not oppositional during class which was a real blessing for me as I could have lost the whole group if I had to fight for control of the class with a child. Win or lose it would have meant that my veneer of infallibility would have been marred for all of them. Aurora received more attention than most for the simple fact of I needed to do that. My teaching of all of them was only as strong as the teaching received by the weakest believer of the class which was her.

On top of this were Aurora's natural social skills. Far exceeding mine she was able to make the newest resident feel at home in minutes. While the other students all learned to not speak out of turn, to not interrupt me, to be attentive; Aurora was constantly talking or trying to. This is something we had in common, to a point. When I was in elementary school my parents had been told during a number of parent-teacher conferences that I was constantly talking. For me that stopped around Grade 6 and was replaced by an increasing sense of shyness. For her the ability to converse and feel comfortable with others only grew with time. Unfortunately, once she finally hit her 16th birthday it was no longer permissible to have her disrupting my classes, she was tainting the adulation I was trying to foster in the young minds of Republica. I began teaching her one-on-one, however her disinterest seemed to persist. I could not even fathom what she was thinking about as she avoided my lessons to the best of her ability. She still did the work, the bare minimum however that only seemed to extend as far as my reach. These were times when I again began to lament at not having announced who I was to her; as things went on it became so difficult to even think about telling her that at times I honestly forgot she was my child.

At some point, I can not totally say when it was, my frustration grew with Aurora to the point that I knew I was likely to react in a manner that would not be helpful and would only create a resentment for me that would be nearly insurmountable in the future. Even with telling her who I really was to her; proving to her that she was not alone and there was someone left who loved her from the start. It is an assumption of course for me that her difficulty with me was due to her believing that her parents were both gone. I cancelled my lessons with Aurora for a week while I tried to think outside the box. I pondered on whether she was lonely, if she was upset at how I acted right from the outset by being grumpy, if she was just moody, if she saw right through my façade and realized I was a bad person. My solution, quite possibly half-baked, was to begin to bring her into my world. To make her my apprentice, everyone else in the community had one why not me. This would give me a chance to cover a number of possible reasons for her indifference. I could become a surrogate father-figure for her, since I was not a real one, per se. I could allow her to see the inner workings of how to govern a community of people; how to make things work, from there she could understand why I do the things I do. I could give her responsibility in order to try to get her to look past any feelings of rebelliousness that she may have had that would have been characteristic of a teenage girl.

I felt the best way to accomplish this was by doing it imperceptibly. Maybe a more direct plan would have seemed less manipulative, but I guess that just wouldn't have been me. What adult male really knows how to deal with a teenage girl? Her lessons began to take a more hands on approach. We would wander up and down the streets checking on this and that. Each day we would do something new. Check on the power plant or water treatment or retirement home, whatever really. It was simply an inspection tour that was held essentially daily. Out of the norm for what I did on a regular basis however as I said Aurora needed to learn something of what I did, on occasion. Princess, still at that point her constant companion would trail a few feet behind us. His muzzle had begun to grey but overall, he was still going strong considering everything. Each day for weeks we would walk around talking to this person and that. People around town were often giving Aurora sideways looks, as if to question what she was doing to which I would often tell them it was part of her education. That would often shut the conversation down; soon she learned to answer that for herself.

It took me a while to notice, probably longer than it should have that Aurora was not disinterested in me or what I was saying. She was, in fact, observing. The day I realized that was one of the most relieving days I had but also one of the most troublesome. Relieving in that I finally understood where her mind was at but distressing in that it forced me to reflect on any of my words or actions that she had observed or heard about from others. Regardless of my 'official' parental status I did still want a relationship with her. I still loved her, in my way, and I craved for her to love me. I missed all those hugs that real fathers would get Christmas morning for getting their only daughter the gift she really wanted. I missed birthdays and boo-boos. And once I was around and able to get all those things I was too scared to say who I was and begin to fulfill the role I should have done. This left me trying to fill the role of a surrogate so I could get what I should have gotten on my own. My daughter's love.

As things continued to progress, after I realized what Aurora was doing, our relationship got much better. She honestly responded to me no longer 'trying so hard'. She was so alike her mother in that all she wanted and needed was independence. On the upside for me I think I learned from the failures earlier in my life that instead of trying to hold on tightly I should loosen my grip a little. It is kind of like that old saying; if you love something let it go, if it comes back then it was meant to be". I do not leave things open to chance like that, in essence, I gave more rope but never let go entirely. With a long enough leash the one on the other end never even knows they are being held back.

There was a point where after our interactions became more mundane and regular that we actually had a conversation about what she was going to do. It was something similar to a parent talking to someone who is starting to date their child. Or at least that was how it felt to me. It was not a normal kind of conversation where we discussed the weather and how the crops were doing and the various bits of gossip. We sat at a picnic table in the center of town eating lunch on a day that we had been doing our inspections around the town. I had been thinking about having this sit-down for a while with her, especially since I realized I was about to quickly run out of things to show her. She seen every little bit of the inner workings of the town. Met every person, shook every hand. Asked every person about their day, their job and their life since coming to Republica. In reality, we needed to have a conversation. I had told her everything about this place and it was now her time to choose; to become my successor or to do something else.

"So. What are you going to do with your life?" She stopped with a mouthful of food and just looked at me with a confused scowl.

"iph-" She held up her hand then covered her mouth as she strained to chew quickly while also managing to not choke on her food. A deep swallow and she again tried to speak before reaching for her glass of water. "I thought you were going to tell me that."

I mused at the thought. With most others I would have had a hand in choosing their path; Aurora was obviously different in that regard. If she had followed along with the rest of the students then perhaps I would have taken a more active role. "Nope. It is up to you... Unless you say something stupid like you want to be a mime or an astronaut. I have my preferences, but I want to hear what you think."

"Astronaut is not stupid. You have to be really smart for that."

"Ugh. Yes, I know that, and I was the one how told you. However, we barely have a working plane so getting into space is not a possibility right now. And stop being a jackass, you know what I meant. So... what do you want to do?"

"Well, I dunno-"

"Don't know. I taught you better than that, at least use real contractions and not slang."

She rolled her eyes. "I don't know what I want to do. I hadn't really thought about it." I looked at her across the table. Continuing to eat, waiting for her to resume talking. After all these years I had come to know her patterns. She would say she didn't know, then sit and mull it over a little bit then come out with her answer. "Well even back when I was a little girl mom always said I should be a lawyer when I grew up. I used to argue with her about everything. What to wear to school, why I shouldn't hit that boy I was in kindergarten with, about getting Lisa to watch-…"She trailed off.

"Interesting. Why lawyer though? You argue enough to not need to do it professionally." My eyes narrowed on her as I spoke that, just a subtle disapproval at her tendency to disagree. "Also, do we even need a lawyer here? We don't have an economy per se. We barely have personal belongings, most stuff actually belongs to the community."

"Yeah. Er, I mean, yes, we do need a lawyer here. It would actually be able to solve a lot of problems people have with each other. Half the time the arguments start as just little disagreements, which turn into bigger things. If someone was able to look at the law and arbitrate for them… then it would solve all the little problems that people have. Or at least most of them." I was done my food and now sitting across from Aurora, in my 'thinking position' with my chin in my right palm. I was looking to see if she was going to give anything away; if there was something more she was not telling me. She on the other hand was looking at me with a cute little expression, like a puppy face. It was at that moment I realized that she was playing into a role, Daddy's little girl. She was asking for the car keys tonight and she was doing everything to ensure that I said yes.

"I don't think I am sold on this. We have the rule of law. We have order here. We have existed for over ten years; built this whole place from the ground up. Well, sort of. And never have we ever really needed a lawyer."

"But we will. Republica is only going to get bigger. We're going to get more and more people arriving, more babies being born. We will need a legal system to keep people civilized. And I want to be part of bringing people back to sophistication."

"The Sophists were just normal everyday Greek philosophers except they charged money for their teachings instead giving it away for free. So, what I am hearing is that you want to make us into a society where money rules us again."

"Yes, I have heard that story before and that is not what I mean. I want to take the best parts of the world as I remember it from before and bring it back. I want everyone to be treated fairly and justly so we can all get along and work for the future."

In my mind I was wondering if she was just repeating things that I had said before back to me. It would be a manipulation that is likely to succeed if that is what she was doing. Daddy's manipulative little angel? Her face was showing me nothing but sincerity so I was forced to put my doubts aside and look at it as a genuine request. "What about taking over running aspects of the town? You have already been doing that with me and you can still have a hand in moving things toward the future. You are number 2." Puzzlement, I had not shown her the population list. "Never mind, I'll explain it later. In any event you are smart enough that you could take over supervising parts of the town, it would make my life easier and then you could still work for the future."

"I think I would be able to better help people with the law, anyone can supervise, I want to help resolve problems that people have." I was in all fairness pretty sold at this point. I was starting to get all proud, like a mother excited her child is going to be a lawyer.

"Slight problem with your plan. We have no lawyers. Who is going to teach you?" I find the fact that we have no lawyers alive in the town to be particularly amusing and here is why. There were always jokes about lawyers being snakes or cockroaches or some other form of vermin; living under rocks or in sewers or wherever. If that were really the case then there should have been some lawyers who survived the flare and made their way to us. The only real determination I can make from that is that they were not quite the vermin everyone thought they were.

"We have a library. Also, all the law books that were in that law office that is next to the post office are still there. I can read it all for myself. You know I am smart enough to teach myself those things." Bah. She was right. And she had expected this conversation at least a little. Or at the very least that question, she had no hesitation in her answers. Daddy's little lawyer.

"You have already been reading the law books haven't you?"

A sly little smirk came across her face; I got her. "Only a little... I just found it interesting."

My look of disapproval appeared before I relented to her. Even if she was not aware that I am her father she definitely knows how to play me the same way. "Mmmhmm. Well okay, you sold me. Since you have already started, here is how we are going to do this. Get me some of the books from the law offices, I'll use them to help you study. We'll get you study plans and assignments and what-not. You are going to be doing reports and analyses. You are going to have to explain your rationale and cite precedents for your decisions. Understood?"

"Of course. I can do all that."

"Good. We should get back to what we should be doing, lest people think we're lazy." I chuckled while she just shrugged. The lack of lawyers left us with a definite problem. Our only would-be lawyer was going to be largely self taught; and therefore her applications of the law were subject to her own perceptions and prejudices on what she believed. I of course was trying to influence her perception of the law but as evidenced by our interactions already that was going to be a tall order for me. As the day started to wind down Aurora appeared with an old rusted red wagon with a large cardboard box inside. It was overflowing with law books for me to read through. I helped her bring them on to my porch; I would be bringing them in later.

Each week I would pick a random book, find an appropriate case study, copy out the relevant details of the legal case from long ago, whether it was a custody suit, or property disagreement, abortion issue or class action lawsuit. I would give her the situation, tell her which side she was on for that case then let her come up with a plausible argument to try to press her issue. She was a pretty good lawyer in my opinion. I would purposely give her the side that lost nearly every case. I didn't want to make it too easy for her. She needed to be able to think outside the box, see things in different ways than others. Look for holes and possible compromises. In my mind she did not win every case I gave her, she was actually batting around .500 but regardless of that every time she was thoughtful and concise with her reasoning. Her points were backed up with precedents and interpretations of the law. Sometimes, though her interpretations bordered on downright devious. Using subtle difference in word meanings and deftly paraphrasing to back up her side when both she and I knew that she was purposely bending the law. I am ashamed to say that I was quite proud of her for that. Not the bending of the truth part but the ability for her to take on a subject and largely learn it on her own to the point that she became proficient enough that she likely could have argued to at least a stalemate with some of the best lawyers ever. Honestly though, I know she only did that to prove that she could, when I gave her impossible arguments to try to support. Most of the time her positions were based on what was best for society as a whole; caring about making civilization better through harmony and living within the rules. In the end, everyone benefitted from having someone around that was concerned with order in accordance with the law; as opposed to my brand of order which was obtained through fear and intimidation. Everyone, except for me that is.

CHAPTER 15 – A PALE YELLOW DRESS

I think this is now the appropriate time to talk a little about Lisa. I am going to assume most of the people who read this are somewhat observant enough to realize that I have mentioned Aurora's mother on a number of occasions but never really talked about her in depth. Funny thing is I don't have any intention of talking of her, I believe that she is long dead. She and Lisa are not one and the same. Lisa was in essence not much more than a babysitter. As I did mention before Aurora's mother was a 'social butterfly'; that seems to be something that extended straight to the end of civilization. I did not get all the details, but it seems that around a week prior to everything happening she went on a vacation to someplace warm, Hawaii or Mexico or wherever; the exact place is irrelevant now. Her trip was bought by her man de jour, presumably someone with more money than brains but that is just an assumption based on my negative opinion of her. Lisa was enlisted as the one to watch over Aurora. This was decided unilaterally by her mother. Lisa was chosen over me. Over Aurora's aunt. Over her grandmothers. There were literally a dozen family members who were more than likely willing and available to take care of her. I may seem like I am being a little paranoid again, only assuming that family members could have kept Aurora safe but at the time of the cataclysm Lisa had only known her for weeks. That, to me, seems irresponsible and careless on the part of her mother. But that is all stuff in the past. And I will admit that as it stands right now I am actually quite happy that Lisa was the one watching Aurora at the end. I was apparently the go-to person in the event of a disaster. Lisa had been told that she was to go with Aurora to Hillview. I was expected to go there in the event of a disaster. Damned if I could remember it, but apparently, prior to Aurora's birth, her mother and I had spent time in the town; I remembered being in the town but until I was reminded I could not remember whom had been accompanying me. It boggles the mind how someone you have known for weeks says "here watch my kid for a couple weeks while I go fuck in the sun. Oh. And in case of a worldwide disaster, please go to this particular town" and you follow the instructions. I mean if I was told something similar I am pretty sure I would have been getting a hold of child protective services to come save this child from this obviously crazy and neglectful mother. Lisa didn't. She took Aurora to where she was told to. They hid in the basement of the church. They survived because of it. And they waited for me.

I know for a fact that Lisa did not expect me to actually arrive. I was presumed dead like everyone else. Aurora on the other hand had been clinging to a thought that I was going to ride up as a white knight right after the cataclysm and save them. Well I was much slower than she had expected. Directly after the flare Aurora was consoled by the idea that I would 'be coming to get her and Lisa soon'; Lisa did not know what else to say. Over time the consolation became 'any day now'. Then she no longer wanted to hear of me coming. I was dead. Like everyone else. In all fairness if I had known I was expected I would have arrived post-haste. However, that was not the case and they had to wait.

There was also the hope that her mother would be coming from whatever far off place that she had gone. I think it would be obvious that never occurred. Whether she survived the flare and made an attempt to come for Aurora we will never know. Chances are whatever plane she was on fell out of the sky as the electromagnetic interference knocked out the computers on the plane. Or it never even got off the ground because of that same problem. Maybe she tried to take a boat from there to here, or at least the nearest point to here on the water, and that boat sunk somewhere along the way. Maybe it was bandits that stopped her from coming. Maybe brigands. Cannibals. Rapists. A starving bear. Maybe a simple cut on her finger got infected and led to blood poisoning. Who knows; it is all speculation. Just random guesses. In all honesty, it was likely the hottest day on record that stopped her from coming. And it is no longer important. What is important is that Lisa sat with Aurora in that church, waiting for something or someone to help them.

It took years for Lisa to work up the courage to talk to me about some of these details. For the most part our conversations had always been rather vague or relating to her. I remember asking to tell me about her once many years ago while we were working at clearing the houses. At that point I had likely been in the town for at least a few weeks, but she had never really opened up. The conversation was really going nowhere when I first asked her to talk about herself. She just giggled and said she didn't know what to say, so I led her with some basic questions. Any brothers? Sisters? One of each. Sister is older, brother was a year younger. Did you go to something like college? No. What did you do, you know, before the flare? Worked as a cashier at a grocery store. Any pets? None. Are you married? In a relationship? No, she was not married, and I got a stupid look for asking if she was in a relationship; of course, she wasn't, everyone was dead. I'm sure she assumed I was trying to get to know her, so I could start a relationship with her but really I was just making chit-chat and those are normal kinds of questions to ask. There were dozens of other questions that I can no longer recall but you get the point. Each question opened the door just a little more until Lisa finally started to no longer need to be prompted. Her favorite color is blue. But not just any blue; Royal Blue. There was a reason for that which likewise escapes me. She had grown up on a "farm"; I use the quotation marks mostly because she did. The farm she spoke of was I guess what would be classified as a hobby farm. Like 6 or 7 acres total land. Mostly enough for a couple horses, a few cows, chickens, pigs, goats; whatever. I don't actually remember what all the animals were. I just remember her talking of her horse, a quarter horse named CeeCee. She had named it when she was still a little girl. She had talked of how she had been so sad when it had to be euthanized, some sort of degenerative joint problem or something. Lisa had hopes of doing some sort of thing related to the rodeo. I am not well versed in the particular events they would have there other than bull-riding or cattle roping. I guess CeeCee dying had kind of taken the wind out of her sails. From there her life kind of spiraled, she began drinking and doing drugs. In her own words she became a bit of a slut. I could see while we were talking of all this that her eyes were starting to well up. Her parents did not know what to do with her. In the end they were essentially exasperated with her and she took the opportunity to leave. When she turned 17 she left home to move to the city; apparently, she and her boyfriend from high school had run off together to live someplace more exciting. Sound familiar? Yeah, that I would assume is how Aurora's mother and her met, in some seedy bar or what-not. She never delved into the story of leaving home much past that although I will assume that their whirlwind relationship did not last significantly longer than she had already told me. In the end she was living alone in a bachelor apartment, working in a grocery store. She had nothing going for herself in any significant way. Perfect situation really for her to just drop everything and watch some random woman's child while that woman runs off to some far off tropical land.

While she never explicitly said to the people in town that Aurora was her daughter she kind of played it that way. When it came time in her mind for me and her to have a conversation where she informed me that she knew who I was; it was understandably awkward for me. I was trying to dance around the truth; which when you know you have been caught is not the most comfortable thing, especially for me. It happened on a day that was near the end of fall. Things had been fairly normal for the couple years prior; food was plentiful. People in town laughed and joked; like before everything got cooked in the flare. I had just come from the back yard where I had been feeding the chickens and the other barnyard animals. I was now sitting on my porch, looking over the garden in my front yard. I watched as Lisa came out of her house that was a little down the street. It was not abnormal to see Lisa; I had been essentially neighbors with her for years. What was different and really caught my attention was how she looked. I was used to seeing a girl who would wear overalls tied around her waist leaving her white t-shirt exposed. Or jeans and some type of work shirt. Really the kind of clothes you are fine with getting dirty. That particular day she was wearing some sort of dress. I really could not even tell you the difference between a skirt and a dress although I am pretty sure this was not a skirt. It was light colored with pinkish flowers, about knee length, straps going over each shoulder and only the slightest hint that she had cleavage. If I had to venture a guess I would say that it was a sundress that she was wearing but that really is just a guess with the only dress descriptor I know. Chances are it was just her "Sunday best". I would say that what it covered said she was going for something that was not provocative but still meant to be appealing. My first thought was something akin to wondering who she was off to go see. She had not dated anyone in the town that I was aware of; I thought she had finally found someone that interested her. I was drinking iced tea; or to be more realistic it was what we had that could pass for iced tea. Let's be totally honest; it was tea that I had forgotten about 8 hours earlier, it was cold enough at that point to seem like iced tea. I was sipping at it, my mind somewhat drifting off about what I would have to eat as I noted that she was walking down the street and crossing the road walking directly towards my house; it had become apparent who she was planning to see. I will admit I got a little tense, and I do not mean that is some sort of sexual innuendo type of way. I started to feel anxious, it is not everyday someone dresses up to come see me.

Through all my time as leader I had essentially cultivated an aura of purity around myself. I tried to make myself seem above sordid kinds of concerns like sex; I was more focused on making Republica a utopia. Even despite my efforts to seem above that kind of thing there were still those who attempted to use their feminine wiles to try to get themselves into a First Lady position within the town. And it was not just women, two men tried to seduce me, likely assuming that since I was not biting on a hook baited with women that was likely due to my having other interests. All attempts at seduction went unanswered. Those that tried often seemed to be new arrivals; I'm sure every one of them had the idea that they could break through my hardened exterior and win me over. I would have hoped that some of the residents who had lived in Republica for any significant amount of time would have tried to dissuade people from trying but likely it was the closest they got to being able to watch a reality show. Post-Apocalyptic Bachelor. Really no harm done either way, just a lot of bruised egos. One would justifiably wonder if the reason I was feeling anxious at Lisa coming towards me dressed up was due to my possibly harboring feelings for her, something I had been secretly nurturing since we had first met. In truth, that is not really the case. Not to say that I did not find her attractive, she was pretty. Her skin looked smooth and was naturally very fair looking. Her hair always had a measure of elegance about it; whether tied in a ponytail or in a bun or just flowing normally over her shoulders; which is how her hair was that day. Lisa had a wit about her that was definitely charming; her voice was just the right tone. I cannot even describe that close to properly; it is as if her voice is in the exact perfect tone that puts it farthest from being high-pitched while still remaining feminine enough to not sound manly. Whatever, that is totally a personal choice anyways. In any event, my and her relationship never got any more intimate than the occasional hug, usually at more festive times like Christmas or our harvest festival but even then it was nothing even relating to her. I hugged pretty much every woman; I shook the hand of every man, I pinched the cheek of every child. I am still ashamed of my thought, oh so long ago, when I had looked at Lisa while we both lay next to the fire in the park and had thought about how it had been a long time since I had had sex. A change in my and/or her actions at that moment could very well have changed the entire course of what happened in Republica. I do not mean anything aggressive in what could have happened; I am not that kind of person, but I would venture we were both lonely at that point and would have liked some form of intimacy. It likely would have been for the better, less tyrannical at least but I am not so sure it would have been the best thing for the town. I believe that I really needed to be focused on the town in order to progress everything as far as it has come. I would say that it is easier to look at Lisa as a friend than anything else.

As she stepped into my yard I could see that Lisa was wearing make-up. I am not a fan of cosmetics, personally. I find that most women look more beautiful when they are natural. Maybe with some slight highlights to accentuate things but generally I will say that women look better before they "put on their face" than after. I think this is kind of where my anxiety was really based; her intentions, clothing, make-up all seemed to point to something other than the relationship that we had already made. I was used to us being friendly neighbors. Or old acquaintances. We had an established way of interacting and it seemed as though things were about to change.

She at least seemed nervous as she spoke, it meant I was not the only one feeling the discomfort as she walked slowly up my stairs. "Um. Hey. I, um... How are you?"

"I'm good. Just drinking my room temperature tea while I rest my feet for a little while. You? Where did you get the dress?" She kind of did a half spin and curtsey at the same time. "It looks nice."

"I found it in the church donation bin years and years ago. Before you got here and started all this." She waved to the town. As her attention returned to me I motioned for her to sit opposite me. I walked inside to get a glass and some more of the cold tea for her. She acknowledged as I poured her the glass. She rubbed the rim of glass as her eyes moved around incessantly. She looked at the glass then me, then the street, and back to me, her feet, my feet, then me. A nervous laugh and back to looking around.

"Soooo. What brings you here tonight?" Her eyes stopped moving around suddenly. I will say it was fairly funny timing as she was effectively staring at my crotch. She took a sip of her tea and grimaced; my guess is she would have preferred it was sweeter. I chuckled a little on the inside.

"I know who you are."

More awkward silence. I stared at her. She stared at my crotch. "Everyone here knows who I am. No one will be overly surprised when you say you know who I am." In truth, I knew what she meant but this was kind of a delay tactic, probably not the best one to use but I needed to keep her talking. It was unclear where this conversation was heading.

"I know who you were before you came here. You came here looking for Aurora. You're her dad."

"Assuming all of that is true…what difference does it make?"

"It makes a big difference to her and will make a big difference in the future." Her gaze had now risen, and she was looking me in the eyes. There was a look of hurt on her face as well as anger. To me those emotions did not fit with her announcing she knew my secret identity. I really hate it when things feel off. "People are afraid of you. No one is willing to say anything but they all think you are crazy."

"They who? And I am still not seeing how this will make a big difference in the future."

She took a deep breath as she prepared to keep talking. This, I would assume, had been on her mind for quite some time. "I said to her mom that I would take care of her. I would keep her safe. I was supposed to bring her to you and you were supposed to take over. Instead, I kept taking care of her and you went off the rails. And now so many people are scared of you that some of them have begun to really hate you. And when they find out who she is they will hurt you by hurting her." I made a mental note to myself that she had completely avoided the first part of my sentence, I still wanted to know who it was that was thinking I was crazy. In this case of deflection; I'm sure it was her plan to just ignore subjects that were off-topic and likely seemed as though it was a really good option for her. All it did for me was peek my paranoia for a little bit.

"Ok, I am a little confused here. How did you come to this whole conclusion anyways? I look nothing like her. And if this was all true then what would be the possible reasoning for hiding it all?" Yes, I was bullshitting. In reality she was right, I could have been a danger to Aurora as people would have wanted to hurt me through her.

"I saw a picture of you." I smirked at her; giving her the old 'yeah right' look. I used to take a special amount of care to avoid cameras. This was especially true back when I let my anxieties rule my life. My goal back then was to just not exist and the best way to be non-existent was not have any evidence that you ever lived. That was ultimately an impossible task. There were security cameras recording every business you could ever walk into. Cameras on the streets. Random people uploading random scenes onto the internet. I controlled my own image as much as possible, but it was likely not enough. "Aurora's mom had a picture of you that she showed me before she left. You were skinnier and shaved and much younger, but it was you. I can tell by your eyes. They haven't changed."

I cleared my throat as I searched for what I wanted to say. I now understood why she was dressed as she was. Her manner of dress had intent behind it. It was meant to convey that she was non-threatening. She was attempting to soften the blow of where I was fairly certain that conversation was about to go. "Ok. I'll play along. Since this seems to be heading towards blackmail…what do you want?"

"It's not blackmail. I want you to do the right thing. To be a father to Aurora. To keep her safe from all the people you frighten. You need to make her the priority for you and stop being the mayor." For the record Lisa was the only one that I can think of that ever used to refer to me as 'the mayor'. Compared to, being 'the leader', mayor actually sounds kind of diminutive. "It is the only way to keep her safe in the long run, you need to step aside and let the council run this place again."

As I already stated, I was not overly inclined towards wanting to give up my position, even for my daughter. At the time of this conversation I had the belief that I would be able to keep Aurora safe, even from afar. I know that my expression was getting firmer. Lisa was looking a little uncomfortable again; this conversation was likely not going as it had when she played it out in her mind while taking a shower. "There is a slight problem with your whole assumption here. Her being in danger is predicated on her being identified as my daughter." My eyes narrowed on her. "There is no one in town that thinks I am her father other than one person. And that person apparently is supposed to be keeping her safe, so it would not even make sense to bring this whole theory up."

"Stop saying it like that. Right now, it is just us sitting here. At least admit that she is yours."

A sigh. "Hmm. Well, since you put it like that. Yes. I am".

"She deserves a dad and you have neglected her long enough. She deserves to know."

"But who are you to make that determination? And what brought this on?"

"It has been years. I have been waiting for you to tell her and you only seem to be going further down a dark path. Further and further from her. She needs a dad. She already lost her mom, it would mean the world to her to have her dad back."

"And her dad has been ignoring her, or to use your word, neglecting her. For years. How fucking happy is she going to be about that?" I noted at this point that there were a couple of women walking down the street, looking at their leader having a somewhat heated discussion with someone. Not the kind of thing that I want anyone to be seeing. Seeing one challenge only leads to more. As I think I have already demonstrated.

"She will get over that. You can make a future with her instead of worrying about the past few years. She needs you."

"What is so urgent that she needs me now?"

"It's her birthday in a week. Every birthday she is reminded that she no longer has anyone to celebrate it with her."

"God. I really should remember that. It was only just Halloween. But that doesn't matter. She is safer right now. And she has you; she cares more for you than me. She doesn't even remember me other than the few phone calls I was able to have with her. She doesn't remember my voice from back then. She doesn't remember me."

"She remembers enough. She remembers that you loved her and you guys can have that again." I sat looking at her. My expression had softened considerably. I kind of felt defeated. Maybe I had been wrong all this time. Maybe I would better protect Aurora by being her dad. Maybe power over others wasn't worth losing her.

"I-" A long pause. I could feel my heart beating. It was an odd kind of sensation though; as if my heart was breaking and reforming with each beat. "I think you're right." A single tear rolled down my cheek. Lisa's maternal instincts immediately kicked in and she rose, wiped away my tear and hugged me. This was the first real intimate kind of embrace I had had in years. It felt super awkward. More than everything else that had occurred so far. "I think we need to talk more first. I don't even know her anymore. How about I announce that I am stepping down after her birthday?"

"I think that would be fine. We can talk as much as you like." Her smile at that moment looked very sweet and motherly.

For the next six days Lisa and I met each evening. Talking of all the things that I have mentioned above about her mother and the circumstances in which Aurora came under the care of Lisa. There were other things we talked of, that were really less important to this whole situation in my life. We spoke for hours every night. It was like I had an old friend come to visit. We had known each other for years. As well there was a subtle amount of vulnerability that started to come out in me as I was no longer playing a part. I was not being the leader I was just being myself. For the first time in years. Each night was filled with stories and laughs. Lisa got to try some of my cooking. My real cooking. Not the whatever we had on hand back around that campfire. Actual prepared meals; spaghetti squash with marinara sauce. Vegetable patties served on cornbread buns with French fries. Baked fish with steamed vegetables. Each meal I tried to go more flavorful, give her something she had not had in years. Something good. I should have put on a cooking class. And I am sure those few people that walked by each night thought she and I now were in some sort of relationship but that is their mistake not mine. Every meal looked like a date while we talked and reminisced.

Our conversation on the day before Aurora's birthday was actually a little amusing. It started simple enough; I asked where Aurora had been this whole week. I had seen her around town but not with Lisa. As Lisa was still her caretaker it was odd to not see Aurora at her place. She said that she had been around all along. I looked at her very confused. My thoughts instantly went to wondering if I was about to no longer have a choice in the matter of when she got told. Lisa giggled a little. She said that they hadn't been talking about our conversations. Aurora had been camping out in the backyard of one of the other little girls down the street; Lisa had checked up on her every night after our conversations. Aurora apparently had always preferred to spend some of the cooler nights outside. Lisa assumed it was due to them hiding out for so long in the church; spending their nights in the dark of the basement. Living in that musty smell of old books and Christmas decorations. Each night they would spend sitting on the mattress that lay in the basement with a little tea light candle sitting on the table beside the bed. Aurora would play with the figures from the nativity scene. First, her narratives were just re-tellings of the birth of Jesus. The random conversations the wise men would have had or at least what a young girl would think their conversations would be like. From there her telling of each night's story got weirder and elaborate. One was a sort of telling of the whole superman story with baby Jesus as Kal-El. There was a version where Mary went shopping for groceries in the manger; the shop keeper was played by one of the wise men while baby Jesus was in the shopping cart. Another was monster story with the lamb having become carnivorous. The wise men were Larry, Curly and Moe and they put on a show for Jesus, Mary and Joseph. I was listening to this and realizing that Aurora, even without my direction was doing quite well. She learned to have skills to cope with negative situations almost naturally. Even in the saddest possible circumstances she was able to have fun and be happy. The night before I had arrived in town Aurora's story of the night was something that looking back seems to have been more prophetic than pure entertainment for the two of them. She was making the baby talk to the Mary figure but in her voice. She talked of all the scary things outside, the weird sounds and people hiding. The Joseph figure then came along and in a deep voice told them that he was "her dad" and that he was here to bring them home. The figures then moved from the front of the manger to inside it. They had already been home. Lisa's eyes got wet as she relayed that Aurora had not done any nativity scene theatre since I arrived. She had no idea what happened to the other figures, but she still kept the three; Jesus, Mary and Joseph. To her Aurora had been holding out hope to have a family again; her, Lisa and me. Lisa held my hand as she looked into my eyes. "She needs her family."

"You are not her family." I said as I took my hand back from her. The conversation had come to its inevitable and abrupt end. I could see her sobbing a little as she walked back to her house; her head was down with her shoulders hunched up a little.

On the seventh day since Lisa and I had our first sit down conversation; Aurora's birthday, the whole town awoke to Lisa's house completely engulfed in an inferno. The black smoke rose into the air and could be seen for miles.

I did not tell Aurora that I was her father that day. I was convinced that she would be fine without me.

CHAPTER 16 – AND A NEW MICROWAVE…

Aurora took Lisa's death like a trooper. She was saddened quite understandably. If she hadn't been I would have actually been more frightened. She still got in essence what Lisa had wanted for her. A family for her. The little girl who she had been visiting that night ended up becoming her 'sister'; her mother adopted Aurora and raised her. That was not her idea; it was 'suggested' to her. I walked past Lisa's house going towards where Aurora had spent the night. It was early in the morning but there were already some people standing on the opposite side of the road. I could hear dozens of gasps, whispers of "oh my god", "tragic", "such a shame". There were others, much fewer in number, that were trying desperately to do something, anything to help the people inside the house. I saw a man trying to dowse the fire by throwing buckets through the window. With a fire that large and out of control there was nothing he could do. Even with a fire truck, it would have been dicey at best.

No one seemed to notice me walking by; their attention was transfixed on the blaze in front of them. The air smelled of smoke, there was the occasional pop and crack as the lumber within the house burned. The vinyl siding on the outside of the garage was melting, dripping in strands. A puddle of liquid vinyl was on the ground at the foot of the wall. I continued down the street, passing more and more people as they went to join the crowd in gawking.

I neared the house where Aurora had spent the night. The house was painted white with trim that was peeling; exposing wood that had weathered to a dark gray color, so the pink of the trim was speckled with dark blotches. I could see the tent in the backyard, blue and green, there looked to have been a rip down the side that someone had fixed with duct tape, the greatest of all inventions. The commotion outside seemed frenzied compared to the quiet emanating from the house. An old stone sat next to the walkway to the house, it had "WALTONS" carved into it, presumably the name of the previous occupants. The woman who lived there now was named Clare Sommers, along with her daughter Beth. Things like that stone, whenever I noticed them, bothered me. Not because of the thought of people that had died; they were long gone as was their claim to things like this house. Instead, it was the idea that people were now being attached to a past that was not their own. They were forced to remember those that they had never met. Everyday Clare would have to walk by that stone and see the name of those people. Even with the clean-up we had done on the house there were still likely very personal items left in the house when Clare moved in, she would have known who the Waltons were. She would have seen pictures stashed throughout the house, found old correspondence, seen the little scratches on the wall noting the height of the Walton children as they grew, used the "His" and "Hers" towels. All of those kinds of things are an anchor for someone who is trying to move on with their life. To make something of their own. To live. I stopped and looked at the stone. It was actually a small boulder I would say, likely weighed a few hundred pounds. I considered what to do. It was a minor thing considering why I was there, but I felt a compulsion to fix it. I could have some men come and pick it up and take it away. It could be smashed into pieces. Carved anew with the name SOMMERS. Flipped over to hide the name. That I could do by myself. I knocked on the door then proceeded to wring my hands together in order to start to get some of the mud off of my hands. I swore at myself under my breath as I would just have to ask to use Clare's sink to wash my hands, the dirt was not coming off easily. Hindsight again being perfect, I should have just turned the boulder over on my way out.

I knocked again, harder. With all the activity outside it was amazing that anyone could still be asleep. I waited, looking off towards the smoke billowing into the sky. It seemed to be lighter now, more than likely all the things made of plastic had completely burned off and now it was just the things like the wood frame burning. Smoke is composed of moisture as well as what I would call impurities. The stuff that did not burn properly; things like plastic, in my mind seem to be composed of more chemicals and other things that just do not burn as nicely. Meaning that natural things tend to burn cleaner than unnatural things. In addition to being the fuel that powered our entire civilization for over a century, oil, was also responsible for providing the materials to make that wonderful miracle substance, plastic. Nylon, plastic, foam, etc. All those give off toxic fumes as they burn; the hydrocarbons that compose them begin to burn as if it was oil again. That is not quite accurate, it does not change back into oil, as far as I know but it does burn with the same kind of properties as oil would. It's funny how most people never understood the properties of the very items that they owned and used; even now I doubt most people would even know that plastic comes from hydrocarbons like oil. Plastic was always seen as some horrible thing because it does not biodegrade; people think that means it will last forever, which is not even close to true. Plastic still breaks down, just in a different process. It photo-degrades. Sunlight, given enough time will break down plastic; or of course you can just have a giant solar flare do it really, really quickly.

I had the time for my mind to drift off into some random thought concerning plastic and still no one had answered the door. Obviously knocking did not seem to be having the effect I required so I rang the doorbell. I really never liked doing that, it always felt somewhat offensive or rude, like honking your car horn at someone. I stood, listening intently to the door for a sign that someone had awoken and would soon be answering the door. I again looked over towards the smoke, it seemed to be even lighter now, and more than likely meant the whole fire itself was running out of fuel and starting to burn itself out. I sighed heavy as I looked back to the door. Still no one had answered. I could sense that I was being watched. I squinted to look through the little window in the door, there was no motion that I could see. The curtains were still drawn on the room to my left, the wisps of smoke were still in the distance. As my gaze drifted to my right I could feel my heart take a giant jump, nearly coming out of my chest before stopping altogether. I stumbled to my left, falling off the single cement step and falling onto my knee which was now crushing some sort of flower in the garden. It was Princess. I had not heard him sneaking up behind me; I had not seen the shadow. There was no warning for me that he was there and I nearly shit my pants because that dog is a sneaky little bastard. I began swearing under my breath about how Princess was a "stupid fucking dog" before I composed myself and took a deep breath. At that moment I was feeling like an old man. Grand scheme of things I was pretty old but landing like I did in that garden made my joints suddenly feel achy and stiff. I grunted as I pulled myself up. Brushing the dirt off I began to see the humor in the whole situation and began chuckling. I tapped my leg and called Princess over; he just stood there looking at me. "Come here boy." Nothing. "Princess! Come!" And he just turned to walk away. Again, I muttered under my breath, "you ungrateful mutt". If I had been more in need of a fuzzy friend all those years ago he would love me right now but instead he is at best indifferent. Suddenly, I wanted a puppy.

I was getting tired of this waiting. I turned the doorknob and opened the door. Republica has that 'small town feel' in that people leave their doors unlocked. The cannibals had long since been turned to paste; there was nothing really to fear but to me it still seemed kind of odd. Notwithstanding all my other seemingly paranoid behaviors from before the cataclysm I have always been one to lock my doors; right from when I moved out after high school, to living with my first girlfriend, to living with 3 other guys in the bad part of town, to living with Aurora's mom to right now. And that is not even counting the veritable fortress that was my bunker/house. It just seems smarter to not have the possibility of people accidentally walking in on you; what if I had just gotten out of the shower? Or what if I decided I wanted to rub myself in jam and pretend my hallway was a slip-and-slide? Or just wanted to watch some horrible old 80s show for the nostalgia of it? Regardless of what depravity or embarrassment I would be trying to hide, it would make sense to at least make it harder than turning a doorknob for someone to discover my horrible secret. For the record, I am pretty sure the only thing that I could worry about is being surprised after having a shower, but if someone was all the way upstairs in my bathroom in order to see me naked, they had better have had a very good reason.

I opened the door, banging hard as it creaked. "Hello!" I know for a fact I was banging that door hard enough that the only ways someone would not have heard it was if they were deaf, dead, had headphones on playing really loud music or were the deepest fucking sleeper I had ever met. I was met only with silence. Silence except for the tick-tick of the clock on the wall; it appeared to be some sort of art deco starburst design. I marveled at that as most clocks still working throughout the town were the old mechanical style, Grandfather Clocks and those types. His was definitely a more modern type that ran on batteries. How it had survived that long I had no clue. Most other clocks like it had been made inoperable during the cataclysm; much like nearly every other electrical thing. I walked slowly through the house, knocking on very door. Every time the same question, "Hello?" No one was here. I was beginning to question whether Clare still lived here. I mean it looked as if someone lived here while at the same time it did not. It was almost like a display home, the kind you would see in some new development. A gated community, filled with cookie-cutter homes. Every home was more alike than the last. Every bedroom had a perfectly made bed; the duvet looked as if it was so tight you could bounce coins off of it. There was no dust to be seen anywhere. At one point after noticing the lack of dust I even ran my finger across the top of a doorframe, only to find that my finger came back just as clean as it had been before. I wondered to myself if I was missing something here. Had Clare and Beth moved? Was this now our display home? I had never been told anything like that. Or was Clare just a super weird neat-freak? Suffering from some type of super OCD. Everything must be clean. Must be tidy. In its place. Everything did seem to be in its place. Nothing looked out of place. Although, if you think about it, when you are in someone else's home everything would likely seem to be in its place. You would have no real reference to where the proper place is; especially if there is no dust to give away the outlines of where the proper place is supposed to be. Perhaps that is why I never used to dust. More than likely it would be that I am 'a guy' meaning that I just did not care about those types of things. And anyways dust in a house is composed primarily of human skin cells. Since I lived alone that would mean that the vast majority of the dust in my house would be mine. So I am just going to put it out there that the reason I did not dust was simply because I love myself so much that I want to keep myself around always. And everywhere. Just an excuse but at least it sounds funny. This house though, there was no one here. No toys or clothes on the floor. I would not have known a child lived here. I became aware as I saw a slight smudge on the wall above the bedroom door that I still had mud on my hands. I walked into the kitchen and turned on the tap. No dishes in the sink. This house seemed more surreal by the moment. I had a further realization that there did not seem to be a towel in the kitchen. I began looking through the drawers where I would have put towels if this had been my house, the ones nearest to the sink. Clare was not me; she did not have the towels in those drawers. As I used my shirt as a towel I looked past the pink lacey curtains into the back yard. Now that I was closer I could see that the blue and green tent had more than just one strip of duct tape, the close side of the tent had a giant asterisk of tape holding the side together next to the door, which was half unzipped. I could see inside the tent; whoever was in the reddish sleeping bag was breathing. As I leaned over to my right I could see that the girl in that sleeping bag had reddish hair; meaning it was Beth. I could not tell for certain if she was still sleeping but more than likely I figured she was. When people sleep their breathing slows considerably, such that the average person takes about six breaths per minute while they are sleeping; I could see that Beth was breathing slightly quicker than that but still fairly slowly. I sighed as I looked out. With the girls still likely asleep I would have to be breaking the news of Lisa's "likely" death to Aurora. Not the kind of thing I am particularly good at, although in all fairness I think no one can be truly good at it. It is near impossible to truly gauge how people will react to getting bad news. Some would begin to sob uncontrollably. Some will instantly look for some form of comfort. Some will simply take in the news and hold on to it to process in their own time. Those same things can persist further than the initial announcement of bad news. Depending on their ability to cope with news like that they could begin the grieving process, hold onto their emotions to possibly deal with at a later time or hold onto their emotions and just let them overtake their whole life in time. People in that last group tend to be the ones that really don't know how to deal with their emotions and subsequently end up by finding means to mask how they really feel. They hide from the negative feelings they have instead of just dealing with them as it seems too painful. Or something like that. All the things relating to emotions are not something that I have a lot of experience with. I have emotions, I am not some sort of automaton, what I mean by I do not have a lot of experience is that I have never had to actually break the news to someone, so I have never had to truly experience trying to be empathetic to someone in that first shocking moment that they learn terrible news. Someone has always done it for me. Or it just went unsaid. Most of the people who died in Republica as a result of something relating to me simply disappeared. There was no announcement of their death. Their mere disappearance was the announcement. The few times I had been somewhat adjacent to people who had recently received notice that a loved one had died, like during our illness outbreak, I had essentially just stood silently while the person began to absorb the news in whatever manner that they did. Sometimes I was close enough that they had instinctively grabbed me in order to get some sort of comforting hug. It was always an awkward embrace as I hugged them while at the same time trying to pull myself away, lest I let their inability to control their emotions spill onto me, causing my veneer of calm and detachment to chip before finally breaking away. More than once during these times I had tried to say something in order to kill that silence that until I spoke was only punctuated by the sobs, sniffles and wails of the mourning. My words were never comforting; often trying to somehow convey a positive side to the death that they were now feeling right down in their gut. "Now they're in a better place." "Now they aren't suffering anymore." "At least they got to live long enough to see their child." They were all acceptable things to say in the moment however to me they always felt hollow and forced. And that is why I would get someone else to deliver the news. Today was going to be the day I would have to buck that trend; I would have to deliver the news myself. I would have to see the emotions streak across Aurora's face. I would have to act shocked.

Faking emotions is actually a difficult thing to do, especially with someone who is an observer. Aurora had known me for so long that she likely could tell what I was thinking by observing the micro-expressions that would flash on my face. I would have to somehow try to control those, which is, in reality, essentially impossible. If you know what to look for you can always know when someone is lying. Their face will give them away. You'll see flashes of emotion, what they are really feeling. Lisa's death was not something I was happy about, I had always liked her. She was at her heart a good person. I was really kind of banking on those emotions coming to the forefront while I delivered the news. That would be the only way that I could seem as surprised and shocked as I should be at this point in time. I took another deep breath and let out a heavy sigh as I wrapped my hand around the doorknob to the backdoor. I was forcing myself to do this. My hesitation is understandable; no one wants to be the bearer of bad news. You are doomed to experience the same feelings as the one getting them. You shared a moment with them. I briefly thought of all the police offers, state troopers and the like that had to deliver the news in much the same way. Difference was I would venture the majority of the time they would not have to be right there seeing the person have to struggle with dealing with those emotions. I turned the doorknob and pulled gently on the door, I was concerned about the door creaking although really; I should not have been. A little noise would have prepared the girls to be awoken. That little queue to their unconscious minds would have been better. Think about it, a little creak, your mind will pull itself ever so slightly out of a deep sleep. That would allow the brain to be able to process things just that little bit better. The other alternative is the first thing their brain would experience from their slumber would be the bad news. I'm sure there would be questions either way as to if the news was real or not. Mescaline is the inability to know whether you are awake or asleep; there would definitely be moments of that happening in the next few minutes. There was not even a hint of a squeak as the door slowly swung open, my thoughts of that little bit of noise were irrelevant; my guess is Clare kept the hinges well oiled. I stepped out into the yard and back into the sunlight.

Again, my heart jumped as I walked out, Princess sat quietly in my path. He still had not made a sound, his tail did not wag. He just sat there, staring at me. I still do not know what exactly it was that day that was so startling to me with Princess being around. I had seen him for years. I never had a fear of dogs. Hell, I have owned a number over the years, ones that by comparison had seemed far more vicious. In actuality they were total sucks, but they just seemed scary. The only thing I can come up with right now is that my emotions were already on edge. Everything I had experienced in the week prior as well as the dread of what I was there to do. It all led me to being more emotional than I wished to admit. I would say that at that exact time I was what I would call hyper-sensitive. Hell, someone could have jumped around the corner and I would have likely had the same reaction as I had to Princess. If someone had given me a birthday cake I would have broken into tears. It was actually just a little while past my birthday at that time, however in being an enigma for those kinds of things no one in the town knew. And not like I was going to announce it. Why seem more human than I have to. Some random creation story; brought by a stork, hatched from an egg, spontaneously combusting out of nowhere are all better and more epic ways to come into being than being born. Like everyone else. I slowly began to walk past Princess, quietly shushing him as I went. He bowed slightly as I laid a gentle pat on his head. Rounding the corner, I was again able to see the tent. I had been able to see from the kitchen window that there was one of those long lawn chairs in the back yard, I don't know what they are actually called and I don't believe I have ever known. Sun tanning was never high on my list of pastimes. Clare was lying on that chair under a bright orange blanket. She had evidently been reading out here last night while the girls were in the tent, book lay on the ground where it had fallen, an empty wine glass sat on the table next to her. Where did she get wine? I would have assumed that all stocks of alcohol would have long been exhausted. Perhaps she had found a stash in her basement, her own personal wine cellar. Maybe she or someone else was making it. Not sure how they could, we do not grow grapes in enough quantity to do so. Regardless, it was irrelevant. Everything in the house suddenly seemed to be less surreal, it was not a fake shell of a house; just a neat-freak's house.

As I slowly walked towards her the gravel ground under my feet; making that characteristic noise. She was suddenly roused from her sleep. A deep inhale, followed by a moan and then a long stretch. As she opened her eyes she was suddenly confronted with the sight of me, standing menacingly over her. It had not been my intent. I was actually hoping to have tried to wake her gently; instead she awoke on her own. Obviously, she was a light sleeper, which is not surprising considering the way her house looked. More than likely I would say her house being as neat, clean and tidy as it was at least slightly based in anxiety, and that would more than probably have led to somewhat interrupted sleep; whether that is in things like insomnia, trouble falling asleep or trouble staying asleep. Her fright at seeing me led her to trying to get up while not being able to. She made a squeaking kind of sound as she fell off the lawn chair onto the ground. I hissed at her "Shhhh. I'm sorry. I didn't mean to scare you." She sat there panting, her eyes opened extremely wide as she appeared to try to collect her thoughts. She was blindly groping for the blanket as she was trying to cover herself up. Another puzzling thing, she seemed to be wearing a house coat over a t-shirt, so it was not like she needed to cover her nakedness or lingerie, but I will just chalk that up to her not having all her faculties with her at that exact second. "Sorry, sorry, I didn't mean to wake you... well I did mean to wake you but not scare you. Umm. Yeah. How about you take a minute to compose yourself and I'll just wait for you in the kitchen, I don't want to wake the girls up just yet." Clare's eyes finally broke from mine and she looked over towards the tent. She still had the look of panic on her face. I kind of chuckled to myself as I walked around the corner of the house and back into the kitchen. Princess had walked off while my back was to him; he was now laying underneath the lone tree in the yard. Still watching me, protecting Aurora. I noted that the smell of smoke persisted, even though the smoke itself was barely visible.

I had never really sat and timed a house fire but for some reason the fire that killed Lisa seemed to have burned out fairly quickly. More than likely I would venture that the reason for that is a combination of things, with a fairly significant factor being related to the solar flare from so many years prior. That house, like nearly everything else on the planet, was bone dry. It was a tinderbox just waiting for a spark. The simple fact that there were not more fires is kind of surprising when you reflect on it; after all everything is dry. An errant spark from a campfire or fireplace. Even just a little heat from some random electrical wiring could potentially reach the ignition point of something that flammable. Maybe I should just knock on wood at that possibility; a fire could still ravage Republica at any moment and would likely leave scores dead and the rest homeless. It would not take much for a fire to wipe this entire town off the planet. As evidenced by some of the "great" fires that occurred in London, Rome and Chicago over the centuries that beast has a mind of its own and an insatiable hunger. I know great in that description means something akin to large or massive but to me it always seemed like they were trying to say it was a good thing. Maybe it was in a way. A chance for cleansing. A flare that was made on earth instead of on the sun.

I sat for what was only a minute or two at Clare's kitchen table before she walked by the window. I saw her stop outside her kitchen door in order to quickly tidy herself up, adjusting her breasts under the shirt and patting the stray hairs that were pointing in every direction. I guess you can still kind of have bed head even if you sleep on a lawn chair. Her hair was fairly nice; it was a shade of brown where it almost seemed to have a hint of red in it; auburn maybe? I had not been able to see under the blanket but see was wearing some very cliché looking fuzzy pink slippers. They were fairly dingy after all this time and I assumed that she had had to have the bottoms replaced due to wear and tear over the many years since it was made in some far-off land by children in sweatshops. She walked in and went directly to the kettle sitting on the counter, then pivoted to look at me, "tea?"

I suddenly had a frog in my throat. I cleared it before speaking. "Yes." Manners, always observe manners. "Please." She turned back to plug in the kettle then reached up to pull a tin out of the cupboard above it.

As she was pulling that tea out and grabbing cups she continued, "What is burning? Is that why you're here?" I let the silence pervade between us as she continued about the task of spooning the tea into an infuser. As she turned around and brought the cups over to the table I finally responded.

"Yes. Aurora's house is gone."

"Oh. That's horrible. Do you know what happened? How it started?" I just shook my head and shrugged. She continued, "Well, I guess that's not the end of the world, there are more houses in town, they can alw-" I cleared my throat loudly. The strength suddenly left her legs and she collapsed into the chair opposite me. "Oh god. Lisa?"

I shook my head again, "She didn't make it out." I was looking down at the empty cup in front of me as I spoke. There are ways to create detachment and distance in body language and this was actually what I think I was doing at that moment. I was separating myself from the situation by not really looking at Clare. We both sat quietly for a moment before the kettle began to whistle. "Sit, I'll grab it." I lightly touched her forearm as I rose and walked over to unplug the kettle from the wall and then brought it to the table. I slowly poured the steaming water into Clare's cup, watching it pour through the infuser. Little wisps of reddish-brown began to flow through the holes and was already starting to change the color of the water into something that looked more like tea. I sat before I began to pour the water into my own cup. I was still concentrating on watching the water, seeing the subtle change as it went from clear water to a darker and darker liquid.

"God, that poor girl. Lisa's all she had. When do you want to tell her?"

It was at that moment that I thought, shit and decided I needed a new plan. Another low rumble as I again had to clear my throat. "Actually, I was hoping I could get you to do that." She damned near spit hot tea out at me.

"Me? But I- I don't-… I don't think I can. What would I say? How do you tell someone that?"

"Exactly. I don't know either. But I think it would be better coming from you because… well… she'll need comfort and ummm…" I shrugged at her. "I have another favor to ask." She sat waiting for me to continue, I let out a little sigh before resuming talking. "Aurora is going to need a place to live and I cannot think of any place better. You obviously have a very nice home. You have the room. Her best friend is here. Oh and Princess is here. There is no one else that I can think of that would have a better possible connection with her and she is going to need some love and support in order to deal with all of this." She was stunned but I could see there was something going on in her mind. She was thinking. She was trying to think of a way to not become Aurora's new adoptive mother.
"Sir. I- Well- Thank you, but I don't know if I can take care of her, sometimes I can barely control Beth. I- Umm. I can't."

"You… Can't?" I was now looking her directly in the eyes. My gaze narrowed as it had so many times before when someone had said something that was running contrary to my wishes. It was at that moment that I seriously began to debate my course of action. As I saw it there were three real ways to proceed. First is, of course, for me to simply dictate what will be happening and only give Clare the freedom in order to figure how she can implement what I have commanded her to do. Second, is to allow Clare the freedom in order to decide whether or not her taking care of Aurora was really viable. Thirdly is for me to go the more civilized route that would still move things in the direction I want it to. Bribery. I could let her see the merits of my side by offering her something. What to offer is the real question in that option. I mean we are fairly simple in what we have available around town. Best that could really be done is to offer more of the essentials. She would naturally get Aurora's share included in that for her and Beth, perhaps I could include Lisa's share in that as well. It could be in the form of food, or clothing; unfortunately for me there was not much else to offer. Against my better judgment I decided to go route three; it is not as quick as my usual way of getting what I want but when it comes to my little girl, well, I'd prefer that Clare not have any resentment that could be directed towards her. If there was to be any it should be directed towards me and herself. Me for suggesting she take her on and her for taking a bribe. "This is very important. Aurora has been here since the beginning. I need her to be with someone who cares about her and will keep her safe. Someone who will instill the values in her that you obviously have. I mean look around here." I waved my arm towards the rest of her house, "This house is immaculate. I don't think I have ever seen a house as well kept. Well, on the inside. Outside, well..." I inhaled through my teeth, showing my disappointment at how it looked. "Listen. How about you and I make a deal? I need to make sure that Aurora is well taken care of. You need something… everybody needs something. What can I do in order to make this work for everyone involved?"

Clare was playing with her teacup, dipping the infuser into the tea before pulling it out and watching the water drip into her cup. I think it was now my turn to feel uncomfortable. I was really not used to asking like this. To have to depend on the whims of other people. "Well I- I could use a new dryer. The old one doesn't really work all that well, I have to run each load like 3 times to get the clothes dry."

"Done!" I was quite impressed. That was easier than I had thought.

She kept talking though, I knew it had been too easy. "And I'd really like a dishwasher, I haven't had one of those since before everything died. Oooo, and actually a new microwave, the plate doesn't turn on this one anymore." I had something of an amused smile on my face as my head started to tilt to the side, like a dog. I think she gathered that she was starting to get a little greedy in my eyes. Lucky for her I know that we do have a building full of new and old appliances; we should be able to find her some new to her items fairly easily. "Yeah. I think those are all the things I need. Wait, actually one more. I need a new vacuum. One of those bag less ones if we can find it, I have been using the same one with the same bag for years; the bag has pretty much completely worn out."

I stopped myself from grinding my teeth in front of her, although I felt as though I had been taken advantage of. In reality none of her requests were that outrageous, it just felt like if I had kept a better poker face she would have just continued until she had a whole new house. "All of that sounds reasonable. I'll have someone come over to look at the kitchen, I'm sure there is going to have to some remodeling in here in order to get the dishwasher in place. We'll get your old vacuum and dryer replaced. What was the other thing?"

"Microwave."

"Yes, you need a new microwave. We can do all that for you. And actually, on top of that I am going to get your outside painted too. I could see when I got here this morning that it hasn't been painted since the cataclysm." Cataclysm is a word that I tended to use mostly in my own head or when I put my thoughts down, like in this; Clare though gave me a funny look when I said the word out loud. I just smiled and kind of waved it off. "Now, just a couple more things. First, this whole thing was your idea. As soon as you found out about the fire you thought that you should help Aurora out. I don't need to be brought up at all in regards to this. I mean, I know she is one of the first people here and I promised Lisa years and years ago that I would take care of her….but it is actually not fair to everyone else that lives in town for me to 'play favorites'. Next, if there are any problems with Aurora that you cannot handle yourself, you come directly to me. You do not discuss the problem with anyone else, nor try to get others to help you solve it. This is my way of fulfilling my promise to Lisa; I will act if and when I need to in order to ensure that Aurora is kept safe and happy. That way I am still able to fulfill my promise, but I can do it from the background. Agreed?"

"Yes. Agreed." She stuck out her hand to shake mine. Suddenly, the whole arrangement felt sordid. I slowly began to rise from the chair I had been sitting in, I had the sudden urge to renege on the entire thing we had just hashed out, declare the whole adoption plan null and void; possibly even break Clare's neck. Even up to the few seconds prior everything discussed had felt like a polite chat about the details of a Gentleman's Agreement that would simply be honored because we said we would; our words were our bond. Now, it felt as slimy and sweaty as her palm was as I shook her hand.

I stepped towards the door of the kitchen, heading back through the house, the safe direction I had come in. I continued talking as I was being led out of the house by Clare. "In keeping with this arrangement, I am going to go. I trust you will break the news as gently as possible. I would suggest you please keep her away from her house until this evening at the earliest. I am not sure how long it will be before we can get Lisa's remains out of their house, but I really think we should avoid any possibility of Aurora seeing that."

"I will. Maybe I'll take the girls out for a walk. We can have a picnic. I'll have a good day with her before I tell her. And that way we can keep her out of town and away from everything."

"That is fine. I'll let you figure out the details." We were now standing in the front foyer of the house, dealing with the last few pleasantries before I departed. "I don't think I have said it thus far but even if I have there is no reason to not repeat it. Thank you for doing this Clare. I truly appreciate it. And I hope Aurora will appreciate it as well; in time."

"No, I want to thank you Sir. I know it is hard on everyone when something tragic like this happens and she has already had enough tragedy in her life. I am happy to help her."

I opened the door and stepped halfway through before turning to her again, "Remember, if you or her need anything come see me and only me. I will sort out whatever needs to be done." Clare was just about to say something as her eyes drifted off to her right. It was kind of comical how she was trying to respond to me while at the same time she was entirely distracted.

"I will defin-… what the…?" I stepped back into the foyer in order to see where she was looking. Following her gaze, I quickly realized the thing that had so captivated her was the slight smudge above one of the doors that I had left when I had run my finger across the top of the door frame. Suddenly I was feeling very meek and ashamed. I had soiled her house. I hissed again as I inhaled through my teeth, again displaying my disappointment, this time at the mess I had caused.

"Oh, yes. I am sorry. That was me. When I came in I had a little bit of dirt on my hand and I guess I had put my hand up. I can clean it up if you'll get me something to wash it with." That was actually a genuine offer. This house was, as I said, immaculate and I was feeling guilty for having tainted that. Even if what I had done was ever so slight.

"N-n-no, Sir. I will do it. I am. I just need. I'll get a cloth after I see you out." She was barely able to pull her eyes away from that smudge in order to actually see me out. As the door closed behind me I smiled to myself. I still felt bad for having messed her house but on the other hand it was quite funny how that little smudge of dirt seemed to break her mind. I had the feeling that she would likely spend the next hour or so before the girls awoke furiously scrubbing every speck of dirt she was able to find. If there was the slightest hint of a shoe print or, god forbid, an actual bit of mud on the floor she was likely to be mopping at a frantic pace to eliminate it all. Everything must be clean. No dirt. Dirt is filthy. Whatever, for me it was just good clean fun.

Princess came around the corner of the house as I was leaving the yard. I whistled at him to come to me; I would venture he had only been coming to see if I was really going but he came nearer to me regardless. I stood waiting for him to saunter his way over to me. He was in no rush; that dog was a Prima Dona; no wonder Aurora had called him Princess. She had him pegged correctly right from the outset. He stopped right in front of me and sat. Damned this is a well-trained dog. It must have been done by his previous owner; I have never seen Aurora do any real work with him, so unless he came preprogrammed out of the box knowing how to act it had to have been done previous to the cataclysm. I knelt, gave him a rough scrub around the ears and neck before patting him on the top of the head. "You're a good boy. Ok, go back to Aurora." He seemed rather indignant that I had made him come all that way; all of 15 feet to see me for only a rough scrub and pat. He trotted 'towards the back yard and disappeared around the corner.

Following this I was in no real rush to get back home. In all fairness I did not have anything of particular note to do at that time. I walked slowly up the street, passing the occasional person returning to their home. Or I was overtaken by a person rushing to get to the scene of the fire before it was no longer exciting. I remember getting a whiff of that particular ham smell that you'll recall I am so averse to. I did however note that the wind seemed to have changed direction and was blowing from behind me. I should not have been smelling anything from the fire at that moment; which meant to me that it was likely just a creation of my own mind. As I neared the house I was finally able to see just what damage had been done, the roof looked as if it was completely gone; the frame was visible in a number of places, blackened but still glowing from the embers burning within the wood. The garage had also ignited at some point although it seemed as though someone had managed to dowse it enough that it did not burn completely. There was a corner of the garage though, the one closest to the house, that looked as if it was completely destroyed. The building would likely be torn down at the same time the remains of the house were removed. There was no real point in trying to keep the garage for a house that no longer exists; we would simply open another house that has been vacant for years.

I was almost completely past the burnt out hulk of Lisa's house before someone took note of me and tried to elicit my direction in what to do. It was kind of stupid really. Wait for the fire to completely die off. Soak any points that seem to be smoldering or glowing. Completely remove any possible sources of re-ignition. Sort through the ashes, find Lisa's body. We would give her a proper service. Let people mourn. I had to reassure more than a few of the gawkers that Aurora was not in that house when it went up. I implied I had seen her going down the street last night and had not returned. I was going to let them do the sleuthing on that. They can find out their own information, lest I seem as though I know more than I should know. I had more than a few people ask if I knew how such a tragedy could come about. I told them all of the time I met Lisa. I made sure they all knew how much she enjoyed reading in bed, by candle light. While I never explicitly said that the fire began due to careless use of a candle that was definitely my implication. When trying to misdirect people it is actually very useful to "not" know something. Let them be the one to figure it out. If someone tries to corner you with the truth you can always shrug and say I never said that, it was so-and-so that figured it out. It comes off as just presenting a theory as opposed to actually having knowledge of something. What better way to avoid having any forms of discussions about the fire then to know just as much as all the other people who know nothing about it? I was fine with not having to discuss it with people, really what would I tell them anyways; nothing that they couldn't observe with their own eyes.

Lisa's remains were pulled from the remnants of the building later that afternoon. There was barely anything left. If I had to venture a guess I would have said that she was in bed when the fire began; although it was sort of hard to tell. The second floor had collapsed during the fire meaning she and her bed had been spilled onto the main floor. The reason I guess she was in bed was that what little bit of her we had found was located underneath the bare bedsprings, as if the bed had overturned when it fell down one level; upsetting her from being on top of the mattress to below. Just another thing that no longer matters; it was more of just something that seemed interesting, so I made a note of it.

I talked to Clare around a week later, asking how the day had gone for Aurora. She said that she had taken Aurora and Beth for a walk along the river. They had spent most of the morning and early afternoon playing in the water. She had made them sandwiches for lunch, accompanied by some fruit and cold tea. Aurora had been particularly taken with splashing Princess in the face, something that would cause him to growl and snap. She seemed to say it like it was a bad thing, like she expected Princess to attack Aurora at any moment. I laughed at the notion; chances are he was one of those dogs that would spend hours in the yard; attacking, biting and barking at the sprinkler. After spending the day out they returned back to Clare's house in order to watch a movie. It was around that time that Aurora began to notice that Lisa had not appeared at all. That was abnormal for her, on any other day she would have at least popped in to say hi, or walked by on some errand, or something. That day there was no sign. She began to look at the clock, that same art deco clock I had noticed. She began to worry about the time. She "had to get home."

It was at that point that Clare finally sat her down and told her. Her house was gone. Lisa did not make it out in time. Aurora instantly had tears dripping down her face. She was not crying exactly, there were no sobs or wailing, just tears. Dripping rhythmically down her cheeks. Beth held her and let the tears soak the shoulder of her shirt. Clare told her that she wanted Aurora to stay with them. She would get a better bed for her to sleep on since she'd no longer be a guest, she'd be family. Aurora just nodded at that, her face was still attached firmly to Beth's chest and shoulder. Princess had nuzzled him up between Aurora and Beth in order to gently lick her hand. The best weapon he had in order to comfort her. I'll say in the short-term Aurora definitely took Lisa's passing as you would expect; she was sad, depressed and sullen. I got Clare to encourage her to work through her grief by delving into her studies. She took her to the town counselor in order to talk about her grief. Little by little things began to seem less dark to her. She began to see the light. She gained an appreciation of being alive herself. Until in the end, I would say she had completely dealt with her issues surrounding Lisa's untimely passing.

All the promised appliances were delivered. The house was painted. The kitchen remodeled. A new mattress was provided. Our deal was fulfilled from my end. Clare stood by her word and did the same from her end.

Clare had complained while she was telling me of how Aurora had handled everything about Princess. She said that she never realized that the dog would be coming along with her. I looked at her as if to say, 'you're an idiot'. Aurora was never seen without Princess. The dog was usually within arm's reach. He was always attentive; watching anyone that approached or interacted with her. For Clare to not know the dog would be part of the package was absolutely stupid. She wanted me to take the dog or get someone else to adopt him. I laughed and told her if she wants the dog out of her house she can try and grab it. I dared her. As calm and placid as he seemed, Princess was not docile. It was plain to see after being around him for years that he was calm when it suited him however he could switch into protective mode in an instant; as with the creeper. Clare trying to take that dog away from Aurora would have only led her to getting bit or even mauled. And I would not have let him be put down for that; the whole reason I gave him to Aurora was to keep her safe. Eventually I summed it up for Clare in the simplest way possible. I told her the dog would not be going anywhere that Aurora was not. I informed her that our deal would not be renegotiated; she had opened her mouth in order to start to make more demands, I was sure of it. I told her if there was such a difficulty with the dog then she should make it part of the chores that I assumed Aurora would have to do. Perhaps she could vacuum since there would undoubtedly be dog hair around. I don't think Clare liked the idea of someone else cleaning her house, however whether she chose to allow Aurora to clean or not was her choice; I simply opened the door for the option. Clare sensed I was no longer in the mood to hammer out a deal and simply took my suggestions and moved on with her life.

CHAPTER 17 – THE PIT

I cannot recall if I have ever made the assertion that I was perfect, it does not actually sound like me but who knows, I have done and said weirder things. I will readily admit right now that I am most definitely not perfect. Having people disagree with me is not something new; I say a lot of things that I am sure others disagree with, generally I do not know that, but I am sure it happens. Having people hate me is not something new either, it happens. Not everyone can like you and I was in charge of people's lives, sometimes right down to minute details; I would be annoyed at that level of micromanagement if not downright resentful and hateful. Few people knew many of the details of my life or my rise to power. The majority of people hear things through the grapevine. And just like the old 'telephone' game the message quickly gets distorted with certain parts minimized, others aggrandized, and others flat-out made up. People coming in to the town had always heard of stories like how I dealt with the cannibals. They heard of little things that happened here and there. Thieves being killed. People getting exiled to certain death. People guilty of sloth being put in the stocks for months at a time. People going missing in the middle of the night. A personal favorite of mine was how someone had their throat slit in the middle of the night. That person bled to death in his bed with his wife lying beside him covered in his blood. It never happened. In all reality if I had had someone killed in that type of fashion I would have had his wife killed as well. It would just be easier to not have someone who I would be certain would be gunning for revenge in the future. But as I said, never happened. The problem with fame, with power, with having an ever-growing number of enemies is that ultimately you are demonized at some point. Much as I am now; the fortunate thing, for everyone except for me is that they are now able to see that I am not the horrible monster they had all envisioned. I am just a man, much the same as any other. I am no more monster than I am angel.

The whole situation with Flynn, Gary, Rusty and the rest really did a number on my mental stability. Not to say that I went off the deep-end, others can say that, but I won't. However, I was definitely not in the best space. I became paranoid. Extremely paranoid. The attempted rebellion was not the worst of it although it was bad. What really hit it home for me was the attack in the park. In those moments I was helpless, or mostly helpless. I had more than one nightmare about a man in a turtleneck advancing on me with a knife. I don't think anyone else saw any noticeable difference, I just kept those feelings inside and I managed with them for quite a long time with no real problems. Then there was the problem with Nixi; this was not particularly dangerous and as I mentioned before it was resolved fairly quickly, efficiently and thoroughly. Problem was that it allowed any latent feelings of anxiety that I had to bubble to the surface. I don't even know how to describe the feelings I was having. When I was younger my family would go the beach. Near the end of the day playing in the water things would begin to wind-down. At that point I would sit down in water that was about waist deep and just let the waves push me back and forth. It is the laziest and poorest massage you can get but at the same time it is wonderful, just a subtle push on you after having spent all day playing and relaxing. Every once in a while, what would happen is a boat would streak by or just a bigger wave than all the rest would come along. It would come overtop and completely envelope you. Just a wave of water, you'd hear nothing but the water as it moved around you. The sloshing sound of the current, as it was churning underneath the surface. You'd see random pieces of seaweed or some other random piece of organic matter move past you as you popped your head out above the surface again. Taking a deep breath as if you had been under for minutes. It had been mere seconds. That was something similar to the feeling I had as my fears and anxieties took over. I began to see conspiracies everywhere. Each time someone waved at me to acknowledge my presence I expected another assassin to emerge from the nearest bush or corner; intent on completing the job that Damian had failed at completing. Each time I locked gazes with someone I imagined they were hatching some plan to kill me. They were sizing me up, seeing what they would need in order to end my life. Any sleep that I was able to get after the affair with Nixi was punctuated by nightmares of being pulled apart by horses, strangled, stabbed, shot, disemboweled, ripped apart by dogs. Those are only the ones I can remember right now. Each time I closed my eyes and tried to rest I was jolted awake; sweating profusely and unable to breath as if I had been running in terror from someone or something. That would be karma finally catching up with me I suppose; I had inspired terror in more than a few people, so I got it back tenfold.

My fears from before the flare began to arise anew like a phoenix from my subconscious. I had not lost my fears, they had been with me all along, and I simply had not been paying them any attention. Now that I was afraid things began to overflow in my mind. Each sound that came from out in the dark at night was a source of concern. Every creaking noise from downstairs was a killer coming to murder me in my sleep. I soon began to fear even going to sleep. Not that I think anyone would be surprised to hear that given how things went for me even when I did manage to fall asleep. I cannot even say how long this had persisted for. The more I was awake the more I began to daydream. Compared to the nightmares I was having these would be what I considered pleasant. I could control them. I was never able to lucid dream that I am aware of, meaning that I was never able to control my dreams. But in my daydreams, I could play things out, evaluate what I should do. Regrettably this only led to my anxieties being heightened. Again, not surprisingly I was literally just sitting there focusing on the things that were making me anxious and trying to manipulate them into something not concerning and the whole experiment did not work. In looking for solutions to my various fears I did come upon the solution to everything. In one plan I could fix all the others. My confidence had been borne out of my feeling secure and safe. At first my security had been something artificial which I then incorporated into myself until that was destroyed by my attempted assassination. I resolved to make myself secure again by somewhat recreating my bunker home. That is not accurate. What I was actually planning was a 'hardened house'. The entire building was to be steel and concrete. Quite simply what I had devised was a plan to create a castle in Republica. This would be better termed a keep though; a castle is the whole structure of a place including the walls, portcullis, moat, towers, gates, etc. The keep was the part at the center. The safest point in the castle, you would need to get through all the other defenses before being able to assault the keep. I know in more than a few medieval sieges the keep was simply surrounded while the attackers had possession of the remainder of the castle. They just laid siege to the keep. They let starvation and disease do the work for them. Instead of trying to assault a place like that they would just wait. Eventually the defenders would surrender. Then they would be taken prisoner or executed. I would of course not leave that as the only option but first there is the problem that I needed that keep being built.

On the first day of spring I began enacting my plans for my new secure residence. The remains of Lisa's house had remained for years after the fire that took her life without being touched. Despite the grandiose plans that were always made for any lots that were opened; usually turning them into some form of garden or park nothing was done to this one. I think in a way it became kind of a shrine for a few people who knew Lisa, including Aurora, as well for things to happen around Republica it generally needed my push for it to really get going and I just did not push too hard on that. My heart was not in it. That morning though I had finally resolved myself to doing something with the piece of property. At dawn I was swinging a sledgehammer, breaking the last few pieces of charred wood apart so they would be removed. I began breaking the cinderblocks that made up the foundations of the house. Once that was done I began to dig out the ground underneath; I was beginning to make the site suitable for the concrete to be poured. I know residents began to peek on what was going on. Some likely thought I was going mad, assuming that those rumors from just prior to Lisa's death, about her and I being in a relationship, were true. I was not dealing with the grief so well. Others likely thought I was angry for some reason and taking out my anger violently on the remains of the building. That would have been entirely out of character for me; as has been evidenced by everything I have said, I take out my anger on people not things. There were likely even a few that thought I was just doing it for the exercise. All of them were wrong obviously. For me though actually starting the whole endeavor by myself was a step towards resolving the inner conflicts I was having. No more was I worried about assassins, random sounds or dark alleys. The thought of having a hard concrete shell around me solidified my courage enough to be able to ignore others. For that first day I worked alone. I talked to no one. I barely ate. I did however drink lots of water; I was thirsty doing all that work. That night I slept and I thought I had happened upon the answer to all of my problems.

The next day as people happened by I began to draft them. I just began calling them over by name before handing them a shovel or a pick and telling them to start digging. The use of their name was intentional. It reminds them I know who they are, where they live and who their loved ones are. It forces compliance by the mere act of calling them. Not one person was able to say they "didn't hear me". Not one person refused to do as they were told. Each one walked over and presented themselves to me before being handed the implement they were to use that day. Most stood there confused for a moment before hurriedly digging at the ground. It was only a few feet down before we began encountering rocks; some were rather large and would take numerous people working into order to break them into chunks small enough to be removed from the pit. Another couple of feet and it was no longer isolated rocks in the soil but actual bedrock. My plan had not been to be as elaborate as with my previous sanctuary but I did still want a basement level; for storage if for nothing else. That means that we had to continue digging into the bedrock. It was much more arduous doing it by hand than it had been for my last home, which had all been dug by machinery. Wonderfully though, I had a large amount of slave labor available to help me. By the end of the third day I was no longer helping with the digging, I had others doing that. All the time I had spent in the preceding months worrying about this and that began to evaporate as my mind began to return to an earlier mindset. I no longer worried about who was looking at me. What they thought. How they were conspiring. Where they would hide the next assassin. I was making myself a new fortress. A place to be secure from all those that could wish to do me harm. Best of all, I would get the very people who I would need to be protected from in order to build it.

In addition to the initial group that I had returned each day I would grab the ones who had the skills necessary in order to complete the tasks I required to be done. We had a man who had worked on foundations prior to the flare; I made him work arranging everything, to properly pour the foundation. I did feel kind of bad making a 69-year-old man work like that however we needed his expertise. No one else could be trusted to do the work; after all it was to be my new home. I deserved something strong and well-built after all the years I had put in making Republica what it is. The wonderful thing about Republica is that at that point I think we literally had every profession more or less covered. Carpenters were conscripted in order to make the molds for the concrete. We had experts in making concrete, a welder who could make the door and window frames, I even found someone who made a kind of bulletproof window. Although in fairness, it was never tested so I was just hoping that it would be bulletproof. I sent teams of people down to the old quarry outside of town. They could get the stone and gravel necessary for making the cement. Everything was moving swimmingly. I heard the occasional grumbling although I let that go. People can be tired and cranky. As long as they still do the work.

It was likely about 3 weeks in that I had been off dealing with matters that concerned the town itself; all the day-to-day minutia that I had been neglecting for a little while. I spent the morning doing my usual kind of rounds; I went from this street to that, checked on the fish hatchery, the power plant, LeAnn and Rita over at the hospital. I saw people tending their gardens; others were working on the community projects like the tropical fruits. I was feeling more and more like my old self. I was talking to people. Instead of wondering who was around the corner, what conspiracies there were out there I just talked to people. I stopped by Ted's yard which was about two blocks over from where my new home was being constructed. I watching as he was planting his seedlings into the neatly arranged rows, each one being set gently into the ground, the dirt piled up around the plant gently with his hands before he would press down making two hand prints beside the plant. It was something so simple and yet I was enthralled with what I was seeing, I stood there with my arms crossed, leaning on his fence with my chin sitting on my arms. I stared at him doing that, moving slowly back towards me as he planted each plant until he was out of seedlings. He stood slowly, grunting like an old man as he straightened his legs and brushed the dirt off of his knees. As he went to walk around the plants he had already put in the ground he spun to see me gazing upon him. He dropped the tray that he had been carrying the seedlings on as he gasped. He stood very straight before saying "Sir" very loudly. I think he even clicked his heels. "I'm sorry Sir. I was just doing my planting."

"Why are you sorry?" I mused as my eyebrow peaked up. He was still standing very tall, for him at least, I think he was only around five foot three.

"Sir. I wasn't working. But Sir, I need to start growing for the year; for the kids you know." I would put Ted as being relatively new; he did not know just how my mind or rules operate. He was probably only in the town for a year or two. I began to shake my head at him.

"I would have thought you were working." His hands were still encrusted with dirt; I could see the dark lines of grime that was caked underneath his fingernails as he fidgeted while we spoke.

"I'm sorry Sir. I will go right now to the quarry." It was at that moment I realized what he was referring to. I had been so involved with the worksite were my house was being built that I completely ignored the fact there were actually a couple of work crews getting the materiel necessary. And of course, I was not familiar with who was working at the quarry site as I had not gone there. After all, why should I? The workers there are simply smashing rocks into gravel to be transported to here. There is no need for my oversight. I will just admit that I felt going there and doing any supervision would be below me. It is not the kind of task that warrants the attention of someone like me.

As Ted scurried out of his yard I said to him "Don't make me have to remind you again." He nodded and almost inaudibly said "Yes Sir" as I watched him speed up the further he got from me. First a quick walk as he neared the end of the block he was jogging, after turning the corner I could only see him between houses, but he seemed to be at a full run then. I looked into the sky, as I stood there still leaning against the fence. I was trying to smell something nice. I had spent so much time recently in the pit of my new house that I had gotten used to smelling dirt and gravel and body odor from dozens of people working on my new project. I think however that it was too early in the season to get a whiff of something nice. All I could smell was the normal sweetness of grass, mixed with the scent of freshly turned earth from Ted's yard. I opened his gate and walked into the yard; I could see the seedlings he had ready for planting were all arranged on what looked to be an old dresser. He had tomatoes, cucumbers, lettuce, corn, squash, etc. All were neatly marked and organized. I enjoyed seeing that level of planning and preparation amongst my flock. It ensured the best chances of us having another productive year.

Each year that produced more food than we could eat was another feather in my cap. That proved that I was the right man for the job. Everything that I had felt, all my plans, every action were all justified by the continuing prosperity of Republica and her people. Nothing could take it away from me.

Before there were hunter-gatherers there were simply gatherers; they would live on whatever they found, there was no real measure of preparation or planning, other than perhaps knowing areas where you would likely find berries or other edibles. Once people learned the skills of planning, weapon and tool making, of tracking they were able to begin to add new food sources into their plan for survival. Gatherers were not as successful as hunter-gatherers; having multiple possible food streams is one strategy for ensuring survival. Once people learned to farm they had a new option. Instead of dealing with possibilities: Would they find game to hunt? Would they find a plentiful enough source of berries? Would they find plants that are edible? The new plan after farming was 'invented' was to take something you already have and make it grow. Controlling what you have and simply nurturing it to thrive is much more productive in the long run. Farming was the base reason for the population explosions that happened all across the planet throughout history. Farming allows for there to be a surplus of food. A surplus of food means that you can have some people not farming, allowing them to pursue other occupations. That is the whole basis of cities. They came about because people no longer needed to grow their own food, the ones who were doing it were able to produce enough for those that did things other than farming. Those people were the traders, the tailors, cobblers, carpenters, garbage men, bus drivers, doctors, store clerks and even the regrettable politicians. And that was my accomplishment, I was the one chosen to lead civilization back to the forefront of the world. I created the soil on which a new society could grow. I was nurturing it through hard work, and blood and tears of my people until we had something to be proud of again.

As I passed to Ted's back yard I noticed that his backyard fire pit was still smoking ever so slightly; a pan lay on the table beside it, if I had to guess I would say he had eggs for breakfast that morning. I shook my head as I pulled a watering can out of the nearby rain barrel and poured it on the glowing embers. I thought of my childhood, always being concerned for the possibility of forest fires. Things were no longer that dry, but it was still a good thing to be aware of. The hiss of the water was all I could hear for a second or two, a giant cloud of steam wafted into the air above me. As I returned the watering can to the barrel I could hear the chirping of the nearby birds resume. There was nothing else. That was not right. There was nothing else. I orientated myself to the south and looked into the sky. I had become fairly adept over the years in gauging the time by looking at the sun and by my guess it was roughly ten. I became a little less concerned; this would be roughly time for a morning break, it was usually earlier but not always. There was not actually a rule about it. At least not one I had instituted.

I hopped over the back fence of the next house and began working my way through the yards towards the site of my new home. I heard nothing. I walked through the next yard, barely noticing what was in the yard. Was there anything planted? I could not say. Was the ground even broken? Doubt it. What color was the house? I have no idea whatsoever. I was focused and driven at that moment. Like every other time something had seemed to be going wrong this just felt off. I entered the backyard of this house; the fence was rather tall. I guessed that this was likely due to a previous occupant, there was a large doghouse in the corner of the yard, it was old and rotten looking but it still stood. Judging by the size of the doorway I would put it as being a rather large dog that had once lived in that house. And that makes the high fence very understandable. I stood beside the gate with my hand on the latch. I felt like I was about to catch the conspiracy that I had been so worried about for so long. My heart was pounding. I struggled to breath more shallowly, lest my breathing be heard by those on the other side of the fence before I wished to make my presence known. I craned to listen, hearing nothing until I got the faintest whisper of laughter. Not hearty laughter though; more similar to the small chuckles you would hear if someone just told an old knock-knock joke. I lifted the latch slowly and swung the gate open. I stepped through only to be standing twenty or thirty feet from the edge of the whole where my foundation was being prepared. I could see no work; hear nothing but the chirping of birds in the distance, I guessed they were still two blocks away.

Nearing the edge of the hole I looked down, nothing had changed since I had left. I immediately began walking around to the front side where the earth sloped so you could reach the bottom of the hole. I stared intently at the group of five people sitting on the half-framed foundation. None had yet seen me. If they had they likely would have begun furiously performing whatever task I had assigned them prior to leaving. Ahead of me there were four more people sitting on piles of timber that had been brought yesterday in order to start the farming work. I grit my teeth as I began checking the faces of every person I could see, I had left Kevin, our oldest carpenter in charge. I was looking for him. I saw him emerge at that moment from the house to the left of my new hole. He was adjusting his pants; I could not tell if he had just used the bathroom or the woman that lived there. Neither would have particularly surprised me although one of them can be put off to personal time, not my time. I recall muttering to myself that for his sake he had better have been going to the bathroom. Turning my attention back to the workers as they obviously had realized I was coming around. And I was walking like a man on a mission. They were all scurrying about, as I had predicted. My pace slowed as Kevin was nearing me; he was now doing a fast walk to get to me quickly, although he still seemed to be having problems with his pants. I never checked before however I became very certain at that moment that he had the proverbial "plumber's butt". I stopped where I was near the ramp into the hole when I came to a complete stop. I turned my back to Kevin and steadied myself watching the activity going on.

"Sir. I'm sorry, I used the neighbor's shitter so I gave everyone a break while I was away." I just breathed, waiting to see what else he would say. He was smart enough to not say anything. Really if he had that would not have been the end of the world, I mean I guess it could have depending on what he said. The main thing that was concerning me about his talking was his choice of words. I have been known to swear but that is usually for some measure of effect or a complete lack of restraint on my part, he was speaking just as a matter of fact. The word shitter, seems so dirty and vulgar to me. I mean you can talk about things like that however there are ways that civilized people can talk about them. Washroom, bathroom, latrine, head, powder room, lavatory. I am sure I could go on if I was too think harder but that is unnecessary, I have made my point. He instantly had become uncouth; I now felt dirtier standing beside him.

"Why was it necessary to give them a break while you were using the washroom? Should they not be able to handle their tasks without you?"

"Ye- Yes Sir. And they were I just gave them a break cause they needed it. Joe said he was exhausted so I let him sit for a minute and since I did that I just let them all have a few minutes. It's no harm done, just a little coffee break." I was measuring what he said, gauging what my response should be. *No harm done.* Possibly, however there is a thing about authority, if you are not enforcing it then you have no authority. And it was *just a few minutes.* But was it? In the minutes I was not standing here the pile of lumber was half gone, the frame was well on its way to being put up.

"No harm done. What's wrong with Joe? Is he okay? ... I should check on him." I began to walk into the hole; I was scanning the mass of moving bodies looking for Joe. He was a relatively young man, I would put him around twenty-five, he was quite fit and much to my chagrin preferred to walk around the worksite with his shirt off. Now don't misunderstand me I am not particularly against him or anyone working with their shirt off. It is actually just something carried over from my childhood. The idea that you don't go out all day without sunscreen. You'll get cancer. We don't have sunscreen so really you would need to just stay dressed, which can be hot in the summer; this however was much too early for it to be that hot. I could see Joe on the far side of the hole, holding up a piece of wood so that it could be tacked in place. I waved him over as I shouted "Joe!" There was a collective silence among all the workers as they shot Joe concerned glances. Each one however tried to avoid my attention by looking busy while not actually doing anything. The uneven beats of their hammers hitting wood and nails had completed ceased.

Joe presents himself to me. I see that he has a tattoo of what appears to be an eagle on his left pectoral; it is kind of hard to tell the artistry is not all that great and the ink seems to have dissipated a little under his skin. Really, it looked like a prison tattoo and in all reality it probably was done in the same way. I am certain that this is not something from before, if he had gotten a tattoo prior to the cataclysm he would have to have been tattooed when he was around 10 and I just didn't see that as a possibility. I made a mental note to look into our resident tattooist when I had the time. I needed to be sure that whoever this was doing the proper steps to sterilize the tattooing equipment. Without properly cleaning things there could be diseases being spread around town; which I could not abide. "Yes?" I just looked at him. Young people, how quickly they forget respect and manners. I hear Kevin cough behind my right shoulder. "I mean. Yes? Sir?" I glance at Kevin over my shoulder. Giving hints, it is like cheating on a test. He will never learn if he does not do things for himself.

"I hear that you are not feeling well. What seems to be the problem my good friend?" Seeing this written makes me realize just how thick I was spreading it on right there, surprising no one else noticed it.

"I'm just tired, I have been out here everyday for a week. I feel exhausted." I recalled at that point that I had seen Joe at more than one of the late-night barbeques that happens every so often around town popped into my head. As I recall from the last one I saw he was one of the people who preferred to indulge in the homemade alcohol a little too much. It just struck me as a very misplaced priority.

"Hmmm. Well on the upside, this will only take a little while in order to get completed. The sooner it gets built the sooner you can have your rest time."

"But that will be a month away. Maybe more. I can't work that long. It's too much!" I can see the rest of the workers in my peripheral vision. All are watching us they are no longer even trying to mimic something that looks like work. I can see a couple workers looking at their nearest partner and exchanging confirming nods with each other. Dissent is always so infectious. One person speaks their mind a little too loudly. Speaking to just a few too many people. This is the kind of thing that needs to be halted quickly.

"Too much? Too much?! For such a strong young man?" Joe's gaze dropped down as he was now pushing dirt with his feet. "We had Randall out here working for how long? And he is like 70. You can do this. You will do this. I am not asking you. I am telling you." Joe just nodded and turned on his heels.

As I begin to do likewise I hear him mutter under his breath, "Asshole". My one-hundred-and-eighty-degree turn becomes a full three-hundred-and-sixty-degree turn. I feel as if I am pirouetting for Kevin's amusement.

"Joe. Come back here for a moment please." He stopped with one foot still in the air. His head instantly receded into his shoulders, like a turtle trying to hide from some threat. There were a couple gasps from the other workers as he turned around and walked slowly back to standing in front of me.

"I'm s- sorry Sir. I- I- I was just upset. It will never happen again." There looked to be tears in his eyes although he was keeping them under control. His chin was belying his emotions though as it was getting very tight with every breath. He could not contain his emotions from becoming completely visible all over his face.

"No. No. No. Joe, I understand we all get upset. Listen though. I get you are tired but here is the thing; this needs to be done. And we need to get it done sooner rather than later." I place my hand on his shoulder as I guide him back to where he had been working when I first called his name. "So here is what I am seeing. There is a lack of motivation on your part and I am going to help you with that. Okay?" He nods at me; a little sniffle escapes him. "Okay. Good. First thing you have to realize is that I have put years into this town and this is the first thing I have really asked for, for myself. Everything else was for the town as a whole. You think I deserve this house, don't you?" Another acknowledgement. "Good, so I want this to be done as soon as possible. Now here is the other thing about motivation, it occurs to me that I have not given you anything to work for. I mean we could get you, I don't know, a new watch? Hmmm? No? Okay, how about a new car? A new house?" His eyes brightened with that one. "Ahhh, so you want a house. Well, let me ask you something first. Do you, Joe, deserve a new house?" His head retreats a little bit again. "Do you!? Answer me?!"

"N- n- n- no." I can feel him shaking under my hand, he tries to pull himself away gently however I just begin to dig my fingertips into his shoulder, I have a firm grip on the actual head of the shoulder muscle.

"No. Exactly. You haven't earned it like I have. And what are you shaking for? I am not going to hurt you. I just want you to realize what I am getting at here. I want this done. Right fucking now." Joe walks awkwardly forward as he pulls his hammer out of his tool belt. I pull my pistol out of the holster on my hip. There is again silence in the hole. Those birds from two blocks away are still chirping in the distance. "I will give you something though Joe. I am going to give you the chance to prove to me that I have not made a mistake here today by trusting you."

"Yes Sir, I'll prove it to you." I nod politely as I return my pistol to the holster.

Now that he seems calmer I continue. "Oh, one more thing. Where did you get that tattoo?"

"A friend of mine did it back in high school."

"High school? What the fuck how old are you?"

"Thirty-six." I will admit I did not think until that moment that it was even remotely possible that he was older than my earlier estimate of twenty-five, but I guess I was proven wrong.

"Huh. Thirty-six." I shrugged as I turned around. Kevin was still standing over by where I had originally been talking to Joe. He was pale. Given the reputation I had cultivated over the years I guess it was not so shocking. I am walking slowly towards him as I point over my shoulder with my left hand. "Can you believe he is thirty-six?" He opens his mouth to say something but never gets the chance as I shoot him in the throat. I continue walking at the same pace. I hear a loud clang from behind me as someone has just dropped some sort of tool. I continue to talk to Kevin as I return my pistol again to its holster. "I left you in charge, so you could keep things moving. I wanted this done soon, not in the middle of fucking winter." He gurgles a little as he is starting to drown a little on his own blood, I did manage to miss the artery though. "You disappointed me Kevin. That pile of lumber never moved from first thing this morning until I returned. You were being goddamned lazy, and you let the rest of them be lazy." I shift my view to my right; my scanning stops on the first person I see. Helen. One of only two women at the worksite. "Helen, come here." She makes the oddest little squeaking sound as she gets off her knees and walks pigeon-toed towards me, her hands clasped in front of her, eyes looking intently down. "You are now in charge here. I want this place being productive from now on. Do you understand that?" A big nod, she truly understood. "Good. Have someone take this out of here and get him burned at the quarry. And that little shit over there, he is firstly going to learn respect. He does not leave here until the job is done. Done! You understand?"

A "Yes Sir." Followed by more furious nodding.

"Wonderful!" I smile at her before I begin walking out of the pit. I look off to the distance to see dark clouds begins to approach. I stop halfway up the ramp and yell back to Joe. "I suggest you get this done quick, the sooner you get the building up the sooner you can get out of the rain!" I chuckled as I walked out of the pit.

CHAPTER 18 – A BLOOD STAIN

I'm sure you may be wondering what exactly fell apart then, what led to my overthrow? To my credit I will say that it was not my inattentiveness that allowed it to happen this time. In fact, I believe that this final revolt was much better concealed than either that came before it. Not only was there no warnings given off for me to act upon there was nothing but I really should have seen it coming. I did see it coming. The incident I just described in the pit of my new house was the direct catalyst for something to happen. I guess they just determined that it was time to stop me once and for all.

After leaving the pit I walked to the garage where Jason worked. He was still my most trusted follower? Minion? Henchmen? Sidekick? I was instantly struck by the smell of oil, coolant and dirt upon walking in to the shop. It was like the smell would only venture as far as the doorway; afraid of the sun even after all these years. I mused to myself upon entering the garage that had really let Jason have a lot of freedom around here. In addition to the old dump truck that sat with a wheel taken off and its brake system entirely sitting on the floor there was what seemed to be an old muscle car sitting in the far bay of the shop on a rotisserie. It was hard to tell as I could only see a little bit of the car but if I had had to wager a guess I would have said it was some sort of Dodge. A Charger, maybe. But not the newer ones, this is one of the old muscle cars from the seventies. Jason hears the dirt on the floor crunch under my feet and slides out from underneath the dump truck. "Sir?" He sits up and begins wiping his hands with a rag; Jason knows that personal visits usually require him to begin working in his other capacity.

I nod towards the truck. "What's wrong with it? We could really use it over at the house."

"The wheel bearings are shot. We've been looking for a replacement but we don't have anything like that here. I've had a few people look around at other places but so far, no-go."

"So? What were you doing down there then?"

"Sleeping." Jason knows he will get that disapproving look from me immediately after saying that, so he just continues talking. "No. Just kidding. I was looking at the possibility of being able to make our own replacement part since that is the only route we can really go."

Impatience now. He knows where he can push and not get me overly upset. "And? Can we make the spare parts ourselves?"

"No. But that has never stopped us before." He is right, we improvise a lot of things around here.

"Good point." We just stand there; he wringing his hands together on a rag watching me while I look over at the truck. This is something I would much rather have been dealing with. It is one of those simple kinds of questions; how can I make this work? Thinking outside the box is just as taxing as other problems but it involves less blood and dirt. My focus breaks as Jason takes the rag and wipes a small spot of blood off my chest, there had apparently been a little bit of splash. "Do you have something to drink?"

"Ummm. Yes, Sir." Jason goes over to an extremely old fridge to pull out a glass bottle with what I sincerely hope is water in it. The fridge would have been considered an antique even prior to the cataclysm, it reminds me of something like an old 50s Chevy. It was large and round and seemed as though it would take a tank to break it; the flame paint scheme over the pearl black paint did not help that mental connection that I made. I sit down in the black leather chair behind the desk. Jason stops suddenly as he turns around with two coffee cups.

"Would you like me to sit in the other chair?" I tilt my head as I speak to him; it was in a way a complete dare. Will Jason oppose me today? I had done this seeming an innumerable number of times before and every time Jason just reaffirmed that I could trust him. That is what I really liked about him. As far as I have always been concerned he was the embodiment of loyalty for me.

"Uh. No, Sir. I, um- I just didn't see you move behind me." A lie, he is more observant than that but this is the tit for tat game we would play at times. He hands me the cup which I immediately thank him for then take a sip. He can see the look on my face as I grimace then swallow hard to get the liquid down. I have never liked the taste of water, I can not say why exactly. City water, country water, Mexican water. To me they all taste the same, as if there was a penny sitting in the bottom of my cup. That is why I tended to prefer things like tea, it masks that weird metallic taste.

"It's warm. What good is a fridge if it doesn't keep things cold?"

"Oh, yes sorry I forgot about that. I keep it set a few degrees warmer than usual; sensitive teeth. You know cold makes em hurt."

"Then why don't you go to get your teeth looked at?"

"We don't exactly have a real dentist, and on top of that we don't have any anesthesia so….yeah, that would hurt if I need to get something done." I roll my eyes at him, he knows better than that. We always make things work and we would end up by just treating anything he needs done dental-wise in the same manner we do when a surgery needs to be performed. We can make things like ether; which while it is not the best anesthesia that was ever made it would be sufficient. All we would have to do is monitor him to make sure he doesn't die mid-procedure from inhaling too much as well as ensure that he doesn't drown in his own vomit after the procedure. It's easy. You notice how I put "we" into that a whole lot, even though I am not the one who makes ether nor am I involved in any manner when it comes to surgeries or the subsequent recovery period. But it is true; we collectively in this town do have those kinds of capabilities.

"I am not going to push this issue right now, but you will be getting your teeth looked at. They are very important for good health and all."

"Uh. Yes…sir… may I ask what is going on?"

"Ah yes, I got all wrapped up in chit chatting. I've had a little bit of a disturbance over at the construction site and I would like you to oversee things there until it is done."

"Disturbance?" I prefer Jason so much more when he does not have questions although in fairness this is something that I had been allowing to happen; if we were alone he was allowed to get clarity. This was the time when he and I were closest to being equals. Almost directly from the outset of his time in the town he always deferred to me. He knew that I was stronger than him when it came to things like drive and will. I will continue until I get my way; whether that means rebuilding an entire civilization from one town up or just in making sure that things run smoothly while building a single house. I cleared my throat before taking another sip of water; I had forgotten that it was not all that appealing. My throat was just feeling dry. I tried to contain my grimace this time; I am stronger than my negative reactions to things like water.

"They were wasting time. Nothing got done all morning while I was out doing my rounds. So.... I felt they needed a little motivation...." Jason knew my code words. Motivation meant instill fear into the people. Examples were those who were punished in some manner, usually very public like being put in the stocks or being expelled from the town. Someone who needed to be forgotten; well, they just disappeared. They were 'Redacted' from the list in black. I had not had to do that for a while prior to this point, a few months, maybe even up to a year; as time has worn on I have become much less concerned with the passage of time. Without somewhere to be time just seems so irrelevant. It just occurred to me that I would need to find out Kevin's last name, otherwise it could take me forever to find his name on the list; also there is the problem that he was not the only Kevin. We have two others so I'd need to make sure that I redacted the right name. "I already have them cleaning the mess. Young Mr. Joe is not to leave the site at all until it is done. If he tries shoot the two people closest to him and put him back to work. I don't care if he eats or not. I don't care if he has to shit in a bucket in front of everyone. He will stay there for the duration."

"I understand." We both stand, I take my cup of water and pour it into the soil of the potted plant he has sitting on the window sill. It looks sick, half the leaves are brown and wilted, the rest are not doing much better.

"What is this?"

"It was my mother's plant; she always had it in the kitchen window. It managed to come back somehow so I keep it going for her."

"Hmmm. Well, that is a nice sentiment. I guess. It may do better if you wash this window." I wipe my finger down the window, through some of the grime although it is so thick and caked on that it only makes a slightly lighter line running down the length of the window.

"I will do that tonight, Sir." I frown a little. I have been pushing for people to be growing food at every opportunity that it seems counter-intuitive to me for someone to be growing any plant that is not edible. I already gave my tacit consent though by seeming to approve of his keeping a reminder of his mother. Not really something to make into an issue though, I have never forced people to try to forget their loved ones before, why would I start now.

"I left… shit, what was her name… damnit. Blond girl…. Holly? Maybe? Bah, whatever. Regardless, I'm sure she'll answer when you arrive. Whatever her name was, I left her in charge. Just make sure that they keep things moving." I turn to walk towards the door before spinning on my heels, "Helen, her name was Helen. In any event, keep them moving, I need to go finish my usual work then I will be back."

"Understood." I walk out into the sun and instantly am overtaken by the brightness of everything. The smells are all so pretty and sweet compared to the dark dankness of the oil and grease that permeated Jason's shop. I stand there as my eyes slowly adjust to the light, even after a minute my eyes are still adjusting and sore from the brilliance of the sun at that moment. The clouds were not closer than they had been. It would still be likely an hour or so before they overtook the sun and darkened the entirety of everything around me. Jason emerges from his shop; I hear a click from behind me. Was it a gun cocking or Jason locking his door? Only a second or so to determine the truth; if it was a gun being cocked really I am already at a severe disadvantage. He would be around 5 feet behind me, even with his arm fully raised and outstretched that would still be around 3 feet worth of distance I would need to cover, backwards, in order to get his weapon from him. The only other option would be to try to pretend I am in the wild west; quick draw, spin and shoot before he is able to shoot me in the back of the head. Both scenarios are not really possible. I know that if Jason has me at that kind of disadvantage I am probably already beaten. If he had cocked his gun, I would no longer be considering what the sound was, I would already be dead.

"Why do you lock your door? Do you expect someone will steal things from you?" I mused to him over my shoulder. My eyes had mostly adjusted so I looked over at him as I waited for him to answer. Jason had changed his clothes, shedding the dark blue coveralls he had been wearing to now be wearing a pair of blue jeans that had long seen the end of their intended life. Both knees appeared to have been patched in addition to what looked like a patch in the crotch. His shirt was obviously something he had had for years as well, the light grey t-shirt was covered in various splotches of dark grey, brown and black where various fluids from the vehicles had spilled on him. Jason was ready to work however; he had his rifle slung over his shoulder and his pistol in the holster on his hip.

"Force of habit. I don't expect anyone will steal from me, but someone may borrow a tool, I prefer to know who I am lending things to."

I chuckled a little at that. "Fair enough. I will be back in likely an hour or less. When I relieve you, I'd like for you to grab a couple of people to follow suit for watching over the site." Jason nodded as he walked off. I was watching his feet; he was no longer waking in that silent manner that I had become accustomed to. He was wearing normal looking work boots. I guess he felt rushed and didn't have time to switch into his ninja clothes.

I walk off in the opposite direction, heading towards the chicken coop, needed to check on one of the protein sources for the town. Coop is likely not the most appropriate word for what we had constructed for these birds. There was a coop where they would all roost, make their nests and lay their eggs but attached to that is a whole enclosure meant to keep them contained and safe from outside threats, although there are not really all that many coyotes or chicken hawks to worry about, it is more of a precaution. An entire lot was taken and fenced. The bottom of each fence was buried so that things could not simply slip underneath the fence, they would have to dig; hopefully allowing us time to stop them. Princess had once, years ago, begun eyeing the chickens. More than likely I believe he had been on his own at least long enough that he had had to find his own food. He never made it near them; it was more of the look. So, better safe than sorry. In addition to the fence there was a net strung over the entire lot; keeping them safe from aerial threats as well as stopping them from escaping. Chickens, despite what some people may think, can fly. Not that well and only for short distances but it can still happen. It is better to save the effort of having to try to round up the chickens from around town if we could avoid it. I wave at Mr. and Mrs. Seltz. They are probably some of our oldest residents and were a couple from before the cataclysm. In order to allow them to continue to contribute and avoid things like bending down they were intentionally set next to the chicken coop. Each day they sit on a couple of old folding vinyl chairs in the middle of the enclosure, tossing seeds to the chickens that crowd around them; pecking at everything and stepping on each other in order to get their food. "How are you two doing today?"

Mr. Seltz stepped off his porch coming down to lean on the fence while we talked. This is something that we had done on numerous occasions, he was an interesting man; I had never delved too far into his past, I mostly let him talk about things that he preferred to talk about although I did know that he had been in the military when he was in his younger years. No idea even what branch, let alone what he actually did while serving but I had always taken an interest in the snippets that he had revealed. He had been able to give us a lot of information about survival skills that we later translated into other things; trapping, tracking, water filtration, etc. There were stories about the 'good old days', I'm sure that means pre-cataclysm but also pre-tyrant. I still liked him though, he had the old-timey feeling you would expect from a grandfather. He likely had been a grandfather which would explain where that sense came from.

Many off-color jokes that would not be heard in polite company. He was definitely not on the politically correct train; I had to forgive him for that. He was from a different generation. An older generation that had paid their dues with the blood of their fathers, uncles, brothers and sons. I on the other hand was not part of that generation. I was in the group in-between them and the millennials. We weren't forged in war; we were cast in the crucible of the cataclysm. Two different generations, both hardened for different reasons, through different processes. "Edith is doing good; I'm a little sore. I can feel the rain coming, we're gonna be in for a bit of a storm." I again look around, the clouds are closer than they had been, and they seemed to be picking up speed. What I had estimated as being another hour of bright sun now looked more like ten or fifteen minutes.

"I definitely see what you mean; I guess it'll be time for me to get heading home. No reason to get soaked if I don't have to but before I go, I just wanted to check on the flock. Everything still going well?"

He smiled and pointed nodded back over his shoulder. "They're fine. Like always, we take good care of 'em but…." I smiled as I knew this meant he had a request, his requests were never anything of real consequence though. I could likely have it arranged in minutes. "I think it's about time we got a new coop. That one has years of chicken shit all over it; I just can't scrape it off anymore." Simple enough to deal with.

"I will see what I can do, will likely be a week or two before it gets built but in the meantime, I'll find some young whippersnapper to clean it out for you. No reason you should be doing it anyways."

"We already got that young boy from down the street helping us here. We give him an extra couple of eggs everyday, so he can help out."

"Hmmm. Good. Good. Well, uh, I got to get moving, um, along. I'll see you another time. Stay out of the rain, Give Edith my love." I was feeling conflicted as I left. Our discussion was much more abrupt than usual. I did not even register if Mr. Seltz had said anything to me as I left.

I'm sure he did, he was never one to forget his manners. I was suddenly feeling kind of sad; maybe ashamed or guilty is a better descriptor. My first reaction to someone, anyone taking from the community, even if it is to give to another for them doing work is still not something I wanted to entertain at that moment. It's like skimming off the till in my mind. Everyone in town gets their allotment; if that boy from down the street is getting more then it begins to move the whole system we have in place off kilter. Not a lot, just a little hair to one side. I was feeling guilty as I know that my reaction, had I not contained myself, would have been to begin to berate Mr. Seltz for assuming he could do that with community food. Grand scheme of things, not a big deal. Something I can deal with another day, it will only take a few words to get him to see where he went wrong and stop the whole practice. I was leaving so I could deal with it in that manner instead of through my typical methods. And like I just said, Mr. Seltz was of a different generation. In his mind what he was doing was no different than giving that neighbor boy a quarter for moving his lawn, just technically it was not his quarter to be giving.

The sky continues to darken as I walk to my house. I am trying to think as I walk what Kevin's last name was. I keep thinking it was something generic like Smith or Jones but that is not it, in lieu of actually remembering his name I try to think about who entered the town around the same time; maybe someone I knew a little better. Closest that I can think of was a man named Reginald...-something. I was fairly confident that they entered within about a week of each other, which did help me considerably. Reginald is a fairly distinctive name, and considering he preferred Reginald to Reggie or Reg meant that he stuck out in my mind a little more. I would be making a black mark about 6 pages back from the current page and adding a new name to my hidden list. From that point on I would be much more acquainted with Kevin's name. The first rain drops begin to fall as I step into my yard. In the few seconds it took for me to get from the street to the safety of my porch the sky opened up, a deluge of water falling everywhere I could see. I retreated to my house, away from the dampness and chill outside.

I enter my study on the second floor of my house to pull out my list of the redacted. I stop before doing so to look out the window, down the street towards the open pit. I see no one so I crane my neck further to the left, trying to increase the angle so that I can get a better view. To no avail. I am not truly that concerned that work continues while it rains, I am more concerned with making my point with Joe and ensuring that he remains where he is until the job is done. I had wanted to avoid being out in the rain unnecessarily, but it seemed that would not be the case today. I let out a sigh as I had been looking forward to being able to sit down, write a name then try to clear my head. Downstairs in the closet, next to the front door, I keep an old rain poncho. I have no idea where it had come from; it was obviously an old army poncho as it was that distinctive olive drab color, I simply liked it because it did not restrict me too much. I always felt with raincoats like I had no ability to move as the material would collect moisture on the inside making it stick to my skin and hold me from being able to be mobile. This poncho still got wet inside but did not hold as tightly. It was old though, after so many years it was beginning to crack and have spots where the rubbery coating was coming off. Little droplets of water could get in, nothing significant though. Not enough to have me "catch my death".

Stepping off the porch I can instantly feel the weight of the rain droplets hitting the poncho; this was a large storm, likely the largest we had had in years. That is good though; every rainfall just made sure that our cisterns, rain barrels, and all the nearby lakes and streams were all replenished. As well with each rainfall there was increased the likelihood that any of the leftover radioactive particles would be washed away. We never really had many problems with radiation here. All the work we had done in pulling off the top layer of soil, washing things and whatnot that we had done after the radioactive dust first began to fall had seemingly worked. No mutants. No mass instances of cancer. No radiation sickness that I was ever aware of. The raindrops now were seemingly huge, as if each one was an entire thimble-full of water. I could feel each hit that I was taking from each droplet.

Nearing the edge of the pit I can finally see that Joe is where he should be. Huddling in the middle of the foundation underneath a tarp stretched across a couple of boards. I was sure he had gotten the message. It occurred to me that I had meant to relieve Jason after I was done my work, he would likely have been expecting me to come shortly after it began raining. I could not see him, I was wondering if he had assumed I was going to take longer than I had expected and had gone to get his own rain gear. Or was watching Joe from the house next door. It did not matter at that moment. I had my own plan for being here.

I stood as close to the edge of the pit as I felt I safely could; about 2 feet back from the edge. I did not want to take the chance of slipping on the wet grass and falling head over heels into the hole. I could see the stain of Kevin's blood on the concrete floor. I had annoyed myself; I knew better than to do that. It is the whole idea of you don't shit where you eat. It was likely going to take forever to get that out of the concrete and even if I did manage to get it out I would have that constant reminder in the basement of Kevin. I already have a means to do that; my list of names. I don't need something extra. I look at the pile of tools sitting on the edge of the pit on the other side of the ramp. Shovels, picks, sledgehammers, pieces of re-bar that we had used as chisels for cutting the stone. None of which were what I was looking for. I wanted a broom; something with stiff bristles. I knew where to find one, I returned to my house in order to get a push broom. As I walked back the first flash of lightning streaked across the sky. It was the kind that does not seem to hit the ground but instead goes from one cloud to another. There was still an accompanying boom from the thunderclap a few seconds later. I stopped to watch the next flash, it took minutes. Likely, five minutes before that next bolt happened. It went from one cloud to another, coming below the clouds in a couple points to make the burst of light even brighter. It was not that late in the day yet still managed to be as dark as it would be just before dusk. The flash woke me from my trance and I continued moving towards the pit. Thunder booms again as I begin to descend into the hole; broom in one hand the other trying to find handholds as I move down. Without warning, although not unexpectedly my feet slip out from underneath me and I'm sliding down to the bottom of the hole. My feet slam into the foundation as it sticks above the level of the rock that makes up the bottom of the hole. I feel intense pain in my left ankle. I know this pain though, I sprained an ankle; I don't even need to get it checked in order to know that. There were no accompanying feelings, like the crack of a bone breaking or the pop of damage to a ligament. I grit my teeth as I roll onto my side and begin to pull myself up. This first step is going to hurt, along with all the others. I feel stupid for having fallen as I brush some of the muck off my pants and see on the side of the pit there is a ladder standing against the side; I could have taken that and not fallen. I could have just thrown the broom down. At least I have a means of egress when I am done with Joe. Hobbling over to the makeshift tent; I can hear Joe sniffling as it was cold and he was lying on cement. His discomfort was not overly surprising and really that was the whole point. He survives this and he will never again have to be taught another lesson. There is also another upside, for me. Leaving him here, until he is allowed to leave only confirms my dominance over him. A man with a broken spirit is malleable. Not that I am looking for another person to help me however they are always nice to have in reserve. After someone is completely broken down; their confidence, feelings of freedom, independence are all stripped away and wiped clean. If it is returned to them, by say someone who has the power to imbue such things, they will be grateful, appreciative and most importantly obedient. This is essentially the basis of any type of 'brain-washing'. Tear them down to build them up.

"Joe." A large sniffle escapes him before he responds.

"Sir?"

"I have a task for you. I want you to use this broom and clean up that mess. It is your fault that it is there, so it's only fair you should scrub it. Don't you agree?"

"B- but it's raining."

"I know, if you didn't notice I am standing out in it. But see the water will help you get this stain out of my house." A pause as I switch gears. "I… Really… Really… Hate stains. Do you understand? I want this scrubbed off today. Now! …. Unless you think there should be another lesson for you on doing what you are told."

"No Sir." Joe pulls himself out from under the tarp. I am not so certain just what he was trying so hard to avoid, he was already soaked under there. I tip the broom towards him as he gingerly takes it from me. I had not entirely thought that through as I was putting a fair bit of my weight on it. I stumble slightly as I reach out for the stack of cement bags. My face contorts into a sneer as I take a deep breath to control my pain. I twist my neck, cracking it as I watch Joe feebly try sweeping the stain.

"For fucks sakes. How did you get to be thirty-six years old and have no idea how to do things? I said scrub it, not sweep it." He begins to bear down on the broom, looking like a curling champion. Furiously scouring the stain with the broom. At least I was right on this count, the stain was already becoming faint. The water around it was turning a light reddish-brown. It was dissipating enough that I would not be seeing only that for the remainder of my life. "When the spot is gone you can stop." I hear something now above the edge of the pit. A weird squishing sound, not unlike walking in a shoe full of water. Or someone stepping into a mushy puddle of muck. As if poetically I look up to see a figure at the top of the ramp, looking down at me as another flash of lightning streaks across the sky behind him. The boom comes instantly afterwards; the lightning happened directly above us. I strain to look through the falling water at the figure standing there. "Jason? Is that you?" No answer but a slight shuffle of his feet. My thoughts drift towards the dummy set up in the park. Was this another trap? I begin to limp towards the ladder, if it is a trap I am not going to just stand here looking stupid. As I walk out of view of the figure on top of the ramp I can hear him yell, before taking the slide down the ramp. He at least had the right idea. Make sliding down your plan; don't let the ramp decide for you what you plan is.

I hear "Stop!" erupt from behind me as another flash streaks across the sky. I turn slowly to see Jason pointing his rifle at me. It would have made more sense for him to shoot me in the back of the head outside of his shop. Or in that back now instead of allowing me to turn. Another positive of the poncho, it hides my hands, he would not even see if I was pulling out my pistol. I stand straight up as I square off with Jason. My ankle is trying to scream at me but I am so engrossed in confronting him that I am barely noticing the pain. He takes a step forward and I undo the button on the holster, pulling the pistol out slightly. "Oh my god. I am sorry Sir, I thought you were that guy I am supposed to be watching trying to escape."

I drop my pistol back into my holster and I angrily gesture over to Joe. "He is right fucking there. How can you see me but not him?"

"You're wearing darker clothes, it's easier to see." Fuck. He was probably right. Rain coming down this heavy and it being this dark would have made it hard to see things at a distance.

"For the record I do not like you pointing your rifle at me." He suddenly realized he was still pointing it at my chest and dropped it down before slinging it over his shoulder again. "Where were you?"

"Next door, watching the site from the window. I saw you get here a couple minutes ago which is why I came out to look, you just disappeared."

I scoffed at such a simple explanation. "I slid down that bloody ramp and twisted my ankle."

"Let's get you to the hospital; we'll get you fixed up." I opened my mouth to protest and tell him that 'I will be fine, it is just a sprain' but nothing escaped my mouth. I only stood there gaping as the ladder was slid up the side of the pit. I hear the metallic crash as the aluminum ladder is dropped on the ground outside the hole. It was a trap and we were stuck at the bottom of the pit, with only a slippery ramp as the possible way to get out. I look angrily at Jason as he looks up to the edge of the pit.

Again, ignoring the pain and the fact that my foot does not want to work I stagger towards Joe who seems oblivious to the current goings-on. I begin to drag his tarp-tent over to the pile of cement bags. I crouch behind the pile, scanning the horizon for any figures above the edge of the pit. A flash of lightning; I would have expected to have seen another person although none appeared. Ten. Twenty. Thirty minutes go by. Nothing. I see no one. I hear nothing. By now, Jason, Joe and I are all huddled under the tarp awaiting the next thing to happen. None of us are speaking. Joe just shivers. We could hear the occasional clacking of his teeth. The rain begins to lighten. It is still raining however is no longer composed of those massive droplets of water; it has turned into more of a nice pleasant shower. Even the air is not as chilly as it had been; there was a warm moistness everywhere. All I could smell was ozone mixed with dirt.

There were no more flashes of lightning happening. I finally see someone. There looks to be a man standing above where the ladder had been. Then another appears, on the other side of the ramp, where I had been standing less than an hour before. More and more were coming to the side, no one was saying anything. They were only looking. I began to feel as if I had begun digging my own grave only weeks ago and now it was about to be filled up above me. A shot rings out, hitting the far side of the cement pile. Cement begins to pour out of the bag in a gentle cascading arch. The bullet had likely only gone an inch or so into that material; it is much too dense to allow a bullet to penetrate all the way to us. And that was all it took. Jason begins fire shots from his rifle at every dark form he can see. I could tell by the third shot he was not hitting anything, whether they were not even real people and just forms meant to get us to waste our ammunition or his aim was just that bad I could not say. I am going to err on the side of, he's a shitty shot. I slap his shoulder and make the cutting throat gesture to him. I just wanted him to stop firing. "You just gave away our fucking position." I was trying to whisper through my teeth although it more than likely only seemed that I was seething. I was, on the inside, but

I was not trying to be that way on the outside. This was an instance where keeping a cool head would be the most beneficial.

I hear someone yell from the side closest to us. "Drop your weapons and come out." I rolled my eyes, another revolt. The last one had been taxing enough I was not looking forward to this one. I was going to destroy half this town. No more bonfires off in the distance. People will be hung from the streetlights. I will flay people alive in the middle of the town. I swear to myself that I will never again go through any dissent again. The price will be so high they will not be able to endure it. We say nothing. I can hear booms off in the distance. They sound odd. Not quite like thunder but perhaps they were, maybe I was hearing echoes coming off the walls of the pit. Four. Just echoes. Six. I'm deluding myself. Nine. Those are gunshots. Eleven. The sounds stop. I hear nothing else. Jason is breathing heavy, almost like a dog on a hot day. "DROP YOUR WEAPONS AND COME OUT!" The people outside the pit seem to have acquired a megaphone.

I pull out my pistol and point it at Joe, inches from his face. His eyes begin to cross as he stares at the tip of the barrel. "What makes you so special Joe?" He is energetically shaking his head. "Don't try to deny it. This is something you obviously did. Or it was done because of you." he continues to deny it by shaking his head; his whole body continuing to shudder. "I have good news Joe, if this doesn't turn out well, I will save my last bullet for you." My wide smile is suddenly lit up by a work light that is turned on outside the pit. Joe begins to cry uncontrollably.

The rain is still lessening; there is no longer the waterfall of muddy water coming down the ramp into the pit. I can see in the shadows of the ramp there are two distinct grooves from where Jason and I had both slid down into the pit. One intentionally, the other…not so intentionally. There is someone standing next to the work light, it was hard to see him although it was apparent he was there. Every minute or two the light would change as something passed in front of the light. Jason again began to scan around for targets along the edges of the pit. The light now made it easier to pin point them, they were ever so slightly illuminated against the dark background. He takes aim as he finds a suitable target. Fires. The muzzle was right next to my ear; which began to ring. I could feel the heat of the flash and sense the burning of the gunpowder. With my other ear I could hear a muffled scream. Volleys return in our direct, each seemingly aimed directly at the cement as nothing else was hit. I hear shouts of "No. No." coming from outside the pit. It was not just one person saying that. It was a chorus of screams, all saying no.

I hear the familiar rumble of someone sliding down the ramp. I look around the side of the cement pile, looking to see who it is. There was no one. A decoy? Toss something down to get our attention looking that direct? I instantly look towards the far end of the pit, there seemed to be nothing happening there. There was not even someone on that side outside the pit. My scanning continues to begin to look around the other side of the pile. Immediately, I begin to turn back, looking to Jason as he again raises his weapon, trained directly beside my head once again. I fire three shots into his chest as I see the flash from the muzzle of his rifle erupt right before my eyes. The gunpowder is blown all over my face; each grain of it is burning a microscopic burn onto my face. It felt as if I had stuck my face into an oven, if only for seconds. My eyes tingled as the burning dust seemingly was beginning to dissolve my eyelids.

I continue to hear screams of "No." Coming closer and closer. The last thing I saw at that moment was Princess, sitting quietly in front of me as Aurora ran down the ramp and stumbled as she reached the bottom.

CHAPTER 19 – A CAGE AND A RAG

I did not miss that old familiar feeling of being hit, hard, in the back of the head. I think it was the butt of a rifle again. I lay there, going in and out of consciousness, soaked from being on my back in a puddle; this entire pit was turning into a pool. Was it to be my watery grave? All I could really do was listen, my eyes still burned. The rain hitting my face was slowly starting to alleviate the sensation that my eyelids were melting but it was going slowly. The first time for certain that I was conscious I was struck at the hint of something oddly salty being present in the air; Jason's blood most likely. I could not place that at the time, I was only confused by it. I had sudden images flash through my mind that I was actually near the ocean. The rain falling was no longer precipitation but instead the gentle beating of the waves rolling onto the beach. Next time I awoke I felt as if I was drowning, the ocean had swallowed me. Overtaken and overwhelmed me. All I could do was try to swim. I spit the water out of my mouth and began to move. I hear shouts from above the surface of the water. 'No.' 'Now.' 'Hurry!' 'What now?' 'Fuck sakes.' 'Not yet.' What do you mean?' 'Yes.' I roll onto my stomach, so I can begin my swim away from the yelling. I only feel pain as my arms are pinned and bent, I can feel metal on my wrists. I still can't see but everything fades to black. Next, my chest hurts. I can feel someone wiping my face with a warm wet cloth; whoever they are they are not being gentle. And they are breathing on me, each exhalation is hot and moist; each of those breaths that I inhale through my nose makes me want to vomit, this person needed a toothbrush. As for myself, I am only able to take shallow breaths, my ribs hurt. I remember thinking at that moment that I must have hit a rock. The shouting seemed so far away. I could still hear it although it was further off. Or it was no longer shouting. I could not tell if it was a volume problem or a distance problem. I begin to have trouble breathing, even shallowly. Everything in my body is telling me to spit out the water. I begin to hack and cough. Each attempt to expel the water only causes me pain. Each spike in pain seems to ease the need to cough more, but it is still all my body wants to do. I want to get it so I no longer feel the need to cough, but the pain is such a high price to pay. Someone grabs me under my arm and lifts me out of the water. I cannot tell if it was the same person who had been wiping my face; it seemed likely they were rough moving me as well. They had dug their fingers into my armpit, it was a nice relief from the pain in my chest and the pain I was starting to feel in my head, the armpit pain only lasted as long as their fingers were jammed in there; the head and ribs, that pain persisted.

I was sitting with my back against something hard. I was not very comfortable; I begin to try to shift myself only to have a foot slammed into my chest. As I begin gasping for air; trying to cough while simultaneously having no air to cough with. My lungs are screaming to breathe again. I began to return to the present; to reality. I was in the pit. I was against the pile of cement bags. I comprehended that what I had smelled was the smell of blood. I could feel someone breathing on my face as they continued to wipe at my cheeks and eyes. My mind comes further towards being able to recognize the world around me. Princess. He was licking my face. Bastard dog; the only time he every really showed me any affection and I cannot even pet him back. I was now fully aware my hands were cuffed behind my back; I try to twist my right hand only to find the cuffs are quite tight. Whoever put them on was quite zealous in making sure I was secure, not very intelligent though. My palms were facing each other, if I had something to pick with there is the possibility I could undo the cuffs. I run my finger over the cuff; I can feel the keyhole. I begin to slowly pat around my waist; I carry nothing that I could pick with. It is not likely I would have been able to do it anyways; I had tried once before, for the fun of it, and was not successful even with my hands in front of me. I again shift my weight to my side as I try to sit a little more comfortably. I again am kicked in the chest, only to hear a shout of "Stop that." The people talking around me are now sounding much calmer. They are closer, clearer; yet I still cannot understand what is being said. Clarity is moving to consciousness compared to mere moments ago. It moves back and forth. As Princess resumes licking my face I begin to try to open my eyes. Everything is still dark and hazy but at least I got something. I can see outlines. Figures. Blobs in the shapes of people. My face is no longer burning as it was; the only sensation is much the same as when you burn your tongue or the roof of your mouth, a persistent tingle that reminds you that you have burned yourself. My chest is still hurting. On my side as well as right in the middle. I must have been kicked in the ribs while I was unconscious. That was my guess at least; it felt like that kind of pain. The middle of my chest was not even a question for me. I felt as if I could tell you what size shoe the person wore who had kicked me in the chest. Ten and a half is my guess. Right foot. I imagine the bruise is already starting to form. I am still not able to see clearly. I can sense the blood beginning to pool on the front of my ribcage. Each cell in my blood having some job to perform there. Nutrients are brought in order to help the healing begin. Platelets begin to clot the blood, my body's attempt to stop me from bleeding to death internally. Red blood cells bring oxygen to the cells as they begin to heal while taking away carbon dioxide, the byproduct of cellular respiration. White blood cells arrive, ready to attack any foreign body that attempts to infect me with some malady. I can feel all these things happening in the perfect shape of someone's shoe. "Bring him."

I suddenly have fingers digging into my armpit as a man grunts trying to lift me. It is kind of comical, I'm not even resisting; he is just that weak. Another person grabs the poncho in their fist, tightening it around my neck as their other hand hooks under my arm helping to lift me. I try to help myself stand up; no reason to be rude now, the polite thing to do would be help these people move things along. As I stand I am reminded that not so long ago my ankle had been twisted there was another mounting pain on top of the others I was feeling. I am half-dragged, half-stumbling towards the ramp. The rain is still falling now, not the heavy rainfall like it was initially but definitely more than the spitting it was doing a little while ago. I could see there were multiple tracks of mud along the ramp, from all the people who had slid down into the pit. My eyesight was coming back however the thumping of my head was making it hard to focus. All I wanted to do was take a nap. I knew what that meant. I have a concussion. Trying to lift my head only seemed to make the pain and the slight dizziness that I felt even worse. They should have just left me to take a nap. It would have been easier to move when I wasn't feeling as I was at that moment. I can see the ladder is now lying on the ramp, giving us the ability to walk back up it in spite of the slipperiness of the rock after all that rain. I struggled to maneuver myself up the ramp; the rungs are still wet. Still slippery. The man ahead of me still has my poncho in his fist; he's still trying to drag me along with it. Choking me. I would presume this is how a reluctant dog would feel when dragged behind its impatient master. My foot slips off the rung and completely off the ladder. It was the same ankle I had already hurt that was now supporting all of my weight, except what was being taken up by my neck. A heavy grunt emanates from in front of me as I am being pulled while a pair of hands push me from behind. My foot flails as I desperately try to gain a new purchase on the ladder. The pulling suddenly stops as I am tossed sideways onto the ground next to the ramp. I sit there a moment, feeling the wet grass in my hands, alternating between coughing and chuckling. I don't even know what I was finding so funny.

My walk to the church was not particularly eventful but still painful. It seemed that every part of my body was hurting in some manner.

Head, check. Chest, check. Ankle, check. Wrists, check. Throat, check. I even became aware that I had scraped my knee at some point during the events of the day; I could feel the raw patch of skin rubbing on the inside of my pants. So much discomfort. Stepping up to the front of the church I was finally being brought somewhere with decent lighting, I was finally able to see someone. The large man that had presumably been the one who wrapped my poncho around my neck was Dale. Another Dale. This was one who spent a lot of his time doing work in the power plant, I think he was something like an electrical engineer. Or electrician; something electrical. Waiting in the doorway of the church is Adam, an older gentleman; he had been deeply religious before the cataclysm only to turn his back on his faith after his family did not survive it. It was different to see him at the church, even though that was no longer what it was actually used for. Adam makes eye contact with me; he looks shocked. I was not overly surprised at that. Given what I know about what is going on, I was not likely to be expected to still be breathing. He darts around the corner back into the church only to return with a bag. It is quickly put over my head and synched up around my neck. More pressure on my throat. I was tempted to tell him this was wholly unnecessary, but I doubt he would have listened. Although, if I had said anything, he likely would have shit his pants. The bag smelled of dirt and mildew and scratched against my face which was still tender from before. I had forgotten about it until the bag began to rub my skin; it was like I was trying to wear a wool sweater after having sustained a nasty sunburn. I could feel every fiber that poked into me; I could feel every thread, every stitch. After so many years spent in Republica I had gotten to know some parts of the town quite intimately, which would most definitely include this church. I counted twenty-three steps from the time the bag was put on my head until I heard a door open and I was shoved through into a room that was dark. I couldn't see through the bag but I could sense if there was light or not. This would have been the pastor's living room another five steps and a quick right turn and I was now in the bedroom. The bathroom would have been another two steps or so; I suddenly became aware that I would like to pee. I would need to request that at some point in the near future; lest I piss my pants and have someone assume that I am so scared I peed myself. Not to say I was not scared but I was just kind of going with it. I had been on the other end enough times to know where this will all lead. Nothing will change that, so really I have nothing to be scared of. Fear only makes sense if there is an element that is unknown. I know this game. I have already lost.

I am callously tossed again, ramming my shoulder into the mattress; I kind of did a half-flop on the bed before sliding onto the floor. I decided I was comfortable where I was and just laid there. I don't even know how long it was. I may have lost consciousness again. As I started to become aware of my surroundings I began to have feelings reminiscent of when I was a child. Remembering the arguments that my parents had had. They fought about all manner of things; bills and money, how my mother was embarrassed by dad when he got drunk at some company Christmas party, a 'whore' from down the street that kept asking for help around the house like getting her lawn mowed or plumbing fixed. Those euphemisms never occurred to me until that moment when those old memories were swirling around inside my head, maybe my parents had more reasons to argue than I realized. I could hear people talking again. It seemed to be the same angry discussion that had been happening out in the rain; chances are they just wanted to be able to continue it out of the cold. And not like I could blame them, I would not have wanted to stay out there all night. I was still soaked and cold but at least I was not still outside. "What do you want to do?" That was a gruff male voice, likely Dale; it seemed to match him.

I cannot hear the response clearly, it is a woman, but all I can get is just mumbles.

"Are you fucking serious?"

More womanly mumbling.

He responds. "That is bullshit. So we are just supposed to do nothing?"

I hear nothing.

"You know what. Fuck you! We are doing this my way." It sounds as if something got tossed across the room. A piece of furniture. Kitchen table possibly. Barking. Good old Princess. Fucking bastard dog. That does explain who the woman is though. Aurora. What the fuck was she doing at the pit in the middle of the rain storm? The door opens slightly, and I can finally hear her clearly.

"We are not doing this your way. We are doing it the right way. It is what we had all decided beforehand. We are going to stick to it. Got it?" I love to hear her talking in such an authoritative manner. To me it means I at least did something right. I'll just have to overlook that she was not only a traitor but actively conspired against me. I was right, there was something percolating under the surface. Not that I can be proud of it. I still got caught by it. And the one person I would not want to have involved was apparently at least somewhere near the epicenter of it.

I am now certain it is Dale that she was arguing with as he growls back as her. "Fine, do it your way."

Without missing a beat, she corrects him, "The right way." I chuckle to myself; I can see the change from light to dark as she steps from the living room into the bed room. I can see a hazy silhouette with a smaller one right alongside through the bag on my head. "He's awake now." I would assume she is telling Dale or whoever else is in the other room. What would it matter though? Awake, asleep, you can kill someone in either state; it does not make much of a difference. I can see Aurora's shadow move out of the doorway, nearly immediately being replaced by a large shadow. Dale. At least this time I was able to mentally prepare; I steeled myself against he manhandling I was about to take.

I was tossed unceremoniously onto a chair in the kitchen area of the pastor's living quarters, the bag is yanked hard. I feel a new flash of pain as the opening was still tight around my neck, pulling the bag had only tightened it instead of removing it from my head. A gruff push on my forehead jarring my head back and I can feel someone fighting with the cord of the bag; the slight tightness that was still there evaporated and for the first time in what seemed to be hours I was able to take a full breath instead of a trying to breath through a constricted garden hose. My face began to burn and tingle as the bag was finally ripped from my head; sandpaper scrapped across my singed face. I sat there while my eyes adjusted to the light, moving my jaw as if someone had just punched me and I was trying to set it back in place. Dale mocked me with a very formal bow while saying "Sir." I only tilted my head like a dog while I watched him, his eyes were fiery and angry, and my lack of any real emotion in these moments only likely heightened his anger towards me.

"Do you know why we brought you here?" My face turns towards the voice but my eyes are still firmly locked with Dale's; it isn't until he blinks and breaks the staring contest that I silently declare victory and look into Aurora's eyes. I would say looking at them that she likely got her eyes from her mother; they were the same shade of brown as mine but the overall look and shape belonged to her mother. I smile at her with my biggest 'shit-eating grin'.

"Breakfast?" Dale takes a quick step forward only to have a hand shoved into the middle of his chest.

"Stop! He is only trying to antagonize you. I told you we are going to do this the way we had all agreed to. Okay? Just be calm." Dale cranes his neck to the side in an attempt to crack it before he nods; he walks across the room and plops himself down onto the easy chair. Aurora's attention returns to me.

"Don't be an asshole. I know what you are doing; your little tricks. They won't work." She seems to be waiting for me to answer but as I say nothing it becomes more of an ill-placed dramatic pause. "We brought you here to keep you safe." My eyebrows perk up as I lean over slightly indicating I want my hands taken out of the handcuffs, she just continues talking. "We are keeping you safe until you have your trial. The people need justice, but they also need rules and laws. Things that you claimed to have given us; everyone here is going to get them for real."

"I have given people law."

"No. What you did was come up with arbitrary distinctions between what is right and wrong and then kill lots of people based on those irrelevant points. Everything you did was on a whim; people lived and died at your pleasure."

"Semantics." I hear a scoff from across the room; although at least Dale stayed in his chair.

"Call it what you want. We are going to have real laws; real justice. A fair process. No one is going to be summarily executed anymore."

I was honestly kind of having fun; this is the verbal sparring that I never did anymore, no one was willing to really disagree with me. It was a nice change of pace. "You are assuming you can keep control of animals like him; people who can't be trusted to conduct themselves as civilized people are the reason I have governed as I have. Without my rules the good people here would have been wiped out long ago and only people like him would be left." Dale began to rise from his chair only to sit back down when Aurora flashed her hand at him. She had some really good control of him, almost as good as the control she had of Princess.

"A lot of the good people *were* wiped out; by *you*."

"Thieves, cannibals, rapists, dissidents. None of them were good people. They all deserved what happened to them."

"I am not going to sit here and debate with you all night, I would prefer to take the first night of freedom we finally have in this place and get some well-deserved sleep. Your trial will begin tomorrow at noon." She stopped crouching in front of me and began to walk for the door. Dale had stood from his chair when she turned back to him. "Dale. Please. Don't do anything, he needs to stand trial. It is the right thing to do."

"Fine." He spoke through his teeth; like an angry child, I think he even kicked his foot like one. I was picked up and moved back to the bedroom. As the door closed I could hear something being propped against the doorknob to prevent it from being opened, likely a chair. I have never actually tried that trick. I have seen it in movies numerous times but never did it myself. I wonder if it is like so many other things that were conveniently exaggerated as a film making device. I lay down uncomfortably with my hands still behind my back to try to get a little rest. I still wanted nothing more than to sleep. Perhaps Dale could get his wish and I would just die from a cerebral hemorrhage in my sleep. That is me fooling myself, I doubt he just wanted me to die; he probably wanted me to be in pain, at his hands. I acknowledged to myself that there could be time enough for that in the future as I finally fell asleep.

I was unable to tell how long I had slept for, if it was day or night. This room was small, only slightly larger than the double mattress I was sleeping on, there was no window. I slid myself off the bed and stumbled towards the door. I made an attempt to open the door but it was still braced shut, I guess that trick does work. I began kicking it, gently at first then becoming louder until I heard someone moving on the other side. "What?" Not Dale, Not Aurora. The guard must have changed.

"I need to use the facilities." Silence. I wait for my guard to ask permission from whomever else is in the room, the wait seems to go on forever.

"What??" It occurred to me that the delay was likely not that he needed to get permission for me to be let out; he did not know what I meant by 'facilities'.

Louder, I respond. "I need to take a leak. Like now. Right now, or you are just going to have to clean up the mess." The chair slides across the floor and the door slowly opens. A streak of light comes through the crack of the door, it is at the very least morning now; probably later, and that concussion put me out for what was doubtlessly a long time. I gently step on the base of the door, opening it quicker only to have a pistol thrust only inches from my face. "Jesus, I just need to piss." He steps back, the gun still trained on my head as I walk to the bathroom door. And stand there. I look over my shoulder at Ivan before I wave my hands behind my back. "Could you get this? It's a little hard to open doors when you're cuffed like this." He takes a wide berth, gun pointing at me the whole time, stretching as far as he can in order to maintain distance from me while still reaching the doorknob. It swings open slightly; I open it further with my foot. I nod towards the bathroom. "Get in there." Ivan looks scared as he cocks the gun. I laugh at him. "How am I supposed to open my zipper with my hands back here? I need you to do it."

"I- I'm- I-… No."

I roll my eyes at him. This guy is so nervous he is as likely to shoot me accidentally as not. "What the hell are you scared of? My problem is that I am handcuffed and can't do anything. Look… just help me take a piss and I'll go back to sitting in my room quietly. Okay?"

He stammers forward a step only to take two back. Another step forward and then one towards the bathroom before he stops. "No."

"Oh, for fucks sakes, fine, I'll just piss my pants right here."

"No, no, no, no, no." He gingerly pulls a set of keys out of his pocket. "Don't make me shoot you."

I turn my back to him and say "I won't." I can feel the right cuff come loose, I twist my hand a little in order to open it all the way. I swear Ivan jumps back five feet when I move. I move my hands slowly up to my shoulders, keeping my palms facing forward, the pair of handcuffs still dangling off my left wrist. "Calm. I am not going to do anything, I just need to take a pee." I slowly shuffle myself sideways into the bathroom. I keep the door open with my foot, so Ivan can feel a little more secure in that he can see me; lest his nervousness take over and he begins shooting holes through the wall.

I have no idea how I did not pee my pants, especially considering the number of times I likely lost consciousness. That was a very long and satisfying pee. I announce to Ivan that I am done and tell him I will be stepping backwards slowly. I keep reminding him to be calm. I really do not want to be shot in a bathroom, it seems rather undignified. Standing outside the bathroom I turn to face Ivan before I lower my hands and pull up my zipper. "Can I ask one favor? Can I put these cuffs back on in front of me? It really hurts to have my hands behind my back like that."

"I- I'm... I'm not supposed to..." I click it closed on my right wrist.

"Oops. Well at least if I need to go to the bathroom again I won't need anyone to touch my junk." I laugh heartily. He looks rather indignant as I wink at him before retreating to the bedroom. I still had no idea what time it was although obviously I would put it at before noon. The chair slams against the door as Ivan places it back where it had been.

It is really hard to properly gauge how quick or slow time is going when there is nothing to look at but four walls and a door. The bed and dresser were both uninteresting. I lay on the bed, gazing off towards the ceiling, lost in my own little thoughts. This seemed like an appropriate time to reminisce about some of the really good old days. Like the time I had gone camping with my family. I had likely been around ten at the time; my aunt uncle and three cousins came along and shared the campsite with us. I remember the smells, the crackling of the fire, roasting marshmallows; the serenity of the whole experience. Waking on the final morning of our long weekend adventure we all got to hear the story of how my youngest cousin, who was around the same age as me, had gotten up in the middle of the night in order to go to the bathroom. After closing the tent, to prevent bugs from getting in, he scuttled off to the bushes. At that moment a wolf howled. He said it was a wolf; it could just as likely have been a coyote, or just a dog somewhere in the campground. Regardless, whatever made the sound it was enough to scare him and he literally ran and dove through the zipped tent door and back into his sleeping bag to hide. He did not venture out again that night. He did not go pee until the adults had started to wake up and make noise. I was chuckling to myself thinking about this story from my childhood as the door opened again.

"What the fuck is so funny in here?"

A smirk for Ivan. "You had to be there." I get waved towards the door so I get up and walk to the living room. Aurora looks down and sees my hands in front of me before darting her eyes to Ivan. Women really are quite adept at 'the look'. "Don't get pissy; I had to pee. No harm, no foul. I'm still here and he's still alive."

"Take him." My ankle still hurts although it is not as pained as it was, it is stiffening up now which is likely not going to make walking any more pleasant than it had been hours ago. Aurora remains in the pastor's quarters to talk to Ivan; I sincerely hope she is not too cross with him. It was my fault and as I had said, nothing bad came of letting me have my hands in front. Dale was again my escort; he was much less hands-on this time, instead just telling me where to go. He was accompanied by Jami, and that is Jami with a little heart above the I. She was a young woman that I had taught in school for her last couple years worth of education. Not one of the ones I would say was my best or brightest. She would be considered average, but she was pleasant. And bubbly. Following her formal education with me she actually started to work in our library, a surprising choice for a girl I never saw reading anything. Maybe she liked the smell of all those books, lord knows I do. Maybe she likes organizing things. Maybe she just wanted a job that involves very little hard labor. Whatever the reason that is what she had been doing for the last number of years. My first thought is that she seemed out of place among revolutionaries although in time it did seem to be more in keeping with the idea. Intellectuals, even ones that are not incredibly bright, are often part of revolutions. They are often the brains behind the movement. That categorization seems a little grandiose for Jami, but who knows, she may have grown since she was a teenager.

I could hear Jami and Dale chatting behind me, their conversation revolved around the events of the previous night; stuff I had not known, although I had kind of suspected. All those gunshots that I had heard while I was stuck in the pit were the people that were known to be loyal to me being executed. I guess the ruse that had been predominantly used was to arrive at their doors while it was dark, mid-storm, banging telling them there was an emergency. Each one would then rush about their house, getting whatever weapons they felt they needed, getting a rain coat then stepping out onto their doorstep only to be shot in the head. Or as they got to the end of their sidewalk. Why I was being treated differently was beyond me. If people were able to accept the killing of my men without any disruptions then they should have been able to accept my death, sans trial, with nary a thought about it.

I was being herded over to the community center for my trial, the same one that had been the initial site of the first uprising against me. Since that day I had not liked this building and preferred to avoid it, if only I could have done that now. I had a serious thought about trying to run so that Dale would be forced to shoot me. We could avoid the whole stupidity of a trial with my death. Alas, my ankle would not have permitted me to make a real attempt at running. At best it would have been a quick hobble, which would have just ended with me getting strangled a little more as opposed to shot. I would just have to deal with my unease and 'face the music'. There was already a crowd inside and outside the center; undoubtedly some were there to see me get justice, some were there for revenge, some were there just to face their fears. The source of their fear being me, of course. Regardless of their reasoning I actually felt glad to see most of them. They were my people, in spite of what had happened previously and what was about to happen.

Contrary to how the room of the community center had been on the day of the first revolt against me there were only two tables set up; one on the stage at the head of the room as well as another facing it. I had the urge to stride up to the stage and sit at that table; it had been where I had always situated myself during the harvest celebrations, so for me it seemed only natural. I know of course that is not the spot set up for me. I had thought that they would be moving me towards the table sitting ground level. In my mind this was looking like a set-up where I would be sitting alone, facing my accusers, with an angry mob at my back. To my surprise I was told to turn right before reaching the first row of seats set up for the gallery to the trial. Not as many chairs as I would have expected, perhaps the plan was to only let a few people be present in order to avoid having a courtroom/community center with more angry people than they can control. I now notice where I am being directed to; someone has constructed a small cage out of steel bars. It is crude looking but will more than do the job of keeping me secure; I am too banged up to try anything anyways, but whatever makes them feel more secure from me, I guess that would be the biggest point for them. I have to duck in order to get through the door to the cage, given that it is only slightly larger than the chair that has been placed inside it, I have a little difficulty maneuvering as I try to duck down over a foot, fit through a door that is not even that wide side to side and still turn myself around. Luckily for me, I still had Dale with me as he assisted me by shoving me sideways into the chair in the cage as he shouted "Sit". My head hit the doorframe, I could feel a small cut had opened on the side of my head. I could feel each drop of blood running down the side of my head, just in front of my ear. I could see each drop of blood as they dripped onto my shoulder. The door slammed shut in front of me. Dale huffed and seemed to puff himself up as he strutted away like he had done something spectacular by putting me in the cage. I decided to let him have it. Moments later there was a hand poking through the bars, touching my head. I recoiled as I had not even seen someone approach the cage. I had been transfixed on the table on the stage, I was waiting for someone to arrive and start this whole thing up. The room was beginning to fill. It seemed that the plan was only to have a few people sitting, mostly the eldest ones, everyone else in attendance would have to contend with standing. The hand was LeAnn, she was dabbing some sort of rag on my head, trying to stop the bleeding. I look past her and I see that Rita is right alongside of her. It was nice to see; she had taken to the idea of adopting her very seriously. LeAnn was very loving and caring for that little girl; in all reality I think it was the best I could have ever done for Rita after her parents had died.

"Sir, just hold still, I'll try to stop the bleeding." She was whispering, undoubtedly to ensure that people did not see her as being contrary to their opinions. I move my cuffed hands up to take the rag from her.

"Thank you, LeAnn, I will hold this, you should go take your seat before they all get filled up. You won't want to miss this."

"But, Sir? I-"

I just cut her off mid-sentence, "It'll be fine, there is nothing more you can do for me right now." I make eye contact with her and plead with my eyes for her to go sit down. "Thank you." She reluctantly begins to rise; she wraps her hand around Rita's as they walk over to the chairs. Rita waves to me with her free hand, I wave with both hands, the blood begins to flow again as soon as I move the rag from my head. LeAnn and Rita end up sitting on the far side of the room, near one of the back rows of chairs, I can no longer see them through the sea of people as soon as they sit down.

It was interesting how now that I was caged, people no longer wanted to give me a wide berth. I would assume it is like being at a zoo; the lions, tigers, bears, oh my, etc., were all seemingly harmless once they were caged. That is a fallacy though. Caging something does not make it safer to be around, in fact it likely makes it more dangerous to be around. Whatever is in the cage feels like it has lost all of its options. The flight response, that I mentioned a great while ago, is no longer a possibility. If they are scared or agitated, they only have one course of action; fight.

I begin to wonder if I am caged for that reason; to keep the people safe from me or to keep me safe from them. Both are likely and both are probably the reason, depending on who you are referring to. Some in town likely still fear me greatly, others, like Dale, want nothing more than the opportunity to tear me apart with their bare hands. My mind drifts further into the randomness as I look around the cage. It reminds me of Andrei Chikatilo, the Rostov Ripper, who was placed in something similar during his trial shortly after the fall of Soviet Russia. Chikatilo had been a serial killer of somewhere around fifty or sixty people, in and around Rostov I would assume. Was his cage to keep him safe until the end of the trial or was it to keep people safe from him? He had been thought to have cannibalized some of his victims; maybe they were afraid of him biting people. My thoughts on the purpose of the cage came to an abrupt end as all those seated rose as someone near the entrance yelled "All rise." It was so surreal; to me this seemed like some court scene on a random TV show or cheap B-movie.

I would like to say I was shocked to see Aurora striding up to the stage with a gavel in her hand but that would be an exaggeration. While not my first expectation, it was top three for me. She was really the only 'lawyer' in town. I am using that word loosely only because I am the one who bestowed that distinction upon her and I think for her to be a full-fledged lawyer would take more than me saying she is a lawyer and then her settling a few arguments among townspeople. Whatever my current trepidation though on her title, she was the closest thing we had to a lawyer and the closest thing we had to someone who was well acquainted with the law. Aurora stood at the table set up for her, tapped the gavel before asking everyone to sit. No one was speaking anymore, they was no random chattering going on in the back ground; the only sounds at this moment were shoes being shuffled about and the slight squeaks of chairs being adjusted by those sitting in them. Princess lies down next to the table as Aurora begins to address the courtroom/community center, "Welcome everyone." Dramatic pause, much more properly placed than her last one. "Today I will be presiding over a historic day for us. Today is the day we begin to live anew. Today is the first day that we are free; for some of us this is the first time we have ever been free. Today we are going to replace the tyranny of the past with the fairness and compassion of a brighter future. We will be making a just society for all, not just for some. There will no longer be an arbitrary set of laws based upon the whims of one man; we will return to civilization but to do that we must first deal with the past, we must wipe the slate clean so that be can begin again." It was a nice speech; I have a feeling that she had not been resting all night as she had said she hoped for, more than likely she had practiced that speech more than a few times.

It was at this moment that I consider yelling out for all to hear who I really am, that I am her father. Demand that this whole proceeding be called off as she can no longer be trusted to preside over my trial. The trial would end but not in the courtroom drama kind of way you would see on TV. Not even close. I think it would create instantaneous chaos within this room. Half of the crowd would begin yelling at Aurora, thinking she had somehow duped them all into not summarily killing me and having some ulterior motive for keeping me alive. The other half would just go directly for me, for my blood. Nothing could be done in that kind of disorder. I would be ripped from this cage, probably dragged outside and lynched. Strung up from some tree or streetlight, more than likely whatever is most convenient would be chosen. However, I felt that urge, to announce to everyone who I am, just drift out of my mind; it was a passing thought. In the end, it would not preserve my life which was the focus of so much of my effort over the years, but it would likely also doom my daughter. Whom in spite of her being a dirty rotten traitor is still dad's little lawyer. Even if she was not doomed by my announcement I feel she could quite likely become a pariah and that is no life for her. It is the exact opposite of what I really did want all along for her, a safe place to spend the rest of her life.

"Randall Omar. You have been brought before this court of your peers to stand trial for your crimes. You have committed crimes against humanity for taking the few who survived the Great Flare and pressing them under your thumb. You are being tried for murder, torture, abuse of power, misappropriation of community resources, slavery." She looks towards the gallery before continuing, "Who would like to be the first witness to testify against the accused?"

There is a collective gasp among the crowd as I begin to retort at her in a yell "What the fuck is this? I taught you better than that! How the hell can you claim to be acting in the interest of justice and the order to law for this community if you have already made up your mind?" A few members from the crowd nearest to me seem to be rushing towards me, not to harm me per se but to in fact silence me. My angrily replying to any of these proceedings could actually damage them, although I do know that. "What is the point of this trial? To get fucking evidence against me? That is asinine and a waste of time. Do this right if you are going to do it."

The door to my cage has been ripped open, there are three or four sets of hands all clamoring to get to me, but the opening is too small for all of them to fit through at once. One hand finally gains purchase on my face, squeezing it to look as though I were making a fish-face. Another hand coming from the other side of the cage grabs me on my left shoulder; I wrest myself away from these hands long enough to make my plea to the court.

"I am guilty! I plead guilty!" The hands all instantly retreat and the door closes. The cut on the side of my head is again bleeding. Once again, I begin soaking the blood with my rag, which is already soaking wet with blood and stained red.

CHAPTER 20 – TELLING THE TRUTH

Should it be considered tragic at how I now exist? It is only temporary. No longer am I in some bunker, or a normal house or even in a church. The clichéd phrase is 'how the mighty have fallen'. The building I now reside in used to be a warehouse; correction, it is still a warehouse. Following the end of my "trial" I was brought over to this building which I would assume was chosen for my imprisonment due to the cement and steel construction of the structure. I could say it is somewhat 'comfortable' in that they did at least convert one of the old warehouse offices into my cell, which is rather roomy by pre-cataclysm standards. No six by twelve cell for me. By putting my feet heel to toe, I was able to estimate that I am living in a sixteen by twenty-four cell; not too shabby I must say. No window but a carpeted floor. A real bed and the old leather chair from my office. A desk along with a number of books; I have not read any of them however. I have been preoccupied with making my own. Honestly, I think they are treating me too well. If this was a normal kind of incarceration I would be quite happy to stay here. I don't have that option really, and at this point I do only have another 6 days and roughly 13 hours left. I do not get the standard steel bars that would be in other cells or had been used to make the cage for my courtroom appearance. I would have to say there were likely not enough steel bars of sufficient size in order to do what they wanted done. We were not really equipped for that, so they made up a cell especially for me. The interior wall of the office was knocked down and a chain-link fence was stretched across the entire opening of the office. While I never made any attempt to escape; and I have no intention of doing so, I did notice that the chain link was fairly secure all the way around. It was bolted; floor, ceiling and walls every foot. Each bolt appears to have been rounded off so that they could not be taken out easily. Not that I would be able to undo the bolts with my fingers anyways, but I do appreciate their zealousness at ensuring that I will not escape. On top of that, I believe there are guards in the hallway, they are not visible from my cell, but I can hear them talking down the hall. I'm guessing there are two there at any given time. As well this is actually a fairly well used building meaning that people walk nearby at all hours of the day. If I was able to sleep normally I would likely be annoyed by all the people moving around. Since my sleep only comes in fits that is not as much of a concern. When I do manage to fall asleep I am completely unconscious. Nothing short of a gunshot could wake me in that precious hour or two of rest that I get.

I have wondered over the past few weeks if there is a sign saying, "do not talk to the prisoner" just out of my view, because there have been few if any words spoken to me. Not that I am begging to have people talk to me; I am relishing the relative quiet. Without people interrupting my train of thought I have actually been able to get my thoughts out so that I can put them here as a final record of the important times of my life. The only things that come close to interrupting my thoughts are my other thoughts, the random ones. On the plus side I never have the problem that sometimes occurs to people where they walk from one room to another and forget the reason they came into the room. This happens due to the brain compartmentalizing thoughts; this compartmentalization also extends to places. In essence what happens is you have a thought in the living room, that thought occurs in the 'living room compartment', when you move to the kitchen you are now in the "kitchen compartment" of your brain; the thought which was generated in one compartment does not translate to the other. It is like the doorway from one room to another is the same doorway that moves from one brain compartment to another. I never leave this room, I never go through doorways; therefore I am able to keep my thoughts moving. It is quite liberating to not have to try to "remember what I was doing".

Now, if you had asked me only one day earlier I would have said that I was done; I assumed I was done. I had reached the end of my story, because there was nothing left to say other than extending my story to my last moments. I was essentially done, all I was going to do was lounge around in my comfy cell until my last day, then a quick wrap-up and then I would be done. I was wrong, in a manner of speaking. This morning I had quite interesting conversation, there is no surprise about whom it was with; everything in my life has involved Aurora since she was born, in some manner.

Every day, at around nine in the morning someone will deliver my breakfast to me. Usually a couple of hard-boiled eggs, some corn bread, some vegetables and a piece or two of fruit. I do not particularly like my eggs hard-boiled however given that the people who bring my meals generally do not say anything to me other than "here" when they drop my tray on the floor means that there is not much of a point for conversation regarding meal choices. Today, my meal was the typical breakfast. Two hard-boiled eggs, cornbread, some carrot sticks, and an apple. I was curious when a second person walked along with Carol as she delivered my food. His name totally escapes me at this moment, David perhaps. Regardless, he stood behind her as she put the food down, picked up my tray from last night and left. He placed a chair in the hallway facing my cell then exited the way he had come. I was honestly a little apprehensive to get my food; the chair made the whole setting change. I was no longer all alone in my comfortable cell; I was now in a cushy zoo exhibit just waiting for the audience to arrive and watch the monster eat. After a moment I reminded myself that I had nothing to gain by being shy or worrying about someone watching me eat. I chew my food the same as any other person. I walked over to the chain link, leant over and picked up the tray. I returned to the desk. The tray was set down before I began to pull the desk back from the wall. I cleared as much as was possible although it was the only flat space I kind of had in the room so it had become the repository for everything that I had scattered around the room. As I was moving my chair in between the wall and the desk Aurora walked slowly into view. I did not actually see her until she was almost at the chair; I am guessing she was walking slowly to try to not make noise. She likely had expected me to be sitting like I normally did while eating, with my back to the chain link. The chair changed the situation so I changed my habit.

"Ah. Aurora. Good morning. How are you today?" She was just too alike me. She only stood there, evaluating what was making me so cheery. Her face was fairly expressionless at this point; stern would likely be the best descriptor. She was going to be difficult apparently. I motion for her to sit then wait for her to take her seat before I follow suit. "I hope you don't mind that I eat while we talk… Would you like some of my eggs, bread or some carrot sticks? I would offer the apple but I am going to take this opportunity to be greedy. I've been enjoying the apples I have been getting lately."

"No… Thank you. You can eat if you want." She sat quietly. I saw Princess come from down the hall. He seemed to be having a bad day today; he was limping slightly. He was getting fairly old for a dog and there was a whole lot of excitement the other day. He must have over extended himself. I stand from my desk, walk over to the bed and grab the blanket that sat on the foot of the bed. When I turned to Aurora she was looking at me funny. It was reminiscent of the time when she used to just sit and observe me. She seemed to be looking to see my motives. As I walked nearer the chain link cage she slid the chair back ever so slightly, but it was enough to make a huge scrapping sound on the floor. I stood for a moment, only a few feet away from her, separated by a fence. Her eyes did not break from mine; her left hand rose slowly to shoulder height, exposing her palm to the guards who I assume were down the hall. She was trying to show me how she was in control, remind me that I was the one on the inside of the cage.

I smiled as I threw the blanket on the floor and kicked it towards the opening that my trays came through. "For Princess, he looks like he could use something soft to lie on." I moved back to my breakfast. The eggs were cold, they were always cold. I began to eat as she picked up the blanket, folded it neatly then placed it in front of Princess. He circled twice before plopping himself down in a huff.

"Thank you." She lightly patted his head before he put it between his paws and closed his eyes. Silence except for my chewing. I was now done one egg and following it up by eating some carrot sticks; each crunch seemed to echo between us.

"Are you going to say something or was this meant to be a staring contest?"

"I have a question. Well, there are a lot of questions, but one in particular that I want answered. Since you made the whole trial a moot point no one ever got to have their questions answered, especially me."

"And you seem to think that I have some burning urge to tell you the truth? To reveal all my secrets?" I laugh at that. "You should know by now, I never lied to you. I always was honest whenever you asked me something." I begin to ponder how truthful I am willing to be at this moment; on one hand my greatest wish is to announce myself to her, on the other hand I think that would not benefit anyone in this building. My mind flips through the catalog of memories that I have, searching for the one question that she desperately needs to have answered. I am kind of stumped. Was she looking for me to explain my rationale for killing hundreds of people in the first revolt? My confusing change of heart by not killing anyone in the next one? Is she looking to find out why I was so brutal with the cannibals? There are so many things that I have done that I wonder if I could explain it to her or someone else for that matter.

"I think you have never been good at hiding things, you prefer to be direct and forthright and make people see your side no matter what. I want that kind of honesty from you now." I jam my whole second egg into my mouth then indicate that I need a moment to chew. At this point I would prefer her to keep talking and she obliges me. "Why did you do it?"

I take a few large chomps to break the egg into smaller pieces, before swallowing it all. It was almost too much for one swallow; I let out a couple hitching coughs as things start to slide down the correct tube. Wouldn't that have been funny, she finally worked up the courage to come and talk to me and I choke to death in front of her without having ever answered her question. And less than a week before my due date, how unfortunate that would be for everyone involved and everyone who has an interest in seeing me die. I wash the egg down with a mouthful of water before my fear of choking to death finally subsides. One more little cough escapes me before I tilt my head like a dog. "You need to be more specific. Do what?"

"Why did you kill my mother?" My mouth instantly gaped open, showing her the half-chewed cornbread I had in there. I was utterly confused, I had not seen her mother for years prior to the cataclysm; I had no idea where she lived, what she did for work (if she worked) or who she hung out with; how could I possibly have killed her. The memories I had from so long ago were all blurry. I recall the tone of my dreams back then had been that I wanted to strangle her at times, a sentiment that came to it highest point after she took Aurora and left. I begin to close my mouth and that seemed to jar my brain back to working order. I felt suddenly ashamed of myself for being so momentarily stupid. Aurora still had no idea who I was. As far as she knew I had never met her mother. She was still going on the premise that had been put forward right from our meeting in the church. She meant Lisa. I knew that. A string of profanities ran through my mind as I silently called myself every name in the book. I chewed for another moment before taking another sip of water.

"I didn't do anything to her."

"You FUCKING liar! Be fucking honest with me. What did she ever do to you? She was nice, she helped people. She never even said a bad word about you. Why would you kill her?" I chuckled. It was nervousness, not because I was particularly amused. This was getting into a territory that I had not wanted to talk about. It was too close to divulging things that she did not want to hear right now.

"Aurora. Dear. Seriously, I had nothing to do with her death." I shrugged at her, she only fumed as she sat there staring at me. Princess had raised his head and was watching me intently although made no movement otherwise. In my mind I was chuckling still. This had not come up in my mental list of questions that she had wanted to ask because I really had not done anything to Lisa. My assumption that she had fallen asleep with a lit candle going was probably correct. I begin to tell Aurora the story about that very morning. "That morning when I got up I looked out my bedroom window and could see that your house was on fire. At first, I was in a panic. I raced downstairs only to stop on my porch." I laughed a little "I was still in my underwear. I was looking at the crowd standing there in front of your house. Lisa was not there." A pause. "I knew right there she was dead, the house was completely engulfed and no one could survive that." I shrugged at her again. I did not know what else to say, that was pretty much everything. That had happened in the first minute of me looking out my bedroom window. She shook her head in disgust at me.

"You're lying. People saw you with her. The night before; every night for two weeks before. They saw her crying the night she died when she left you."

I coughed before correcting her, still had a little tickle in my throat from that egg. "It was one week, not two. And yes, I had been talking to her. We were talking of old times, talking of how we both got to where we were. And yeah, she was crying that last night, and it was my fault that she was crying however, here is the point I have already told you, I didn't kill her."

"Assuming I believe you, then tell me why was she crying?"

"In short, cause I said I wasn't interested in her." She began pointing her finger furiously at me.

"You see! You see! That is how I know you are lying. She wasn't interested in you. How could she be?" That one kind of hurt. I know that I am a 'monster' but really, I am not so ugly that someone being interested in me could be so unfathomable. I felt the first tear in years begin to well up in my eye. It would seem that being deposed, imprisoned and sentenced to death, kind of takes the wind out of one's sails. I was defeated, and so was my spirit. My resolve was not what it had been. Obviously, the part that made this the most poignant for me was who it was coming from. I still felt a little betrayed by her. I took a moment before trying to respond

"I don't know what to tell you. She was interested at least a little, but it was not going to go anywhere. When I told her that, well… she got upset." I was feeling fairly confident right now that I was going to be able to skirt the issue I most needed to avoid.

"I know my mom, she was not interested. Which means you are lying. So… just tell me… why did you kill her."

"I am lying? Really? How about for a second here let us get to what you are lying about."

"What's that?"

"Lisa wasn't your mother." It was her turn for her mouth to gape a little. She didn't have a mouth full of food, so it did not have the same effect but still, she was not expecting me to pull that on her.

"She was- I mean- She did- She was my- wait- what? Who said that?"

"Lisa told me… amongst our weeks' worth of chats… that your real mom was in Mexico."

"Dominican Republic." She corrected me. At least that pretense was done.

"See. Now who is the liar?"

'She was like a mother to me, so she was close enough. She was all I had left. Until you killed her."

I sighed as we obviously had not reached the point where she understood enough of the story to accept the truth. I had nothing to do with it; it was a very beneficial coincidence in terms of keeping Aurora's parentage a secret but as far as I know it was entirely accidental. "Is this the whole reason that you didn't let Dale just rip my head off like he so wanted to do? I don't know what to tell you that you will believe, but I want you to look at me, see if I'm really lying like you are so convinced I am. I did not have anything to do with Lisa's death. Nothing at all." I think this is what would be referred to as a 'dead-pan' delivery. Practically monotone, very direct; I took out any of my normal inflections. If I was lying and it was going to show on my face then she would see it. I watch as her lips purse together; she believed me. Or at least she knows I'm not lying. She may not even believe what she has seen for herself but she likely will in time. "And since we are on the subject of the truth about Lisa's passing how about I offer up something I would guess you didn't know. I was the one who arranged for Clare to take you in. Did you not think it was strange that she knew that Lisa was dead without having ever left the backyard? She slept in that lawn chair while you and Beth were in that ratty old tent with all the duct tape on it. After I realized that Lisa was dead in the inferno I went over to talk to Clare. I arranged for her to adopt you. Hell, I gave her a whole pile of new appliances and whatnot because I knew having another child would be extra work for her." A slight lie there, Clare was much greedier than I was portraying but Aurora does not need to hear that right now; I have already turned enough of what she believed on its head.

"You didn't. She cared for me. She was told that Lisa died, someone came by-" and the wheels have started to gain traction. I can see her mind grinding over all the points I have said. She was likely remembering all the appliances being moved in, the house being painted, the new bed, etc.

"Clare was a neat-freak. Do you think she would have allowed a hairy dog like that to live in her house without someone telling her that she would need to keep the dog? Not really. I had promised to keep you safe from the first day I met you and Lisa in the church, it was a promise I intended to keep. I knew you would not stay with her if Princess was not there so….I had to arrange for a vacuum, so she could keep the dog hair to a minimum."

A slight giggle from Aurora. "Clare vacuumed every day. Two or three times a day. As soon as she saw a single dog hair."

"I am going to venture that while you do not totally believe me, yet I have given you enough that you can go ask Clare. I'm sure if you tell her you talked to me she'll tell you the truth." I felt tired at this moment; apparently telling the truth as a little taxing. "So, I answered your question, do you feel better?"

"No, I don't feel better." He voice was indignant. I toss my hands up.

"Okay, so what do you want to know now?" I was not looking forward to more truth. At this moment all I wanted was to take a nap.

"What was that bullshit that happened at the trial? First you start an outburst then you just plead guilty. What game are you playing?"

"No game. All the charges you said I had committed, therefore I am guilty. You can't claim to be trying to establish a society based on law and order if you are going to fuck up the simplest part of the trial. There was no organization. It was going to be a whining and complaining session against me with people just coming up and saying how they were wronged by me. That is not a trial; that is a self-help group. And you never even gave me the chance to plead guilty or not guilty before commencing that part. Like it or not I saved you. I saved you from embarrassing yourself by conducting a half-assed trial." I made the air-quotes gesture as I said trial.

"Excuse me? Who the fuck are you to judge me on the proper conduct of a trial? You have never done a trial, you only ever killed people or exiled them after making some speech that was just a random assortment of reasons for doing what you were doing. You had no consistency; one thief dies, the next is thrown out of a plane? How does that make any sense?"

"Difference is, I never claimed to be making some sort of just society. I was making civilization out of nothing. At any cost." This conversation was spinning out of control. I was trying to defend my position, even though I knew I couldn't. The mere fact I had plead guilty kind of takes the legs out from underneath anything I was saying at this moment. I began to think of a way to end this conversation. It is like when you are losing a game and know there is no hope for winning, at that point you can only have one of two real plans. First is to try to end it looking respectable, so people can say that you made an effort and didn't give up. The other option is to essentially give up and just try to get the game to end as quickly as possible. Lessen the hit to the ego by reducing the time spent getting humiliated. That was what I was looking for here; I was looking for a way out. I wanted to take my old man nap.

"Exactly. At any cost. You crippled this town with your purging of so many people. All they wanted was equality and justice and you had them all wiped out. Those fucking bonfires. You know I can still see them clear as day in my mind. That is when I knew you were evil. Before that you were just a super asshole. After that, you just looked evil."

"They deserved it. Every last one of them. And I would do it all again."

That did it. She could no longer stand to look at me. I have never seen her upset this bad, her face was flush and I could almost see a vein popping out of her forehead. Same location as the one I would see in my father's forehead when he was angry, genetics I guess. At any other point, under any other circumstances, I would likely have told her to calm down or she would have a stroke. Right now she would not listen and my suggestion would likely only put her closer to that possibility. She screamed at me "Just tell me how you want to die?!" Before she stormed off down the hall; followed closely by Princess who was struggling to keep up. The door to the hall clanged loudly as it closed.

I was no longer hungry. I did not have much left on my tray but that did not matter. Even the apple, which I had so selfishly refused to offer Aurora, no longer held any appeal for me. I could have sworn that I felt a tear roll down my cheek but when I went to wipe it off my hand was dry. Is there even such a thing as phantom tears? I seriously did not know where to go from there. I moved my desk back to where it had been, pushed the tray and the remaining food out through the gap in the fence then laid on the floor and strained myself to reach far enough to get the blanket I had lent for Princess' use back. There was a shout from one of the guards at seeing my arm sticking out of the fence, however there was no follow-up. They likely assumed that I was doing exactly what I was doing, retrieving my blanket. I began pacing back and forth around my cell with Aurora's last words still ringing though my mind. Those words echoed through my mind for hours. It is like having a song stuck in your head. I could not get them out, which is why I am writing this down; hopefully I can get them out by putting them on paper.

CHAPTER 21 – LET US HAVE A PLAIN DISCUSSION…

My impending execution. Where should I begin on this subject? I had not really been thinking about my execution because I had honestly assumed it was something that was out of my control, something that I had no say in. Now that I am contemplating it, it is an interesting idea to have to consider. Execution is not like suicide; that is something that is borne out of utter sadness, out of hopelessness and despair; maybe mental illness. However, I think I am actually wrong in that regard. Both suicide and execution come from the same things.

Hopelessness and despair are kind of the same things although in my mind I see them as slightly different while still connected; somewhat akin to two sides of the same coin. Hopelessness is the feeling of being without hope while despair is a sadness associated with being hopeless. If someone is hopeless, they literally have no hope for the future, no hope for things to get better. So, technically you can be hopeless without having despair; I might even be able to venture that you could have despair without being hopeless, although I'm not really seeing how; you would probably need to change the definition then. Regardless, they are connected as I stated. Hopelessness can be interpreted as the reasoning for both suicide and capital punishment. People wishing to die see the vileness of their life or the circumstances as never being able to change. That is generally a complete fallacy but that is how they feel. For someone who is suicidal that is something completely internal, they feel despair at their circumstances or their past or their prospects for the future. And in the end, for the person who is contemplating suicide all that matters is how they feel. If you feel that something is horrible past, present or future, and continue to view it as that then there will be an utter feeling of hopelessness that would manifest as despair. Much the same as it is with any emotional reaction. If someone is scared, hurt emotionally, angered, in love, etc. all that matters is how that person feels. While the other person(s) may have intended to scare or piss off or invoke feelings of affection it only matters how the person feeling it feels. If the intent was to make a joke but the person is angered; it is not their fault, per se, for misinterpreting it, really it would have been the joker's delivery or choice of joke that is to blame. Execution or as it is also known, capital punishment, has always been seen as the 'ultimate punishment'. Going from the side of the authority or law or however you would prefer to categorize them, they would see the offender who deserves that ultimate punishment as being hopeless for rehabilitation. So, executing people is also borne out of hopelessness; society has no hope of getting anything from them, so it is a better result to remove the person from the population of living people.

I will take a slight aside here to comment on myself. Looking at my own recollection of what capital punishment is for and in short how it is to be used, I can see where I went wrong. Not that any of this can be changed now. If I had applied those standards to the people of Republica I would likely not be sitting where I am. I may have been the revered leader who brushed the radioactive dust off of civilization after it had been buried on the microwaved world. However, that is not the case; according to my detractors I am the reviled tyrant who used people to keep grinding civilization into the ground after a great worldwide cataclysm. I may have to agree with them although, I don't really have enough time for all the regrets that would entail so I will just shorten the whole process to admitting I made mistakes. Perhaps, I really did a disservice to the people of Republica by ruining the trial that had been arranged for me. I still do not believe that it would have been anything other than a farce, some kangaroo court; however, it was not *for* me. It was for them. Like a funeral, the person being buried has no idea what is happening, it is solely for the friends, family, acquaintances, co-workers and neighbors to begin to get closure from that person dying. I am not going to go off on a discussion of atheist versus religion here, so for simplicity let us just assume the deceased is not aware of what is immediately going on around their body. If there is a soul it has ascended or descended as that person's religion would dictate as soon as they died so they were not present for their own funeral. By ruining the kangaroo court I took the chance for my former people to begin to get closure from the era that had been my tenure as leader. I guess in a way they never really got to grieve over all the ones they lost. They were just redacted from history. Everyone will get their closure and a chance to grieve; in only a few short days. Aurora can be less pissed off at me then, she'll give the people what they need.

So… on to the most pressing question. *"How do you want to die?"* It still feels hard to think about, I was so worried about being alive for so long that it requires me to really switch gears in my mind in order to accommodate the concept of dying. The question itself still seems to be echoing in my mind. I'm still trying to write it out, which is why I am just continuing to do this. I don't remember if I said that I was upset that Aurora had said those words to me or it was just implied or if perhaps I had only thought it. I was hurt by it. I had begun to mentally prepare myself as soon as she was born for the day, likely when she was thirteen or fourteen, after she had discovered boys (or girls, I'm not about to be judgmental about that) when she would throw a fit or temper tantrum or whatever you'd like to call it and she ended up telling me she hated me. I was prepared for it. That she wished I'd die. I could forgive her for saying it. That she never wanted to see me again. I could survive even if she really meant it. All of those would have hurt me to my core but I could have tried to press on, make our relationship work. For any of those things to happen though would have required so many of the circumstances that brought us to the present to have gone completely differently. No fortified house in the middle of nowhere; her mother not leaving me and taking her away; the cataclysm not happening. As well I would have to dodge so many other things; getting my arm ripped off by some random piece of machinery on my land and then bleeding to death; getting some random illness and then becoming frail and weak, or better yet dying outright.

If you really examine how many things have to line up just so you can end up right where you are, it is astronomical. I think it is what was referred to as the butterfly effect. Meaning that everything, even a butterfly on the other side of the earth can affect how things turn out. This is a very complicated kind of theory; I am not even sure it is even provable but let's just for arguments sake say it is true. Pick one day at random. Let us say that the defining moment out of that day is whether or not you get hit by a bus. Getting up and out of bed at six in the morning or six-thirty, could effect that fateful meeting with the bus. With a six in the morning wake up you have time to shit, shave, shower, feed the pets, read the newspaper, make breakfast, etc. However, when you are looking at a six-thirty wakeup then suddenly you no longer have time for everything, you would have to prioritize so that you are not late. If you leave late suddenly you may be directly in the path of that oncoming bus. You miss the article in the paper about the buses in the city being poorly maintained. You don't see the job posting in the classified sections asking for bus drivers; they are getting paid poorly and have shitty benefits meaning that no one decent wants to drive a bus and the people driving the buses are possibly less skilled. Maybe the problem is you are distracted because now the cat will not get fed until you get home in about twelve hours and it bothers you. You don't see that bus as you step off the curb. Perhaps, you step off the curb in order to cross the street to go to the coffee shop across from work in order to get coffee and breakfast. Although what if your destination is the pharmacy to buy deodorant so you don't stink at work from having not showered. All of those things line up just right and you die. Or just wrong and you live. Or maybe you are sitting at your desk and a scene from Speed is being reenacted and then a cop drives a bus through your office at 70 miles an hour and you are crushed between the vending machine and your computer monitor. Should have just woken up late, if you were late for work you would have been at the coffee shop at that exact moment instead of dead. So many things could change and have still led me here, while countless others could have been slightly different and I would have died years ago. The tyrant died before he became feared. I would have moved on before Aurora got a chance to hate me. Regardless of my philosophical thoughts, I am still facing an impending execution date and I have not even figured out what I am to wear. Hood or no hood? Noose or not? My Sunday best or a crown of thorns. So many decisions.

I guess I might as well start with my first decision. The only one that matters and the root of the question that haunts me. How do I want to die? Top of my head I can think of a great number of ways to die that have been used before. Shooting, firing squad, hanging, lethal injection, electrocution, stoning, beheading (which would include the guillotine), being drawn and quartered, and there are likely more but those are the only ones that came to me at this exact moment.

Earlier I mentioned Andrei Chikatilo; that Russian serial killer/cannibal. Following his trial he was taken to some dank and dark room, put on his knees and shot in the back of the head. That was a quite popular method of execution, as far as I understand it, in Russia. I mean that is even what would be described as 'execution style'. The pro of this for me is that it would likely be painless or nearly painless. I would have to hope that the person doing it would be able to hit the back of my head from a foot or two away. Should be easy, although with people being nervous and shaking, who knows. Since we do not generally bury people in Republica and I have mentioned before that I should be cremated it would not matter if my face was destroyed by the bullet. The cons however are kind of important. Firstly, in order to ensure that I do die as intended the caliber of the bullet should be fairly significant. Russian spies, possibly American and British as well, preferred to use .22 caliber pistols for discretely executing people. The weapon would be easily concealable and the bullet itself is quieter when fired than larger caliber bullets. The downside for spies was that those bullets are not as lethal as larger ones meaning that their target could technically survive. And therefore I could technically survive. Since concealing and minimizing noise is less of a concern for us here they would likely go with a larger round. Possibly .38 or .45 or something in between like a nine-millimeter. If that was the case I would assume someone will probably use my own weapon against me, try to make it some sort of karmic revenge. Those larger bullets are much more likely to exit the front of my skull; the .45 I would say would likely guarantee that. An exit wound means a mess. If there is a mess expected then they are less likely do it publicly so there will be less of cathartic effect for the crowd. Also, whoever is the one to do it, regardless of if they absolutely hated me or not will likely have some psychological effects. I know from experience, after all of these years being a tyrant, even when you feel you were right you still have lingering doubts. You still have nightmares. You still have trouble sleeping. Murder is not natural for humans, even though we do it so naturally.

This leads to the main benefit of the next method. Firing squad. From my understanding this was the popular method utilized for army deserters and spies captured during wartime. Differences are that you will generally have five men, each with a rifle. Four of the five will have live rounds; the fifth will have a blank. So the benefit is that every one of those men can hold on to the possible belief that they had the blank. They did not have a part in killing the person. What that does is it diffuses the blame from one person to five. Each one gets a psychological out, thereby doing less damage to them. It is a great concept. Negative for me, is that I have to hope that at least 3 of the 5 are able to shoot well. Traditionally the target that they are to all aim for would be placed over the heart. This would be good for hopefully reducing the amount of mess that is made but if the people are not good shots, then really I am left tied to a pole waiting to bleed out. I would suppose this is also more acceptable for the general public to witness so there is that benefit as well. In my mind, I will put firing squad as a definite possibility while I am going to put bullet in the back of the head execution style is a no.

Hanging was the next one I mentioned. I am torn about this one. Benefit for the people is it can be done publicly and has been done publicly so many times in the past that it could not even be counted. There will need to be a gallows constructed but that would not be a concern. I'm sure with the people in this town that are skilled with woodworking they could have one built in only an hour or two. The largest problem as I see it is that the people in town do not know the formula for hanging people; I assume that since I do not know it. I am probably correct that no one knows it, although they could very likely guesstimate it and get it pretty close. I am sure at this point you may be wondering what formula I am referring to. That formula relates to the length of the rope being used to execute someone. Most of the time the people representing the justice system would prefer the death to be quick, painless and acceptable for viewing by all ages. A hanging done in the proper manner will allow for that. The trap door on the gallows will drop, the person will fall, reach the end of the rope and the sudden stop to the fall will break the neck. Simple enough. But what if something goes wrong? What if the rope is too long? The person will gain more speed than the human body can take and their head can quite literally pop off as if it were a dandelion. That is not suitable for viewing by all audiences. Most children and likely more than half of the adults would be fairly traumatized by watching someone's head just pop off their body. I would also assume there would be an accompanying sound which would be rather disgusting; perhaps a sound similar to pulling a boot out of very deep mud. Or maybe the sounds of the saliva vacuum from a dentist's office followed by a loud pop. I would not even know how to describe it; I've never seen it so I am just assuming what it would sound like. What if the rope is too short? Well, what you have then is the condemned flailing and twitching as they are slowly being strangled. This is similar to another method of killing someone that I would not like; the garrote. In both instances the person is simply left to suffocate to death. With the garrote there is the extra caveat of there being one person standing there behind the one who is dying and their whole job after beginning is to simply stay there and keep pulling until the person stops fighting back. I would say all of these possibilities; my head popping off, my just dangling at the bottom of a rope that was too short to break my neck and being garroted are not something I want to experience so I am going to say that right now firing squad is still top of my list.

Lethal injection. This was very popular in the United Stated in the years prior to the cataclysm; in the states that still practiced capital punishment. I don't recall there being all that many states that were still doing it and when they did they would literally take decades to get around to executing the person. In truth, it seems rather silly to do it that way. The biggest pro of this method is that it is supposed to be painless. First chemical number one knocks the person out; second chemical numbs them and third stops the heart. I don't believe that is actually what each chemical did but it something like that. Point is that they effectively put the person to sleep. Like a pet. I like this method; even with the few ones that were messed up in the years before the cataclysm, it is still a good choice. Alas, the main problem with lethal injection for us is we do not have a sufficient amount of any substance to put me to sleep and that is why I am going to discount it without further consideration. Likewise, with the other mechanical form of execution, the gas chamber. I am not certain if we have enough of a toxic substance to allow me to be gassed to death. Carbon monoxide poisoning would be a welcome alternative however I am unsure if the bio-diesel that we use in our vehicles puts out enough toxic chemicals to kill me. The exhaust itself smells somewhat like French fries. Really, trying that as a method of killing me could just turn into a five-hour session of me sitting in a booth that smells like an old fast food restaurant really, really wanting a burger to go with my fries. In conclusion, I like lethal injection but it is not feasible and I would be willing to try carbon monoxide poisoning however I am not convinced it would be effective, meaning I am still leaning towards firing squad. This is somewhat depressing, I was hoping to at least be able to have more of a debate with myself however so far it is fairly cut and dry.

I guess I may as well use that as a segue into beheading. In the middle ages this method was reserved for those of a higher social standing; lords, ladies, royalty, etc. Again messy. When this was most common it would have been done with an axe. Further into the Industrial Revolution you would expect more technological innovation, hence the Guillotine. As far as I know we do not have any axes with an ample axe head to be able to cut my neck in one swing, meaning multiple swings. This is something like what happened to Mary, Queen of Scots. It took multiple strokes to cut her neck, in the end the executioner actually had to use the axe in a sawing motion to get the last little bit cut for her head to be fully disconnected from her body. Not a pleasant thought. I am sure she did not necessarily feel past the second stroke but still, this would not even be pleasant for the audience. Guillotines made the process better by automating it in a way. I do not recall ever hearing of a botched beheading on a guillotine, meaning each time the blade dropped it was assured the person would die as a result. It is effective and reliable. Exactly what you want when you want to kill thousands of people. It would be my choice right now if it were not for the story I had read from the French Revolution. A condemned man was convinced to try to help someone determine how long a head survived after being severed from the body. There was some sort of set questions they had arranged and he would blink to respond. From what people believed, the head would only be aware of its surroundings for something on the order of ten to fifteen seconds after the severing stroke. This experiment had it lasting closer to two minutes. Another instance from the same period involved someone slapping a severed head across the cheek; the look returned from the head in the basket was one of indignation and contempt. As if to say 'how dare you, I have already had my head cut off, leave me in peace'. It sounds utterly maddening. To have two whole minutes of my head in a basket or being held aloft of the masses to see. The entire time I would know I am already dying. I am just waiting for my consciousness to die out. I have never understood how losing blood flow from your head for only a few seconds can lead to one losing consciousness yet a severed head, with no blood flow whatsoever is able to continue 'being alive'. In any event, that story truly has me scared shitless for this method. I will say however that this is actually my second choice right now behind firing squad.

Electrocution was on my earlier list. This one is totally plausible for us; we do generate enough electricity in order to be able to accomplish it and I have never heard any bad stories about it. Well none that I am aware of that were based in fact…in fiction however they are more able to have any conclusion they could wish. The particular horror story I am thinking of involved someone not getting the necessary liquid placed in between the condemned and the electrode. The condemned essentially just had to burn to death instead of being electrocuted. To me it seems highly unlikely and overall being electrocuted should be fairly effective. My understanding of how it works is that the electrical current passes over the heart of the condemned, thereby stopping it. Their consciousness is affected as well by the electricity, since that is all our nervous system is, a series of electrical impulses. In short, the person never wakes up. This is now my new top choice being followed by firing squad and beheading, although I do have a lingering doubt about why they started to phase out electrocutions. Oh well, it is probably nothing.

Last on my list I am going to consider and quickly ignore the possibility of using are some of the more brutal methods from the past. Stoning, and being drawn and quartered. Stoning is pretty much as it sounds, the person is buried in the ground then people throw stones at their head until they are dead. It seems stupid, brutal and wastes completely too much energy. Drawing and quartering involves the person being hung, then cut down, disemboweled, their entrails burnt in front of them, then their head is cut off and the body is cut into four pieces. The point of this was all meant to a warning to people who may rebel against the crown in the future. The head was placed on London Bridge on a pike while the four parts of the body were taken and displayed at the four corners of the realm. Perhaps I should have done that instead of the bonfires, I may not be here now. Either way you look at it; these are not methods I would vote for. There is also crucifixion. Than could be fun; at the very least to discuss it.

Christians have an idealized version of this method of execution. Each crucifix is more or less the same, a lower case 't' with Jesus nailed to it. His feet crossed on a little stand made for him. In antiquity it would have been more likely to see a 'T' shaped cross as they would only have to lift up the top section as opposed to lifting the whole cross. They would just drop it on top of the upright, which would be reused over and over again. The neatly crossed feet, which may have been done, were less likely. Much more probable would be nailing a man to the upright with an ankle on either side. All of the nailing was only a way to keep a person there until they died. Funny thing is they do not die from blood loss (there is surprisingly little blood) or exposure to the elements. In fact people tended to die from suffocation. As I had mentioned when discussing Damian, people need to use their diaphragm to breath. When nailed to a cross you can not use your ribcage to breath as much as you normally would. Meaning that your diaphragm does more work. That however requires you to not be slouching, so you would literally have to hold yourself up by the nails through your hands and feet. That would be excruciating. But people would instinctively do it, until they are completely exhausted, then they stop lifting themselves up and asphyxiate.

My methods are also out. Flaying would likely not be high on what most of the crowd would like to see and I honestly would not suggest being trash compacted, I have claustrophobia.

So, I now have it narrowed down to firing squad, beheading and electrocution. As much as I have been thinking on this; I know that I do not have one hundred percent of the final say in my mode of death. I know, I do not. There is a matter of practicality. Could they make, for example, a guillotine? Likely they could. Would Aurora and the others on the new ruling council allow someone to be guillotined? I would put more money on no than yes.

Electrocution; could it be done. Yes. Would they allow it? Probably. Will they get it right the first time, I'm not so sure. Thomas Edison advocated direct current (D/C) for use in homes while Nikola Tesla advocated alternating current (A/C). In Edison's effort to discredit A/C he went about demonstrating the dangers of it by advocating its usefulness for executing people via electrocution. In order to prove this he electrocuted an elephant. For the record, I hate Edison. The reason I bring all this up is not a convenient way to mention my disdain for Edison but instead to note that we do not have an elephant, or any other suitable large animal that electrocution could be tested on. Therefore, I would be the guinea pig, and that is not a good place to be if you are looking to just be killed.

So, the old front runner turns out to be the winner, firing squad. It should be effective. I can ask that the shooters all practice for a while beforehand taking that concern out of the equation. We have two doctors right now, so they should be able to locate my heart quite accurately. I can wear something dark, so it is not too gory for the children. Everyone will get their catharsis when they see my head droop down after the shots ring out. All the shooters will get their slight reprieve for their psyche. I see no real downside, other than my death. Fortunately, I think I am pretty prepared for it.

It has been two days now since Aurora was here and asked me how I wanted to die. I am still waiting for her to return so I can give her my answer. I hope she returns. She has no idea how much it would mean to me to see her before my death. I am ready now. Come on death.

CHAPTER 22 – CONDEMNED TO BOREDOM

It astounds me at just how quick things have been proceeding. Like the old saying goes, "time flies when you're having fun"; I am not exactly having fun, most of the time however my mind is occupied enough that time is flying by. My musing about execution methods took much longer in reality; a couple days as opposed to a few pages. I guess the joke I could make here is that I am making possibly the most important decision of my life; certainly one of the last.

I was again left sitting in my chain link cage with nothing to do but wait. I was still awaiting Aurora's return so I could give her the good news; or waiting for her designate to find out my answer to her question. Each meal was arriving as clockwork; it was the only thing that broke up the monotony that I was experiencing. I wondered how people who had to serve years in incarceration managed to do it. For me this was maddening, and I only had to do a month. Even with books and other things around to do, I truly lacked the motivation necessary to occupy myself with those distractions. The largest thing for me prior to being imprisoned was the need to constantly improve myself. To know more. To learn more. In short, to be a better person. I am, of course, referring to my knowledge base and not where I fall upon a scale of good versus evil. When you are living within a finite timeframe there is a very well-defined lack of opportunity to improve yourself. I could have learned all I wanted within that 30 days, it would have meant nothing. Best I could have hoped for was to glean something astounding, like discovering the secret to cold fusion or time-travel or some other seemingly impossible achievement. That is not possible however. As smart as I may have convinced myself that I was, I was not necessarily smart enough to solve those questions. I mean I guess there may have been a possibility, but I am secure enough in my own self-image to say that things like quantum physics are not my area of expertise. Hell, it is not even an area that could be considered as a strength for me. And I am fine with that. There is really no shame in admitting that I have limitations. I have interests and while time-travel may be interesting, so many great stories have involved it, however it is not the kind of puzzle I would actually be interested in trying to solve. I would prefer to leave travelling through time as something that happens in stories; anyways if the time-travelling paradox is true there is nothing that I could do about what has already happened anyways. God, what could I really do that would be of any consequence anyways. Start telling people years before the cataclysm that they need to get underground to survive it? No one would believe me, and I would just be locked up in a psychiatric facility. Go back in time to kill Hitler before he can begin the Second World War and the Holocaust. Go further back in time to solve the mystery of who was Jack the Ripper. Go further back and see who the model was for the Mona Lisa. Buy a first edition of the Gutenberg Bible. See the real Jesus of Nazareth. Meet Julius Caesar then stick around to hear what his true last words were. See if I could arm wrestle a caveman. Go on a Jurassic safari and see what massive dinosaur I could hunt. Visit the big bang. Of course if you recall my earlier thoughts on time travel you will remember that I think it would be near impossible to calculate, meaning if I was to even succeed in figuring out time travel I could not carry the two at some point then find myself a few hundred feet under the ground, or floating in space hundreds of miles from anything, only to suffocate to death in the vacuum of space. All completely riveting thoughts, yes?

Staring blankly at an old copy of Homer's Iliad, my eyes scan over each sentence over and over again. I am not really reading anything; I had not flipped past the fourth page. I was planning on just reading something not for the sake of learning anything but just to try to engross myself in an ancient epic, give myself something else to concentrate on. I was unsuccessful in distracting myself in the manner I intended; instead I found my mind wandering to the randomness of thinking of time travel and learning and wondering about existential kind of things. I am not a philosopher. These kinds of things are out of my purview, they interest me so I speak on them however I cannot say I am an expert. In any event, having my mind go off on these little trips seems to make me want to return to my story.

On that note, where I had once been staring blankly at the Iliad, now I stare blankly at a keyboard. Without being too interested in what I am doing time is running slowly and quickly at the same time. It feels as though no time is passing at all and yet I can look at the clock and it seems to have gained an hour from the last time I looked. I have written next to nothing. What else is there to say?

After six hours I am beginning to wonder why I continue to sit here. There is nothing more to say. As I stand and stretch I crane my head to the side. I am listening down the hall; lately the guards have been having somewhat interesting conversations. Mostly just the latest juicy gossip that is going around town. This person sleeping with this other person. Another guy made himself a still and is now getting drunk constantly; some people are worrying that he won't have any food later in the year since he has done nothing in terms of planting. A girl has been getting into public arguments with her boyfriend. All bullshit. All the kind of stuff that I have never really involved myself in. Well, not totally true. I would likely have involved myself when we have someone who does nothing but brew alcohol, but I am not in that position now. I am no longer truly allowed to care. At this point I only truly crave to hear about my people. In spite of whether I care or not, I have still been a part of the lives of all these people for so long I find myself wondering and worrying about them. I almost feel as though I should be a part of their lives still. I briefly had a thought where I wondered if any of the people who until recently had been my charges still had thoughts of me. Other than thoughts about watching me die; I am certain there must be at least a few of those thoughts out there.

Tonight, the guards are speaking of something boring; comparing long dead quarterbacks from football teams that no longer exist. I never followed football enough to even recognize half of the names being tossed about. The tone and subject suddenly changes; no longer is it a debate, now I am hearing greetings, and general mundane chit-chat. "Hey. How are you doing? How is the weather?" My interest is piqued. Who is here in the middle of the night? Why are they here? "Why are you here?" In my ever-advancing age I am unable to hear the replies clearly. Something is said about bored and wanting to say hi, which seems very odd. It is a girl's voice. My chest begins to tighten as I slowly walk closer to the chain link; each step is soft and measured to try to make as little noise as possible. I am already having enough difficulty hearing what is being said. Is this the lynch mob finally coming to obtain their justice? It would seem odd to wait so long for this, I have been in this cell for over 3 weeks and I am only a few days from my execution date. Perhaps impatience finally got the better of them. The conversation is turning again to a different tone. More like the football conversation. Something of a discussion. A debate. Are my guards being persuaded to step aside and just let the mob take me? A giggle. Another thing that is out of place.

"Here, try these, I made a bunch." Was that voice Suzanne? No. It can't be. Too high pitched. Amy maybe or possibly LeAnn. "They're good, my mom's old recipe." Definitely LeAnn. That however is confusing too. I would not put her as the kind to be part of a lynch mob.

The conversation continues. There is another voice now, a man; if I had to hazard a guess I would say it was Ronnie. I did not know him too well however I had heard in the last few months that he was now dating LeAnn. "You look tired…Go. GO!"

It is now clarified for me. This is not a lynch mob coming to take me out to in order to obtain justice on their terms. This is a rescue. Or a jail break. Both terms I think would be accurate at this point. I chuckled to myself while simultaneously rolling my eyes. Ronnie runs down to the front of my cell, instantly grabbing at the fencing like it would have just been that simple to open it as if it were a gate. His eyes are darting up and down the fencing, presumably looking for the door. "Am I to assume you guys did not being a pair of wire cutters?" This haphazard rescue was fairly amusing so far.

"I- Uh- Shit! LeAnn! We've got a problem." That was an understatement. I did not know this guy from a hole in the wall and I have an instant dislike of him. To me it would just seem to be common sense when trying to enact a prison break you come prepared for a number of eventualities. Or do some investigating as to what you are up against and pre-plan to deal with those problems. I am being too hard on him, which is not out of character for me I guess; if anyone is to blame for this botched prison break I would venture that it was LeAnn being all nostalgic and still having a crush on me. Ronnie's eyes are still scanning the edges of the fence and can see the way the fence is bolted to the wall around the entire perimeter as LeAnn comes jogging down the hall. "I- Uh- Jesus! What the hell do we do now? You said this would be easy!" I couldn't help but laugh at them through the fence.

I addressed her since I knew her personally, "I am sure in all my lessons I said something about planning ahead. Knowing the challenges, you would be facing and tackling them. This seems ill planned."

"Sir. I'm sorry." Her voice was becoming as panicked as Ronnie's was. "I thought they would have a way to open the cell." She looked as if she was about to burst into tears as I shook my head disapprovingly at her.

"I'll go get something to cut this with!" Ronnie sprinted down the hall. I could hear him slam into the door then thumping footsteps moving away from the building.

"LeAnn. This is not a good idea, you need to just walk away right now like nothing happened. You guys cannot do anything for me."

"But Sir. I…" LeAnn knew my look of derision well enough to know that I was not approving of her plan at this moment, whatever thought she had been having dissolved as I looked into her eyes. Her mouth continued to move slightly, as if she were talking to herself. Perhaps she is trying to think of ways to counter what I am telling her. Or telling her she needs to listen to me. Either way at this point in time she just looks like a goldfish, taking breaths of water.

"There is nothing you can do. This fence will not come off easily. There are people all over this place all you are going to do is earn yourself a seat in the next room over. Let it go." I can hear a door somewhere within the warehouse slam. It is not something uncommon to hear. This was the constant noise I had referred to earlier that did make it a little hard to get any rest around here, until my mind finally crashes out and I sleep. So, needless to say, having doors slamming has been a fairly regular occurrence during my imprisonment. The slam is likely some heavy metal door that just closes heavily as opposed to someone angrily slamming it. The sounds are too frequent for that. "See." I point to the warehouse on the other side of my inner wall. "Someone will happen by here soon enough. You too will be thrown in here beside me. Think of Rita, she needed a mom which is why you adopted her. She does not need to see another parent die."

"But…Sir. You don't deserve this. You've done so much for me. For all of us. You saved us from the brink of destruction. You rebuilt after the cataclysm. You stopped the cannibals from eating us all. You gave us food. Water. Power. Medicine. Education. Strength. The strength to rebuild." Shit; she is using my own propaganda against me.

"I did not do any of that. I simply made people think I did it. You all did those things. Now shut the fuck up and go before someone catches you." A blank stare. "Jesus. Fuck… do as you are told. Move it." Ronnie crashes back into the hallway. He seems to have found some old pair of garden sheers. My dislike of him has been reinforced. He is kind of an idiot. I cannot see him getting enough leverage in order to be able to cut any of the links that comprise the fence. That idea is irrelevant anyways though, the sheers are so old and rusted it does not even look like he can open them. He stands there in front of my cell swearing as he tries desperately to pull them apart. "Ronnie. Stop that. You and LeAnn get the fuck out of here. Seriously, grab her by the scruff of her neck and take her out. Now. Someone is coming!" I did not really know if someone was coming but I needed them to get a sense of urgency. She was not listening.

This is the problem with having 'tunnel-vision'; you get so focused on the goal that you have no idea of what is going on around you. No clue what things are coming up from within your blind spots. This is the prime way people get caught when doing something they should not be. Really, these two are just being stupid; there is nothing that can be done for me. I have lost most of the support of the people; my henchmen are all dead, including my most trusted man. LeAnn helps Ronnie pull on the handle of the sheers and they manage to finally have them pop open. The blades are deep orange with rust; jagged and dull from years of corrosion. I can see flakes and powder of oxidation drop onto the floor. With each passing moment they are making it more likely they will be caught. More likely I will have neighbors for a few scant days. That is assuming I am not determined to be too much of a threat. If that is the case then I will not be allowed to live just waiting for my execution date. It will be getting bumped up earlier. Each moment that they are more likely to be caught they are also leaving more evidence of their attempted break-out plan. The pile of rust powder on the floor now has some very visible shoe prints in it.

Ronnie is opening and closing the sheers trying to get them to move more fluidly, which he has somewhat managed to do. Ronnie is trying futilely to cut the wires with the fence. Nothing is working. As I expected he can just not get the necessary leverage to cut them; also the blades are too dull. It is almost as if garden sheers were not designed to cut thick metal wires. LeAnn shoves Ronnie's shoulder; in order to get his attention. "You need to get something else, these won't work." More tunnel vision. I just want to slap him as he continues to try to cut the fencing. I shrug at her then gesture in his direction, as if to ask where she found this guy. Ronnie stands there, frozen, holding the sheers, staring at LeAnn as if asking her what to do. "GO! Get something else." She commands him as she rips the sheers out of his hand.

Ronnie runs back down the hall and I call out behind him. "If you cut open this fucking fence I will break your fucking neck as soon as I get out of the cage!" She grabs the chain link, pulls herself close to it and begins whispering to me.

"Sir. Please. You need to let us help you get out. You don't deserve this. You're a great man. We can get you out."

"I am not a great man; I just play a great man on TV." Probably not the best time to be making jokes but it kind of slipped out. "And I do deserve this. Have you asked anyone else in town if they think I should not be here? I doubt anyone will say that I should be allowed out. You saw how the trial went; people were after me from the outset. I need to be here. I plead guilty because I cannot argue against any of the bad things that people can say against me."

"But-"

"Fucking shut up. Do you want to know really why I am here? All the bad things that happened in this town…all the things they say that I did. Well, I did them. And there is more stuff that has never even come to light. When people get angry and start rioting in the middle of the harvest celebration that was because of me. I hurt Rita and then killed her parents because of it. I killed other people because of what they knew. I am not a good man. I am the worst kind of man you could ever know." If you have been paying attention all along, and I will hope that you have been, you will know that I just lied to her. I needed to crack through the façade that I had created. My armor was too shiny and perfect. She needed to see the nicks, dents and scrapes or in lieu of that if she would not see the real ones I was just going to make ones that she could see.

It is hard to describe the look on her face at that moment; shock mixed with a little disbelief and a whole bunch of broken-heart. I stood there on the opposite side of the fence, looking into LeAnn's eyes as they began to well up with tears. Her eyelids were quivering and a tear began to roll down her cheek. "What?" Her voice was so soft and quiet; it was breaking slightly as if she had been yelling so much that she had lost her voice. That was her idealism being broken though. I was at a loss for words. Probably one of the few times I can really say that has ever happened. I couldn't hold on looking at her anymore. I bowed my head before turning around to wipe my eyes. I guess that by putting dents in the armor that she could see, also made actual breaks in my emotional armor. I remember the feeling that I had in my chest as her expression changed; it was the same kind of feeling you get when you girlfriend tells you 'we need to talk' just before she announces that she is taking your daughter away from you. Your heart just drops out of your chest like it is not even attached anymore. It was not said but I felt as though LeAnn had said that she was 'not mad just very disappointed in me'; I felt as though I was getting the worst guilt trip ever.

I turned to face her; my cheeks streaked wet with tears. "I'm sorry. You need to go." And that was the last I saw of her. Her shoulders heaved and shuddered as she cried her way slowly down the hallway. I heard the clank of the sheers hitting the floor just before she opened the door and left.

I had seriously almost forgotten about Ronnie until he burst back into the hallway; he had apparently found something actually made to cut wires and began snipping them. "Ronnie. You need to stop." A link is cut. Clink. "Ronnie! It's over. LeAnn is gone." Clink. Clink. "Ronnie! What the fuck are you doing? You need to go." Clink. Clink. "It's over. You'll just get yourself caught! You'll end up here with me!" Clink. He is not listening to me. I have no idea at all what is going on in his mind, but it is very apparent I will be free in a matter of moments. I begin to think about where I will go after the fence is opened. To one of my old weapon stashes, of course. How else I am I going to properly effect a prison break then by being able to defend myself. Clink. I take a deep breath. The hole is almost big enough to squeeze through. Clink. Clink. The whole fence is rattling now as it is no longer holding itself up and is slightly sloughing in on itself; its own weight is pulling it down into the hole. I crouch down as I pull myself though the opening. I grunt slightly as I stand up straight; I have not really moved more than laying down in bed or sitting at my chair in over three weeks, I was a little too stiff to be crouching. I pat Ronnie on the shoulder. "Well, I was wrong. I guess we could get out." He smiled at me as I turned him to begin making our way out of the hallway. I could see that the two guards are both slumped in their chairs. From here it looked as though they were still breathing. As it happens, I kind of hoped they were breathing as there was no reason for them to be killed, not when they were just doing their job. I again grabbed Ronnie across the shoulders as we took our first couple steps towards my freedom. He leaned in to me as he accepted my hug. My right hand slid off his shoulder coming up underneath his chin before I slipped my whole arm around his neck. I began to squeeze as strongly as I could, pulling Ronnie backwards. We both fell somewhat awkwardly as he crumpled like an accordion. I came to a rest sitting on his calves, his whole body contorted into some weird pretzel shape. I was again feeling someone's pulse as I was choking the life out of Ronnie. In all fairness; I had told him I would do this. For a moment I had considered the other possibility. Escaping, leaving town then returning later on in order to exact my revenge. That is not who I am though. Even with all the bad things that can, have and will be said about me; conqueror will not be one of them. Psychopathic killer, while not totally accurate, will likely be used on more than a few occasions. Ronnie is taking his last few stabs at trying to break my grip; his fingernails are digging deeply into my arm. It feels like I am being scratched by a cat. The reason cat scratches hurt so much is that despite the fact that their claws look and seem sharp they are not. Well, they have a sharp point but are not little blades in a cat's paw. And that is the reason those scratches hurt so much, it is a tear in your skin as opposed to a slash. Same with why paper cuts hurt. The edges of sheets of paper are more like a saw blade than a knife blade; although you cannot really know this until you look at it microscopically.

As Ronnie's fingers finally begin to loosen I begin to think about how dirty his fingers probably are. Did he get rust from those dirty rusty sheers underneath his fingernails? Am I going to spend my last few days with lockjaw, suffering horrible spasms before my execution? I don't think that tetanus really has anything to do with rust; it is more of just associated with rusty nails and that spilled over into just rusty objects. The bacteria that causes tetanus does need an anaerobic environment, meaning that for it to have the best chance of multiplying in a body it needs to get deep inside, like in the wound made when someone stupidly steps on a rusty nail. I have no idea how long the bacteria takes in order to fully mature but I will suspect that even if Ronnie did manage to get that particular bug inside me I will die of other means before I succumb to a simple bacteria. Getting a nasty infection is more likely. I shrug to myself as I pull Ronnie's body off of me; it has been likely a minute since I last felt a heartbeat; I was feeling fairly confident he was dead. As I stood I realized that Ronnie had let go of his bodily functions when he died. I crawled back through the hole in my cage in order to go wash myself up and change out of these dirty clothes.

Now some reading this may understand my reasoning for what I did, others will not. There was of course my need to remain a man of my word, and I did say I was going to kill him if he cut the fence and let me out. But that is only part of it. In fact, quite a small part of it. There is a much larger concern that I had to worry about. I had been somewhat painted into a corner at my trial; or more accurately following my trial. I was not present for the sentencing portion of my trial; I was simply informed of the outcome. That was easy to foresee as being an outcome considering the mayhem that likely would have happened had the trial continued with everyone expressing all their hurts and fears regarding me. Therefore, ultimately, I am fine with just being informed of my sentence; I had nothing that I would have brought forward as a mitigating circumstance nor did I have any allusions about clemency possibly being granted to me. Nope. I knew I was going to die, as much as did everyone that was involved in the deliberations. The caveat and the reason I feel as though I was painted into a corner was that Aurora, as trustworthy as ever in wanting to serve justice in a calm and orderly manner; had required that I be incarcerated for one month prior to my execution. As the presiding judge over the case she was given the latitude to require such a thing. God knows why she wanted to do that; it worked out for me in that I have had the opportunity to put in writing all of my experiences, thoughts and motivations. Perhaps Aurora's justification was to force people to perform actions based on calm rational processes, instead of letting people's emotional state dictate the course of the punishment I was to receive. To me it seems perfectly sane and quite a safe plan. Unfortunately, despite the soundness of the plan I had heard a few rumblings from the guards in my first few days in this cell where they lamented that they had to stand guard instead of just hanging me as soon as the trial was done. People want their justice; and it simply does not feel 'just' to have to wait. It is however a sign of maturity to be able to wait and delay gratification. Whereas children often want things now and therefore need them now, adults who have reached a proper level of maturity, should be able to wait for the appropriate time for such pleasures. She was trying to make the whole population act more mature. It is kind of an ingenious plan if you think about it.

I do not however believe that was her motivation though. I believe that her main rationale was to be as different from me in the style of government. She wanted the people of Republica to be as different from me as possible in the implementation of justice. If it was me that was ordering the execution would I have waited a month or would I have just simply ordered the accused to be killed immediately? From all that I have documented here it seems pretty obvious I would have eliminated the person without a second thought; without a second wasted. Because that is how someone who acts on emotion works. So it is completely logical and reasonable to take your time. Make a plan. Wait until there is a little less emotion bubbling just below the surface and met out punishment in an orderly manner. Not as a mob pulling me out of the cage in the community hall and out to the nearest tree. Aurora had accomplished that which I could not. As much as I may have aspired to not act in an emotional manner I had failed miserably in the enacting that aspiration. All the people that I had killed or ordered killed had died based on what was my emotional instability. My inability to control my fear, my anger and my impatience; was the ultimate reason that so many died in this town.

My dirty pants were placed in a heap on the far side of the hallway, opposite the opening in my fence. The smell of urine was everywhere in my cell. My pants had been soaked in it, there were likely droplets everywhere from when I returned to my cell furthermore there was the puddle of urine sitting underneath Ronnie's corpse. There was also a fainter smell of shit coming from Ronnie however his pants seemed to have contained at least some of that unpleasantness. If I had believed there was a possibility that Ronnie was only unconscious and not dead, that was no longer possible. The side of his face that lay closest to the floor had begun to turn kind of an odd combination of colors; gray and white blotched with purple. His blood was pooling at the lowest points of his body. As I noticed that I began to wonder how long that usually took for the color of the deceased persons skin usually took. I had never paid attention. Was it a long process and my mind had just drifted so long that it was now happening? Or was it that fast and I am just stunned by the speed of it? Like everything else I would venture it is somewhere in between.

Rigor mortis has likely started to set in as well; I am not about to go and check though, I am not truly all that concerned about it. The only thing I would like to change is the smells although I have no plans on moving Ronnie myself as I will be a good little prisoner and just wait for someone to notice. I will sit in my cell.

Remember earlier when I had mentioned that there seemed to always be a constant flow of people around here, well today seemed to be some sort of holiday as I sat on my bed for a full twenty minutes before someone opened the door to the hallway and came across the guards. At first the tone of what was said was good natured. "Hey. What the fuck are you guys doing? You shouldn't be sleeping." Then everything started to become more urgent in his voice. "Guys? Guys?" Presumably they were being unsuccessfully shaken awake. I can only imagine what happened then. I would guess that my chance visitor saw Ronnie's body slumped in a heap down the hallway next to my cell. After adjusting his position slightly he was able to see there was a hole in my fence. I know that he did not venture very far down the hall, if at all. I saw no one appear in front of my cell. I saw no shadows and heard no approaching footsteps. Whatever he saw or thought he saw, what followed I was not prepared for. The most loud and shrill scream I had likely ever heard in my life. And keep in mind; I have heard someone being killed by a trash compactor. The door out of the hallway thudded open with a metal clang which was quickly followed by more panicked screaming. I am not sure who the man was down the hall, but the screaming was comical; I am fairly certain most women would not have been able to make such a sound. And please do not take that as being some sort of sexist joke; it is a fact that women in general have a higher pitched voice then men. This sound was that piercing, it felt as though it would poke right through your ears to you brain.

Things moved much quicker after those screams had raised the alarm. If I had been paying more attention I would likely have been able to count the number of seconds before people began bursting into the hallway on the digits I have available to me. Within minutes there were half a dozen men standing outside my cell, all with guns pointed through the chain link directly at me. I heard six distinct clicks as each of their guns were cocked when I rose and walked towards the hotplate next to my desk. "Would anyone like some tea?"

CHAPTER 23 – ONE FINAL TRUTH

I am now writing of the last happenings of my life. My execution is now hours away. Should I be excited? I almost feel as though I am. I have been mentally preparing for this for a month. I have likely been ready to die for longer than that, even though I was trying so desperately to avoid it. In my last musings I need to talk of my final conversation with Aurora. As expected she appeared shortly after I began making tea while six men pointing guns at me. She was out of breath when she finally stopped in front of my cell, at first only looking dumbfounded between me making tea calmly in my cage and the gapping hole in my cell and the corpse smelling of shit in the hallway.

"What the fuck is this?!"

I take a sip of tea, grimace then grab some sugar which I begin spooning into my tea before I answer her. I point using my tea cup. "Well, my dear. That appears to be what we would call a hole." One of the men standing guard snickers which is almost immediately met with an ice-cold stare from Aurora. Apparently, I can still manage to be funny.

"I can see the goddamned hole. Why is it here? And why is this guy dead? Who is this anyways?... Guys?" She looks around at the men standing beside her.

"That is Ronnie Meltar." Her gaze returns to me as I take another sip.

"Okay, so this is Ronnie Meltar. Why is he dead outside your cell? And why are you still in it?"

"Well obviously I did that. I warned him. I said I was dangerous and unstable and if he tried to let me out I would kill him. So, uh, yeah…. Would you mind taking him out of here? He kind of stinks." It was almost amusing how three of the men in the hall lowered their weapons and began to move towards the body before realizing who they were listening to. Apparently, it was that ingrained in them to listen to me that they started to do it instinctually. Aurora nodded at two of them to continue. "Also. How are the guards? I never checked on them, it didn't feel right to leave my cell for more than a couple seconds."

Her eyes looked down the hall past the two men who were now carrying out Ronnie's contorted body. "They're unconscious by the looks of it. Still breathing. What is going on here? And just tell me the truth for once."

"Tsk. Tsk. I have lied very sparingly over the years when it came to you. This is not a time to be bothering with falsehoods. He was trying to enact my escape from here. I chose to not go and he would not accept that and proceeded despite my objections. So…. Also, could you also have those pants that are on the floor behind you taken out, they are covered in his piss."

"Ugh. I thought that is what I smelled." She looked around at the men standing with her. "Daryl, go get some heavy-duty wire or something so we can close this hole."

"We're just going to close up the hole? And leave him in there? Are you crazy?" I am not sure who that particular gentleman is; Aurora did not seem overly impressed by his questioning her.

"Yes, we will close it. If he wanted to leave the cell he would have done so already."

I laugh. "I was waiting in here for someone to notice what was going on for probably half an hour. If I wanted to do otherwise there is nothing any of you could have done. I chose to be here."

"Daryl. Please. Wire. And the rest of you just lower your guns, he isn't going to try anything."

Daryl sighs as he holsters his gun and walks away. He seemed to have the same kind of attitude as a younger brother might when he gets excluded from everything fun that happens. "You'll be pleased to know I have an answer for you." Aurora's attention snapped back me as she looked at me with a slight look of confusion. "How I want to die. I think firing squad would work."

"The gallows have already been built."

I was feeling a little betrayed and hurt at that moment. "...Then why did you ask me how I wanted to die?"

"I was angry, and it was a rhetorical question. I was not actually expecting you to give me an answer." My chest was tightening as my mind began to race. It was becoming hard to breath. I weakly clutched at my chest as I sat down in my chair. "When it was decided that you were to be executed it was also determined that you would be hung."

I spoke quietly, almost inaudibly to anyone other than myself. "Hang by the neck until he is dead." I could not stop myself from fidgeting at that moment. All the things that I had previously thought about how I wanted to die was now coming back to haunt me. I had so convinced myself that I would be able to control aspects of my life up to and including my method of death, I suddenly had lost the last bit of control that I was grasping to. Quiet reigned in that hallway for the next few minutes; the only sounds were the occasional cough or a foot scrapping along the floor. I could not stop myself from fidgeting. I was completely aware of it but just could not stop. I was fully embroiled in a panic attack, something I had not felt in what seemed like forever. Daryl returned with something that they used to begin to repair the chain link. The fence rattled with a distinct metallic sound as they stretched everything back into place so it could be restored as close to its previous condition as possible. By the time they had finally got the last few links repaired I had managed to compose myself enough that I was able to not be incessantly wringing my hands together.

A chair was brought in front of the cell as the men departed down the hallway. Aurora sat opposite me again, much as she had done not so long ago. It would seem she still had more to talk about, yet she did not speak. She only sat there observing me, like an exhibit in a zoo. It felt like déjà vu all over again.

"I asked Clare if you had her adopt me. She said you did. She said she did not know why you asked. Why you insisted. Or why you picked her but did admit that she was given a bunch of stuff for taking care of me."

"It is not quite like that. She wasn't given things for taking care of you; there was going to be an extra strain on her and her resources, so she was given things to help compensate."

"Sure, that makes sense. After all the paint job on her house was totally necessary."

I sighed a little at that, Aurora still seemed to be in the mood to argue with me. "It was not necessary but seemed appropriate. She did not have the ability to do it herself and the house could use it. I am not totally sure just why you are upset about her getting her house painted though."

"I am not upset. Let's make that clear." I nod to her in agreement. "I still do not understand why you did that. I asked around. No one thinks that the fire that Lisa died in was an accident. This only leaves you or one of your guys starting it as a possible explanation. So, if you did that then why get me adopted. It was the same kind of thing that you did with little Rita" I could see we were only going to run around in circles here however I had said I was going to be truthful, so I was not going to change my story now.

"Look in my eyes. Do I seem to be lying? No. I am looking you dead in the eyes. I. Did not. Have anything to do with Lisa's death. Nothing from me, and not a word to anyone else."

I could see the disgust on her face. It was not exactly disgust with me, well it may have partially been that but I think it was more her being displeased that she believed me. I had changed the monstrous image she had of me in her mind, even if it was just a slight change. She grit her teeth together as she said "Fine" between them.

"Wonderful. Now that that is cleared up; how about we just have some tea and talk? Like we used to do."

"We never used to talk. You used to talk. Ramble for hours about this and that. I don't even know if there is anything else to say to you."

"It is up to you, however I will be here. And I would like to remind you that I was not all bad. Did I not do good things here?" I could feel my face lighten as I pulled out the 'puppy-dog eyes'.

"There were good aspects. But those were outweighed by the negatives." I slide a tea cup under the food tray slot under the fence along with the little bowl of sugar that I have. I forget just now what kind of sugar this is. We do not have any refined sugar; that has long since been used and we don't grow sugar cane. I think it is some sort of tree sap derivative, like maple syrup sugar. Whatever. I don't need to know where it comes from, we have a couple chemist people who do shit like that. I return to my teapot and add more water to my cup of tea. Aurora is still sitting in her chair looking at the cup like it is poisoned.

"You cannot be serious, as if I really remained in my cell so that could have the slight possibility of poisoning you hours before my execution." She was still well aware of my 'looks' and she knew the one I was giving her at that moment said I thought she was being a moron. She picked up the tea, added two spoonfuls of sugar, was about to drop in a third before putting it back in the sugar bowl, she stirred it, tapped the rim of her cup four times then put the spoon back in the sugar bowl. It was a pattern that she had; I had seen her repeat it as long as I have ever seen her make tea. When I first noticed it I had wondered if she had OCD or something, as it seemed to be very ritualistic as she performed it exactly the same every time. If she did suffer from OCD I could not pick out any other rituals she did; I would have to put her tea making as just some weird habit as opposed to a mental disorder compelling her to do odd things repeatedly. She pushed the bowl with her foot back under the fence before returning to her seat.

"So. Do you plan on telling me just why you are still here? "I am extremely curious as to why you stayed in your cell. You could have run." She suddenly began to look around herself, sniffing slightly.

"It's the piss covered pants you smell. You never had them taken away like I asked." She looked a little relieved that she now knew what the smell was although she did seem to be off her tea; the cup sat half full in between her hands which sat on her lap. I continued to answer her question "Where was I to go? Would you have preferred I tried to start a riot, maybe a little civil war in my town? I have rebuilt everything you know. Here. There is nowhere for me to go that is not here."

Aurora nodded in reluctant agreement. "So, what about that guy?"

"I told you the truth. He was warned to not let me out. He ignored me, so I killed him. There is no good in my being let out." I chuckle a little. "I told him explicitly that if he let me out I would break his neck. I kind of lied there, I did not break it, but I did still kill him. Thing is, as far as I can see it, the last good thing I can do here is die. To make everyone in Republica have the ability to start to sleep soundly. Wouldn't you agree?" She acknowledged me but seemed to be thinking a bit. We were on either side of the cage, nothing but chain links between us for what felt like a very long time. "Anything else?"

Aurora still took a minute before answering. "I am still upset with you."

I laughed fairly loudly with that one. "As is everyone else around here."

"Not that, when you first came into this town, I was scared of you, after I realized you were just a man I came to like you. I loved you. You were like a father to me. Then you just…"

"I just what?" I could feel my pulse through my thumb as I held my now empty teacup. Each heart beat just reminded me of how much time was flowing before Aurora finally continued her thought. I put the cup down onto the desk.

"You turned dark. All the patience you had was gone. You got angry. No one could please you. And I knew there was something wrong. I feel like you broke my trust."

I was having another person tell me they were very disappointed in me. I managed to keep my tears in my eyes, although they were definitely welling up. I could not hide the sadness and regret on my face as my bottom lip began to stick out slightly and quiver. And then she dug the knife deeper. "Despite what you say, there can be no good from you. Even in death, you are more evil than anything and that cannot be erased by killing you." I pawed at my eyes with a small rag that I had been using as a face cloth; I was drying up my tears while they were still in my eyes. It was hard to keep up. I felt like a fool. My staying in this cell had not been assuring that the people here would sleep more soundly; it only prevented them from having a convenient boogie-man for their scary stories. "And the worst part was that way back then, after there was that guy in the night, you had told me that you would keep me safe. I would never have to be afraid of anything or anyone as long as you lived. Except you were what I was afraid of."

"I'm..." Deep breath. "Sorry." It was a meaningless gesture. She could not even hear me I was so quiet. Another deep breath. "I'm sorry."

"That's wonderful. But you have no idea of the lasting damage you have done to me and everyone else. Sorry just will not cover it. Do you remember Joey? He was the young man you killed Kevin over in the hole where you were having them start your new house. He is terrified of everything. Every noise shocks him. He is constantly scrubbing the floor trying to make sure there are no stains. Apparently, that is your handiwork, something about 'he hates stains'; that is all he fucking repeats while furiously scrubbing a clean floor. You broke him. He is not the same man I fell in love with and I don't know if I'll ever be able to bring him out of it. Did you know he has not been able to sleep since that day? Every night he sits in the corner of the room under a tarp like he is still in that pit. On the off times when I manage to get him try to fall asleep and he actually manages to fall asleep he wakes up screaming. Every night." There was nothing I could say at that point. I had not even had an idea that she and Joe were together. Chances are the look on my face was blanker than I had meant to show but I was caught out in left field. The tears that had just moments before been flooding my eyes, obscuring my vision were now gone. The feelings of sadness and regret were oddly displaced with the same impatience and rage that I had felt roughly a month ago in that pit. I cannot now explain just why I felt that way, nor could I possibly explain why those emotions again began to bubble to the surface. My mind was back as if I was standing there being furious at his laziness.

"Firstly, I did not kill Kevin over him; Kevin was punished appropriately for not doing his job. Secondly, how could you possibly fall in love with someone so useless?"

"It was not fucking appropriate! They are people, not slaves. They get tired and are allowed to take breaks. If you were still a person you would know that. Jesus! I never totally realized just how crazy you are. You actually think that you did the right thing. Killing a random person. Over nothing. He had a family you know. You took him away from them because you had a tantrum!" Aurora rose from her chair; her hands were clenched in fists at her sides. "And I love Joey because I know him for who he is and that is all you fucking need to know. You are no longer in charge anymore!"

I had held out the faint hope, far back in my mind, of telling Aurora who I was in our last conversation; not as a means of gaining clemency or anything like that, but just to tell her. It was not something for her really; it would have been for me. To get that one last secret off my conscience. Stop it from weighing on my heart before I died. I could not even fathom the idea of saying to her as she stormed off down the hallway. Perhaps I should have done more anger management with her when she was younger; not that it would have really been helpful at this point however I have a feeling she will be fuming all the way until she knows I am dead. The door down the hall sounded as if it had been torn open before slamming heavily a second or two later. After a moment or two a guard, someone I had not seen before came down and claimed the chair as well as the teacup. I would have told him that was for the cell, but it was not important anymore. He could take it perhaps so he has a souvenir from the tyrant's cell. He placed it on the seat of the chair as he took it down the hall. Far off I could hear the cup fall and break. So much for him having a keepsake, now he just had a mess to clean up. I began to write furiously so this could be preserved.

I looked around the cell for a few minutes, taking in my surroundings, imprinting them on my mind, I needed to preserve this moment; as it would be one of my last. These walls, this room would be my final sights. I found as I got closer to writing events of the present I began to talk while I wrote, like someone who cannot think without speaking.

My name is not Randall Omar. I was pressed to give a name when I met with Aurora and Lisa and all I could think of were names like John Smith. John Johnson. Plain and boring names. The kinds of names there were hundreds of in any old phonebook. I needed something randomer. It is kind of stupid, I know, but that was how I settled on the name that I used for years. Rand-omer. I used this name so much so that I effectively became someone else by assuming a new name. All I can say was I was not the man I once was as soon as I became a new person. Randall Omar was a mask I wore for much too long.

Arthur Stanley Harvard. There is no longer any point in apologies or explanations. As well I no longer have the time to try to dispute any of it. It is what it is. Anyone who reads my testament can take the entirety of my life for what it is and make their own determinations on whether the things I did were right or wrong. Perhaps Aurora was right, and I have become crazy. It would be comforting to say that it was just me getting older and going senile, but I think I have been drifting off this way longer than that. Perhaps, it is happening all the way back when I began to build my house off in the wilderness; that was when I was becoming unhinged.

It would certainly seem so if you follow the bouncing ball through all of this.

EPILOGUE – THE ADORING PUBLIC

I am guessing I will just start this off by continuing to document Randall's life, since it would only make sense. For posterity.

The morning of Randall's execution, things around the town seemed to have a relative calm. The usual hustle and bustle that typically happened early in the morning just did not seem to be there. People still went about their business though there seemed to be a more somber tone about it. There was less jovial chatting among friends. Less conversation at all as far as I could see. Everything seemed to be business-like; that could just have been when people were around me or maybe it was just my perception. I'm not sure which and I am not sure it matters, all that does seem to matter is that everyone seemed somewhat subdued, which when you think about it kind of does not make sense. People would be expected to be happy now that their oppression was over. It would seem however that people were preparing for the event to occur later in the day; hastily clearing off their obligations for the day so as to not miss the show. As for myself, this rang true as well; all the little details that needed to be attended to were dealt without a word being spoken. In fact, I do not think I spoke a word until it came time to bring Randall out from his cell to the gallows. I walked through the town square; I watched as the trapdoor was dropped, sending a large bag filled with rocks crashing down before coming to a sudden stop at the end of the rope. This was followed by a subtle creaking sound as the bag was swinging slightly at the full extension of the noose. I heard one of the men on the gallows shout "Perfect. Let's reset it and try one more time." The words he used do not match the tone he spoke in however; he spoke in a much more monotone kind of delivery; more matter-of-fact. From there I moved along to the church. There was no movement outside the building; the other members of the ruling council were likely inside discussing some minute detail of governing the town; I was not part of any of those discussions, not at that point, as I had been designated as the one who would be bringing Randall to the gallows. I was the judge and I am to lead him to the next person in the chain of justice; the executioner.

The sun had lifted over the horizon a fair while ago, but it was just now beginning to feel warm on my face. Up until that moment it was almost as if things seemed almost cold, I was unaware of the chill though; my mind was justifiably elsewhere. Also, I had this funny feeling about the sun and how it was shining this morning. I am not certain how to describe it but it was really feeling brighter to me; like the dawn of a new day, I would venture however that it was not the sun that was brighter, just my view of the world that brightened. Experience has taught me that I really don't want the sun to get any brighter. I inhaled deeply before I continued on to get Ivan and Dale. They were to be the escorts to bring Randall to his execution. I knocked on Dale's door which opened a moment later. I told him "it's time." Dale nodded and stepped out into the light. He tried to make small talk by asking me "how's it going?" I could only look at him sideways as we walked to Ivan's. He got the message I was not really in the mood to chat. I repeated the same greeting with Ivan after he answered the knock at his door. Dale and Ivan followed behind me as we walked to the building that had housed Randall for the last month of his life. I could hear them whispering behind me however my mind continued to be elsewhere. They could talk amongst themselves; I did not want to be part of their conversation. Randall had made killing people something that was normal to deal with; he was able to rationalize and justify it to himself. For me this was a new experience. And I was not certain I was up for it or if I was going to be able to handle it. Even if I could handle it; I honestly was not looking forward to it, I never wanted to have anyone's blood on my hands.

Randall sat quietly in his cell; the hall still smelled of urine to me, who could say though if the smell was really still there or if it was just part of my memory of this place. I almost considered asking Randall although I was uncertain if he would even have smelled it anymore after having spent hours in that smell. It was likely that the smell was still present, even if it was very faint; the only reason it was so noticeable to me was that my mind was very aware of my surroundings at this moment. It was a new experience and for better or for worse I was likely going to profoundly remember it for the rest of my life. I would say that is likely very true as even with the time that has passed between his passing and my writing this, that hallway still has that lingering smell to me. It has diminished greatly but there is that ever-so-slight hint of salt and urea in the air. In the end I chose to not even mention it to Randall or anyone else; if it is only a memory then it is mine. If the smell is there no one really wants to talk about it anyways. Dale pulled a pair of wire cutters from one of his jacket pockets and began to cut the links on the fencing. Randall smiled and chuckled to himself. I looked curiously at him to which he beckoned me over towards where he was sitting. "The last time I heard that clinking sound I was being given freedom; this time it is going to be something entirely different."

"And last time this fence was cut you killed someone. Is that the plan for this time as well?"

"Not quite. Someone will die, but it will not be at my hand." He winked at me. It sent chills up my spine. I think that was one of the most unsettling things I had ever experienced. We sat for a moment with only the clinking of the chain links being cut punctuating the silence. Randall sighed before turning to me and asking "Do you think you are doing the right thing?"

"Yes." I spoke so meekly. I immediately began to regret not sounding more confident in my answer. I had not expected him to ask that, although I really should have. I knew him well enough to know that he likely had been waiting for hours just to ask that. I wondered if he was trying to sow the seeds of doubt in my mind as I reminded myself that I was doing the right thing. There was always that lingering doubt in the back of my mind though. The fence was halfway done being cut open. Ivan had pulled a pair of handcuffs from his back pocket and seemed to be readying himself to have a struggle in order to get them on the prisoner. They did not know Randall as well as I knew him. He would not try to fight. For him that would seem rude. I composed myself and reasserted to him "Yes, we are doing the right thing." Randall almost seemed disappointed at that answer, his bottom lip pouted out a little as he nodded.

"Good. Don't forget that." A slight pause as he seemed to be thinking of the next thing he wanted to say "Your mind will try to make you think that you did the wrong thing. Don't second-guess yourself. It will drive you insane if you dwell on your apparent mistakes." I did not understand why he was telling me that at the time. I did not gain the understanding of it until after I had read this memoir of his. Then it became clearer and I began to understand. I was being given sage advice on how to follow in his footsteps. He looked from me over to the hole in the fence. Dale was cutting the last few links to open the fence completely; most of it was already drooping down. Unlike the hole meant to allow Randall to escape this one completely opened up the fence and would allow him to walk out as opposed to crawl. Which I guess would be necessary if he is going to be cuffed. His gaze returned to me as he stood. Randall's height seemed to vary at times and this was one of the times it seemed to be most apparent to me. Don't get me wrong, this was not a real thing; it was more of something that I perceived. At this exact moment he seemed to be almost a giant compared to me. It was as if I was feeling small and that somehow translated into him seeming larger. As I steeled my resolve again that we were doing the right thing the height difference between us become less apparent to the point were we seemed to be looking eye to eye. "You'll have to excuse me. My adoring public awaits." I always hated his stupid jokes, they always seemed ill-timed. In his mind however, these were the most appropriate times; when the situation called for anything other than humor.

I watched as Randall strode over to the hole in the fence as Dale cut the very last link. Ivan looked nervous as his hand quickly moved to his hip, onto the grip of his pistol. It was hard to see from my angle, but it seemed that he put his finger directly on the trigger; you know one of those things you should never do. I expected to hear the pop of a gunshot while his gun remained in its holster. I was very grateful when Randall turned his back to the two and put his hands behind himself. At the very least it allowed Ivan the opportunity to breathe again without his heart in his throat. He seemed to have suddenly realized where his hand was and jerked a little as he let go of the pistol. I shook my head as I regretted bringing Ivan to do this, for him Randall was some sort of supernatural demon, he could not just look upon him as a normal man. Dale took the handcuffs from Ivan's hand as he was now staring intently at Randall, frozen in place. Dale was a good choice; not just due to his physical size but also his calmness with the whole situation. As long as nothing was said to upset him that is. He still had a burning hatred for Randall, which was not to be unexpected, given that his girlfriend had been caught in one of the purges. I wonder even now how well Randall knew the people he had killed; if he knew about their lives. Did he even know why Dale hated him so much? I would venture he did not know but there would not be any time to find out the answer it so that will just have to remain a mystery. I did have confidence in Dale that he could control himself enough to get done what needed to be done; he would get his justice for how he was wronged. I could see him firmly grip Randall's hand and affix one cuff before the other. Randall stood there, seemingly determined to take the whole situation in as dignified a manner as possible. As he was turned around and led out of the cell by Dale I could see that his eyes were looking bloodshot. I would guess that he had likely been crying before we arrived. Or had not slept. Probably both. His head hung low as we walked to the end of the hall. As the door was opened and we all stepped out Randall seemed to take a deep breath. He was inhaling the freshness of the outside air, something that had been denied to him for a month. That is of course assuming he was telling the truth about how far he got down the hall during his "escape" attempt. He raised his chin up as he stepped into the brightness outside, letting the light shine on his face and warm it.

The walk to the town square and the gallows was not exceedingly long. As we walked there seemed to be an ever-growing crowd behind us; like a parade that gets bigger and bigger the longer it proceeds. I am not sure how much Randall was aware of though as he seemed to be walking with his eyes closed. I would assume it was due to not having been outside in the light for so long, but it is also possible he just did not want to see anyone or anything, like he was trying to preserve as much of his old view of the town. He tripped over a curb, only to be dragged back up and along by Dale. The whole procession came to an abrupt halt when Randall reached the bottom of the stairs to the awaiting noose. Randall almost fell over again as he did not stop in time and tripped slightly over the bottom stair. Dale kept him mostly upright. I don't know if it should seem comical or not, but it became obvious as Dale stood there holding his arm that the stairs would not be wide enough for the both of them to go up at once. "Stairs." He announced gruffly and then let go of Randall's arm. Randall finally opened his eyes and began to walk up the stairs. Each step seemed to be slow and measured; like his biggest concern was to make sure that he did not trip and fall. Randall stopped a few steps after reaching the top, allowing Dale to come up behind him. He was then given a slight nudge to continue walking. His first few steps after the pause seemed stilted; as if he was learning to walk again.

Martin stood on the opposite side of the noose. He was wearing a piece of black cloth across his face, like a bandana. He was looking more like some sort of outlaw than the executioner. I feel that this was something that was not well planned out on our part; I am not trying to be too judgmental although I would say that it looked kind of tacky. The overall mood of the crowd still remained rather subdued. And I was really impressed with Dale. While he did not have a different attitude than usual he was able to be more professional in his demeanor than he was when he had escorted Randall to the church after his apprehension. Randall was moved onto the trapdoor; Dale still gently held his arm while Martin looped the noose over Randall's head. I was not able to hear the exchange from my position at the bottom of the stairs, but I did see Dale look him in the eye before nodding slightly, patting him gruffly on the shoulder like old friends before walking off the platform. I asked Dale some time later what Randall had said to him; he replied that he had apologized for calling Dale an animal; he said it was unfair and had been done in the heat of the moment. There was another man on the far side of the scaffold who I could not see from my vantage point that began to read off the crimes Randall had committed. At the end of the list he made the pronouncement that "Randall Omar, you have been sentenced to death by the people of Republica." There were a few quiet claps. Given how much people wanted him dead only a month ago this was feeling very anticlimactic. "Do you wish to speak your last words?"

Randall took another stilted step forward; he looked as if he was about to begin a great impassioned speech. "I- …." His voice cracked while his face contorted into some strange look of disgust. Another chink in the armor was showing. He cleared his throat before beginning. "I have spent the better part of my life in this town. With you people… I brought you together; I gave you all shelter, food, medicine, jobs. I gave you all life… I am the reason you are all here… and you should thank me for that. I made your lives better. I gave you *everything* back that the sun had taken from you. I gave you civilization again. You would have nothing without me giving it to you." A sneer appeared across his face. "Instead this how you all repay me. It was me that saved you from the cannibals. You worthless pile of ingrates. Without me half of you would *be* food right now. Every last one of you is like a little fucking child. You want to know why I acted as I did; because you fucking deserved it. You want to act like spoiled children then you will all be treated like children. None of this is free; it requires hard work, and structure and discipline. Laws for fucks sakes. I have spent the past month thinking about what I have done for this town… for you people and… and… fuck."

There were a number of sideways glances between people in the crowd. I had seen the overall mood in the crowd starting to ramp up as he was berating the people more and more. If he had kept going I would have had to worry about people rushing the stage and lynching him; as if they would bother to drag him away to the nearest tree with the noose from the gallows still around his neck. Reflecting on the whole situation I wished that I had not been feeling as though I was frozen in place so I could have gone up onto the scaffold myself to stop him from talking. But I couldn't. I was in all honesty mesmerized by what was going on; as if I was just watching it like it was some old movie. He seemed as though he was getting the crowd all riled up intentionally. If that is the case then I think I know what he is doing. He was trying to take away any feelings of guilt or second thoughts they may have had by making himself into the monster that everyone feared; to get everyone to feel as though they have done the right thing. Like what he said to me. Although if that is not what he intended to do then I really have no idea just what he was doing. And then his tone changed. I came to realize later on that like all the other chinks that had appeared in his armor over the past month he was just not able to project that same level of confidence in what he was saying as he had before he was arrested. I think it was that he didn't believe his own lies anymore. He could not continue the smokescreen that he had been using for years. He closed his eyes as he collected himself and continued "You know what, I am done. There is nothing I can say to you people other than I'm sorry. Anymore, than that would just be extra words. You were the ones who made this place, I was just here first. Without you there would have been nothing to work for. I- I'm… I'm tired…. I'm done. I- uh… I'm sorry." He stepped back, the leaned over to Martin. I could not hear what he said but presumably he was asking for the hood. A hood was slipped over his head. A breath was collectively taken in by the whole crowd as Martin pulled hard on the lever to the trapdoor.

Nothing. Randall continued to stand there; a hush was covering the crowd like a fog. Everyone held their breath. It felt as though time had stopped for a moment. Randall had always made stupid little comments when he was teaching about being prepared for everything. Double and triple checking everything to make sure that nothing ever went wrong. Really, I am not sure why he said that, the best thing he ever did in terms of preparedness was survive the Great Flare and that was more of a fluke than something intentional. In any event, this was definitely one of the times that I wish people had kept checking and made sure that the trapdoor worked every time.

Randall turned his head inside the hood as if to look at Martin "Seriously? Are you going to say this is my fault for shooting an actual competent carpenter in the neck?" People were starting to move about now. I could feel a slight breeze on my cheek, it came at a time where it felt coincidentally like everyone in the crowd exhaling. We were no longer stuck in a momentary time-warp waiting for the condemned to fall. I could see the hood moving as Randall was shaking his head. "You guys kind of suck you know. They used to make toys for three-year olds that were more deadly than this contraption. And this smell is fucking horrible, what was in this-". Martin shushed him and I could begin to hear other things that were going on. I could hear various people around the scaffold of the gallows muttering to themselves, I could hear faint whispers of people in the crowd, and I could hear the slight brush of the wind. All of that was just noise. There was only one sound that my ears were waiting to hear; the heavy wooden 'thunk' of the trapdoor being tossed aside as the weight of the man standing on top pushed it down and out of the way.

Randall stood there, now strangely compliant after having been shushed, shifting his weight back and forth on his heels, almost like he was comforting himself by trying to rock himself to sleep. Or he was subtly trying to get the trapdoor to drop. I wondered what was going on his head when he suddenly turned his head towards Martin again who was pulling the lever over and over again to try to get the trapdoor to drop. "I'm bored." Randall snickered a little under his hood. That kind of answered my question about what was going on in his head. "Is this going to take long? I have other executions to get to. People are expecting me." He was shushed again and I was able to hear the people grumbling to themselves around the gallows.

Now they were now getting louder. They are shouting *to* each other as well as shouting *at* each other. Some are assigning blame; others are looking for a solution. From underneath the platform a man yells out "got it", Randall suddenly stands stiffly upright, like he just came to attention at that pronouncement.

I think I heard him say "Come on death". Slightly odd to have as his last words but not completely out of character for him; although he could have said "apple sauce slip-and-slide" and I would not have been terribly surprised. There is a loud crack that echoes out from underneath the scaffold as the man who has *got it* seemingly hits a hammer to fix the problem. I see Randall begin to fall; time has slowed down again. He is tipping forward slightly, from my vantage point it seems as if his face is only going to miss the edge of the hole by inches, if not less. He disappears from my view; the stairs are obscuring the sight of him coming to a sudden stop at the end of the rope. I can however see sunlight is shining through the hole, with his shadow resting in the middle of the square of light under the gallows.

After all that waiting for the trapdoor to drop I cannot now remember if I had heard the heavy wooden 'thunk' sound that my ears had been waiting for. Not that it mattered, the result was the same. I do remember thinking that it was almost disappointing to not have things turn out as you expected them to. That was wrong though; the events of the day proceed almost exactly as I expected them to, with the exception of the trapdoor malfunctioning and that was what was disappointing. The problem for me was that the catharsis I would have expected from Randall's death was not there; everything went "as planned" and I did not feel any better… I did not feel a sudden relief at having played my part in removing a tyrant. I was not overjoyed to have sentenced someone to die. To have essentially killed someone. I took no joy in any of that. And I felt no weight being lifted off my shoulders after his death. In fact, I felt heavier as I was weighed down with the sudden burden of what I had done. Few people within the town know but I had in fact objected to his sentence. Not on the grounds that I felt he needed to live but more on a moral stance; I was overruled however. I did not feel that we should be in the habit of killing anyone; that is the kind of thing I wanted to remove. It was likely more of a burden at that moment to have a conscience than not. I walked away from the scaffold wondering if I was any better than Randall. I considered if I was ever going to be the same as I had been; it seemed less likely with each step I took away from the town square that I would be the same person.

I was walking back to Randall's cell at the warehouse. I knew that he had been writing; it seemed to be the only thing he did while he waited for his execution. I was hoping that I would get answers to all the questions I had had over the years. I have now read this entire manuscript twice. As well I actually waited months before writing of his final day. Lisa would have said that was just the introvert in me coming out. I sat on what I knew about him, about myself, about the town, about everything and kept mulling it over. Looking at it from different angles. Reconstructing it as needed. Re-evaluating each of my conclusions. I was not certain that I would be able to write anything, so I wanted to make sure that I had my thoughts and my feelings in order so that they made sense to me. If I could not even justify things to myself how could I ever put them down and have them potentially make sense for anyone else reading them.

The first time reading this thing only fueled my anger and almost completely wiped out any apprehensions that I had about having done the right thing. It felt like I was reading some tacky propaganda book meant to sway my feelings towards following the 'party line'. Right up until the end I was just angry having to see things from his perspective like they were the real way that things were, as if they did not differ completely from my recollections of what happened. And then the assertions of who Randall really was only seemed to prove that he was not in contact with reality anymore. And that is where he kind of got me. He was not insane in a sense, as he pointed out. But he was delusional. Like an old man who was starting to suffer from dementia. Some of his memories were spot on; some were just a little off. Little details were off, but it was more than that as I think he was really getting to the point where he had a tenuous grip on reality. The little mistakes were nothing; James Thomas not John Thomas; the Parmons not the Perlmans. In the end, we are all talking about people who have died so it is not particularly important. The real thing that showed me that he was no longer the same man he was during his 'tyrant' years was when I went to see him while he was in his cage. He offered me a blanket so Princess could lie down. I distinctly remember that whole exchange. It was at that moment that I began trying to commute his sentence; I needed more time to think. I had to decide if it made sense to leave him in that cell for the remainder of his life. I was overruled however. The problem you see is that Princess had died, years prior, of old age. He even remembered me patting my dead dog's head. He was offering to make my dog more comfortable when the dog was long gone. My confusion at that moment had led me to wonder if he was just trying to come off as crazy so I would doubt myself; reading this however only reinforced that he sincerely believed that Princess was still guarding me. I have been conflicted ever since that day. On one hand I do think that he deserved to be punished for his crimes against the town that he was likely fully aware of although, on the other hand, it could be argued that he was not necessarily the same person if he was living in a fantasy world. I think I was really just trying to avoid having to look at myself and wonder if what he did still warranted the end that he got, considering he was not necessarily the same person. His killing someone in the hallway of his cell certainly helped me reach the conclusion that he was indeed dangerous, regardless of how in touch with reality he was. I will likely always have a slight feeling of regret deep in my gut but I think that in the end I did do the right thing for the people of the town. At the very least I ensured that they will be safe from him.

So that is what I got, this rambling record of a madman who seemed to hold just enough onto reality that he was able to seem like a normal person, at least some of the time. I had to re-read everything only to see if my recollections matched up with what was written. In a way I can almost say they are true, the problem is that I am looking at a coin; he saw it from the heads side, I see the tails side. Same issues and same situations however they are distinctly different when looking at the surface perspectives. One is a face; the other is whatever, a building, a bird. We don't even have money anymore. Overall, I will have to say for the most part though things were close to what happened.

I am certain after reading this memoir through to the end that his whole intention of writing this was to get me to understand why he did what he did; for me to acknowledge that in the end he did the right thing and profess that I love him for all he did. That is just not something I can do; it has been a struggle for me even to accept what I read, let alone believe what I read may be the actual truth. There are lots of things to try to reconcile in my mind; on one hand there is the fact that for the majority of my life I loved my father and missed him as I believed that he had died along with everyone else. I was so young when I last saw him that I couldn't even remember what he looked like. To me he was only a voice that told me he loved me, and I loved the voice for that. On the other hand, if Randall really was my father then he was wrong in so many ways from a moral standpoint. He let me spend the majority of my life thinking that he was indeed dead meanwhile he was alive and in front of me all along. He was just too scared to "out himself" for who he truly was. While he may have given this town a foundation on which to build, he, in fact made it considerably weaker through fear and through making people disappear. I am sure if anyone from a later generation who was to read this would wonder why no one left the town. Randall seems to have purposely left that as ambiguous for whatever reason. People did leave, more than I can count, although there was a reason why banishment was a punishment that was used. Up until the few years before his execution there were still large tracts of land that were scorched, being out somewhere else may be freer but it was not necessarily safer or ensured that you would survive. Republica was a home to a lot of people. People had made lives and friends here; they had grown roots. Not everyone was willing to just discard that all. It is unfortunate that the 'first revolt' as he referred to it was not successful. In the end it would have saved a lot of innocent people. After my initial reading of the manuscript I had gone to Randall's home to search for his hidden list of names. I found the names of 'the redacted ones' just where he said it was. For me, him calling them that only helps prove his disconnect with reality; those were people not simply entries on a list that could just be erased. The list did seem to have been thumbed through numerous times; there was a slight amount of grime on the edges of the pages; it is possible he had poured over the list as he said he did, as if that was a measure of contrition for what he had done to those people. In his paranoia though he hurt many people who had nothing to do with that 'revolt'; I would say after he killed everyone at that cabin he was having people killed indiscriminately. It worked for what it was; a fear tactic to keep people scared and in-line. It worked for years. In my way of looking at it the final act he did through this telling of his life only served to taint the memory that I had of my father as someone who was a decent, albeit misunderstood man. It would really be impossible, given the things he admitted to doing in this memoir, to say that he was still a decent man. He was not misunderstood. It would seem that my mother ended up making somewhat the right decision in leaving him and taking me with her, although who knows. I could speculate that given the influence of me and her on him he may have taken a more fatherly tone in his rebuilding of things as opposed to the dictatorial method he chose to employ. Maybe it was our leaving that caused the first real cracks to appear in a broken mind.

As for his final day of freedom I don't know what it was that really set people off when Kevin was killed in that pit. That particular death was no more significant than any other that happened. I can venture a guess that it was the callous nature with which it was carried out. Or maybe it was the fact that it didn't even have the usual semblance of being a justified murder. There was no 'trial', no judgement; just a one-off random decision that resulted in a man dying. And he was not even the offending person; he was just there, ostensibly 'in charge'. In that context it could be anyone next; they simply have to be in the literal wrong place at the wrong time and they would succumb to the same fate. It could have been that Kevin was so universally liked that Randall's actions were deemed by the populace as a whole to be so abhorrent that his abuses could no longer be tolerated by the people. Perhaps it was all the witnesses, it made his abuses become real, and visible. All that was ever really seen by the people at large were the far-off bonfires. So much of what had transpired, before happened off in the woods, in a cabin, in basements, etc. It was never seen as being something that you could see as a seemingly 'normal' occurrence that could happen on any given day. And that led to the tale of Kevin's death spreading like wildfire through the whole town. I would say that it is all of those things in part; certain things factored more for certain people while his other abuses triggered others more severely. In the end it seems that people were completely fed up with having their lives controlled and monitored by him and his thugs. This is a thought that does not matter now. Whatever it was that proved to be the impetus; it was obviously long overdue. Not that anyone can blame us for taking action, even it seems to have come too late for some. As he pointed out a number of times, fear is a great motivator as well as a great hindrance. Fear can stop someone in their tracks if they let it. Even I let it for a long time.

Joey is recovering, if you could call it that. Every day is a struggle for us, for him. Loud sounds like dropping a book on the floor cause a loud yelp followed by at least an hour of sobbing. Other sudden sounds only cause him to grasp at his chest like he is having a heart attack. A thirty-six-year-old man is not having a heart attack; his anxiety is just that severe. He has compulsions to clean things, to scrub them clean in a manner that goes far beyond just wanting things clean. His mind was broken by Randall, which as he said was partially what he wanted to do. He wanted to indoctrinate himself a new follower, take away his own self confidence and replace it with what he gave him. "To grant Joey a gift of strength." Such bullshit, I really think Randall just liked making people scared. Despite my and other people's best efforts there has not been an easy rebuilding of his psyche; progress is exceedingly slow in getting him to be comfortable again. Two or three times a week there is a quivering mass on my floor. It had been daily, and then went to four or five times a week before it kept dropping. The hope is soon he will be able to control his anxiety enough that he will not need to worry when sudden sounds happen. He talks with Dr. Sanders weekly. He has been eating his lunch closer and closer to the new machine shop; the sounds of the construction, while rhythmic are still loud. He's working on those things. He still hates the rain, still shakes when he hears thunder in the distance. He still has not taken a shower, he can only take baths; the falling water is too close to rainfall, to that night, he just cannot stand the feeling; the sounds of water falling.

In my mind, this is the legacy that Randall truly left to the people of Republica. An entire population who has been traumatized in one way or another and now have to deal with it. While not being better than the alternative (Randall still being in charge) we have begun to encounter problems which have not been something that we really had to deal with on a large scale here. There does not seem to be much in the way of drugs within the town which I am thankful for although a number of people seem to have constructed themselves stills for making alcohol. I would presume they have been built since Randall's capture but I am not entirely sure they could have been made prior to that, when he remained in power. There is debate among me and the other civic leaders about how to properly handle this. Some have actually begun to reminisce about the "good old days" when things like that were much less common, and even if they existed were kept under tight control. I will admit there was no crime really back then, no drunkenness or the like. Everyone contributed their fair share. That seems to be waning somewhat. I miss the stability but I just cannot bring myself to think that what had happened before was a good thing, I am sure there has to be a happy medium somewhere in there.

Joey and I have talked of getting married recently although I worry that he has begun discussing it mostly because I think I am pregnant. I only assume I am pregnant because of the morning sickness. I am not sure how far along I am and I have not even gone to see Dorothy yet, it is on my list of things to do. I will say however that I will not let LeAnn touch me. While Randall's portrayal of LeAnn's attempted break-out is damning but it is not what we could really call evidence; it is he said-she said and one of those people we cannot ask for clarification and even if we could talk to him it would be debatable how reliable the words of a madman would be. What we are left with is a story which LeAnn denies and the guards are not able to break the tie as they cannot recall anything. What am I to do? No one else in Republica is really in a rush to condemn her. She is technically our future doctor, pragmatics have somewhat taken over. Regardless, I will not let her touch me. I will wait for Dorothy to have the time and she can do my ultrasound and tell me about my baby. It is so cliché but I really could care less if it is a boy or girl, as long as it is healthy. As long as it does not turn out like its grandfather, things should be okay. I have decided that this will be the last time I write my last name as Harvard. From this point forward I will Mrs. Joseph Smith; Aurora Dawn Smith. A boring name by Randall's standards but that is who I am now and will be for the future.

I am sure there may be people reading this who wonder if Randall was truly my father as he claimed to be, especially since I continue to refer to him as Randall. Part of me wishes to just deny the whole idea and emphatically say it is not possible. I feel that would be too easy for me to do, in a way. While on the surface it does seem incredibly unlikely that he is my father although for me it does not feel like a lie. Or a mistake. Or a misdirection. The mere fact he knows my father's name would lead me to believe it is likely true; I never spoke of my father to him that I can remember. And I certainly never told him his name and even if he had fabricated that identity for himself from things that Lisa had told him he just seems to know more than even she would have been able to tell him. I would put it as being more likely to be true than a fabrication. However, the reason I continue to refer to him as Randall as opposed to *Dad* or *Arthur* is that they are not the same person. Even if they had inhabited the same body at different periods in his life they are not the same person. So as a result, for me, it actually seems quite easy to separate Randall and Arthur. For me, they are two totally different sets of memories based around two different people. I remember reading something years ago about multiple personalities. While it was hard to prove that he had multiple personalities it almost did seem to be possible. The extra 'personalities' would appear when some people are confronted with an extreme trauma that they could not deal with so their mind would make a whole new personality that was able to handle the horror that they had experienced. I think that is where Randall came from. He was the extra personality that was brought out by trauma. My father's entire world was scorched and cooked above him while he was hiding in his basement. Up until he found me he likely believed that I was dead. I think it was survivor's guilt that broke him, it likely happened in the first moments after emerging from his home and even finding me alive never quite fixed it for him. That is the only way I can reconcile in my mind that they could possibly be the same person.

-Aurora

About the author:

L. Edward Toole was born in Winnipeg, Manitoba and has lived in various places throughout Canada before returning to live in the city of his birth. He has been writing for his own amusement since he was 15 or so, often making little short-stories about whatever random idea popped into his head. His first novel, Memoirs of a Tyrant, having much the same beginning, being written in a notebook while he rode the bus to and from his job at a call center. When writing he tries to bring the experiences he has had to life including insights garnered from his studies as he earned a degree in Psychology and interactions with people dealing with addictions.

You may wish to follow the author on Instagram, Tinder, Facebook or the Olive Garden Review however those likely will not be helpful in the slightest. For the opportunity to see the author post something that may/may not be interesting, funny and/or relevant you should probably just follow him on Twitter: @L_Edward_Toole